The Romance of William and the Werewolf

The Romance of William and the Werewolf

(William of Palerne)

Translated and illustrated by
Michael Smith

unbound

First published in 2024

Unbound
c/o TC Group, 6th Floor King's House, 9–10 Haymarket,
London SW1Y 4BP

www.unbound.com

Typeset in 10.5/14.5pt Palatino LT Pro by Jouve (UK), Milton Keynes

A CIP record for this book is available from the British Library

ISBN 978-1-80018-369-8 (hardback)
ISBN 978-1-80018-370-4 (ebook)

Printed in Great Britain by Clays Ltd, Elcograf S.p.A.

1 3 5 7 9 8 6 4 2

MIX
Paper | Supporting
responsible forestry
FSC
www.fsc.org
FSC® C018072

To the memory of my brother, Stuart.

When old age shall this generation waste,
Thou shalt remain, in midst of other woe
Than ours, a friend to man, to whom thou say'st,
"Beauty is truth, truth beauty, – that is all
Ye know on earth, and all ye need to know."

John Keats, "Ode on a Grecian Urn"

CONTENTS

HISTORICAL INTRODUCTION

Preserved in the library of King's College in Cambridge, England, is an intriguing bound volume of considerable literary significance. Showing evidence of once belonging to a chained library and now catalogued somewhat drily as Cambridge, King's College, MS 13, this obscure codex comprises two – originally separate – manuscripts on parchment: part of a medieval *South English Legendary* (a collection of hagiographic texts) and, that which concerns us, an almost complete mid-fourteenth-century English translation of a twelfth-century French romance known as *Guillaume de Palerne*.* Commonly referred to as *William of Palerne* (William of Palermo), the Middle English text misses two passages, including its opening lines, which scholars nonetheless have been able to recreate by reference to the French source. The extant manuscript is important for two reasons: it is the only surviving medieval redaction of this text written in English and it is also one of the earliest Middle English romances presented in that distinctly English style, the alliterative long line. Indeed, it is often seen as one of the earliest, possibly *the* earliest, texts to appear in what is frequently referred to as the Alliterative Revival of the Fourteenth Century.[1]

The romance as we know it today was first laid out effectively for the modern reader by the great palaeographer Sir Frederic Madden.[2] In his publication of it for the Roxburghe Club in 1832, and reflecting on the subject matter of the narrative, Madden gave the romance the title *The Ancient English Romance of William and the Werwolf* (sic). Three decades later Walter Skeat, in his EETS[†] edition of 1867, developed Madden's work by incorporating the missing elements from the French source[3] so

---

* The complete codex has been subject to a modern rebinding; for a full description of the MS, see Bunt, *William of Palerne*, pp. 1–10.

† Early English Text Society.

1

that for the first time the modern English reader could understand the text in its entirety. In deference to scholarly cataloguing whilst also respecting Madden, Skeat published the poem as *The Romance of William of Palerne (otherwise known as The Romance of William and the Werwolf)*. It seems that although the werewolf of its content lived on in the title, Skeat felt drawn also to classify the work in the same way as the French. By 1985, when Gerrit Bunt published his modern critical edition incorporating a raft of new scholarship, all trace of the "werwolf" had disappeared from the title.

Yet, as we know from the lais of Marie de France,[4] werewolves are a theme in romance, being representative of outcasts in society, exiles unable to return. In such romances werewolves, lacking the clothes and other symbols of civilisation, are condemned to roam the world as dumb animals, deprived of human company through being unable to speak even though they may fully comprehend the words of other humans.[5] It is this theme within *William of Palerne* – two princes exiled through familial mischief, one of whom (Alphonse) is turned into a werewolf and rescues the other (William) – that allows us to refer to the story by Madden's name with some legitimacy. By calling it *The Romance of William and the Werewolf*, we are at once drawn to the mystery it holds, intrigued by the ambiguity of the story and the morals it may divulge. In so doing, we perhaps gain an insight into how medieval audiences were attracted to the content of the stories they enjoyed. For what is clear is that this was a story for enjoyment; its survival at Cambridge may be unique to us, but the tale represents, by the very fact that it was translated from French, a window on the literary world well known by contemporaneous English writers and their audiences.

The Romance of William and the Werewolf, as it survives today, offers a tantalising and unusual glimpse into this interconnected world of patrons, poets, scribes and audiences.* This is a story that was wilfully chosen not just because it was attractive but because it was well known: someone owned a copy in French, someone wanted it translated into English, and someone had the skill to translate it with an audience in mind – and to do so in a distinctive poetic style. At a later date, perhaps

---

* See Appendix 1: The Character of the Narrator in *William and the Werewolf*.

only a decade or so after the text was created by its original poet-scribe, a further scribe then copied it; this is the manuscript at Cambridge that survives today. In retaining and abbreviating the core plot of its tail-rhyming Old French source, and then fundamentally re-writing it in a non-rhyming, long-line alliterative form, the romance also reveals a remarkable innovation on behalf of its poet and reflects a demand for such work by his patron. Most strikingly, given that medieval alliterative romances are frequently coy about their writers and their patrons, *William and the Werewolf* names both: the poet-scribe was a certain "William" and his patron was none other than the hugely powerful Humphrey de Bohun, 6th Earl of Hereford and Essex and sometime hereditary Constable of England.

Humphrey, as we shall see, was a man renowned for overseeing the beginning of an operation that was later to produce some of the finest medieval codices ever created in England during the Middle Ages. "William" on the other hand, while notionally a poet or "princepleaser", may also have been someone with a much closer relationship to his patron, one much more significant than just servant and master. Crucially, the naming of his patron by the poet-scribe also means that we can date the work much more accurately and establish it more firmly in the literary canon to which it belongs. With Humphrey's death in 1361, we can say with some certainty that *The Romance of William and the Werewolf* was created in English sometime during the period when he was earl (1336–61). This in itself also provides an avenue for investigating the original poet-scribe.

Patron, scribe and circumstance

Although immensely powerful and well connected (being both nephew to Edward II and cousin to Edward III), Humphrey was an accidental magnate, inheriting his earldoms following the early deaths of three of his older brothers (Edward, d.1334; John, d.1336; and another Humphrey, who died young).[6] Despite this, the family's power, lands and indeed its hereditary status as title-holder of Constable of England were not necessarily guaranteed, not least because Humphrey's father had taken part in the baronial revolt against Edward II and had been killed at the battle of Boroughbridge in 1322.[7] It was only after

Edward's death, and in particular when the young Edward III finally wrested control from his mother Isabella and her lover Roger Mortimer, that the status of the de Bohuns as earls of Hereford and Essex was restored.[8] The re-emergence of the family and its willingness to show loyalty to the Crown may well account for Humphrey's subsequent reputation for the aggressive and stringent maintenance of his Welsh estates.[9]

Yet such a reputation seems in marked contrast to the Humphrey we know through his unique artistic and literary legacy: the creation of a manuscript workshop that was later to produce some of the finest medieval illuminated manuscripts ever created in England, including the magnificent Egerton Psalter and Hours.[10] These religious codices, produced by a dedicated workshop deliberately assembled in the shadow of the Black Death in Humphrey's relatively remote *caput* at Pleshey in Essex, hold the key to understanding the inner earl; they may also go some way to explain the sentiments exuded in *William and the Werewolf*. Despite his hereditary power and huge estates, Humphrey was not a well man and was subject to an unknown and clearly debilitating infirmity that significantly affected his power to exercise his duties. His condition appears to have been such that even as a child he required a separate teacher, Houard de Soyrou, to that of his brothers.[11] In 1338 he resigned his role of Constable in favour of his younger brother William, Earl of Northampton,[12] "*tam ob corporis sui inbecillitatem, quam propter infirmitatem diuturnam qua detinetur ad officium Constabulariae exercendum*" (both because of a weakness/infirmity of his body, and because of the *prolonged infirmity* [my italics] by which he is afflicted to perform the office of Constable). Humphrey's condition may also explain why he never married or had heirs and why he was subsequently to devote his life to his manuscript workshop, his library and his faith. It may also hold the key as to why *William and the Werewolf* itself emerged as a "sanitised" redaction of the French text, removing particularly graphic depictions of violence[13] and toning down some of the romance's more erotic passages.

Despite his reputation in Brecon in Wales, the Humphrey of *William and the Werewolf* is seen by his own poet-scribe – whom we shall call Scribe William – as a man worthy of praise and deserving of prayers. Early on in the romance, Scribe William tells his audience:

And ȝe þat loven and lyken to listen ani more,
all wiȝth on hol hert to þe heiȝ King of hevene
preieth a pater noster prively þis time
for þe hend Erl of Herford, Sir Humfray de Bowne,
þe king Edwardes newe at Glouseter þat ligges.
For he of Frensche þis fayre tale ferst dede translate,
In ese of Englysch men in Englysch speche;
And God graunt hem his blis þat godly so prayen!

(ll. 162–9)

(Lit. And you who love [this story] and would like to listen to more of it, please, with your whole heart, say a quiet paternoster now to the high King of Heaven for Sir Humphrey de Bohun, the high Earl of Hereford, the nephew of King Edward who lies buried at Gloucester.* For [Humphrey] first ordered the translation of this fine tale from the French for the pleasure of English men in the English tongue; And may God grant those His bliss who will say such prayers!)

This dedication is rendered even more emphatic because Scribe William returns to Humphrey at the end to remind the audience of his generosity:

but, faire frendes, for Goddes love and for ȝour owne mensk,
ȝe þat liken in love swiche þinges to here,
preiȝeþ for þat gode lord þat gart þis do make,
þe hende Erl of Hereford, Humfray de Boune;
þe gode king Edwardes douȝter was his dere moder;
he let make þis mater in þis maner speche,
for hem þat knowe no Frensche ne neuer underston.
Biddeþ þat blisful burn þat bouȝt us on þe rode,
and to his moder Marie of mercy þat is welle,
ȝif þe lord god lif wil he in erþe lenges,
and when he wendes of þis world, welþe with-oute end,
to lenge in þat liking joye þat lesteþ euermore.

* Early commentators suggested the scribe implied that Humphrey himself was buried at Gloucester; Edward II is clearly the subject here, as rightly stated by Madden in the introduction to his edition for the Roxburghe Club. Humphrey was buried at Austin Friars in London.

> And God gif all gode grace þat gladli so biddes,
> and pertli in paradis a place for to haue. Amen.
>
> (ll. 5527–40)

(Lit. But, fair friends, for God's love and your own honour, all you who like and love to hear such things, say prayers for that good lord who ordered this [book] made, the high Earl of Hereford, Humphrey de Bohun – his mother was good King Edward's daughter – he ordained this story to be written in this manner of speech [i.e. English] for those who know nothing of French nor understand it. Pray to that blissful Man who died for us on the cross, and to his mother Mary, that fountain if mercy: "Give that Lord a good life while he lives on earth, and when he departs of this life, grant him wealth without end, to dwell in that blissful joy which lasts unto eternity." And God openly grant a place in paradise for all who so gladly pray this. Amen)

Dedications to patrons are not unknown, so it would be wrong to suggest that Humphrey has been singled out for special praise. However, it is worth comparing this latter invocation to that which appears in Scribe William's French source, *Guillaume de Palerne*, whose patron is also named at the end of the romance:

> Cil qui tos jors fu et sans fin
> Sera et pardoune briement,
> Il gart la contesse Yolent,
> La boine dame, la loial,
> Et il destort son cors de mal.
> Cest livre fist diter et faire
> Et de latin en roumans traire.
> Proions Dieu por le boine dame
> Qu'en bon repos en mete l'ame,
> Et il nos doinst ce deservir
> Qu'a boine fin puissons venir. Amen
>
> (*Guillaume de Palerne*, ll. 9653–63)

(May He who was and is eternal, and is quick to pardon, protect the Countess Yolande, that good and loyal lady. And may He protect her body from evil. She ordered this book to be written and made and translated from Latin into romance (French). Let us pray to God for the good lady that He grant her soul to rest in peace and that He gives to us this reward so that we are able to come to a good end. Amen)

Despite the fact that both patrons lived well over a century apart in time (Countess Yolande of Hainaut is thought to have died some time between 1202 and 1223), the English invocation at first glance appears to be formulaic in following the French. However, where it differs is in emphasis: unlike in the French original, Humphrey as patron is twice remembered by his scribe – at the beginning and at the end – and in an almost ritualistic way as his qualities are again stressed: his royal background, his wish to see the work translated, and his seeming concern for his subjects to gain access to a story previously only understood in some form of "higher" tongue. The English text is also specific in stating that the translation is for the benefit of others, those who neither speak French nor understand it; the motive appears to be significantly more altruistic in intent than that of the *Guillaume* scribe. In particular, however, the English redaction is unique in further reinforcing the second invocation by prefacing it with the (self-deprecatory) words of the manuscript's own scribe:

> In þis wise haþ William al his werke ended,
> as fully as þe Frensche fully wold aske,
> And as his witte him wold serve, þouȝh it were febul.
> But þouȝh þe metur be nouȝt mad at eche mannes paye,
> wite him nouȝt þat it wrouȝt; he wold have do beter,
> ȝif is witte in eny weiȝes wold him haue served.
>
> (ll. 5521–6)

(In this way has William ended his work as fully as the French source would ask, and as his wit would serve, albeit feebly. Although this poem may not be to the pleasure of every man, do not blame him who transcribed it: he would have done better if his wit in any way might have served him so.)

The emphasis on Humphrey and the work of Scribe William in trying to undertake his patron's command suggests that *William and the Werewolf* is written with a specific purpose in mind and by a man who fundamentally understood his lord and his wishes. Thorlac Turville-Petre, noting what he saw as the Gloucestershire dialect of the poem and highlighting the spread of the de Bohun estates from Essex to Gloucestershire and the Welsh Marches, suggests the romance was intended not for Humphrey himself but to have an educational function – a guide to the values of courtesy and manners – for managers and others in his distant estates.[14] Elizabeth Salter, writing around the same time as Turville-Petre, seems supportive of the view that aristocratic audiences preferred to read in French, arguing that English books were rare in the libraries of the nobility, where French texts were seemingly preferred.[15]

Certainly, the notion that the text was transcribed for "those that know no French" appears to suggest a different social class of readership. However, to go to the lengths of completely rewriting a French poem of great length into a substantial alliterative romance for remote tenants seems a singular and extravagant act of centrist lordly propaganda, particularly given its core theme of the importance of good lordship. Gerrit Bunt, in his critical edition of the text from 1985, argues that the audience for the poem probably did include Humphrey, in addition to those in his service.[16] In this light, what is perhaps more compelling is that Humphrey was aware of the significant social change brought about by the Black Death and its potential impact on his status. As an invalid lord living remotely from some of his estates, he may have wished to connect more closely with those managing his estates by sharing with them the *Werewolf* text and the themes of lordly tolerance and duties it extols. It is notable that in 1362, a year after Humphrey's death, the Pleading in English Act had been passed that ensured English courts heard and decided upon cases in the English tongue, and within fifty years the Chancery Standard of English had emerged in official documents. English, it seems, was becoming ever more the language of everyone; the need for laws to reflect this suggest long-standing social undercurrents.* The social context of English society was changing;

---

* Larry Benson, discussing Geoffrey Chaucer (c. 1340–1400) and his decision to write in English, not only cites his upbringing with English poetry and his love of the English language but also the contemporary forces at work in the background that enabled him to come to the fore (Benson, "The Beginnings of Chaucer's English Style", pp. 246–7).

knowledge of French had become considerably less important to justice and administration while ignorance of it was no longer deemed a barrier to successful prosecution nor, seemingly, social elevation. English at the highest levels was here to stay.

In this context, the dialect of the poem is of great interest. Gerrit Bunt has analysed conflicting academic opinions and has concluded that its language reflects dialects from the West Midlands, eastern England and possibly Norfolk.[17] In a separate, later analysis he also argues that the poet-scribe was from southern Worcestershire or Warwickshire.[18] It is also clear that what survives is very close in date to the lost original[19] and may be a relatively uncorrupted version of the "autograph" copy in Scribe William's original hand.* This is attractive because it suggests that, despite the varying dialects it contains, the text may have accidentally retained clues as to the identity of Scribe William: someone who was perhaps operating at one time in the western Midlands but who may later have worked in eastern England. This could to some extent mirror the broad spread of the estates owned by the de Bohuns; Scribe William may have been a trusted servant of Humphrey himself, someone who had travelled with him from estate to estate, betraying subtle changes in his dialect during his career as he worked in different communities. An alternative possibility is that the Worcestershire or Warwickshire dialect of Scribe William may, during the copying of his text, have been altered by the dialect of the (unknown) copying scribe. This may have been carried out in the East of England, possibly by one of Humphrey's own scribes working from Pleshey.

The de Bohun workshop and the search for Scribe William

In order to understand who Scribe William may have been, and how significant he was, we need first to understand Humphrey de Bohun's

---

* Popular texts were serially copied by scribes, leading to numerous variations, textual additions, and texts appearing in dialects of either their copyists or those of their intended audiences. *The Awntyrs Off Arthure*, a fifteenth-century stanzaic romance, survives in four different manuscripts, all of them different and none of them true to their lost original (Lincoln Thornton MS 91; London Lambeth Palace Library MS 491; Oxford, Bodleian Library MS Douce 324; and Princeton University Library MS Taylor 9 [the Ireland-Blackburn MS]).

life at Pleshey,* a place where in later years he was to create a specialist workshop dedicated to the production of exceptionally fine illuminated manuscripts. Humphrey's family was no stranger to literature; his own father had nearly seventy liturgical texts attributed to his library,[20] while an inventory of items held at Pleshey in 1399 listed copious religious texts and more than eighty other texts, including romances and works of history.[21] Humphrey's own will, strangely, mentions only two minor volumes, both of which relate to use within the chapel at Pleshey; but this is not the only story. If lacking detail of his own literary possessions, the will more than makes up for this by showing Humphrey's motivations, in particular his intense personal devotion and who he instructs to ensure his wishes are carried out. It is here that we are introduced to his confessor and executor, a certain William de Monklane, who is instructed in particular to oversee masses to be sung for Humphrey's soul. Significantly, Humphrey rewards him not only with £100 in silver but also a number of gifts and a request for him to have a permanent "beautiful and respectable" chamber at Pleshey in which to carry out his work. A further bequest of £10 is given to a certain John de Teye – described as "our limner" (illuminator) – to pray for Humphrey's soul, with an additional 40 shillings left to a "Johan Luminour", possibly also de Teye or another illuminator.[22]

De Monklane's own position as executor, and the bequests he receives, reveals his importance to the earl; it has been argued he may even have been Humphrey's nephew.[23] The personal bequest to de Teye reflects his value to the household as an in-house illuminator at Pleshey; he was also a man in such demand that, long after Humphrey's death, he was still employed at the castle in 1384 and training an apprentice.[24] It is thought that both de Monklane and de Teye were such integral members of the Bohun household that they enjoyed significant status and understood Humphrey's needs intimately.[25] Their status as Augustinians is also informative; Humphrey's own grandfather founded the church of Austin (Augustinian) Friars in London around 1265[26] where,

---

* Excavations reveal the keep upon the motte at Pleshey was more palatial than military. In Humphrey's time, what seemed like a single tower in fact comprised a substantial wooden inner structure encased by thin walls of clunch and flint containing chambers, a hall, and a kitchen built around a central courtyard (see Allen, "Rethinking Pleshey Castle").

as Humphrey's own will reveals, he wished to be interred and to which he bequeathed generous sums.* It is in this context that William's importance is significant; he was a key player in the origin of the famous de Bohun Manuscripts, a collection of psalters, books of hours and prayer books so richly decorated that they have been described as "the most important group of English illuminated manuscripts of the second half of the fourteenth century".[27]

What appears to have drawn the production of these manuscripts to Pleshey is a combination of four factors: de Monklane's closeness to Humphrey; an existing industry of illuminators in East Anglia; de Monklane's knowledge of de Teye's work at one of these workshops; and the impact of the Black Death, in particular on the workshops of Cambridge.† De Bohun, perhaps driven by his own infirmities and sense of mortality as much as his religious devotion, seems to have been compelled to establish a workshop far away from the risks to life brought about by the plague in urban centres, bringing to Pleshey the best talent he could find. Certainly, the earliest of the Bohun Manuscripts coincide almost exactly with the arrival of the plague in 1348 and again in 1361, perhaps not coincidentally the year of Humphrey's death.[28] By then, Pleshey had become a centre for lavish book production[29] and was to remain so perhaps until the late 1390s when the castle's assets were dispersed following the death of Thomas, Duke of Gloucester, husband to Eleanor de Bohun.

A feature of the earliest Bohun Manuscripts is their celebration of Humphrey's forebears, in particular the marriage of his parents and his mother's descent from Edward I,[30] which, as we have seen, is highlighted twice in *William and the Werewolf*. It has been argued that in an age of the fragility of the male line, items such as books were designed to outlive their patron-creators and to eternalise themselves, their ancestors and their familial connections.[31] In this light, the establishment of

---

* Austin Friars in the City of London today reveals little of its former medieval glory, and none of the original medieval friary remains. Subject to the Blitz of London in World War II, in the 1950s a new church, known as the Dutch Church, was erected on the site of where part of the main friary building once stood.

† See Dennison, *The Stylistic Sources*, p. 272. Philip Ziegler (Ziegler, *The Black Death*, pp. 178–9) writes that in East Anglia at this time there were 2,000 vacancies in the priesthood as a consequence of the plague; a figure that increased to 2,500 if Cambridge was included.

his prestigious manuscript workshop and the intimate involvement of William de Monklane in the execution of Humphrey's will are fundamentally linked to the eternal preservation of the earl's memory. Whether de Monklane was himself of royal blood[32] or a nephew of Humphrey himself (see above), what seems abundantly clear is that he was a close confidant of the earl and knew him well. Although it has been speculated that Scribe William might be William Langland,[33] or a member of Humphrey's household or even an Augustinian friar at Llanthony priory,[34] the intensity of the relationship between de Bohun and the Herefordshire-born William de Monklane offers the possibility that *William and the Werewolf* may well have been a work of his own hand. De Monklane's spiritual closeness to Humphrey, his fundamental involvement in the establishment of the de Bohun workshop, and his trusted status as the earl's confessor and executor all point to a man with an intimate understanding of his lord. If indeed de Monklane was of royal blood or noble, his knowledge of French and his ability to translate *William and the Werewolf* on behalf of his patron – combined with the profound knowledge of courtly life portrayed within the romance – would have been fundamental to its successful execution.

Scholarly reception

If the well-connected William de Monklane was Scribe William, and despite the scribe's own tongue-in-cheek acknowledgement that the poem may not be to everyone's taste (l. 5524), he might nonetheless be disappointed then to learn that *William and the Werewolf* is often dismissed by scholars, irrespective of its status as one of the earliest surviving works of the Alliterative Revival. As early as 1935 the leading scholar J. P. Oakden, while describing the poem as "eminently readable", regarded it as "trifling and only remotely interesting" before going on to dismiss the fourteenth-century redactor's attempts to translate the work from tail-rhyme French into alliterative English as seeming beyond him.[35] As we have seen, Thorlac Turville-Petre, one of the greatest scholars of Middle English alliterative poetry of recent times, also found himself conflicted by the poet's quality. In describing how Humphrey de Bohun may have commissioned *William* not for himself but for his estates and its workers in the west, he argues that its romanticised portrayal of courtly life may have had a specific intention to make his workers more aware of a higher way of living, to "polish up" these "rough diamonds".[36] In other words, a more sophisticated French telling of the romance was then rendered into English to create some form of "dumbed down" text to educate lesser folk in the unattainable lives of their social betters. Writing in 1987, W. R. J. Barron dismissed the romance as "plodding" and even grandiloquent in its use of the alliterative form;[37] as recently as 2014, a scholar examining whether William Langland may have been the author of *William and the Werewolf* describes it as "jejune" and the "oddest duck" of all Middle English alliterative works.[38] Even if a connection between Langland and the *William*-poet is accepted by scholars, it is one whereby *William and the Werewolf* as a literary output represents some form of apprentice piece,[39] a lesser work designed to hone skills for better things to come.

Although *William* may be decried by these scholars for its seeming lack of sophistication compared to works such as *Sir Gawain and the Green Knight*, and while others have arguably seen it as an alliterative outlier,* what cannot be denied is that this is a work of dedicated technique: it is translated from French rhyme to English alliterative poetry to *satisfy* the demands of an audience. The poem's appeal cannot have been related to its alliterative form alone; its subject matter is also seen as important – and important enough to have generated nearly 6,000 lines of seemingly innovative poetry in the process, and to have been copied at least once (and most likely numerous times, given what is known of its popularity).[40] If the narrative is read correctly, as Arlyn Diamond argues, it reveals an examination of the interdependence between the social order and the happiness of individuals – and does so with an attractive and varied use of vocabulary.[41] More generally, Nicola McDonald, inspiring us to understand the contemporary attraction of such works, reminds us that Middle English popular romances are relatively under-studied and that they present a real opportunity to understand how medieval people imagined and thought about their world.[42] It is by understanding the potential themes behind *William and the Werewolf* that

---

* Nikolay Yakovlev has described *William* as being among a number of poems that are "metrically deviant" from the corpus of long-line alliterative work (Yakovlev, *The Development of Alliterative Metre*, p. 25).

we will be able to understand it for what it is: a work with appeal and relevance.

Themes within the romance

The trajectory of the plot in twelfth-century medieval romance has been described as a journey by the lead character towards self-knowledge, often supported by a framework of chivalric concerns such as love, martial prowess and recognition.[43] At its most basic, *William and the Werewolf* is a romance around a single, even conventional, theme: the exile and triumphant return of two princes who eventually inherit the kingdoms denied to them by the machinations of others.* Yet as we explore the romance more deeply, we begin to see that it contains a number of themes, many of which are still relevant to the reader today. In the injustices done to William and Prince Alphonse, we are shown how those seeking power (William's uncle; Alphonse's stepmother) will do anything, to anybody, in order to achieve it. In showing Alphonse's transformation into a werewolf, as well as depicting William and Melior disguising themselves as bears (and later as a hart and a hind), we are introduced to how society judges exiles: as rejected, landless and invisible. Although some scholars reject the notion of disguise in this particular romance as comical,† Morgan Dickson explains that a number of twelfth-century texts (of which *William*'s French source is an example) use the theme of disguise to interrogate the integrity and identity of a given character; in the process, a character's self is contrasted against its social identity, the part it plays in society.[44]

The role of women in the romance is both profound and complex too, far more so than the archetypal "damsel in distress" figure seen in many texts of the period. In the romance's "bad girls", Braundine, Gloriande and Acelone, we are shown how appearances can be deceptive, reversing the stereotype of the gentle woman, maiden or damsel and showing how disguise can be insidious rather than obvious; the enemy within need not

---

* Exile and return is a theme of many medieval popular romances, including *Bevis of Hampton*, *The Romance of Horn* and *Guy of Warwick*.

† One scholar, George Kane, rejects the animal skin disguises of the characters as improbable and even preposterous (see Dalrymple, *Language and Piety*, p. 69)

be a werewolf but could just be one of us, walking about in plain sight. We see this when the romance asks us to compare its two enchantresses: Braundine the "accursed stepmother" (ll. 130–32; 146) and Melior's "amiable" (l. 586) and "lovely" (l. 965) maid (and cousin) Alisaundrine, who uses her powers for good. Whereas Braundine uses her "black magic" (l. 119) and agency to convert Alphonse into a werewolf for the benefit of her own son (ll. 133–41), Alisaundrine instead has the power of dream management; revealed twice (ll. 651–8; 861–8) as controlling the thoughts of William as he sleeps and turning them towards Melior. By contrast, the dreams of women, in being freely formed rather than magically induced, reveal an agency fundamental to the romance; the women have an ability to understand events and shape things for good in spite of their surroundings. Twice, during their elopement, Melior dreams of the dangers confronting the lovers (ll. 2293–2313; 3104–9) while, besieged in Palermo, William's mother Felice dreams of her saviours coming to rescue her dressed as a hart and a hind (ll. 2869–2916). Women influence the outcome of the narrative through the power of their dreams.

Despite the romance's focus on its heroes William and Alphonse, it is clear throughout that feminine power is fundamental to their success. In Melior's rejection of the arranged marriage her father is planning with the son of the Greek emperor, we are shown the agency of women to choose for themselves and reject the patriarchal domination of society.* Indeed, Melior's elopement with William suggests an even stronger agency; under medieval laws of marriage, by asserting their love and promising themselves to each other, the couple – in the minds of the audience – are already married.† Women's power within marriage is

---

* The romance is not unique in portraying the power of women; the character of Josian in the Anglo-Norman *Bevis of Hampton* has a unique agency. In one redaction – contained in Edinburgh, National Library of Scotland, MS Advocates' 19.2.1 (the "Auchinleck Manuscript" of c. 1330) – she is shown to have been educated by Italian scholars brought to her native (Muslim) land of Ermony to school her in medicinal crafts (*Bevis*, ll. 3671–6).

† Irrespective of whether a couple solemnised and therefore consummated their union, they were in fact already married under the terms of what was known as "present consent"; a medieval audience may well have seen this as substantiating the anger of both the emperors of Rome and Greece on hearing of the elopement. Although William and Melior do marry later in a formal ceremony, the notion of the emperor's consent as a condition of the union did not require the vows to be renewed. The reader is referred in particular to Helmholz, *Marriage Litigation in Medieval England*, pp. 25–73.

also revealed on three occasions when Melior (ll. 5115–35), Florence (ll. 5204–8) and Alisaundrine (ll. 5156–60) are each given advice on how best to support their husbands. Whilst seemingly both patronising and patriarchal at first glance, this advice, when read within the Augustinian framework of the English telling,* reveals the weakness of men and the fundamental power of women in ensuring the practice of good lordship in the eyes of God.

As if further to emphasise this point, the romance reveals a profound and haunting example of unequal marriage, where women are merely trophies to achieve imperial aggrandisement. Here, when Alisaundrine explains to the Roman emperor why his daughter has eloped rather than marry the Greek emperor's son, she states that Melior had heard that in Greece wives are locked up in towers to live their lives alone (ll. 2010–21). Melior, in repeatedly giving sound advice (ll. 1806–13), discussing ideas (ll. 2562–6) and offering reassurance (ll. 2358–61) to William during their elopement, as well as being revealed as ensuring good lordship through her marriage (ll. 5485–90), is shown to be a woman of independence, justice and moral influence throughout the romance.† If William is to be seen as the perfect lord, he is made so by Melior, yet even here both characters are overshadowed by another woman's notable and empowering dream. At the very end of the story, it is the dream of Queen Felice – the female victim of a predatory brother-in-law and the consequences of his action – that is seen as having been materialised most joyously; her son is now Emperor of all Rome and her daughter the Queen of Spain (ll. 5491–5506).

In much the same way, the romance's depictions of ordinary folk – the cowherd and his wife, William's boyhood friends, the charcoal burners and others – reveal yet another interesting facet of the story: a desire to show its audience the importance of everyone in society. Whether we see this as an example of the medieval poet creating a pastoral opposite of the courtly world in order to comment on it,[45] or as preparation of a

---

* See Appendix 1 for more detailed insight into the narrator, scribe and the influences in the romance.

† Independent women are far from scarce in Middle English romance; in the fifteenth-century *Sir Degrevant* the character of Melidore (a name curiously similar to the heroine in *William and the Werewolf*) is revealed as highly intelligent and discriminating in terms of the man she chooses to marry.

prince in his education in fitness to rule,[46] the lives of the less fortunate are nonetheless fundamental to an understanding of the story and its message. One of the poem's most compelling themes is the importance of good governance; when William becomes emperor at the end he never forgets the cowherd who looked after him in the forest as a boy (ll. 5361–94) and who first advised him on good lordship (ll. 328–44), while, as we have seen, Melior, Florence and Alisaundrine all receive instructions to shape their husbands in such a way that will encourage the poor to respect them.

A strong Christian ethos is prevalent throughout the romance via an extensive literary use of pious formulae; whether through its characters or the voice of the narrator, the text's use of "Creator-formulae" seems fundamental to the narrative's evocation of a benevolent God.[47] In this context, we might read the romance almost as a world watched and judged by God above, its pastoral landscape perhaps some form of Garden of Eden where those who are seen as corrupt, deceptive and arrogant are despised and ultimately rejected in favour of a fair and just society shaped only to please God. Yet even here, we ourselves are not allowed to be the judges of those whose performances we watch; in showing the forgiveness meted out to the stepmother Braundine (ll. 4327–4420) and to the two women instructed to poison William and his father (ll. 4767–4804), both William and Alphonse (and indeed their courtiers and friends) are ultimately revealed as generous and reflective, not spiteful and vindictive. Indeed, even at his most angry, William himself is not permitted by the narrative to have Braundine burned to death if she refuses to return to Palermo to disenchant Alphonse (ll. 4259–61; 4365–7), nor Gloriande and Acelone for their crimes (ll. 4772–4). Instead, all three women realise their mistakes in their own ways and come before William begging forgiveness while, at the same time, relieving him of the need to show cruelty as a lord. In *William and the Werewolf* one bad deed does not necessarily deserve another; if it is at all possible, the characters in the romance are all subjects for redemption rather than punishment. Whether wicked stepmother or "hag", puffed-up Spanish king or marriage-seeking, empire-building prince, all must ultimately be subject to God's law in a land free from flatterers and false men, liars and sweet-talkers (ll. 5480–81). If we accept Roger Dalrymple's position of the benevolent deity, we must also not forget the romance's central,

Augustinian, theme; that in order to enjoy the benevolence of God, all must do their best to please Him.

A romance for today

Richard Holloway, in his foreword to *Others*, a collection of essays edited by Charles Fernyhough examining life as seen by immigrants, writes, "By revealing the complexity of the human condition, [great novelists] get their readers to understand what makes their characters behave the way they do, even if they don't like the result."[48] Hence, the themes, language and messages of *William and the Werewolf* do not rest statically in the fourteenth century; they are eternal, along with the behavioural traits of their characters, and reside in the mind of the reader. The world of Humphrey de Bohun, and that of the later medieval period, was not a fixed social entity with established strata but one that was both complex and constantly shifting; generalisations about society are difficult to assert.[49] We must no more see medieval romances as fixed in their time than any other work of literature from any period; the issues these narratives raise are part of the complex, vibrant and unending struggle of life and the difficulties it throws at us. In early 2020s Britain, we live in a society where honours and seats in the House of Lords are given out for the most darkly hidden of favours rendered; where great offices of state are gifted to sycophants of questionable levels of capability; where public money intended for public contracts ends up in the private bank accounts of the wealthy; and where a Prime Minister lies to Parliament and, when ejected from office on the judgement of his peers, still protests his innocence while holding his own judges in contempt. What medieval scribes called "surquedry" (overweening pride or arrogance) we may call governmental arrogance, hubris or even corruption. We may even call our governments medieval, although that, as we have seen, would be unfair. To those in medieval times.

Medieval romances – like modern novels – enabled their writers to portray the deeds and motives of others and for their audiences to consider them in their own time and space, far away from the machinations of those who would prefer to suppress them. So it is that lest we think the characters in *William and the Werewolf* are somehow quaint examples of a world so far away, the modern world has a way of telling us otherwise. For the modern reader, in making us experience the lives of William and Alphonse as exiles, *William*'s author enables us to consider the plight of refugees and migrants today – seemingly unwanted and distrusted, with all society's media tools launched against them. Alternatively, thinking of Alphonse's transformation into a werewolf, we might reflect upon the fate of those prisoners who are wrongly convicted of crimes they never committed, languishing in gaol for years until the wrong done unto them is finally exposed. Even if we deem it incredible that two medieval nursemaids responsible for looking after a young William might ever poison him to death, we only need to turn our heads towards Manchester, England, where in 2023 a thirty-three-year-old children's nurse was sentenced to multiple full life prison sentences for the murder of seven babies and the attempted murder of six others in a manner described by the trial judge as "deep malevolence bordering on sadism".

Thus, this so-called "jejune" medieval text, this childish "odd duck", seemingly beyond the competence of its redactor to translate from French into English, is far from being an irrelevant dead end in the history of medieval English literature, a stepping stone to something better. Translated at a time of dramatic demographic shifts, when the shadow of death was omnipresent through plague, life expectancy deeply uncertain, and public order fragile, *William and the Werewolf* was a cautionary tale against excess, oppression, injustice, prejudice, corruption, pride and tyranny. At the same time it is a story of inner truth, of goodness and service. In a way, it may also have been some form of "last stand" by its aristocratic and deeply religious patron, hoping for his own salvation while seeking still a retention of the Old Order and its values in the shadow of a new, more commercial and litigious world engendered by the Black Death. But nonetheless Humphrey de Bohun's inspired commission, in its simple demands for justice and fairness and frequent calls to God and a deeper morality, still calls out from those far-off days and sings anew its message. *The Romance of William and the Werewolf* may be set in the past, its language religious or quirky and its characters arguably stereotypical, but its relevance is profound, cautioning us always to think more deeply about the human condition, about how we act and who we choose to be.

THE STORY

William is the only son of King Embrons of Palermo and his wife, Felice, daughter of the Emperor of Greece. Embrons' brother seeks the kingdom for himself so he persuades and bribes two maids, Gloriande and Acelone, to poison both Embrons and William. While the family is relaxing in the walled garden of the castle, a wolf appears who snatches William away and, despite being chased by Embrons and his entourage, manages to escape and crosses the Straits of Messina with the child, eventually stopping in woodland outside Rome. The wolf looks after William until he is discovered by a cowherd and his dog; the cowherd takes him home where he and his wife look after William, who enjoys an idyllic, humble boyhood in the woods hunting and sharing his wins with his friends. Before William is taken in by the cowherd, the narrator also tells us that the wolf – now described as a werewolf – is Alphonse, the son of the King of Spain. That king's first wife (Alphonse's mother) had died; when the king remarries, he has a second son by his Portuguese wife, Braundine. In order for Braundine's son (Braundinis) to inherit the kingdom, she turns Alphonse into a werewolf using a special ointment.

One day, the Emperor of Rome is out hunting when he is separated from his party and eventually comes across William in the woods via a subtle intervention of the werewolf. Seeing him as a fine, handsome boy, the emperor negotiates with the cowherd and arranges to take William to court so as to learn its ways. At court, he is made page to the emperor's daughter Melior and quickly proves to be exemplary in his work, learning the ways of the court with such grace that he is admired across the kingdom. Eventually, William and Melior find themselves attracted to each other and, via the intervention of Alisaundrine, Melior's cousin and closest confidante, they are brought together although their love remains secret. It is then that Rome is threatened by an invasion from the Duke of Saxony, who has attacked the kingdom burning and destroying many towns; William asks the emperor to knight him, after which he proves himself in battle by defeating the duke and his army and taking hundreds of noble prisoners.

After the battle, the feelings of William and Melior for each other grow stronger but they discover that the emperor has arranged for his daughter to marry Partenedon, the son of the Emperor of Greece. William believes Melior prefers Partenedon and becomes dangerously ill; it is only when Alisaundrine intervenes further that the two lovers realise they must elope; Alisaundrine helps them to escape, as they disguise themselves in two white bear skins. The Emperor of Rome, furious, spreads the news of what has happened throughout the kingdom so that anyone who sees the "bears" will know who they are and report them. Meanwhile, during their elopement, the werewolf watches over the couple acquiring food for them and later helping them avoid capture when workmen spot the lovers in a quarry outside Benevento. The couple realise that the werewolf is friendly and possibly human beneath the skin; eventually, with the help of the werewolf, William and Melior swap their bear skins for the skins of a hart and hind before eventually crossing the straits of Messina to Sicily.

We now learn that William's father is dead and much of Sicily has been laid waste; William's mother Felice, alongside Florence (her daughter and William's only sister) is besieged by the King of Spain in Palermo and is about to surrender. William and Melior eventually reach the city, where Felice dreams of a hart and a hind sent to help her rid her land of its foes; Moyses, a priest, interprets her dream and tells her that help is on the way. When Felice sees a hart and a hind in her gardens she disguises herself as a large hind so she can get nearer to them. On discovering they are not animals but people, and that they will help defeat her enemies, Felice brings William and Melior into her stronghold where they are finally disrobed of their skins and are revealed as a handsome and fair couple. Queen Felice, still unaware that William is her son, asks him to nominate the arms he should bear in battle and he chooses the face of a werewolf, symbolic of his own outlawry as well as that of his saviour.

William organises the defence of Palermo and eventually defeats the besieging King of Spain and his son, Braundinis; both are taken prisoner by William. When the werewolf appears before all the court and the queen's prisoners and then bows at the King of Spain, the king realises that he is his son who has in the past been converted by his wife Braundine. William commands the king to have Braundine fetched; when she arrives she converts the werewolf back into Alphonse. When Alphonse is introduced to the court as himself, he then reveals that he was the werewolf who stole William from his parents as a boy; to the joy of Felice, William is revealed as her son. In a wedding attended by the Emperor of Rome and Partenedon of Greece, William is formally married to Melior. William's sister, Florence, is married to Alphonse whilst Braundinis, his stepbrother, marries Alisaundrine. On the death of the Roman emperor, William becomes Emperor of Rome; meanwhile Alphonse becomes King of Spain after his father becomes too old to continue. William puts in place good laws in his land and removes those that were bad; the cowherd and his wife who had looked after William as a foundling are given a castle and an earldom. The narrative concludes by praising Christian values before commending to God its patron, Humphrey de Bohun.

NOTES ON THIS TRANSLATION

The preparation of a complete alliterative edition of *The Romance of William and the Werewolf* has not been straightforward, not least because the extant Middle English text is ancephalous; its opening passages are missing, as well as a further short passage as the story progresses. So, while I have based my translation of the text on the two Middle English critical editions of the poem produced by Sir Frederic Madden and William Skeat in the nineteenth century, and on Gerrit Bunt's up-to-date edition of the 1980s, I have had to resort to the Old French tail-rhyme edition of the poem to fill in the gaps and complete the English text. In so doing, I am indebted to the 1876 edition of *Guillaume de Palerne* prepared by Henri Michelant on behalf of La Société des Anciens Textes Français, which enabled me to undertake first a translation and then a restructuring of the Old French text into a style that matches the rest of my work with the extant Middle English text. Leslie Sconduto's verse translation of Michelant's *Guillaume* has also been useful when checking for sense. The original Old French text from Michelant, and my accompanying translation of it, can be found in Appendix 2; any errors in that translation are my own.

Translation, tense, punctuation and stress

With the exception perhaps of large illuminated capital letters randomly spaced within them, Middle English romances are notorious for having very little, if any, punctuation. I am grateful therefore that scholars such as Madden, Skeat and Bunt have, in their presentations of the Middle

English text, inserted modern punctuation at points that they see as fundamental to an understanding of each line. Depending on the needs of expressing modern English, I have either followed the punctuation suggested in these critical editions or have re-punctuated the relevant lines for sense. Notwithstanding, I have translated the text according to the extensive glossaries provided in all three critical editions while also falling back on Stratmann's *A Middle-English Dictionary* when necessary.

It will be realised immediately that medieval poetic delivery was, and remains, a singular activity. Both the Old French and Middle English redactions of *William* place strong emphasis on a fictional narrator (see Appendix 1), a person who speaks at once in the present tense and then in the past; often he changes tense within a sentence (he enters the room and he spoke to the king). Where it makes sense to do so without affecting the clarity of a line, I have retained these elements; I regard these variations in tense as part of the experience of medieval texts, bringing the narrator into the life (or lives) of the reader(s).

A similar quirk surrounds the use of the apostrophe; these do not exist in Middle English. However, the use of the apostrophe is clear in how words are set out (the "kingeȝ chamber" [the king's chamber]). In my 2021 translation of the fourteenth-century *King Arthur's Death* (the *Alliterative Morte Arthure*), I attempted to structure my translation so that the apostrophe was redundant; I believe now that in doing so disrupted the flow at key moments so this translation incorporates apostrophes where necessary while avoiding their excessive use.

Finally, any reader of Middle English alliterative poetry will be familiar with its use of a caesura in each line. The alliterative long line comprises two verses – the longer a-verse and the shorter b-verse; these are separated by a brief pause – the caesura. While the a-verse is flexible in length, the b-verse (in the Middle English form at least) is rigorously controlled, with metre determined by the stress placed on each syllable or not (the "dip"); it is typified by a short dip, a stress, a dip, a stress, and then either a short dip or no dip at all. The stresses are usually provided by the words that alliterate and, typically, there will be two alliterating words in the a-verse and two in the b-verse. Having said that, sometimes there will be more than three words alliterating in the first line but, for metrical purposes, only two of these will usually be stressed.

In the example below, taken from line 3 of the Middle English section of the poem, the dips (the unstressed syllables) are shown by "x" and the stresses (the stressed syllables) by "/".

a-verse					Caesura	b-verse		
Hit	be<u>f</u>el	in	þat	<u>f</u>orest	--------	þere	<u>f</u>ast	by<u>s</u>ide
x	x /	x	x	/ x	--------	x	/	x / (x)

Stress pattern of the Middle English alliterative long line.

As can be seen in this example, the stress falls on the alliterating letter /f/; what is also clear is that in this case the final stress falls on /s/; I have underlined the stressed letters. What is not clear is whether the "final e" is pronounced in "byside" (hence (x)) but, even if so, this would receive a short dip and not be stressed.* The example above highlights a further problem for all involved with alliterative romance; the alliteration is variable. Sometimes, for example, there will be four words alliterating (*aa-aa*) and sometimes, as here, three (*aa-ax*). Sometimes the a-verse alliterates on one letter, the b-verse on another (*aa-xx*); there are many variations and sometimes (although very rarely) the poet decides it's all too much and doesn't alliterate at all!

The rules followed by the poets seem to have been flexible, but my intention with this translation is to replicate as much as possible the correct alliteration and to envisage a caesura within each line. In my translation of *King Arthur's Death*, I created a visible caesura within the text to enable readers to see the structure; with this translation, to avoid too prescriptive a reading, I have not signified the caesura but leave it to the reader to find their own flow on the understanding that there is a rhythmic delivery based on the underlying principles. I acknowledge that the re-creation of the rigid b-verse stress/dip structure has not been a fundamental principle of the translation, but I hope the reader will nonetheless find a rhythm based on the rules I have outlined and which re-creates a modern equivalent.

---

* For a thorough assessment of the stress patterns in Middle English alliterative poetry, the reader is referred in particular to Putter, Jefferson and Stokes, *Studies in the Metre of Alliterative Verse*.

General layout and line sequence

The original poem is written as one continuous work, broken up by illu-
minated letters, some of which were never completed and a gap was left
in the manuscript for the illuminator to create. For completion, I have
incorporated illuminated capitals into this edition in all positions
intended by the scribe, including those where they would have been if
the illuminator had completed his task. As with *King Arthur's Death*, my
illuminated capitals take the form of linocut prints, based on the stand-
ardised letter form of the Macclesfield alphabet. To help readers referring
to either Skeat's or Bunt's edition I have numbered the lines in the poem
by every fifth line to match these texts. Where I have translated the Old
French, these two distinct passages are shown with two sets of number-
ing, A- and B-, and reflect the numbers given in Michelant's Old French
edition (so A 101 equates to l.101 of Michelant's *Guillaume de Palerne*).

The illustrations

Readers familiar with my earlier translations of *King Arthur's Death* and
Sir Gawain and the Green Knight will know that I produce all the illustra-
tions for my work using hand-cut linocut plates printed manually from
a Victorian Albion press at the Essex studios of my friend and tutor, Sue
Jones. My influences over the years have been various, including Edward
Bawden, Käthe Kollwitz and some of the interwar printmakers such as
Cyril Power. For this edition, I have tried to find a distinctive style of my
own for some of the larger prints and to create more integrated illustra-
tions to encourage the reader to think beyond the image. I hope you
enjoy them and that they add to your overall experience and personal
interpretation of this magnificent medieval romance.

Michael Smith, Summer 2024

The Romance of William and the Werewolf

(William of Palerne)

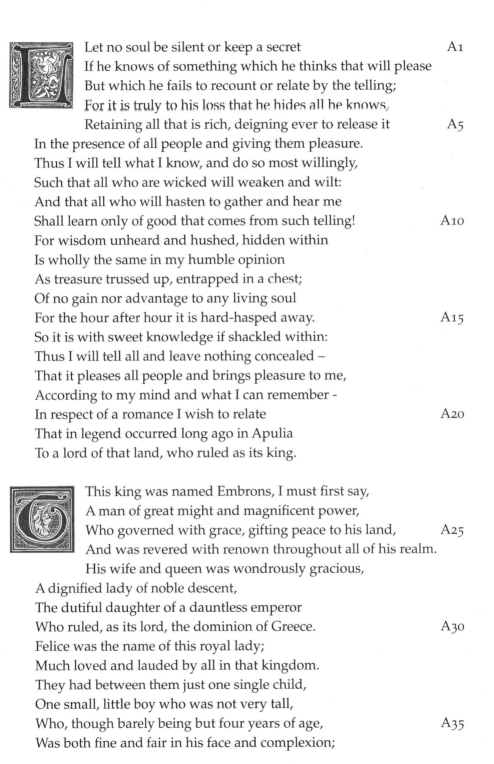

Let no soul be silent or keep a secret   A1
If he knows of something which he thinks that will please
But which he fails to recount or relate by the telling;
For it is truly to his loss that he hides all he knows,
    Retaining all that is rich, deigning ever to release it   A5
In the presence of all people and giving them pleasure.
Thus I will tell what I know, and do so most willingly,
Such that all who are wicked will weaken and wilt:
And that all who will hasten to gather and hear me
Shall learn only of good that comes from such telling!   A10
For wisdom unheard and hushed, hidden within
Is wholly the same in my humble opinion
As treasure trussed up, entrapped in a chest;
Of no gain nor advantage to any living soul
For the hour after hour it is hard-hasped away.   A15
So it is with sweet knowledge if shackled within:
Thus I will tell all and leave nothing concealed –
That it pleases all people and brings pleasure to me,
According to my mind and what I can remember -
In respect of a romance I wish to relate   A20
That in legend occurred long ago in Apulia
To a lord of that land, who ruled as its king.

This king was named Embrons, I must first say,
A man of great might and magnificent power,
Who governed with grace, gifting peace to his land,   A25
And was revered with renown throughout all of his realm.
    His wife and queen was wondrously gracious,
A dignified lady of noble descent,
The dutiful daughter of a dauntless emperor
Who ruled, as its lord, the dominion of Greece.   A30
Felice was the name of this royal lady;
Much loved and lauded by all in that kingdom.
They had between them just one single child,
One small, little boy who was not very tall,
Who, though barely being but four years of age,   A35
Was both fine and fair in his face and complexion;

This young lord was hailed by the name of William.
But that most royal queen, peerless in her realm,
Consigned him to the care of two courtly women
That came from her country as it is recounted. A40
One of those women was called Gloriande,
And the second was known as Acelone.
She assigned both of them to watch over her son;
To teach and to train and to educate him,
And explain all the law to enlighten that lad, A45
As is right and proper and pertaining to princes.
That queen called them friends and confided in them
But she was tricked and betrayed by these two women
And she was direly deceived with much disgrace.
Harken now unto me and I will tell you how. A50

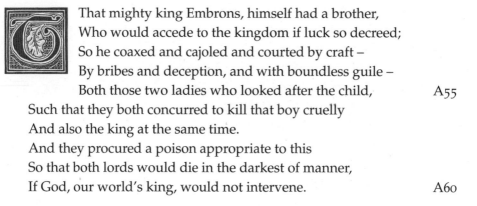

That mighty king Embrons, himself had a brother,
Who would accede to the kingdom if luck so decreed;
So he coaxed and cajoled and courted by craft –
By bribes and deception, and with boundless guile –
Both those two ladies who looked after the child, A55
Such that they both concurred to kill that boy cruelly
And also the king at the same time.
And they procured a poison appropriate to this
So that both lords would die in the darkest of manner,
If God, our world's king, would not intervene. A60

They had dwelled and resided and lived in Palermo,
For more than a month in that mighty city,
As part of the court of the king and the queen.
Below the great keep, which was built of marble,
Was a choice and cool orchard of the most charming trees A65
Encircled all round with walls of worked mortar;
Within this walled pound were many wild animals.
One fine and fair day – a high Festival day –
The king came to that place in pursuit of his pleasure.
His top knights and best townsfolk, A70
And many nobles came too,

And also the queen, that lovely lady.
Now, those women who held William in their ward –
Inflamed by foul evil and their own wicked fire
Although yet to harm him, that happy young lad –   A75
Have brought the boy with them to be with the others.
But if only they all could have known the lamenting
Which that day would unfold on account of that child!
As that king seeks the shade under cover in the orchard,
And likewise the queen, so carefree and happy,   A80
They know nothing of the grief and the great numbing sorrow
Which will fall before them, in front of their eyes!
Thus, as their child goes to gather some sweet garden flowers,
Running quick between blooms and bright to another,
The king and the queen look now at the bushes: A85
A wolf, mouth wide open, wildly leaps with a spring
Like a terrible tempest into that garden,
And all turn to avoid this startling creature.
Right before the great king, and as bold as brass,
It takes hold of his son in its huge mouth   A90
And runs away from them all before up rose a cry
Which was rapidly raised to rally the people.
So rises such grief, and such anguish and agony
For the son of that king whom this wolf has taken.
The queen cries and exclaims and repeatedly calls,   A95
"Holy Mary please help me, hear me I pray!
Retainers and servants, what are you all doing?
I shall kill myself if my son is not rescued!"

The king calls for his horses, crying aloud
For his men and companions to mount at the ready.   A100
Now all in that city are in tumult and torment;
They run as quick as they can at the cries of distress.
  With a prick of his spurs the king pursues that fierce wolf;
Although the wall of that orchard enclosed it all round,
That wolf was wily and slips well away,   A105
Passing onto the plains as it escapes.
Often howling and weeping, the boy wails in distress;

The king, at the canter, hears his cries
And spies them quite clearly as they climb a mountain,
So summons his men to ride even more swiftly.   A110
At that call and most quickly those men are encouraged
But away flees the wolf with that woeful boy.
Away flees the wolf followed by those men
Who are anxious and eager to capture that creature.
They chase that wolf to the Straits of Messina: A105
It leaps into those waters along with the child.
Its swims the Straits swiftly and so is now lost
To that much-concerned king and all of his company;
And so, in this way, that wild beast escaped,
This fierce, wild wolf with the child in his mouth.   A120
The king halts and turns back, he can do no more,
Greatly saddened and sorrowful and in deep distress
For his one single son who has been lost;
He and his retinue return to the city.

The queen is much maddened by her own mourning;   A125
She wants only her death, such was her woe;
She weeps and she wails often with howls of lament,
For her sweet only son whom that wolf had stolen.
"Oh sweet son of mine," said that queen in distress,
"Of rosy complexion and such a tender mouth,   A130
You most saintly of souls, of such divine spirit,
Who would ever believe that a beast or a wolf
Would wish to devour you? Oh God, what misfortune!
Alas! Why should I live or make my life any longer?
Oh my son, where might I find now your sweetest of eyes,   A135
So pure and so innocent, unsullied by pride;
Your fairest of foreheads, your finest of hair,
So fair it seems spun from strands of pure gold;
Your tender expression and your shining face? –
Oh my beating heart! How can you bear this strain? –   A140
My boy, what will become of all of your beauty:
Your fine noble body, and all of your brightness;
Your nose and your chin, and your enticing mouth;

Your much-favoured form, your fabulous features;
Your wonderful arms and your whitest of hands;   A145
Your bewitching waist and your handsome hips;
Your lovely fine feet and your fairest of legs?
Alas! Oh what sorrow, what dolorous woe!
It was intended without doubt that you were solely made
For the partaking of pleasure, and as a pleasure to be shared!   A150
Now you are for the gnawing of some wayward werewolf;
Oh my dearest child, what direst misfortune!
Yet I cannot conceive, not on any account,
Why any such wild wolf would be so wanton
As to tear and torment such a tender young body,   A155
To wound or to worry it, or cause it to bleed;
I simply will not believe it would give Lord God pleasure
Nor that He would consent to such dreadful cruel things!"

 And thus is this lady so deeply bedevilled
And so, in this way, she laments for her son   A160
And weeps in her woe and bewails his fate.
But she is so reproved, restrained and corrected
By the king that her sadness, her harrowing sorrow
And her sobbing recede and her worries ease;
And so in this way is that royal queen soothed.   A165
But now is the right time for me to tell you
What becomes of that wolf which made off with the child;
He had carried him a great distance through day and dark night,
And had criss-crossed completely large tracts of the land
Until in the countryside, close near to Rome,   A170
He finally stops in a great leafy forest
Where many a wild beast walked freely abroad.
There he rests to recover for fully eight days.
No matter what the boy wanted, whatever his needs,
That wolf never ceased to endow him with it: A175
And thus it was so this child wanted for nothing.
The wolf dug a deep den down into the earth,
And the loveliest grass he laid within it,
And fine bracken and ferns which thrive in the forest,

Which it has spread about inside, like a nest.   A180
At night the wolf lies alongside that child,
Such that he embraces the son of the king
With all four of his feet to comfort the boy.
And so in this way that princely one
Comes to trust it well, and is wholly pleased
With whatever that wolf will do for him.   A186

*

And that prince was well pleased with such provisions,   1
And was wisely obedient to what that beast willed.[1]

Now it befell in that forest that fast nearby
There lived a worthy old fellow who was a cowherd,
Who for a fair many winters had kept in that forest   5
Many cows in that country, in herds of the common;
    Thus at that time it betided, as our books reveal,
That cowherd came once to be keeping his beasts
Fast by the earth-barrow which this boy slept within.
The herdsman had a hound with him, light like a hart,   10
And trained to bring back his beasts when they broke away;
The herdsman sat with his hound below the hot sun,
Not fully a furlong* from that fair child,
Clouting his shoes, as he was accustomed, and as befalls his craft.
All that while the werewolf went about hunting,   15
To bestow on the boy what food it might bring.
The child dwelled in his den, hidden singly in secret,
A big and bold boy, very brave for his age,
Who had swiftly learned to speak and move speedily around.[2]
Although that lair was lovely, he was lonely in there   20
And the bushes soon beckoned him blossoming green all about,[3]
Which looked sweet and lovely and lent great shade,
And where birds, most boldly, sing on their boughs.
With the melody they made in the May season,

---

* 220 yards, the length of one side of an acre or an eighth of a mile.

That little child became listless and crawled out of the cave,   25
So for to fetch flowers which he sees before him,
And gather the grasses which were green and fair.
And when he went out he liked it so well,
The scents of that sweet season and the song of the birds,
That he fared fast about to gather those flowers   30
And played for a long while to relish that mirth.
Now the hound of that herdsman, as so it would happen,
Swiftly sniffed out that child and follows its scent;
And soon he sees it, to speak the whole truth;
He began to bark at that boy and stand at bay from him,   35
Such that he was nearly witless for worry and fear,
And comes then to cry so keenly and shrill,
And wept so wonderfully fast, I would truly tell you,
That quickly his crying was heard by the cowherd,
Who knew straight away it was the voice of a child.   40
So up he rose rapidly and ran there swiftly,
Drawn towards that den by the noise of his dog.
By now that boy, on account of that barking,
Was driven back to his den and hid still in its darkness,
And wept, as he would, vexed wild through fear,   45
While the hound at the hole held itself in abeyance.
And when the cowherd came there, he cowered low down
To behold in that hole why his hound was barking.
Then swiftly he saw that seemly child,
Lain lovely, yet weeping in that low filthy cave,   50
Clad in comely clothing, fit for any king's son;
In good clothes of gold and dressed richly and gaily,
With prize stones and fine pelts, as would be right and proper.
That churl chastised his dog, shocked by this chance find,
Bade him cease his barking and spoke to the boy,   55
Encouraged him to come to him and called to him often,
And offered him some flowers, with fair behest,
And bade him to have hastily what his heart might want;
Like apples and all things that children adore.
Soon, I speak truly, that churl enticed him so well   60
That the child came from the cave and stopped all his crying.

The churl, with great cheer, took that child in his arms
And kissed and caressed it and thanks Christ often
Who had sent this God-send as such prey to be found.
He quickly went with that child home to his house,   65
And took him to his wife at haste to take care of.
A gladder woman under God there never was on this earth
Than that wife was with this child, I would have you know truly.
She called to it most kindly and asks of his name,
And it answered swiftly, saying "My name is William".   70
Then that good wife was glad and began to bring him up well,
Such that he wished for nothing; he might have all that he wanted,
And they would find none fairer for as long as he stayed here,
And none better, be you sure, for they had been blessed with
      no children
Brought forth from their bodies; here had dwelled bleak sorrow. 75
So, in truth, they decided he should share all their goods,
And live as heir to their lands once their days were all done.

But we must now change our tale from the churl and that child
Because I will, for a while, now speak of the werewolf.

 When this werewolf returned to his wondrous den,   80
Bringing food for the belly for that boy to eat,
Which he had won through hard work far and wide thereabout,
He found a nest, but no eggs, for nothing was left there.
 And when he saw that boy missing, the beast bellowed so much
That no man on Mother Earth might know his deep woe.   85
He ruefully roared and rent his hide,
And often ate the fair earth and fell down in a swoon,
And made the most woeful moans that man might devise.
That bleak-hearted beast then went looking about
And found the fresh footprints from when that cowherd   90
Had borne that boy away to be better cared for.
Quickly, that werewolf then followed the scent
Hastily to the house where that herdsman lived.
There he walked round the walls to win a better view
And, truly, at last, he finds a little hole.   95
Then he peeped and he pried and openly beholds
How the wife of that herdsman hugs and worships the boy,
And how finely he is fed and so fairly bathed,
And how she warmed to him well as if he were her own.
Then the beast was blithe and pleased for the sake of the boy,   100
For his main wish was always that the boy be well-warded.
Now heartily, from happiness, he looked heavenwards,
And thanked God most thoroughly many thousand times,
And so went on his way, to wend where he liked;
But where I would not know, I will tell you truly.   105
But now, my noble host, hold yourselves still;
And how that beast, through bad works, was brought to be so,
I will tell to you swiftly, most truly for sure.

 This werewolf was not always of this kind,
But had come from a kin both courtly and noble;   110
For his kindly father was the acclaimed king of Spain.
By the grace of God, the king's first wife begat him

But that bold lady died giving birth to the boy.
And so that extolled king, as he thought best counsel,
Wedded another wife, a worshipful lady, 115
A prince-daughter of Portugal as is truly proven.
Yet truly, as a young lady, she had learned much mischief,
For she knew well enough all the workings of witchcraft;
There was nothing more she need learn of the art of black magic[4]
For in the competence of witchcraft she was very well
    educated;[5] 120
That bold queen was called Braundine by courteous nobles,
The first child of the fair king was fostered, as best,*
And he had lords and ladies to host him with love,
And that fair boy began swiftly to grow up fine and proper.
In time, the stepmother queen had malevolent thoughts, 125
On seeing how formal and fair and well-formed the boy was.
And thus she thought thoroughly that never could her
    own son
Come to be called the king there, as heir to that country,
While the king's first son was still thriving and alive.[6]
So she earnestly studied – as all stepmothers will – 130
How to do secret damage to spite her stepchild;
In faith, among fourscore, you would scarce find a good one!†
Thus, truly and fast she took to learn how
To bring that boy hopeless woe, never able to mend,
So he would never in this world ever wear the crown. 135
And so she made an ointment of such great strength,
That by charm and enchantment – may chance bring her evil! –
When that woman therewith had that worthy child
Just but once well-anointed with that potion all over,
He became wholly a werewolf quickly thereafter 140
Such that all his manly form was misshapen by her.
Yet his wits were still there, just as well as before,
But truly, all other likeness to men was now lacking,

---

* Sons of nobles (for example, William Marshal, Earl of Pembroke, in his youth) were often sent away to learn skills from other lords.

† This view of stepmothers is not present in *Guillaume* and is peculiar to the English poem.

And as a wild werewolf he was always to seem.
And when this full-witted werewolf was so transformed,   145
He knew it was by the craft of his accursed stepmother;
And before he went away he thought how he might
Work some wicked revenge, no matter what happened.
And so with no block to bind him, he bounds at the queen,
And he grabbed her with haste to strangle her horribly,   150
So she was near done to death, I truthfully deem.
But in disquiet she cried out, so keenly and loud,
That maidens and mighty men came to her immediately
And would have beaten that beast had he not been so fleet,
And fled fast away into fields afar.   155
And plainly into Apulia he passed at that time
When such fortune befell as I have told you before;
Thus was this wise beast, this werewolf, first formed.
But now I will stop telling of this severe beast,
And talk instead of the attractive child I told you of earlier.   160

Thus this first Fitt has passed of this prize poem,*
And you who love this and would like to listen to more,
All, with a whole heart, to the High King of Heaven,
Please quietly pray a paternoster, at this point,
For the high Earl of Hereford, Humphrey de Bohun,   165
Nephew to King Edward who lies at Gloucester.
For he first ordered translated this fine tale from French,
For the ease of Englishmen, into English speech.
And may God grant His bliss to those who pray so devoutly!

 Lovely lords, now hear more about this little boy,   170
Who the kind wife of the cowherd kept so fairly.
She reared him as well as or better than if he were her own,
Till he was big enough and bold to labour in the field,
And could know all the craft of keeping their beasts,
And bring them to the best pastures when such needs became
    necessary;   175
And he watched them so wisely that they wanted none other.
The bold boy at that time had a bow bestowed on him
And he learned to shoot in the wood's shade so sharply and well
That he quells with that bow many birds and small beasts
And so plenteously in his play that, to speak plainly,   180
When each night he went home while he drove those beasts,
He came so well bedecked carting conies and hares,
And pheasants and fieldfares and other great fowls
That the herdsman, his wife and the whole of their friends,
Would by then be fed fully by that boy with his bow!   185
And he had many fellow friends in the forest each day,
Young bold boys like him, who also kept beasts;
And each boy was as blithe as he best liked to be,
And followed our fellow freely because of his fine ways.
For what things William won each day with his bow,   190

---

* A fitt, or fitte, is a term sometimes used in Middle English poetry to suggest sections or episodes of a romance. In the Blackburn-Ireland MS redaction of *The Auntyrs off Arthure*, the scribe not only divides the work into three distinct sections but writes "a fitte" at the beginning of each one, presumably to assist a household reader.

Be they some feathered fowl or four-footed beast,
Never would this William keep what he caught,
Until his friends were all first favoured to their pleasure.
He was so kind and courteous since he came to that place,
That all loved him who lived there who looked on him but once;   195
They blessed who so had borne and brought into this world
So much manhood and mirth as was manifest in that child.

After some time it betided, as so our books tell us,
That as this bold boy blithely kept his beasts,
The royal Emperor of Rome rode out to go hunting   200
In that fair forest, I tell you faithfully,
    With all his much-esteemed men who were mighty and noble.
Then they found, as befalls, full soon a great boar,
Which they heartily pursued, hunting with hound and horn.
The emperor eyed a good trail, eager to approach   205
And to butcher that boar, once brought to abeyance;

But he mistook a trail mark, and rides so manfully,
That each way that he went he knew not where he rode.
He was so far from his men, I tell you faithfully,
That he might not hear the sound of neither hound nor of horn, 210
Nor of any living soul; he was left all alone.
The emperor, on his stout steed, then strikes down a way
Listening out for his hounds or the shrill of a horn;
But then so comes a werewolf, right in his way then,
Grimly after some great hart as God would allow, 215
By chance chasing it to where that child played
Who kept the beasts of that cowherd I spoke of before.
The emperor than hastily followed that huge beast
As stoutly as his steed might stretch itself to run;
By now he stumbles on that boy and looked all about, 220
The werewolf and wild hart had both run away –
He knew not in this world to where they so went;
Nor where he should seek to see more of them.
But then he looks all about and observes that boy;
How fair and fine he was, and nobly formed; 225
Such a fair, seemly boy he could not recall seeing,
In look nor in build, there was none quite like him,
Nor of such stately semblance; not that his eyes had seen.
The emperor wanders in wonder, in awe at the child,
Who, in faith, seemed a faerie for the fairness it wielded, 230
And for its courteous countenance which so caught the eye.

 Directly, the emperor draws closer until
The child gamely counters and greets him with courtesy.
In haste, the emperor responds honourably with
   his greeting,
    And then quickly afterwards asks the boy his name, 235
And he commanded him tell of what kin he came from.
Then the child said, seriously, "Sir, at your will,
I will tell to you promptly and assuredly the truth.
Sire, I am known as William, by all around here;
I was born here close by, by the side of this wood. 240
My kind father, sire, is a cowherd of this country,

And my esteemed mother is his meek wife.
They have fostered and fed me fairly to this time,
And here I keep all his cows each day as I can;
But, by Christ, of my kin, sir, I can tell you no more."   245
When the emperor had heard all his words wholly,
He was in awe at his fair speech, as well he might be,
And said, "Dear bold boy, be quick I pray you,
Go, call that cowherd to me, he you claim as your father,
For I would talk with him and ask him some questions."   250
"No sire, by God," said the boy, "of this you can be sure!"
"By Christ, who is crowned the High King of Heaven,
I shall not have him harmed, never in his life!
And maybe, by God's grace, it could be good for him;
Therefore, bring him here, fair boy, I pray you."   255
"I shall then, sire," said the child, "but I hope for his safety
I may hold you to your word to work him no harm."
"Yes, surely," said the emperor, "as God gives me joy!"
The child then wanders off swiftly, without further delay,
And quickly calls for the cowherd when he comes to his house;   260
He goes faithfully forthwith to where his father was;
And said then, "Sweet sir, as Christ so help you,
Go yonder to a great lord who is gaily attired,
And one of the fairest of fellows, in faith, I have seen;
For he willingly wishes to speak with you;   265
For God's love, go now quickly, lest he be aggrieved."
"What, son," said the cowherd, "did you say I was here?"*
"Yes, certainly sir," said the child, "but he formally swore
That he should not harm you but, most high and nobly,
Prayed that you come and speak to him and seek him
　　　there swiftly."   270
The churl goes forth grudgingly with the good child,

---

* Both the cowherd's uncertainty to have his location revealed, and William's initial unwilling-
ness to reveal it (l. 251) hint at medieval uncertainties about who to trust and whether, in this
case, nobility can be trusted. The subsequent description of the conversation between emperor
and cowherd reflects two key themes of the romance – that things are sometimes not what they
seem and that good lordship respects the poor.

And they promptly appeared before the emperor.
The emperor then, right as soon as he sees them,
Called the cowherd to him and courteously said;
"Now tell me fellow, in faith, and have no fear,   275
Have you ever seen your emperor, may Christ so help you?"
"No sire, by Christ," said the cowherd, "who is King of Heaven,
I was never yet so hale to be near him so highborn
So that by spending such time I might recognise him."
"Certainly," said the emperor, "you should truly know,   280
That I am that very one, I would have you know well;
And I wield by right all the royal rule of Rome.
Therefore, cowherd, I counsel and also command you,
By virtue of that one thing you love most in the world,
That you tell me promptly, and truly in faith,   285
Whether this bold boy be actually yours,
Or comes from some other kin, so Christ help you!"
The cowherd began to quake, for concern and for dread
When he was aware that here was his lord,
And briskly be-thought that if he tried to bluff him,   290
He would promptly perceive this, he plainly thought.
Thus he told him the truth, truly and swiftly,
Of how he found him in the forest which grew fast beside,
Clothed in comely clothing, fit for any king's son,
Under a hollow oak, through the help of his dog,   295
And how he had fairly fed him and fostered him seven winters.
"By Christ," said the emperor, I convey great thanks to you,
That you have spoken surely the truth about this seemly child,
And all your troubles and travails have not been in vain!
For he shall wend now with me, I would have you know truly;   300
My heart wills so hungrily that I have this boy,
That I wish that in no way you remain as his ward."
When the emperor had so spoken, I tell you surely,
The cowherd was disquieted, and who could blame him?
But in no way could he withstand the will of his lord,   305
And so gave in with goodness, on God's holy name,
So he might work his will with him, as a lord would his own.
When this worthy child William was aware of the truth,

And knew that the cowherd was not his kind father,
He was wholly in wonder and began to weep sorely,   310
And said sadly to himself, very soon thereafter,
"Ah, gracious good God! You the greatest of all!
Much is Your might and mercy, Your esteem and Your grace!
I'll never know in this world now from whom I was born,
Nor what destiny is due me, so let God do His will!   315
Yet I know well and truly, and without fail,
That I am most beholden to this man and his meek wife;
For they have fostered me full fairly and fed me for years,
So may God through His great might yield goodness to them.
But I just don't know what to do by wending from them,   320
Who have kept me most kindly; how can I repay them?"
"Boy, be calm," said the emperor, "please break from your sorrow,
Because my hope for your whole kin, hastily hereafter –
If you would give in to goodness and such grace as may befall –
Is that your friends, for their fore-deeds, shall be fully repaid."   325
"Yes, sire, if Christ wills it," said the cowherd, "then let this
        case be so;
And let God lavish him with the grace to become a good man."
And then promptly he taught the child the following advice,
Saying, "You my sweet son, since you shall wend there,
When you come to the court, among those kingly lords,   330
And come to know all the customs which belong to that court,
Be both obedient and affable, so each noble will love you.
Be meek and be measured, of minimal words,
Be no teller of tales but be true to your lord,
And be prompt in the proffering of help to poor men,   335
So they recount of rich folk in words right and reasonable.
Be you fully generous and faithful and always of fair speech,
And be of service to the simple as so to the rich,
And be a fellow of fine manner as befalls your estate;
So you shall gain all God's love and that of all good men.   340
So learn, son, this lesson, which I learned from my father,
Who came to know courtly ways by long service at court,
And hold it in your heart, now I have told it to you;
May the best things befall you, and never bad deeds bestowed."

 The child wept all the while, wondrously fast,   345
But the emperor had a good grasp of the advice the
   man gave,
And commanded the cowherd, fairly and with courtesy,
To heave that high child up behind him on his steed.
And surely he did do so, although dolefully,
And beckoned him to Christ, who suffered pain on the cross.   350
Then brightly that boy began now to be glad
That he should ride so royally; so readily and with haste
He comes now with courtesy to take leave of the cowherd
And said then, "Sweet sire, I beseech you now,
For the great love of God, please greet my good mother,   355
Who has so fairly fed and fostered me until now.
And loyally, if Our Lord wills that I should have life,
Her travails have not been futile, I say to you truly.
And for God's love, good sire, also greet well and often
All my free fellows that fare in this forest,   360
Whom I have often played with openly in many places:
Hugonet and Huet, the kind-hearted dwarf,
And Abelot and Martinet, Hugo's happy son;
And Akarin the Christian, who was my kindred friend,
And a true kinsman to any pagan's son,[7]   365
And all those other fine fellows whom you fairly know,
May God make into good men to grace Himself much."
The emperor took note of the names which he named,
Then with glee took great pleasure as he greeted all those
Of his country companions most fairly with courtesy.   370
Then he beckoned that cowherd to Christ and all saints,
And forthwith bustled brightly on his way with that boy.
The cowherd went back to his house with care in his heart,
A heart broken and burst on account of the boy.
And when his wife knew, I would tell you truly,   375
How that child, from her ward, was gone away for ever,
Then no man upon earth might tell of but half
Of the woe and the weeping as made by that woman.
She would have slain herself there, sure and swift I believe,
Had not the kind cowherd given her his best comfort,   380

And put her in hope to have great rewards later.
But it is truly now time to leave them in this tale,
And begin to speak next of the emperor and bold boy.

Lords, listen now to this, please, if you will!
The emperor, blithe with that boy, rides on his
    bold horse 385
Fast through the forest till he found his fine company,
Which had taken in that time a great tally of game,
Both boars and bears, by many a cartload,
And harts and hinds and a host of beasts too.
And when his lovely people see their lord arrive 390
They were glad beyond gain and greeted him finely,
But they were all in wonder at the boy borne behind,
So fair and so fine and of such noble form;
They asked fairly and affably where the emperor had found him.
Against this he gave answer; that God had sent him, 395
Beyond that no one knew of those who had first found him.
Then he rode forth with this party right into Rome,
And always the bold boy sat still behind him.
Thus he passed into the palace and promptly alighted,
And William, that choice child, was led into his chamber. 400
Now, this emperor had then a dear damsel daughter,
She was the fairest in form a fellow might ever see;
And truly, William and she were both the same age;
As equal as anyone could adjudge by sight.
That eminent maiden was known as Melior; 405
A more courteous creature, more wise and clever for her age,
Was unknown at this time by anyone in this world.
The emperor goes meekly towards that maid,
And led William with him, that worthy child,
And said, "Dear daughter I would like to declare 410
That I have a prize present for you to please your heart.
Take here this bold boy and be meek unto him,
And keep him cleanly, for he is come from good stock;
I have earned this through hunting such that God has sent me";
And then promptly he told her the whole story truly, 415

49

Of how he had mislaid his men and meandered about,
And how the werewolf went by him with a wild hart,
And how swiftly he pursued him to slay that deer,
Until they brought him to where that boy kept his beasts,
And how his prey disappeared, suddenly from his sight;   420
And how the cowherd came to him and truly recalled
How he had found that fair child at first in the forest,
And how he was clothed as comely as any king's son;
And how the cowherd, from concern, became most sorrowful,
When he knew that the child was to go from him then;   425
And how boldly that boy then bade that cowherd
To greet well his good wife and gamely thereafter
All his free fellows, as I told you before.
"And therefore, my dear daughter," the emperor said,
"For my love do look after him, for truly I think,   430
By his eminent manners and manly mien,
That he comes from good stock, I hope by Christ . . .

*

. . .Now, dear daughter, the name of this noble young man?   B690
He is known as William," says the emperor with warmth.
"I believe by the venerated holy Father most virtuous
That he hails from a family of high noble lineage,
For he is fine and fair, and handsomely favoured
In form and in face and in all of his features;   B695
We know not at this time, but I hope we soon will,
From what kin he comes and from which family's stock.
So, dear daughter of mine, pray devote yourself
To this child whom I chanced on and place in your charge."
"I give you great thanks for granting me this,"   B700
Said that maiden Melior. "My dearest father,
I will mind this young man and do so with much willing."
Then she takes that child and leads him towards
Her private chamber as is pertinent and proper;
She has some robes readied to wrap that boy well   B705
And has him most comely clothed and suitably cared for.

When he was dressed and donned in the dearest of robes,
And fittingly fashioned with the finest of shoes,
That boy looked so noble in form, so fair and so fine,
So formal and frank, and so dignified,   B710
   That none more comely nor keen could be seen as his equal
Anywhere in this world, where so the sun shone,
Or who seemed of such beauty or such wondrous appearance.
And Melior the maiden, she of much noble merit,
Summoned a servant and requested of him   B715
That he fetch some fare, some food for the boy
Who, being so hungry, consumed it with haste.
Now let us turn for a time to the boy's duties.
Because if this boy is the son of some noble king,
So I believe this: it would not be ignoble   B720
If he should serve the emperor at his palace and court
And such a maiden of fine merit and mind
As the amiable Melior, so eminent and lovely.
Thus, William her ward remained with her,
As you will learn if you will listen longer.   B725
He makes every effort to serve her to this end
And all others also and in the same manner.
He finds out how to do this in ways fair and fitting,
In the same way as anyone who has never been
Neither nurtured by nobles, nor brought up at court.   B730
Yet nature, by nature, unravels his grace:
And he, above all those who serve at that palace,
Pays close attention and puts all his whole heart
Into whatever task is granted to him to tackle;
More than any such squire in service anywhere   B735
At that royal court so regal and rich.

That child put his heart so wholly into his tasks,
And was so active and attentive and fully accomplished,
That barely had he been there but a full year,
He had grown so adept, so adroit and able,   B740
   That no peer, prince or person could possibly fault him,
No matter how closely he monitored him

In any of his actions, or attention to duty;
For mistakes he made none, nor did he misbehave.
You may have heard long ago, habitually said, B745
That the noblest of birds, of the gentlest breed,
Learns often alone and all by himself,
Without critical correction by some harsh instructor;
And so as you shall hear, and in such a way,
Did William that wise boy teach himself well. B750

 And in this way William works and lives at the court;
In all those things admirable by which others applaud him,
He does nothing to displease in conducting his duties.
He is gentle and gracious and of noble good will;
Soft-spoken and willing and suitably wise; B755
He makes himself much loved by all men and women;
And is generous and giving, the best he can be.
And know this well, too, that there was no need
To find any fault in the form of his speaking;
For foul words he spoke never nor talked as a fool B760
But was charming and cheerful, and completely enchanting.
He achieved more in chess and the playing of checkers,
In hawking and hunting in woodland or holt,
Than any living soul in all of Lombardy's land.
Nor is there any resident in all of Rome's realm – B765
Be he some household servant, or great lordly son,
Or peerless high prince proved royal by birth –
Who when William sits on his horse in the saddle,
With his shield to his shoulder, shining lance in his hand,
Seems of such fierce features and so finely formed, B770
So erect and so regal, so ready for battle.
I know of nothing more that I might mention to you,
Except that all seem so base when set beside him –
Whether resident of Rome or one living in Lombardy –
He seemed so well to be sire of them all! B775
Neither throughout the kingdom nor the whole Roman empire
Is there any that I know, neither low nor high born,
Who bears so well – do I boast? –

Such very great virtues, however so voiced:
All recount their own tale when talking of them   B780
All the people and public as one praise him well,
And likewise the emperor, in a similar manner,
Holds him in high esteem and loves him as dearly
As if he was of his own boy, and born of his own wife.
And when he so wishes to seek pleasure away   B785
He always takes William along with him too;
Whether on state business or lesser assignments,
Whether near, far or wide, William came too.
And the folk of that kingdom and country about,
Those ruling as lords, or as noble barons,   B790
For love of their lord, that lauded emperor,
All acclaim and applaud that boy with approval,
And also, much more, his great magnanimity;
A particular asset gaining praise and applause.
And what, might I say, of all those maidens,   B795
Those dear noble dames or young damsels at court?
I vouchsafe this with certainty, may God grant me sweet joy:
I simply do not conceive that any who see him,
Or who hear of his deeds or of his honour hailed –
No matter her status, her merit or eminence,   B800
However handsome in beauty or highly esteemed,
Whether noble or not, in nurture or nature,
Whether heedful or haughty, or held to be clever –
Will not wish to be with him and want of his love!

He is revered with regard throughout the whole realm;   B805
And his renown by repute spreads all around.
Thus William was at court wholly three complete years,
Residing right there amongst all the Romans
As I have so told you, and as you have heard.
He grew well and noble, of wondrous refinement;   B810
A youth good and graceful, and always so gracious;
Strong, of fine form, handsome and fair.
His work in the chamber was wondrous to behold;
The maidens and damsels, above all I deem,

Accord him accordingly the greatest acclaim,   B815
For his generous largesse and his vice-less virtue.

 When Melior, that maiden and eminent damsel,
Hears recounted the reverence with which he is regarded,
His qualities and character and noble condition,
And she sees there is no one so fair in this world –   B820
No man of such merit nor so matchless in virtue,
Whether called a king's son or crown prince of an emperor,
One so rich in renown or esteemed in repute –
Then soon her whole heart and her inner hopes
Turn quickly towards him in eager attendance.   B825
Thus she now became sad and inwardly pensive;
And her thoughts cannot think of anything else!
She berates and she blames and belittles her heart
And she frequently cries, "Heart, what have you become?
What have you witnessed, what have you seen?   B830
What is it my eyes have sparked within you
That you so prick and pain me and place me on trial
Such that I do not know what so wracks me within,
Nor what great ambiguities make me so anguished,
And to lament so much more than is normal for me?   B835
Lord God, what curse plagues me to bring me such grief,
That works me to such worry, to writhe without end,

*

Such that I sigh and sing at the same time
Melting nigh into mourning then making much joy?
Though, my heart, you can heal me of all hardships I feel,   435
I suffer still a fierce fainting which often afflicts me,
And takes me so terribly, to tell you the truth,
That I am muddled and maddened nearly to mourning;
Yet you rescue me readily when I sink into sickness,
When I happen to hear of that man being hailed,   440
He who so torments you but whom you hold so noble,
He, that flower of all fellows of fairness and might![8]

No prince is his peer, no angel in paradise,
For that dear man seems so fair in my sight!
I have pitched and painted him so deep in my heart,   445
That he sits in my sight, I think, surely forever!
And so fair is this figure fastened in all my thoughts,
That no cunning nor craft can thus scrape him out;
And if I might try to do this, Oh, Mother Mary, truly,
I would not do so for the world so well do I like it,   450
For such work would win me only bottomless woe!
I have so much love and liking when I see that lord,
That I would rather have that love than lose all my sorrows –
And since this is surely so, to speak the whole truth,
Then I have done a great harm in blaming my heart;   455
So I will celebrate it, and any work that it weaves,
For I would have no other, in all the whole world!
Who then should I blame but my own wicked eyes,
Who led my heart, through their looking, to suffer such misery?
Had they not done their peeping, I may have dodged such pain;   460
Therefore readily, I reason, to rebuke them instead!"
But then she thought this through, in this way, as follows:
"But my eyes surely are subjects in service to my heart,
And bound then to its bidding as a boy to his master;
I would therefore blame wrongly the work of my eyes   465
For, though it may seem so, I may not be so sure
Because I know that my sight is servant to my heart
Just like my other proud wits, and work at its behest.
For although I set my sight steadfast on a thing,
Be it bright or brown, of beauty or plain,   470
My sight may in no manner work me any harm,
Unless my haughty heart gives its hard assent!
So surely my sight is subject to my heart,
And does nothing but its duty, as destiny decrees?
Thus it is my hasty heart that be wholly wrong;   475
I must lambast and blame it, though it may blunt my woes,
And which has so strongly set itself on so strange a fellow,
Whom no one in this world knows from whence he came,
Except that my father found him with a forest cowherd,

Keeping men's cattle in the country without.   480
What? Fie! Should I be so taken of a foundling so fair?
No! My will shall not give way to my wicked heart!
Acclaimed kaisers and kings would consider me craven;
I will not lay my love so low now at this time;
My disgrace would be dire if I did such a thing,   485
I will break from this troubling and blame my heart!"

She tossed and turned in such torment, attempting to sleep,
That of her heart, seriously, she said she would make amends
For the wrong she had wrought it; so quickly thereafter
She said to herself, sighing, in this same manner: 490
    "Now I am but wholly witless – and wondrously foolish –
And heinous and hard to blame my heart thus.
But to whom might I talk to make amends,
Since I am his sovereign, myself in all things;
Surely, in all circumstances, he works at my behest?   495
By comely Christ, I know well, for all my melancholy,
My heart wants for my renown only, nothing more, I believe!
I see well he has set himself in a fine noble place –
Which is peerless among people, praised above all,
Fashioned most fairly and of the finest manners;   500
For no king, nor no duke, is more courteous under Christ.
Though he was found as a foundling in the wild forest,
And kept the cows of a cowherd, to speak but the truth,
Each creature there knew that he came from good stock.
For when he was free in the forest, and first found in his den,   505
He was clad in fine clothes that were fit for a king.
When he first came to this court, he showed by his comportment
That his manners were majestic and none might amend them.
From that time until now he has not lost his teaching,
But has borne himself beautifully such that all nobles praise him,   510
And every man in this world worships him all as one,
Whether king, courtly duke, keen knight or another.
Though he came from no such kin, being cultured by a churl –
Yet as I wholly know he was never of such kind! –
I think that I might well love him, and with much worship;   515

56

Since he is peerless and praised above princes and others,
And each lord of this land is pleased wholly by him
As a most seemly man, of superior manners;
Thus I have wrongly denounced the work of my heart
For he has done his duty, as he ought, with due dignity! 520
He serves me more worthily than any woman on earth,
Through the kind lineage of Christian law;
Thus has my heart so worked his will highly
As to set himself surely on the most special man
Who lives in any land, and who is lauded by all! 525
I have no worldly knowledge how my heart might any better
Work for me in this world to secure my renown;
For if any man might on earth be more worthy than he,
My heart is so haughty he would make his man higher!
And I have so wrongly worked to blame him for my wounds; 530
I greatly beg his forgiveness for my guilt in this case,
And vow to make full amends for my mistaken slander!
I will wholly hereafter, without further delay,
Work to what my heart wills, whatever so happens,
And lay my love on that lord loyally for ever. 535
God has given me a gift, it shall not come again;
So for as long as he lives, I grant that man my love."

 And when she had thus assented, she said soon afterwards,
Sadly sighing and sorely for the sorrow in her heart,
"Alas! This bitter heartbreak will bring only disaster 540
For I know not in this world how that worthy boy
Shall ever know of my woe without me telling him!
No! I myself know for certain I shall never tell him;
For that would win such woe it would never be mended!
For he might, full well, hold me for a fool, 545
And loath my love so much that I would rather die!
No! Best it be not so; better things might befall;
I must work other ways if I want to succeed.
Suppose it were such, should it happen so,
That I were so unsound that I would speak to him, 550
He who is the most seemly, so to save my honour;

57

And that I told him truly my troubles and woes,
And what a life of love-longing I lead for his sake?
He would think I was mad, or I openly mocked him,
Or my deeds were done from spite to do him dishonour;   555
Such would be shocking and shameful, and shame me for ever!
What if I said to him seriously that instead I was sick,
And told him most truly my sickness's symptoms?
But he knows nought of such craft, by Christ, as I trust
Thus he would in no way understand what I meant;   560
So that, when I had bemoaned my woes, he could say no more
Than "certainly sweet lady your sorrows grieve me".
And my woes would then wax once again all anew,
Then my sadness would double for I dare not show it!
Alas! Why, he knows nought of the woe which ails me,   565
What sorrows and sickening I suffer for his sake!
I sail now in the sea as a ship with no mast,
Without anchor or oar or any seemly sail;
So high heavenly King send me to a good haven,
Or else shorten my life in no little time!"   570
Thus Melior, that maiden, lamented all morning,
And it held her so hard, I tell you the whole truth,
That soon within seven nights she was unable to sleep,
Her want for all meat or mirth went missing for a while
And she succumbed to such sickness, to speak of this truly,   575
That no healer in the land might be sure of her life,
For none can, by their craft, conceive of her sorrow;
Thus doleful she pined, day after day,
And all her clear colour came simply to fade.

 Then this eminent Melior had many maidens   580
Assigned to serve her, and assist in attendance;
But among all those maidens there was one she loved most,
A most dignified lady, as I deem to be true,
Who came from the same kin, a close cousin indeed;
A duke's daughter, of Lombardy, dressed in fine clothes;   585
And that amiable maiden was called Alisaundrine.
And from the time when Melior began mourning most strongly,

That woman was ever by her, and busy to please her;
More than any other maiden, she loved her so much.
So when she sees her so sick, she said one time,   590
"Now Madam, for Mary, the mild Queen of Heaven,
And that love which you laud her with, most loyally on earth,
Say to me what sickens you; what sorrow grieves you.
You know I am your close cousin, by Christ in heaven,
So by seeking my counsel, I could help to heal you –   595
And be trusty and true to you for evermore –
And so help you to regain your health, and with haste,
If you spell out your sorrows so I might best solve this."
When Melior, that meek maid, heard Alisaundrine's words,
She was greatly gladdened by all her good promises   600
And said to her then, with some sad sighing; –
"Ah, courteous cousin, may Christ bless you well
For the kind comfort given in what you now declare;
You have warmed me well, with your pleasant words!
I give myself to your grace to help regain my health;   605
As you have asked me here about what hard pains ail me,
So I will tell you of my troubles, whatsoever betides.
For certain, this sickness which so sorely grieves me
Is more fevered than any soul has ever suffered.
Often it takes me some nine times each day –   610
And ten times at night, not even one less –
All caused by a throbbing thought which thrills my heart;
I would tell you all of my matters if I might, for shame,
And will not hesitate in doing so, of that you can be sure.
Yes these hard pains which haunt me, which are so harmful,   615
They come from keen thoughts which capture my heart
Of that bold noble William, who is praised by all men;
No man on earth wins more worship than that man does.
I have so properly painted him, portrayed in my heart,
That he seems in my sight to sit most humbly.   620
Whenever I meet a man, or I come to speak with one,
I think thoroughly each time that he is William instead;
A fair few times I have tried to flit him from my thoughts
But, without doubt, all my work is always in waste.

59

Therefore, courteous cousin, for heavenly Christ and His love,   625
Acquaint me with your kindness and counsel me for the best;
For if my heartbreak not be cured, within a brief time,
I will be as dead as a doornail – please do all that you can!"

Then afterwards Alisaundrine, in answering this,
Was greatly in wonder and wrestled in thought   630
How to comfort her completely and calm all her sorrows;
Then she said to her softly, some moments later;
"Ah, madam, cease mourning, for the love of Mary!
For this is no sickness that ails you so sorely,
I think that, through craft, I can help you recover;   635
I will go and gather a herb, which I know will bring gain!
Used selectively, it is said, and taken just once,
The taste which sits in its roots, its scent and its sweetness,
Shall in my view, through virtue, make your sorrows vanish!"
She would not, however, let her lady know   640
What means she meant to use, lest she were aggrieved.
Then Melior, most meekly, thanked that maiden,
And privately prayed her, with piteous words,
To go and gather that good grass as soon as she might.
And so Alisaundrine answers and said,   645
"Madam, I will do it immediately, without one more word."
Then this maiden Melior began to mend her cheer;
Thus, her sad sorrow ceased for the first time.
Then Alisaundrine, in all ways, after a while,
Besought herself busily how best to work,   650
To make known unto William the will of her lady,
Properly, unperceived, however later reproved.
She was crafty and cunning and clever in all things;
Of charms and enchantments to challenge all afflictions;
Thus, through her knack and craft, to speak of the truth,   655
As William, that worthy lad, slept through the night,
With nobody in his bower but himself all alone,
A splendid sweet dream she set him to have:
That her sweet maiden Melior, meekly and alone,
Clad in most comely clothes comes to kneel before him,   660

All weeping with woe – or so he thought –
And sickening full sadly she said this to him:
"Lovely sweetheart lad! Look now upon me!
I am Melior, near mad, man, all for your sake.
I place myself at your mercy for only you might save me! 665
Lovely lord, my sweetheart, clasp me in your arms,
And work your will with me, lest wholly and fast
My life is truly lost, I am so lovelorn for you."
Thus William thought wholly and quickly on this,
As a man greatly glad for the grace which befell him; 670
He hoped to envelop that lady most lovingly in his arms –
Although he instead clasps a pillow, greeting it properly –
And welcomes her worthily, for wholly he thought
That it was the maid Melior, that eminent lady!
He clasped that pillow courteously and kissed it full often, 675
And made the most mirth with it that any man might;
But, in his uttermost ecstasy, he then awoke softly.
Yet he liked this leisure so much, his play with the lady,
That long after he was awake, a full while indeed,
He writhed wholly as if she were still in his arms; 680
But, by Peter, it proved to be nought but his pillow!
Yet when he was fully awake, he now looked all around
To have beheld that beauty and increase his bliss.
Then he perceived that pillow all plain in his arms;
Otherwise there was no one within that chamber. 685
Then he bustled from his bed, as a boy much amazed,
And looked for that lady, in all truth he so went
As if meanwhile she had hid in some private hollow
To grieve him in her game, as if to beguile him.
But when he was aware that he was wasting his time, 690
He became sick with sorrow and said in this way,
"Ah, Jesus Christ my justice, judge this to be right;
How falsely has fortune left me foundered now!
Why is my eminent lady, Melior, not here,
Who humbled herself to be my lover, and lay here in my arms, 695
And who also said surely that she would rather die?
Yes, I know it was she! I know it well and true;

In no manner might it be that this was but some dream,
For that lady was lovely, us delighting each other.
Thus surely so, I would think, it is some splendid marvel, 700
Where that lady has wandered who has vanished from here."
Then he leaps up lightly and looked all about,
But faithfully, all was falsehood and all was in waste.
Then he said to himself, sighing full softly,
"In truth, I am mad, I may well know it now, 705
For to wonder whether this would be more than a dream!
My heart is too haughty in climbing so high
So to lodge with that lady that would lower herself –
She the heir to an emperor and even his peer -
To come to such a cur! No! Christ forbid 710
That my mistaken mind dwells more on this matter!
For there is no lord in any land that wields any life,
Whether called king or emperor, crowned and with wealth,
That surely is not too base, to wed that seemly one.
So, without doubt, I am mad to hold such a view, 715
Through a much-muddled dream, that such a maid would
Lay her love so low as to call me her lover!
No, I have worked all in waste; I will not any more
Lay my love so high to win her for my lady –
Though it yearns for none other, no one upon earth – 720
While I know not myself from whom I am descended.
I know not my own kin, my home country neither,
Therefore, it behoves me obediently to behave
As one who, otherwise, was with his own friends.
For if I worked otherwise, and it was perceived, 725
And discussed in this court, my concerns would be greater;
For, in faith, I have no friend who would speak for me
If the emperor were wrathful and worked his rage on me.
So it behoves that my heart be not haughty but chaste,
And I bare myself blandly, till better things betide." 730

 And so in this way, William worked to escape his woes,
But surely that seemly one still sat in his heart;
For the joy made with Melior, the beauty in his dream,
Hangs so heavy in his heart, and cleaved so hard,

That nothing in this world would drive it away.   735
He was, from time to time, so distracted, often seeming in study,
That truly, little by little, he sunk so low in malaise,
That he mourned to near madness and refused all his meals,
And, wearied through woeful wandering, he wakes often at night.
Such longings of love had so engulfed his heart,   740
He knew not the best way to abate his bleak yearning.
But in his immense mourning, he rises on the morrow
On account of his heartache, and clothed himself quickly.
And when he was graced so gainfully, he then grabbed his cloak;
As a most woeful man, he wrapped himself so within it   745
That no man whom he met would know of his mourning.
Then that gloomy one goes now into a garden,
A fine, peerless place, fit for any prince on earth,
That was wound all about by a wondrous high wall.
That private play place, to tell you the truth,   750
Was joined well and just close to Melior's chamber.
So William went there, I would have you know truly,
And took a seat quickly beneath a fine apple tree
That had branches full broad and bore great shade,
And was set right below Melior's window;   755
So obsessed was William, bound up in his woe.
That fair tree was so full of leaves, so bedecked with flowers,
That none might see William unless they were nearby,
Yet, by looking up at the window, William wholly might see
If Melior and her maidens sat there in a meeting.   760
Once William had taken his place under that trusty tree,
He set his sight surely and securely on that window,
Without flinching or fainting, from morning till night.
But often his cravings recur and his colour changes,
So sorely he longed for that seemly lady.   765
Such sorrow he suffered some seven nights full,
That never might that man take meat into his body,
Yet was fully fed to his fill just for to look
On the room of his maid Melior, for whom he so mourned.
And when it neared night, and he was still numb with grief;   770
He would wander to his chamber and still make great woe;

But no soul who served him might surely know
Why he was so woeful, nor where he spent his days;
None dares, for dread, to keep watch on him discreetly,
So they let him work his will, as well as he would.   775
Thus, he dressed quickly and deftly each day in the morning,
And faithfully, without fellowship, would walk frantically,
And then go to the garden, his grief for to slake,
To wait at the window, where his woes would awake,
And he would sicken so often and sometimes quake;   780
Such dolorous dread drove to his heart,
That he never should in this world win her whom he so yearned.
Through the sorrows that he suffered, so truly to tell,
All his clear colour comes thus to fade;
He grew so feeble and faint from waking at night,   785
That no one in this world might know what distressed him.
But then it happened one time, as this tale tells,
That William went to this garden, his woe for to slake,
And under that trusty apple tree turned to sit down,
As one kept awake by his woes of a night;   790
And as he waited by the window, as he would always do,
He slipped slumbering down, into a fast sleep,
As one so woe-weary with being so long awake.
But we must now speak of Melior, who was also in mourning;
Like him, sorrowful or more so – if such might be so –   795
For the love of lovely William who lay so nearby.
Then she asked this of Alisaundrine, as so it happens,
Just as woeful William was fallen sleep,
Whether she had gathered that grass which should heal her grief.
"No, madam, not yet," said that maid then;   800
"Though I have been fixed on finding it a full many times,
But my work was all in waste: I am sorry to say.
But, if it were your will now to work as I advise,
Let us go to the garden, I think good may come of it,
For we shall find some fair flowers, and hear the song of fowls,   805
And come to catch such comfort through what happiness occurs,
That it will hopefully heal you by the time you come home."
And so that eminent Melior meekly followed her wishes,

So to work at her will, as she would advise.
Then, right away, she arose and they both readily walked,   810
Gaining that garden quickly by going down some steps;
Bare of ladies or bearers, but just themselves alone.
In advance, Alisaundrine had in fact rightly arranged,
On account of her craft that she had contrived before,
That they would certainly then come to meet with William.   815
And when those gracious girls had come into the garden,
They found there fair flowers of a full many hues,
That were so sweet to savour and so splendid to see;
And each bush bloomed with birds which most blithely sang,
Both the thrush and the throstle, some thirty of both,   820
Made melody full merry in all manner of ways,
And all finely those fowls sang in that fair park;
They made so much noise, for the mirth of that May time,
That it would gladden anybody who heard their glee here.
But despite all that mirth, Melior mourned so strongly,   825
And so hard had her love pains pierced her heart,
That no glee under God might make her glad;
For faithfully, in feebleness, she soon started to faint,
And she sat down to rest beneath a seemly sycamore[9]
And beside that bright maid who knew all of her troubles.   830
Then, when Melior bemoaned all the mischief which ailed her,
That other then countered with comfort and joy,
And both examined the matter that concerned them the most.
Then Alisaundrine, by her wiles, looked slightly away
Towards where William had waited so long,   835
For she knew full well the place where he lay.
Then she said swiftly, to that seemly maid,
"Madam, dear Melior, by Mary in heaven,
I think I see a young soul asleep near beside,
Whether he be knight or bachelor I truly know not,[10]   840
But he seems, by his semblance, to be sunk in sickness,
Therefore, lady, let us go and see what sickness ails him,
And who that somebody may be, that lies troubled with woe."
Then that eminent maid said meekly to Melior,
"Ah Madam, Melior, now may this mend your cheer,   845

For surely, who is it but William, whom you so well love!
He has had some harsh sickness and come here from some sport
So to lessen his melancholy, and thus he lies here sleeping
To savour the sweet scent of these seemly flowers."

 Then the eminent Melior was very much gladdened, 850
And both go to that gentleman at a good pace.
And on coming towards him, to tell you the truth,
They sit down softly before him in a most seemly way.
And when that maid Melior might see his face,
She thought thoroughly at heart that she would prefer 855
To be with him always than be queen of the world,
Because she thought that this fellow was so fair in his features.
And, in faith, she would have folded him freely in her arms,
And cuddled and kissed him most keenly right then;
Yet she dared not do so for dread of spies seeing her. 860
And so Alisaundrine assembled her thoughts,
And quickly, with her wiles, caused William to dream,
Such that he then dreamt that Melior most high
And Alisaundrine alone had come to him,
And that this maid Melior had full meekly brought to him 865
A most regal rose, which he takes readily;
And when he had it in his hand, it seemed wholeheartedly
That he was safe and sound, free of all his sorrows.
Thus his melancholy was so lifted, and he felt such delight,
And so greatly was he gladdened that he began to wake up. 870
And when he sees her so seemly sitting before him,
He was all of a wonder, and swiftly gets up,
Then, kneeling through courtesy, he greets that comely one,
And Alisaundrine afterwards, as is appropriate.
And then that maid Melior most meekly said to him, 875
"My sweet lovely beloved, our Lord give you joy!"
And when William was aware of the words that she said,
That she had called him "beloved", it so lit up his heart
That truly, without doubt, for a while he was speechless,
And he stared on her stupefied, so stunned by joy 880
That his complexion lost colour, he became all pale,

Then became, in a short while, rose-red just as swiftly.
So wholly did that word work its way to his heart
That, amazed and near mumbling, he seemed almost mad,
So wholly had Love loosed an arrow on him   885
So hard through his heart; all because that high maid
Called him "dear beloved", he seemed to lose all his might.

 But Alisaundrine was wise to that which so ailed him,
And said to him seriously these self-same words:
"Sweet William, see here, what sickness grieves you?   890
Your fair hue has faded so much through your affliction,
And if I might amend it by any manner, I would."
Then William, with speed, answered in this way,
Sickened most sadly by the sorrow in his heart,
"My dear good damsel, my death is inevitable;   895
For such a bottomless blackness binds me so deeply
That never did a fellow have such a fierce fever!
For it makes me ignore all mirth and all meat;
I might not sleep, be assured, so sorely it grieves me.
And all this much mischief is made from a dream   900
Which came on me at night – accursed be that time!
And such hard hurting pains have held on to me since
That I know not in the world what it is I should do!"
"Now, sweet man," said Alisaundrine, "say to me thus,
How these harsh pains afflict you, and the hurt that they yield."   905
"Without fail," said William, "I will conceal nothing.
Sometimes it holds me with heat, as hot as any fire,
But just as quickly and keenly cold comes thereafter;
Sometimes I sigh and sing at the same time,
And then such anxious thoughts pierce my heart so thoroughly,   910
That I know not in the world where so it might wander,
For in faith, in myself, I then feel but nothing."
Then Alisaundrine in answering said afterwards,
"William, I would ask you that you will tell me
How come all your sickness is caused by a dream?"   915
"No, assuredly, sweet lady," he said, "I shall never do that,
No matter the mischief that might fall upon me!

I would rather conceal it and live through this melancholy,
Though by enduring this distress I may die at the end;
Thus none in this world will know why it comes on me!" 920
Then Alisaundrine said, "What ails you is deadly;
What power it wields, I would know for sure!"
"Yes, truly," said William, "it grieves me wickedly,
For though my sickness and sighing is sometimes assuaged,
I also mourn many times, much more than before." 925
Melior, that mild maid, thought on this meanwhile
And said to herself softly these self-same words:
"A gracious God, greatest of us all!
Take heed of Your handiwork, and help us two now!
For sure, this same sickness also grips me, 930
In all ways and worse, I know, as it does William.
And I see well how that sickness grips him most sorely;
It has plagued him so piteously who once seemed so peerless
In both fairness and feature of any known fellow.
But alas! He knows not the woes which I too endure, 935
And have suffered loyally for his love for such a long while!
And if he would know of it, well then, I am undone,
For I dare not, for shame, show him what I wish,
Unless he would, in any way, show his hand first!"
While Melior, in this manner, lamented thus to herself, 940
Alisaundrine meanwhile assembled all her thoughts:
She could see in each countenance how they looked at each other,
So she said these words, quickly, to William,
"I see well by your semblance what sickness ails you:
No matter how hard you hide it, I wholly know 945
It is the sweet lock of love which hold you in its clasp.
You are like weights in the weighing, and I know well
How they bow back and too in lively balance unending.
And, since I see this is so, I shall thus let you know
That, little by little, I'll soon bring you relief." 950
Then William well understood that she knew what ailed him,
And knew all his kept secrets despite his concealment;
He was in dread of death in case she worked to his detriment.[11]
Then, supplicant on his knees, he said softly to her,

"Eminent maid, have mercy, for love of Mary in heaven!   955
I give up all to your grace to help me in my grief,
For you might lengthen my life, if you will it, and soon."
And Alisaundrine then said in answer as follows,
"How might I help you? What have I to cure you?"
"Well, if you cannot," said William, "I will never be healed.   960
My life, ill fortune and death rest all in your hands.
For if I have not the succour, soon, of that sweet maid -
That comely creature whom you keep as your ward -
Than all of the surgeons of Salerno will not save my life.
Therefore, lovely lady, all my hopes lie with you;   965
You might spare me or spear me, with equal speed, as you will."

 And then Alisaundrine answered and said,
"Now, surely, William, I will tell you honestly,
Since you have steadfastly told me the truth of your secret,
And have told me truly that you trust me to help,   970
Then if I might mend your sorrow, in any manner,
But not busy myself to it, then blameworthy am I!
Therefore, be you sure and certain, since it may not be otherwise,
You will quickly have all my help, and most wholly."
Then William was greatly glad and thanked that lovely lady.   975
And then Alisaundrine, as she was so accustomed,
Called that maid Melior meekly towards her
And said, "Take mercy, madam, on this man here,
That is near driven to death and all for your sake!"
"How so for my sake?" said Melior then,   980
"I know I have never wronged him, in word nor in deed."
"No certainly, madam, that is so," said that other,
"But he has languished for your love for a good long while;
If you do not grant him your grace, and help him with great speed,
And let him be your beloved, loyally for ever,   985
He will not live through this misery any longer than tomorrow.
Therefore, comely creature, by Christ who made you,
Let him not lose his life yet for a little while;
Since he loves you so loyally, please take him as your love!"
Then Melior, most meekly, spoke to that maid,   990

And said most seriously, smiling a little,
"Now, by God that gave me my spirit and my soul,
I care not for no creature to call me a murderess;
I would much rather prefer to save a man's life!
Since he is made so maddened by me, and suffered much for
    so long,   995
Then willingly, as you have prayed so, and also for the peril
Which I see besets him, thus – to save his life –
Here I grant him graciously, in God's holy name,
My loyal love for ever, for all of my life,
And give this vow to God, and to His good mother,   1000
That I'll never love any other, for as long as I live!"
When William heard these words, I will tell you truly,
He sank quickly to his knees and thanked God full often,
And said, "God, who made man and all of Middle Earth,
You have wrought for me now a mighty miracle indeed!"   1005
Then he humbled himself to Melior in every manner,
As the gladdest and most gleeful man God ever wrought.
And, in the same way on her side, she responded likewise,
To work with all her will to give him what he liked.
Then both held the other hastily in their arms,   1010
And came to greet each other with so many keen kisses
That neither might desire more such mirth in the world.
Quickly, each came to tell of their troubles and woes,
Which they had long suffered sadly for the sake of the other.
And, at this time, Alisaundrine acknowledged this truth: 1015
That her mistress and this man might not miss her now,
So she walked for a while away from their sight;
For she truly believed, to tell you the truth,
That were she out of the way, then William would find
Time to play in that place the private love game.   1020
So she took herself meanwhile to seek pleasure elsewhere;
She goes about in the garden to gather some flowers,
And to watch so that no one would walk therein,
For dread they discover the doings done there.
Then William with Melior played at his will,   1025
And each loved to their liking, all the long day,

Till the sun was nigh set, surely, to rest.
At this point, Alisaundrine approached them with caution
And meekly to Melior, "Madam," she said,
"Did you get that grass which you asked me to gather?   1030
I truly trust at this time that your woe has departed!
Both of you, I believe, is like each other's physician;
All the surgeons in Salerno could not have worked sooner
To alleviate your lamenting, this I surely believe!"
Then William grew quickly and wholly ashamed   1035
And Melior and he meekly asked for her mercy,
That she conceal their conduct well, whatever might occur;
And they thoroughly thanked her many thousands of times,
For she had brought both of them from bleak woe, they said,
And lengthened their lives for many a long year.   1040

 And then Alisaundrine, shortly after that,
Promptly asked Melior to cease her mirth-making
And said, "It is so near to night that needs must you part;
I dread you being discovered, for you have dwelled here
    awhile!"
"Alas so much mischief!" said Melior then,   1045
"This day is so much shorter than it first seemed!"
And William, surely, said the same at that time
But Alisaundrine afterwards answered and said,
"Make not any mourning, for you may meet often –
Discreetly each day, henceforth, whenever you dare –   1050
Therefore, high ones, please make haste and depart."
Then both see no succour; they must separate and split,
So, with clasping and kissing, they then took their leave
And each took themselves promptly to their own chamber,
Both of them so blissful that their bleakness was cured;   1055
Henceforth and so wholly they had quickly recovered!
And thus for many years, with love's many amusements,
They played privately together, and unperceived,
Such that none under the sun suspected any guile.
William was so well beloved by rich, poor or whoever,   1060
And so free with his fellows in endowing his fair gifts,

That, assuredly, the emperor himself loved him supremely,
And so did everyone else who saw him with their eyes.
And Alisaundrine always served them at each turn
And in such ways so discreetly that no evil was suspected,   1065
And all gave good words whose company they graced.

It betided after some time, as the tale tells,
That the selfish duke of Saxony drew into that land
With an august great host of good men of arms,
To wage war wrongly with the emperor then,   1070
    And with boasting and bluster he burnt several towns.
No strength could withstand him of any stout walls,
And he beat down many boroughs, and brutalised many people,
Such that much distress was dealt as so wrought by those deeds.
When these tidings were told to the Emperor of Rome,   1075
He was greatly aggrieved – no one thought him guilty –
That anyone in this world should make war on his land.
He then sent his messengers swiftly all about,
To all the lords of his land, the lesser and the great,
That owed him service through homage or other allegiance,   1080
And warned them, to wit, why he had sent for them,
And had them all hurry to him as hard as they might,
Well-equipped for war with noble horses and arms.
When the command of the emperor was called all about,
Many was the bold noble that busked to him quickly,   1085
Kings and acclaimed dukes and excellent knights,
And other bold nobles, about sixty thousand,
All bound ready for battle in the brightest of arms:
And right into Rome all these ranks draw
To work the emperor's will, however he thought best.   1090

When William that worthy one was aware of these
    doings,
There was no gladder man that God ever made.
He went straight to the emperor and said straightaway,
    Kneeling calm on one knee, courteously as becomes,
"For the love of God, good sir, pray grant me this boon: 1095

Dub me into knighthood to do battle for you,
And I hope by heaven's King that my help shall never fail you,
And that with my manly might I will maintain your rights."
The emperor was greatly gladdened and granted his will,
And made him a knight on the morrow and, for his sake,
    made more   1100
Of the sons of proud princes, the doughtiest in the world –
Some full fourscore for the love of William –
And had them all horsed and armed as a high lord should,
And made William their warden, as well he might,
To guide and to govern those gallant young knights.   1105
And when the host of the emperor was wholly assembled,
He told those great men before him all his troubles and harms:
Of how the duke of Saxony had done him great wrong,
And had burned all his boroughs and quelled his nobles,
And he commanded them kindly to give him their counsel   1110
As to what were the best ways for him to work his revenge.
And all said with one voice, "Sire, we advise,
Sally forth with your host, stand back no longer,
And do unto that duke what deeds that you may;
Hem him in so hard that he is driven to some place;   1115
Pursue him to some city and besiege him there,
Until you have defeated that fellow, with much fine force."

 When the emperor knew well the will of his counsel,
He directly made ready and advanced on his way,
With the whole of that host which he had assembled.   1120
And they were well furnished with abundant supplies,
So plenteous that his people might pass where they would.
And they headed out so hard, I have to say truly,
That all his well-equipped company soon came to that place
Near where that doughty duke had wrought such distress.   1125
It was quickly told to the duke, I tell you truly,
How the emperor and his host had come to them here,
To right himself of the wrong which he claimed was wrought
    there;
So, with boast and bluster, he swiftly sent nobles,

As evil envoys to the emperor, and egged him on swiftly*   1130
To bring himself to battle by a certain day,
Or else shortly he would, he sent them to say,
Brutally kill all his nobles and burn all his lands.
These tidings were told to the emperor quickly;
And at once, when he knew this, he called for William,   1135
That bold young bachelor, and told him before long
How disdainfully the duke had told him of his desire
To be bound on a set day to bring him to battle.
Sir William, most wisely, then said these words,
"Sire, God through His grace grants you to speed well,   1140
To abate all that boasting of this brash duke.
And so I well hope, sire, we shall emerge the best."
The emperor, with eminence, then said to the messengers
He would blithely be ready to fight that bold battle;
So they departed in haste and soon told the duke.   1145
Then both parties, promptly, prepared themselves
With all the trusty attire needed to do battle,
And they made themselves merry in the meanwhile,
Till that self-same day came which had been truly set.
Then both parties prepared themselves, at that place suitably
          chosen,   1150
On a fine fair field, to tell you faithfully.
Then their battles busked here in the best fashion;[12]
And when the ranks were arrayed, readily as appropriate,
Buglers and trumpeters began to blow quickly,
And all manner of minstrelsy was made there then   1155
So to harden the hearts of those high nobles.
Then the battle began, most boldly indeed;
Many stunning strokes were given out sternly,
And many a bold noble was brought out of life.
But shortly, to tell you the shape of this tale,   1160
The duke's men were much bolder, if I dare speak the truth;
He had many more than the emperor, and they fought so manfully

---

* The text reads "enviously to þemperour, and egged him swiþe" (lit. "maliciously to the emperor and taunted him swiftly").

That the first battle, horribly, was much bludgeoned to death,
And then fast, out of fear, began to flee where they might;
But the Germans chased swiftly and slew them right down.   1165
When the emperor saw this sight, his men all so quelled,
He was wondrously woeful, I will tell you truly,
And full piteously he prayed to the Prince of Heaven
For Him to grant the good grace to safeguard his men,
And said, "High King of Heaven, by Your holy name,   1170
Please do not favour my foe, who so falsely ruins me.
Dear God, why? I never induced nor gave any reason
For him to work me any wrong nor make war in my land!
And lord, he is my liege man, as You know loyally,
For wholly all of his lands he holds of myself.   1175
Thus more wrongly he works, as all the world knows,
Therefore, to my mind, Lord, for the love of Your mother,
Help me have the upper hand, in my rights hereafter!"*

 William, that young knight, was so near to hand
That he heard the pitiful pleas which the emperor
   had made,   1180
And he sickened for sorrow and was sad indeed.
   So quickly he called all his young knights to come,
And said, "Loyal lords, listen to my words!
Now let us confirm our claim to be called knights, by Christ!
Look, our folk begin to fall through default of help;   1185
On your lives, don't be slow in helping your lord!
With haste, and good hearts, hurry now to the deed:
And whoso fails for his cowardice, let wild fire burn to death!"
Then without any more words William gallops off at once
Fiercely towards his foes as a fellow near deranged.   1190
Where the press was most perilous, he pricked his horse foremost,
And blessed so many with his broadsword about every side
Such that any warrior so wrought by it never rose again.

* The emperor, in outlining the case for his actions, is asserting his right to pursue a Just War against the duke. See Appendix 1 for more insight into Just War philosophy in the Middle Ages.

And surely for to say, within a short while,
William plied so wonderfully with his own hand,   1195
That he slew six of the greatest, I can assure you,
And these dead were the doughtiest in the host of the duke:
The first one was his nephew, a noble knight of arms;
The next was his steward who administered his retinue;
The others were lords of that land, the best and most loyal.   1200
And when the duke was aware of how William demeaned him,
And how brutally he'd battered his nobles to death,
And, in particular, his nephew, whom he held nearest to heart,
He was nigh out of his wits, both for wrath and with anger,
And called on his courageous knights who were keen and noble,   1205
And said, "My lords, for my love, do not stall any longer,
But seek out that keen knight that works such carnage on us.
Look how loathsomely that lord lays into our men!
None may withstand the strokes which he strikes so sternly."
Thus the duke then declaimed and raved with such disdain   1210
That his knights swiftly swore that, whatsoever occurred,
They would take William at once, whether quick or dead.
Then a great retinue of rich warriors all ride together
And went straight to Sir William and beset him all round;
But with doughty great blows he long defended himself.   1215
But, surely to say so, he was soon outmatched,
And they, with fine force, withstood all his fair strokes,
And wounded him wickedly, and won his steed from him,
And soon bound him briskly, to bring him to grief,
And drew him to the duke so to learn of his doom.   1220
But William's own retinue were soon aware of this,
And with doughty conduct dealt out many great dints;
Those brisk, keen young knights were so acclaimed for their
      strength
That at once and swiftly, they worked many a wide way
Till they had pierced through the press to reach their master
      plainly,   1225
And rescued him readily from those warriors who held him.
Then they unbound him briskly and brought him his steed,
And he was expertly attired in his trusty fine arms:

His shield on his shoulder, a sharp sword in his hand.
And when William was ready, he watched all about; 1230
Fiercely, like a lion, he leaps into the press,
Promptly, right where the press of the people was thickest.
Then he lent such lusty blows to those lords he assailed,
That he soon lays low the life of any lent such a blow;
And thus he drew to the duke, dealing such payment, 1235
And as soon as he sees him, he seized a spear,
And addressed himself to the duke, desiring promptly to joust.
And when the duke was aware that he would come forth,
He fearlessly, too, fastened his spear to the fewter*
And so grimly, with great courage, each goes at the other. 1240
And William, by good will, hit the duke so well,
That the sharp spear gouges through both shield and shoulder,
And wholly he hurled both horse and man to the ground.
Then he leaps lightly down and lets out his sword,
And he said devoutly, directly to the duke, 1245
"Sire, you said not long past that you should conquer me,
And had made your men bind me and suffer me mischief;
But greatly I thank God, Who granted me my escape,
And if you wanted your will, well, you have thought wrongly!
Thus sire, in the same way are you beset now, 1250
And I am pressed as your prisoner to pay you my ransom!
Yield to me in reply, or you shall quickly die,
For all the armed men on earth may not now prevent it!"

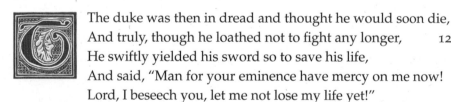

The duke was then in dread and thought he would soon die,
And truly, though he loathed not to fight any longer, 1255
He swiftly yielded his sword so to save his life,
And said, "Man for your eminence have mercy on me now!
Lord, I beseech you, let me not lose my life yet!"
Then William at once, as a high lord would,

---

* A fewter in the late medieval period was a small hook fitted to the breastplate to bear the weight of a lance. In the twelfth-century *Guillaume* and perhaps at the time of de Bohun's translation, the word carried a more generic meaning, possibly suggesting resting the lance in a horizontal position on the saddle ready to joust.

Received his sword regally, from that royal duke. *   1260
And thus he hurried to the emperor with that man then.
When the emperor sees William come to him with the duke,
He was the gladdest of magnates that might go on earth;
And he wends forward to William to welcome him again,
And clasped him kindly, and kissed him many times.   1265
Then William at once, as well he ought,
Proffered him the prisoner, promptly and freely,
For to do with the duke as he best deemed.
The emperor gave thanks often for Sir William the worthy
Which the great grace of Lord God had so gloriously bestowed;   1270
And no more strokes were dealt once that duke was taken,
For all his folk began to flee as fast as they might,
And he who had the best horse held himself best saved.
But the men of the emperor manly chased them in rout,
And slew them down on each side, those whom they might take,   1275
Unless immediately and meekly they cried for their mercy.
And as always it was William who went among them,
To the boldest of nobles as he had done before,
Who truly, dare I say, sought his succour then;
Right few went away unwounded or captured.   1280
Had that day lasted longer, I say to you loyally,
No one would have escaped I would say well and truly;
But the night was near nigh, that none might see another
For a fourth of a furlong further from him;†
And in that dark many men of that duke withdrew   1285
And whoso harried them the hardest held himself not beguiled.‡
With much mirth, the emperor then spoke with his men;
And when those same were assembled, surely to tell,

---

* William, although he has defeated the duke, is lower than him in feudal rank and, under the
laws of chivalry, treats his captive with due reverence.
† A furlong measures 220 yards or 660 feet. The text therefore suggests that visibility was down
to 55 yards or 165 feet.
‡ The MS reads "and ho-so hardest miȝt hiȝe held him nouȝt bigiled" (lit. "And whomsoever
hardest might hurry did not feel deceived"). The poet appears to suggest that it was only the
darkness which prevented the victors from capturing more men; there was no trickery involved
on behalf of the duke's fleeing soldiers.

They had taken that time three great lords
And a full five hundred full noble prisoners,   1290
Bar counting all those others who had died in the battle.
Then the emperor was greatly glad, and thanked God often,
And William too for his work, which had succeeded so well;
And then he with his whole host hastened to their tents
With mirth and with minstrelsy, and made themselves at ease,   1295
And turned to rest for a time, until early the next day.
And then when they were awake they went off to church
And heard their holy mass, and quickly hereafter
The emperor called all of his counsellors to him.
And soon, by their assent, at that same time,   1300
Just as William had willed, who had well advised him,
All those doughty dukes and lords who had been captured
He had fetched before him and swiftly asked them
If they would hold in his name the whole of their lands.
And they granted this gracefully, glad so to see fit,   1305
And all of those there, at once, paid him homage;
Then, with due love of loyalty, the emperor released them
And sent messengers with them to Saxony then,
Announcing homage in his name, concealing nothing,
Right across that royal realm, to rich and poor alike.   1310
When that deed was done, as privately commanded,
And all his just laws were set in those lands,
And all those people were pleased to enjoy their peace,
Then the emperor was well pleased with all of his work
So he lovingly travels with his lords to Lombardy   1315
With all the mirth that mankind might devise for his folk;
And he set off for that land, faithfully, with his close fellowship.
The doughty duke of Saxony, for the distress he caused
And for his people so slain, was sent into prison
And knew well how his actions had been wrought wrongly
      through pride;   1320
And such distress dwelt in his heart for all his wicked deeds,
That on the fifth day he died, to tell you the truth.
When the emperor knew this, at once he commanded
To bury him as appropriate for such a noble great baron,

With due worship and honour, and this was done quickly.   1325
Then the emperor rode from there and on towards Rome;
And boldly William went with him, who was sorely wounded;
But, truthfully, learned doctors looked at his wounds,
And said he should be safe, and soon be healed sweetly.
Then the emperor sent out his most manly messengers   1330
On to his dear daughter to inform her duly
That he was coming with his company, all safe as Christ willed.
Immediately those messengers then sped to Melior,
And graciously greeted her when they see that good lady,
And imparted their message to that high maiden,   1335
How her father would come home in good health to her,
Faithfully in a fortnight with all his bold fellows.
Melior gave those messengers a most cordial welcome
On account of the tidings which they had told her so promptly.
"Now, fair friends, by your faith, did you find any defiance   1340
From soldiers on the other side as so set against you?"
"Oh Madam!" said the messengers, "what may we now tell you?
Since Christ died on the cross to save all mankind,
You may never have heard of so hard an encounter,
Nor of so many fine nobles slain in one battle."   1345
"Tell us what so befell," said Melior then.
"Madam," said the messengers, "by Mary in heaven,
That duke had such a great host of good men of arms,
That, surely, all our side might soon have all been slain,
But for the succour of one sire who dwelt in our midst,   1350
And who has lengthened all our lives, I truly believe,
Through all those doughty deeds he happened to do there."
"Sweet sire, who is he?" said Melior swiftly.
"Well indeed, it is William," he said, "who is newly knighted;
He may be held a lord truly, a real leader of people,   1355
For to wield all the world, to rule wisely and well;
For there is no king under Christ he could not overcome.
For sure, we might now all be forsaken had it not been for his work,
Your father, and his folk, might have all come to grief,
And all here who now live would soon have been destroyed."   1360
Then swiftly they told her all the certain truth,

83

Of how much mischief at first confronted their men,
And how then at once William went to their foes,
And delivered them from the duke, to tell you this first,
And how he caused those great lords to give their lives in vain;   1365
And then they truly told her how he was taken himself,
And how he was readily rescued by his retinue later;
And then the deeds he then did: how he took that self-same duke,
And brought that battle to an end through his bold deeds,
And how the duke from distress died in his ward,   1370
And how all of Saxony was set well with sound laws,
To work her father's will through William's deeds.
And when this tale was told, Melior said swiftly,
"Loyal heralds, for my love, do please tell me truly,
Does William come with my father, is he well and healthy?"   1375
"Yes, certainly madam," they said, "he is beside your father;
But he is not wholly well, for he was sorely wounded,
Which grieves him gravely, yet God may still help him."
"For the love of Mary," said Melior, "may he be healed?"
"Yes certainly, madam, for he is so sound now,   1380
That he may readily ride and roam where he likes."
Then Melior made great joy with all those messengers
For the tidings they told as so touching her father;
But in her heart I tell you, she held such bliss,
That no woman in this world might wield any more,   1385
Because her lovely beloved had won such lauding,
As to bear best in battle by his brilliant deeds.
Then they all made merry, to make short of a tale,
For seven nights surely, and so at last
The emperor and his people all came to the palace.   1390
He was received by the Romans royally as their lord;
Then Melior, most meekly, with her many maidens,
Fared out to her father, and greeted him finely,
And then her lovely beloved whole-heartedly after;
And she made so much joy as might any woman,   1395
Kindly clasping her father and kissing him also.
And with a courteous countenance came to William next,
Such that none who might see them would suspect nought but good.

But privately, unperceived, she then whispered to William
To come softly to her chamber as soon as he might.   1400
And, by cunning clue of the face, he assented to come,
For he dare not do this openly lest guile be opined;
In any case, through her cunning, she knew his will at once.
It would mostly be a long matter to make known all the joy
And rich array which those Romans laid on for their lord,   1405
And the unmeasured mourning they made for their friends,
When they wholly knew which of them had died in battle;
But they soon caught much comfort from the conquest achieved,
And so they made themselves as merry as any men could.
And, when he saw it was time, William then went to Melior   1410
And longed there to his liking with that fair lady,
In the delights of love, a long while unperceived,
And so discreetly that no soul suspected any ill.
And Alisaundrine, as always, served them with due will,
Such that none knew their secret save for those three alone.   1415

 But then some time later, it soon betided,
At Easter, while the emperor remained encamped in Rome,
That in that sacred season he summoned all the greatest
Of the lords and the ladies who lived in that land.
And all then came quickly upon his command   1420
And dearly that day were served with delicacies.
As that meal reached its merriest, to tell you most truly,
Some thirty busy nobles, barons most bold,
Came in manfully with a message, from the Emperor of Greece,
Who was then known by his birthright as keeper of
    Constantinople.[13]   1425
Most truly, the messengers were right royally arrayed
All in glittering gold, and most grandly dressed;
It would be troublesome to tell of all their rich attire!
But they advanced in earnest, straight to the emperor
And, courteously on their knees, they came and crouched to
    greet him   1430
With grace from the Greek emperor and his good son.
And the emperor, most seemly, then said to them,

"By He that made all men, may He save your lives,
And may Christ give much joy to all your courtly company,
As the most eminent messengers ever to come before me!"   1435

One of those bold emissaries began to tell of their errand,
He was a great lord in Greece, known to all as Roachas,
And said seriously to the emperor in this self-same way,
"Liege lord and your followers, listen to my speech!
The good Emperor of Greece, the greatest of us all,   1440
Whose messengers he made us to make you know his will,
Sends us to say to you that he has a dear son,
One of most excellent in existence, in all doughty deeds,
That any man upon earth might ever hear of,
And who shall be, as his heir, emperor by inheritance.   1445
He has often heard things said of your seemly daughter,
How she is fair and fetching, and beautiful in form;
So for the acclaim laid upon her, and for the love of yourself,
He prays, lord, you vouchsafe that his son should wed her.
Begrudge him not this your gift, graciously I ask;   1450
Favour, please, this fair union to be swiftly fulfilled.
And if you do this, I dare say, and surely commend it,
She shall wield at her will more gold than your silver,
And have more splendid cities and seemly castles
Than you truly have small towns or houses of the poor!   1455
So of this, sire, we would wish to know of your will.
To the great lords of your land who are lodging here:
We must at once know your will, and what you advise,
And we wish to know swiftly what will be your answer."
The emperor called his counsel to know of their consent   1460
And with grace, and ungrudging, all granted this quickly,
And set a certain day to hold that celebration.
So this pledge was assured, on both sides then,
To make that eminent marriage the following midsummer.
And so these messengers were made mild at ease   1465
All the while they dwelled there and truly, when they went,
They were given great gifts of gold and of silver,
And they went home quickly, with joy and much mirth,

And told their high emperor the answer they had.
Great merriment was made from that mission in Rome   1470
And word went far and wide how the maid was to be given,
Right throughout Rome, and everyone was in rapture
That the mild Melior should come to be married
To the heir-Emperor of Greece, and every man with great joy
Passed the news to another, swiftly all about.   1475
But worthy William knew nothing of this,
For he was with his bachelors, battling at a joust.*
And when he was told these tidings, I tell you truly,
He soon fared fairly quickly from his knightly fellows,
As meekly as he might to avoid any mistrust.   1480
But, once departed from those people, he pressed on as fast
As he might with his horse through the hurt of his spurs,
He was so near wiped of his wits by woe at that news;
For should he lose his beloved, he would loathe his life.
He was so crushed and downcast when he came to his rooms,   1485
That briskly, for heartbreak, he took straight to his bed,
And sighed so much for sorrow, to tell the truth surely,
That each one who knew of it thought he would not recover.
And when it was known in Rome that William was sick,
Much was he lamented by all and sundry;   1490
For a better-beloved noble was never born on this earth
Than was known by any fellow while he lived in Rome.
These tidings were then told swiftly to the emperor,
And he near swooned for sorrow and seemed nearly to die;
But his courteous knights caught him, to comfort him better.   1495
And when he, through their comfort, came to recover,
He at once went to William to know how he fared,
And his knights followed forth, some five or six of them;
And, as he came to him, he asked how he fared.
"Sire," he said softly, "I am certainly so ill,   1500
That I believe that my life will not last till tomorrow.
But God, sire, for His grace, might He grant you joy,
For all the past worship that you have bestowed upon me."

* Bachelor: see note to line 840 above.

When the emperor had heard wholly all of his words,
And sees him so sick that indeed he seemed dead,   1505
Such sorrow sank to his heart that he might not suffer
To be there, unless somehow his heartbreak be becalmed.
He at once took his leave and went home again,
Weeping as he would, near mad with sorrow and woe.
And directly, distressed, he told his daughter,   1510
How William, her worthy foster-brother, was nigh at death's door;
And she comforted her father, as fast as she might,
Though no woman felt worse for the woe in her heart.
As fast as her father had fared elsewhere,
She wept and she wailed as if she would have died,   1515
And swooned countless times, ceaselessly, as she might.
But Alisaundrine at once, who knew all her anguish,
Comforted her as she could with all kinds of speech,
And urged her at once to wend there, to know how her man fared.
"And, surely, madam, I say it may so betide   1520
Your care will help him recover and slake his sorrow."
Then Melior, meekly, called all her maidens,
And many of her company, for dread of any calumny,
And at once they went to William's chambers,
For none of them knew how it was that he fared.   1525
And when she drew to his chamber, directly she asked,
Her maidens and company then meekly to stay there,
All but Alisaundrine. Alone then, those two,
Then went in to see William, without any other,
And bustled quickly to his bed, and began to sit by him, 1530
And soon she said to him softly, "My dear, sweet beloved,
I am come alone to see you, except for Alisaundrine,
So to know of your woe and what so ails you.
My peerless paramour, my plaything and joy,
Speak to me speedily lest my life is fast spent!"   1535

 William turned around promptly and took heed
     of her,
And swiftly said, "Welcome, sweetheart!
My dearest darling and my dear heart,

Both my bliss and my sadness; barring help I am doomed!*
But comely creature, for heavenly Christ's love,   1540
For what manner of misdeed have you forsaken me,
Who has loved you loyally, and thinks of you always?
Faithfully without falsehood, you have failed me now,
And have turned your intentions towards another!
You have wrought me great wrong, great sin well and truly,   1545
To do me such distress that I die for your sake.
But lovely beloved, our Lord wishes it
That your worthy will was to come to me now;
And you have lengthened my life and lessened my misery
Through the solace of seeing you, my dear sweetheart!   1550
And when Melior had heard wholly his will and words,
She sickened for sorrow, and wept well and sorely,
And so lovingly said, "Believe this, truly, my beloved,
All the men upon earth should not save my life
If you were to wander from this world, and I not follow you!   1555
I have no knowledge of this, loved one, believe me truly,
For though my foolish father might affirm agreements,
Why now suppose that I would perform his will?
No, by God who gave me the Ghost and my soul,
His travails are for nothing no matter the outcome!   1560
For there is no man on earth that shall ever have me
But you, love and loved one, believe me most truly;
In faith, they will have to kill me, fast and swiftly,
Or bury me deep down alive, or draw or hang me!"
"Ah, know this," said William, "and do so without doubt,   1565
I am healed of all my harms right now, hearing this!"
"Yes, by Mary," said Melior, "never misread me;
I will fulfil my affirmation faithfully and by deed!"
Then was William right glad, I will tell you truly,
And both kindly clasped the other, and kissed well and often,   1570
And wrought what they willed for a good pleasant while.
And truly, when the time came for these two to depart,

* The line is difficult to translate effectively: "Mi blis and mi bale þat botelesse wol ende!" (lit. "Both my bliss and my sadness which, unless remedied, will end in disaster!").

Melior and her maidens then meekly went home;
William's woes were soon vanquished in that very room,
And he was now fully healed of his heartaches and horrors.   1575
All the surgeons of Salerno could not any sooner
Have lessened his melancholy and saved his life,
Than did the maid Melior in so short a time!
The word soon went far and wide that William was healed,
And everybody was glad and thanked God often.   1580
Then the next day William went well attired
In gay clothes of gold and other fine gear,
And came straight to court as a knight cured and whole,
Where they hailed God highly for his life that was saved.
And surely, as soon as the emperor sees him,   1585
He hails him with haste and holds him in his arms,
And clasped him and kissed him, most kindly and often;
And they were left much light-hearted for a good while after.

 But now to mention more of those messengers from
    Greece.
As fast as they truly had told to their lord   1590
Of their fine royal reception in regal Rome,
    And of that gracious grant they had gained from their
    errand,
The Greek emperor was gladdened greatly at heart.
He swiftly sends messengers to summon at that time
All the great folk of Greece and other grand people,   1595
Such that no man on earth might know of their number;
Men could hardly describe all those regal ranks,
Nor the provisions that promptly were bestowed on those people.
But surely, at sunset, with sumptuous merriment,
This grand gang of Greece began riding to Rome,   1600
Riding in royal array right to that city.
To recount that array who rode forth at that time,
Well, all men known to man might not describe it,
It was so well arrayed, and in all ways,
With plenteous provisions provided as right!   1605
When the Emperor of Greece neared nigh unto Rome

With all his bold nobles, behind him for three miles,
The Emperor of Rome readily rode out towards him,
With the most striking company a king had ever led.
When both courtly companies came close together,   1610
The sight was most seemly and lovely to see,
And when both of those emperors were at last stood still,
One first kissed the other most kindly then,
And so just as swiftly did the same to the other;
No man might describe all the mirth at that meeting!   1615
Those rich parties ride forth together into Rome;
There each street was festooned and strewn all with flowers,
And richly adorned with hangings right royal,
And all manner of minstrelsy was made all for them;
And fancy-dress dances done with due pleasure,   1620
And splendid songs sung, to sweeten their hearts,
So that, surely to say, if I sat for ever,*
I could not tell of the mirth that was made there;
Thus, I choose not to mention any more of this matter.
But all that gang from Greece was gaily received   1625
And made at home with haste, I have to say truly,
In a place where great tents and pavilions were pitched,
By a side of that city to house so many people.
For all those that see it, surely, spoke of this as true:
That place of pavilions, and of those prize tents,   1630
Seemed as much a sight as the city of Rome!
The emperor and every man was placed right at his ease,
And had whatever they wanted, at once and at will.
But now I will for a while stop talking of these wonders,
And mention now Melior, that blissful maiden,   1635
And so too, worthy William, who was her dear sweetheart,
And tell this tale truly of what then betided.

* Here we learn that the storyteller sits, rather than stands, to deliver his story. In Syrian culture, for example, storytellers sit high on a seat while the audience smokes or drinks coffee below them. The Frontispiece of Chaucer's *Troilus and Criseyde* (Cambridge, Corpus Christi College, MS 61) reveals Chaucer himself sitting in a chair while his audience rests on the ground.

When these people were housed well at their ease,
William quickly, at once, and wholly alone,
Mourning beyond measure, wanders to Melior,   1640
And, sighing full sadly, said to her soon,
"Ah worthy one, now I am truly woeful:
My dear, destiny ordains that I die for your sake!
I cannot bear that I was born to abide this time,
To lose she whom I love and live all my life for!   1645
How foully you fed me with your fair words,
When I near died from distress, many a day since;
But yet God, in his grace, has given it to be!"
Melior said meekly, "Why so, my dear heart?
What I formerly affirmed, I still hold to this fully,   1650
I swear by the High King, who holds all of heaven!
Therefore cease all your strife, let us study instead
By what way we might best burst free from this land."
When he heard these words, William was happier
And said, "My honey, my sweetheart, how whole you make me   1655
With your comfort and kindness in all my cold distress."
Then steadfast, stuck in thought, they studied together a while
By what way might be best to break free of that country,
Privately and unperceived, lest they be caught and punished.
But their thoughts were in waste, it was beyond their wits.   1660
So they called Alisaundrine quickly for counsel,
And told her truly what they both intended,
And wished to know of some way to escape that land;
And upon her charity they pleaded, for the profit of love,
To declare some cunning ruse, of which she could conceive,   1665
To allow them to wander away, unperceived.
Alisaundrine then answered and she said thus,
Weeping most wildly because they would leave,
"By that blissful Lord who redeemed us on the rood,
I cannot conceive by any craft the best way   1670
How you might hasten uncaught or escape without harm.
For once everyone was aware that you had run away,
Then in every country well-kept by courteous men,
On every bridge, every path, and on every broad way,

Neither clerk, courtly knight, nor country churl   1675
Shall pass unperceived but be openly searched.
And even if you were disguised, dressed in any way,
I would wholly think that you would be recognised.
Since it cannot be otherwise that you wish still to elope,
Then I will now make clear a much cleverer scheme.   1680
In the kitchen, I know well, are copious skilled men,
Who fare fully all day flaying wild beasts:
Hinds and harts, with hides most fair,
And bucks and bears, and other wild beasts,
And all such fair game that befalls to be eaten.   1685
But the most brutish beasts are the bears, I would say,
Which grow ghastly and terrifying in the eyes of good men.
Might we, by cunning, come by two skins
Of such brutish bears and besew you therein,
There is no living soul that would wish to know you.[14]   1690
But hide away from high roads, I advise, to avoid mishap.
There is really no finer plan by any reasoning I know,
Than to be so disguised as such bloodthirsty beasts,
For in how they seem they are most like men."*
Then William at once, and his worthy maiden,   1695
Thanked her fully and thoroughly many thousands of times
For her clever counsel, and kindly besought her
At once with some will to win them two skins
Of those brutal beasts – as bears are so called –
Privately, unperceived, lest peril should befall.   1700
And so Alisaundrine, as an honourable maid,
Said she would do this directly with all of her might
So to save them from sorrow, or she would die trying.

With no more words, and at once, she went forth quietly
And briskly, from a cupboard, borrowed boys' clothes,   1705
And attired herself elegantly and promptly in them;
And she bustled to the kitchen dressed as a boy,

---

* The poet appears to suggest that a bear skin, as well as frightening off men, might also be the
best disguise because bears can walk on two legs ("most like men"), enabling the exiles to cover
more ground quickly than had they to walk continuously on all fours.

There, folk were busy and laboured at skinning those beasts,
And she promptly employed herself helping those men,
Until she found the right time to take what she sought.   1710
And she waited well for the best white bear skins,
Which were lovely and large enough to clothe her friends in;
Then she went away swiftly, well unperceived,
And flew to her lady and her dear beloved,
And said softly, "Now see how swiftly I've sped!"   1715
Full glad of this garb, they thanked her greatly,
And profoundly they prayed that she wrap them therein,
So exactly that no soul might see their clothes.
And she motioned for Melior to be made up first,
And fastened her in that fur with a good many thongs,[15]   1720
Above her true day attire to tell you the truth,
Such that no man on earth might think otherwise
But that she was a bear fit to bait at a stake,
So justly joined were those seems, by Jesus in heaven!
When she was sewn in as she should be in that attire,   1725
Melior in her merriment said to her maid,
"Dear Alisaundrine, for your love, do you like me now?
Am I not a bold beast, which seems most like a bear?"
"Yes, madam," said that maid. "By Mary in heaven,
You are like some grisly ghost for a man to gawp at,   1730
For I would never, for all the good that God ever made,
Meet with you on some broad way by a large mile,
So brutal a wild bear that you now resemble."
And then Alisaundrine, again in the same way,
Enrobed William then in that other bear skin,   1735
And laced well each limb with long-lasting thongs
Above his clothes craftily, which were comely and rich.
And when he was sewn in, as best as could be,
William then said to Melior, in a most merry manner,
"See me, lovely beloved, how do you like me now?"   1740
"By Mary, sire," said Melior, "that mild Queen of Heaven,
You seem such a bold bear for a noble to look on,
That I am aghast, by God who made me,
To see so hideous a sight as your seemly face!"

Then at once William said, "My dearest sweetheart,   1745
Let us head hence with haste, I hope it be for the best,
This evening exactly, when few men will be walking."
And she agreed at once to work as he willed.
Alisaundrine, as soon as she then saw them leaving,
Wept as if she were mad, both for woe and for sorrow,   1750
But briskly, nonetheless, she brought them by some way
Privately to the postern of that peerless arbour,
Which was choicely adjoined to Melior's chamber.
And Alisaundrine, as soon as they should depart,
Swooned and fell several times and thence, when she might,   1755
Prayed most piteously to the Prince of Heaven
To look after those lovers and guard them from any ill fortune,
Which might put those paramours in such great peril;
And surely for to say, they then parted asunder.
At which point Alisaundrine returned again to her chamber,   1760
And mourned nigh from madness for Melior her lady.
Now, truly at this time, I will leave tell of her;
And I will tell of the bears, and what happened to them later.

William and the maiden, now dressed as white bears,
Go forth through the garden at a good speed   1765
Fiercely on their four feet, as befitting such beasts.
Then a Greek groom drew near, enjoying the garden
And beholding the flowerbeds and arbours so fair;
And, as he went, he became aware of the white bears;
They went away at a gallop, or so it seemed.   1770
And, near worn out of his wits, he was nigh full of dread,
And fled homeward as fast as his feet might drive him,
For had he not run away at once they would surely have followed
To have made him their meat and murdered him direly!
When he found his fellows, they were fascinated by his look;   1775
Why he was, in that way, so worn out;
And he told them promptly how those two white bears
Had gone into the garden and made him aghast;
Had he not run away they would have slain him at once.
"But they did not see me, surely I hope;   1780

They showed little interest in me, but went forth on their way,
Wilfully to some wilderness, where they might dwell."
Then his fellows were gleeful as to his fear,
And they laughed at this lark! But I will leave them now,
To tell more of what happened to those bears afterwards.   1785
Now they go on from that garden, at a good speed,
Towards a fair forest which grew fast beside there.
At times they went onwards on all fours like wild beasts,
And when they were weary, they went forth upright.
Thus they went through that wilderness all that long night,   1790
Till the dawn of the day and the rise of the sun.
They drew to a hidden den for dread of being seen
And hid under a hollow oak where it formed a huge den,
As luck so fairly befell, which they found to rest in.
For it was far from anyone, and fixed in woodland so thick,   1795
That no one in this world would seek them there;
And, I will tell you truly, being awake so long wearied them.

And they hailed God highly, at this chance happening,
That they had discovered such a den so hidden to rest in.
Then William said seriously to Melior so high,   1800
"Ah, my lovely beloved, Our Lord help us now!
He who was born in Bethlehem and who redeemed us by death,
Shield us from blemish and shame on this earth,
And show us in some way how we may win some food;
For, beloved, I dread we should die of hunger."   1805
Melior said seriously, "Sire, leave off your words!
We shall live off our love, loyally at best,
And will gather what we can, through the grace of God:
Bullaces and blackberries, which grow on the brambles,
So that we shall never be harmed from hunger, I hope;   1810
Haws, rose-hips and acorns, and hazelnuts,
And all the fullness of fruits that grow in the forest.
I say to you, on my life, sire, this life I like truly!"
"Most certainly," said William, "my worthy sweetheart,
But it behoves things be better lest you become sad   1815
For hitherto you have never known of such hardship,
But were brought up in bliss, as befits such a lady,
With all manner of meats; and to miss them now
Would be unbearably bleak; better things I intend.
I will wander to some pathway, anywhere near here,   1820
And wait if anyone comes walking alone,
Either churl or child, from a fair or cheap market,
Who might bear about him either bread or drink;
And I would rob him readily and return again swiftly.
I can think of no other craft which would keep us alive."   1825
"No, sire," she said, "you shall not work as such;
For such misdeeds meted here would make a great noise
And be recounted readily all over Rome!
Thus we might, through such happenings, have harm in that way.
Therefore, it is best we stay quiet and live off the fruit   1830
That we will find in the woods as we wander about."
And both then brightly agreed, in a brief time,
And clasped each other kindly and kissed full often,
And lay hidden in that den all the day long,

Sleeping well sweetly at the same time together,   1835
As however they would. Yet we will now leave here,
And for a while I will turn again to the werewolf,
Concerning this tale and as tells this true story.
On the same night that William went with his dear heart,
The werewolf, as God willed, knew well of their story   1840
And what fortune might befall them for their deeds later.
When they went on their way, he follows them closely,
Briskly behind them, but they did not know.
And when the werewolf knew where they would rest,
And heard how hungry they were and how they lamented,   1845
He goes to a great highway at a good speed,
To meet maybe some man and win from him some meat.
Then by good chance it befell there came a cheap-market churl,
Who bore bread in a bag and fair well-boiled beef;
The werewolf, at once, went swiftly towards him   1850
With a loud ringing roar, like to rip him apart,
And brought him down by the breast, bolting him to the earth.
The churl knew full well that death awaited,
So with a whole heart he prayed to God for his life,
To escape unscarred from that scary beast.   1855
He broke from that beast and began to flee
As hard as he might so to save his life.
His bag, bread and food he left with the beast;
Glad that he was gone without greater harm.
The werewolf was glad too that he had won the meat,   1860
And thus went at once to where William rested.
Before both him and the maid he laid that bag,
And before saying a word he busked away briskly,
Now that he knew well that they had what they needed.

William wondered greatly about that wild beast;   1865
What he brought in the bag and why he would not bide.
He brought the bag to him and opened it briskly,
And found the bread and the beef; he was then greatly blithe
And said meekly to Melior, "My sweetest heart,
Behold what great grace God has bestowed on us!   1870

98

He knew well of our work, yet is so well pleased,
That he sends us a servant to succour us in our need,
So wondrous a wild beast which possesses no mind.*
Such a wonder, for sure, I have never seen;
Let us hail God most highly to whom we are beholden." 1875
"By Mary," said Melior, "you speak so much truth;
I would not like, for the world, for our work to be undone."
William, most meekly, then takes out the meat,
And said, "Loved one, my beloved, of what our Lord sends,
Let us make ourselves merry for we have meat at will." 1880
They eat at their ease, as well they might then,
Without salt or sauce or any seemly drink;
Yet hunger had hold of them, they held themselves contented.
But be well aware, the werewolf knew what was missing;
He went straight to the highway to await good fortune, 1885
Then it betided at that time, to tell you the truth,
That a country clerk was coming on his way towards Rome
With two flagons full of the finest of wines,
Bought from a burgess in a nearby town borough.
The werewolf waited for him and then went towards him, 1890
Bellowing like a bull, bent on death to man.
When the clerk saw him come, for concern and for dread,
He let those flagons fall and began to flee fast,
The lighter to leap so to save his own life.
The werewolf was delighted at the work of the clerk, 1895
And flies to the flagons and grasps them full swiftly
And then wends towards William at a wondrous speed,
And to his mistress Melior; and most mildly then
Sets those flagons down fairly right in front of them,
And then went away quickly without further ado. 1900
William and his fair woman were both delighted,
For the help they had gained from this wild beast,
And they prayed full privately to the Prince of Heaven
To save that beast from sorrow which had so helped them.

---

* At this stage, William considers the werewolf to be only an animal, allowing the true condition of the beast to be realised later on.

Then they made themselves merry in all manner of ways,   1905
And both ate at their ease and drunk afterwards,
And so pleased themselves until they wished to sleep.
Then either clasped the other full lovingly in their arms,
And their dread and distress was soon duly forgotten;
And they slept so soundly in their seemly den   1910
Until night neared so closely it might be no nearer.
Then at once they awakened and went on their way;
They fared forth at night finely on their two feet,
But when it drew to the day, they then fared as beasts,
And forged forth on four feet in the form of two bears.   1915
And always the werewolf followed them without fail,
Most nobly behind them, though unknown to William;
Yet whenever they were lodged where they thought was best,
Then all manner of things, and meat which they might need,
The werewolf won for them and brought to them at once.   1920
Thus they lived this life for a full long while,
And crossed many countries as so was the case.
So let us leave now their story, and learn of another;
For I can return to them when the time so befalls.
I will tell more of a matter that I mentioned before,   1925
Of the royalty arrayed in Rome for her sake,
And of that worthy wedding which was granted before
Between Melior that maid and the Prince of Greece.
Now listen, dear lords, as I start to relate it.

Immediately on the morrow, when that marriage
          should be,   1930
The royal emperors arose and dressed themselves in rich array
With all those worthy clothes which such men should.
          No man upon earth may ever imagine
Men more richly arrayed, to recount everything,
Than each Roman retainer and the riches they displayed;   1935
The greatest, by their degree, dressed the most gaily,
The more minor men as they might, to make known the truth.
And the season was seemly, the sun shone most fine.
The Emperor of Greece and all his regal group

Hurried then to their horses, with haste and quickly. 1940
But to tell of the attire of that prince at that time,
He whom all that royal array was arranged before
And who would, at that time, be wedded to Melior,
It would lengthen my tale by a good long while!
But surely to say, he was so well dressed, 1945
That he might in no manner be in any way improved.
And when those great Greek men were all on their horses
And the Romans similarly arrayed, to reckon their number
Would truly be twenty thousand, attired at the best
And all stoutly horsed on stalwart steeds. 1950
All manner of minstrelsy was then quickly made,
And all the merriment that man might ever devise;
And soon those retinues began all their royal revels,
Riding forth through Rome, to relate matters truly,
Right to the chief church, as so chosen before, 1955
That is called throughout Christendom the church of Saint Peter.
The Pope with many prelates was there as appropriate,
With cardinals and bishops and many abbots,
All richly robed to hold that royal ceremony,
With due respect for that wedding which they would conduct. 1960
Then the Greeks go to that church quickly and grandly,
To wait there for that bright bride Melior.
The Emperor of Rome was then completely ready,[16]
And all the best barons, the boldest of his realm.
But the emperor was wondering, I will tell you truly, 1965
Why his daughter that day was delaying so long,
Because the great men of Greece have already gone to the church.
Then he bade a baron to bustle to her chamber
To hurry her hastily and bring her to him,
And he wends there at once, I will tell you truly. 1970
He found neither bride nor boy in that bower then,*

* The MS reads "He fond þere burde no barn in þat bour þanne". Given that the noblemen
would expect only to find Melior in the room, the phrase "burde no barn" ("woman nor child"
or "woman nor young man") is an idiom akin to the modern "neither hide nor hair" or "neither
sight nor sound". The phrase is repeated at line 2008; given that the audience know already
what has happened, the poet may have been punning on the phrase.

And could find no one to speak with in spite of his cunning;
And so he nimbly runs back to tell his lord directly.
The emperor, when he knew this, waxed near to madness
So he went, full of wrath, to his daughter's bower, 1975
And drives in at that door, like a devil from hell.
He began to call and to cry and to curse fast,
"Why the devil do you dwell for so long, you damsels?"
Alisaundrine, as soon as she heard him there,
Was distressed and in dread of the death she might suffer; 1980
So by cunning contrivance she quickly considered
How bold she might be in her best excuse,
So the emperor would not suspect that she had assisted
His daughter who, with William, had gone away.
With a mild mood, yet boldly, she bustles from her chamber, 1985
And comes quickly to the emperor and greets him with
 courtesy,
And at once she asked what he wanted there;
And so he said swiftly, "Certainly, I am in wonder
Where my daughter today dwells for so long;
For all the people have passed to church in their pomp. 1990
I have sent others to seek her for some while since,
But no fellow could find her, therefore I am troubled."
Then Alisaundrine answered and said as follows,
"Sire, those barons are to blame, who lie so blithely;
For my lady lies sleeping, I say to you loyally." 1995
"Go at once," said the emperor, "and waken her quickly;
Bid her bustle from her bed and be attired briskly."
"I dare not, for sure," said Alisaundrine then;
"She is wrathful with me, God knows, for some small sin."
"Why so?" said the emperor. "Tell me now swiftly!" 2000
"Full gladly, sire," she said, "by God that made me,
If you would not be wrathful when you know the truth."
"Most certainly," said the emperor, "therefore, speak swiftly!"
And so Alisaundrine, in this way, soon after
Said, most seriously, with sore dread in her heart, 2005
"Sire, for certain, I am duty-bound to speak truly.
Last night, my lady made me linger with her awake,

With nobody nor boy but just our two selves.
Then she told me her tidings, as before told to her,
By one acquainted with the customs of the country of Greece,   2010
How every grand Greek man, who was a great lord,
When they wedded a wife, no matter how noble -
Kith of emperor or king – who comes into Greece,
That she should soon be shut up on her own,
In a trusty great tower, fully timbered too,[17]   2015
To live in lonely sorrow for the rest of her life
Never once any more to wield one jot of joy.
Therefore, I assure you, she was greatly sorrowed,
And so she swore for that sake that she would suffer any pain –
Whether to be hanged upon high, or drawn by great horses –   2020
Than be wedded so woefully to anyone from Greece.
She would rather be wedded to someone much simpler,
That she might lead her life in much happiness and laughter.
And also, sire, certainly to speak the whole truth,
She told me another tale, which troubled me sorely,   2025
Whereby I won her wrath when we parted company."
"What so?" said the emperor. "Tell me now swiftly!"
"Be assured, sire," said Alisaundrine, "to spare you your honour,
I will tell you at once what trick she has worked.
She called me to her counsel when she knew of the case   2030
That she should be wedded, and so said to me then
She had laid her love in a place which she liked the better,
On one of the boldest of nobles ever to bestride a steed,
And of the fairest of face; so I asked her of his name,
And she said to me shortly, the sure truth to be known,   2035
It was that worthy man William whom everyone loves,
Who stopped you from being beaten by his own mighty strength.
And when I knew of this work, I will tell you truly,
I disliked this very much – no might man blame me –
And I manfully admonished her, as is my manner,   2040
And warned her at once, without deceiving you,
I would let you know soon of all of her work and deeds.
And, when she knew that, through unbridled wrath
She told me directly to depart her chamber,

Howling at me never to be so foolhardy as to come before
    her again.   2045
And I bustled quick from her bower – she barred it soon after –
And I have not seen her since, sire, I say to you truly;
I dare not, for dread, draw towards her again
Therefore, you yourself sire, must awaken her softly,
And feed her with fair words, befitting your eminence,   2050
So this marriage can be made, and concluded with harmony."

When the emperor had heard wholly all of these words,
He was driven near witless with wrath at that time,
And, deranged with distress, he dashes to her chamber,
And bustled right to her bed, but there he found nothing 2055
    Within her comely curtains but for her warm bedclothes.
At once, like a wild man, he opened the window,
And scanned around steadfastly for his seemly daughter;
But all his work was in waste, for that maid was flown.
And when he might, in no manner, find his daughter Melior, 2060
He was deranged like a devil and dashed out again,
And asked Alisaundrine again after this,
"Damsel, directly, do tell me now fast,
Where has my daughter fled to? She is not in her bed."
Alisaundrine was sorrowful at heart because of his distress 2065
And said, "Sire I have not seen her since midnight at least;
I think that she went to William in wrath at my words.
Send men swiftly there, to seek her at his chambers;
And if William has not flown, you must know this truly,
Then my lady, I tell you, still lingers in the city;   2070
But if William is away, never think otherwise
Than that my lady is with him, come what so will."
The emperor behaved like a tyrant, through torment and torture,
Near worn out of his wits, and said with great wrath,
"Ah! How that untrue traitor has now betrayed me   2075
For the wealth and great welfare I wrought upon him,
Whom I fostered from a foundling to be the finest in my land!
Thus, for his deeds today, I am undone forever!
As things fall, every fellow will hold me as false,

And the Greeks in great anger will begin war on me,   2080
And everyone will think this wrongdoing is mine!
Therefore, by great God that granted me to be born,
And bitterly with His blood absolved us all on the rood,
Let every man know that nought must happen but this:
That if this traitor be taken, before I eat today,   2085
He shall be hanged upon high and then drawn by horses!"
The emperor, most keenly, called many knights to come,
And other seemly sergeants, some sixty well-armed,
And had them go at once to where William stayed,
And if they found that fellow, however fate betides,   2090
They must bring him back briskly, tightly bound before him.
They dared not do differently but drive on their way,
But sought him with sore hearts, because they loved William so well;
When they could not find him, in all faith, they felt glad,
And returned again to the emperor, and told him he had flown.   2095
Then he brayed mad with brain-rage and rent all his robes,
His beard and his bright hair he twists from bleak woe,
And he swooned some six times for sorrow, and also from shame,
That he should be found false; and "Alas!" he said often
And blamed with bitter cursing the day he was born.   2100
Then kings and acclaimed dukes tried to bring him comfort,
And bade him cease all his sorrow and swiftly to go
And tell the Emperor of Greece, truly the truth,
And implore him for mercy for all these misdeeds;
And after quickly consulting a counsel on this case,[18]   2105
He goes to the Greek emperor all gloomy at heart,
And kneels crouching before him, cowed and crying for mercy,
And told him all the truth, quickly and instantly,
Of how his daughter had flown with him whom he had fostered;
And he pleaded, through charity, if he would let him know   2110
By what way that he might work best to avenge him.
And when these tidings were told, if the truth be known,
There was soon in that city many a sorry fellow;
Because of that missed marriage, all merriment now ceased
Right throughout all of Rome, and great sorrow arose.   2115
The good Emperor of Greece was sorely aggrieved

At such misfortune befallen; but from seeing that other
Imploring so meekly for all that misfortune,
The lesser he lamented but, scowling, he said,
"Sire, by God who gave me the Ghost and my soul,   2120
Now I know wholly that this was all wrought through guile!
Let no living men make it seem otherwise;
Thus I will not burn your boroughs nor quell all your barons,
And I shall not seek of you your shameful destruction;
For I wholly think that this guile was never wrought by your will, 2125
And so I quickly convey to you this, my own counsel:
Let it be swiftly declared through each country in your kingdom,
That any baron and burgess, noble or bondman,
Who is in any way nimble and can walk or wander about,
Must wend at once wide all over your realm,   2130
Through woodland and wasteland in all manner of ways,
To seek out that soul who has so betrayed you,
And that mild maid with him, your daughter Melior.
And, to make each of those men more eager in will,
Promise whosoever finds them that he'll gain such winnings   2135
As to be rich and royal for the rest of his life;
And who so fails to hasten hard to work at your behest,
Order him be hanged quickly and drawn by horses.
And look to see that all herdsmen keep common ways watched,
And each bridge thereabouts that anybody may cross,   2140
And to search in each city and every small hamlet;
They shall not pass unperceived, if your people be true."

That royal Emperor of Rome then thanked him readily
For his careful counsel and for his kind will;
And then both sides brightly let messages be sent.   2145
As hastily as men might hurry, all worked at his behest,
And soon such a host was assembled to seize that pair,
That never no noble brought such people to battle.
They searched so closely through cities and small towns,
And in woodland and ways that were thereabouts,   2150
Such that no soul should escape them by any sleight.
And yet, by the grace of God, no man might grasp them;

There they lay in lovely sleep, held in each other's arms.
But when these findings were brought to both of the emperors,
That no one in no way might ever find William, 2155
Nor that maid Melior by any manner,
There came a good Greek man – may God give him sorrow! –
He who was terribly afraid of those white bears;
Soon he said to those emperors, "Sires, will you hear me?
I saw something mysterious myself, yester-eve, 2160
Well within night-time as I walked in the garden:
Two of the most brutal bears that a man might behold,
As seemed so in my sight that I have yet seen.
I ran directly for dread of suffering death,
But truly those bears took no heed of me, 2165
But departed in private by the postern gate;
Yet, to where they went, alas, I know no more."
"By God," said the Greek emperor, "who gave me to be born,
I dare lay down my life that this was that foul traitor
Who went away in that manner so that no one would know him! 2170
Let us swiftly know from the kitchen whether they miss any skins."
When men came to the cook it soon became known
That some boy bore away two white bear skins.
Then it was keenly commanded for a cry to go up
That everybody should busily search for two white bears; 2175
His trials would not go unmerited, he who tracks them down fast!
Then on horse and on foot each hurried hastily,
Hunting with hounds through all the high woods
Till they neared upon nigh, to mention the truth,
To where William was lying with his worthy loved one, 2180
Both readily but a bow-shot beyond sight of their hunters.
But when that wise werewolf knew they were so near,
And sees those bold bloodhounds seeking them busily,
He thought he would do all he could, while his life lasts,
To save and to serve both those seemly bears; 2185
And promptly put himself, on peril of death,
Before those hearty hounds which howled so loud,
So to win them away from those two white bears.
When the hounds had the scent of that high noble beast,

They ceased all their seeking and pursued him swiftly 2190
Over mountains and mires for many a mile.
And all men who might hear all those merry hounds,
Swiftly pursued them to see that merry chase,
And left those lovely white bears to lie at their rest,
Who knew nothing of this work going on all around them. 2195
So those people pressed forth and thus missed their prey,
For God granted the werewolf the gift of such great speed
That neither horseman nor hound might hasten to take him!
When the emperor was warned that they had laboured in waste,
All the Greeks, out of grief, began to take their leave 2200
And went back to their country, downcast and troubled.
But though watches were set up all about, far and wide,
Of bold nobles at arms, so to seek those bears,
That good-witted werewolf helped them so well,
That no one for a good while might know where they dwelled, 2205
And hastily, when they had need, he helped them find food,
And showed them all the best ways to wander by night;
And for when the day dawned, he taught them discreetly,
By careful craft of his countenance, where they should take rest,
And busily, himself, he would be near on each side 2210
To help them from harm should any mishap arise.
And so that wise werewolf trained them in his ways.
Thus they passed through Lombardy, travelling at night through lands,
And came into the marches of the kingdom of Apulia.

It so happened one time that they travelled all night 2215
Far from the forests and parkland and all the fair woodlands;
No cover might they catch, that country was so flat.
And as daylight dawned, to tell you the truth,
They saw a most seemly sight; a city most noble,
Enclosed all comely about with fine castle walls; 2220
Nobles knew that rich borough by the name of Benevento.[19]
When William was aware of it, he was full of dread,
Lest any soldiers from that city should see them then,
And he said meekly to Melior, "My own sweetheart,
If our Lord so likes it, pray save our lives now! 2225

For I know not in the world where we might hide.
Peerless Prince of Heaven, by Your pity and grace,
Have mercy and save us that we be not slain!"
"Amen, sire!" said Melior. "Mary grant us this,
Who loved that blessed Boy whom she bore in her body!" 2230
Then within a short while, as they waited without,
They soon see beside them a fine seemly quarry
Below a high hill, all hollow and new-dug.
Directly they hurried there, from dread without doubt,
And crept into a cave, when they came to that place, 2235
All weary from walking to take some welcome rest.
Locked in their lovely arms, they lay down to sleep,
All bound in their bear skins as they did so before.
And that wise werewolf who was always beside them
Crouched under a crag, to keep watch on those bears. 2240
But they had not really rested for very long
When some workmen soon wandered to work at that place,
Stoutly, with strong tools, to start digging stones.
And as they came to that cave to commence their work,
One of them soon saw those seemly white bears, 2245
Lying lovely together, locked in each other's arms.
Then faithfully and fast, he said to his fellows,
"Harken now, high sirs! You may have heard often
Of that cry which is called across many countries
At the behest of the emperor who happens to hold Rome, 2250
Concerning any man who so might find anywhere
Two brutal white bears? Well this cry baldly states,
He should win a reward which would last him forever,
Through the great wealth of gold which he would be given!"
"Yes, truthfully," said his fellows, "we know that full well, 2255
But where did you see such, so God help you?"
"In truth, fine fellows, I shall tell you full soon,
If you attentively, together, stay true and loyal,
I will win our reward, for I know where they are!"
"Yes, certainly," they said, "we will be so true 2260
That not a foot shall we flee no matter what befalls!"
"Well, sires," said that other, "may Christ save you,

"Stand still here a while, staying in this place here;
I will bustle to Benevento to tell of these bears
To the provost and other people and have them press in haste   2265
To come here and catch them, for they lie in a cave
And sleep surely together; I saw them just now."
Thus his fellows were told in full and they bade him run fast,
And they would boldly bide there so to keep the bears there.
That other went at once to warn the provost   2270
How he had truly seen, in that quarry hard by,
The two white bears, and bade himself swiftly
To come with great power and catch them quickly.
"Are you sure," said the provost, "that they are still there?"
"Yes, certainly," he said, "I saw them both just now;   2275
And five of my fellows are waiting fast by them
So they would not wander off while I came here."

Promptly, the provost then warned all the people,
On pain of losing their lives, their lands and their goods,
That they all hurry hastily, on horse or on foot,   2280
And most securely surround all that quarry swiftly,
    In order to take those two white bears at once,
As the emperor had proclaimed across all that country.
Soon each man that might then armed himself manfully,
And those that had a horse hurried hastily to it,   2285
And fellows on foot followed swiftly after,
So that country was alive quite soon with that cry;
And quickly keen men-at-arms encircled that quarry –
Some twenty hundred and two truly in number –
To take those bears briskly. But God help them now,   2290
Slain while they sleep! Yet hear now this miracle!
As those two bold bears slept so near to oblivion,
Melior by a dream was driven mad for fear,
And her sorrowful fantasy meant she was soon awake.
And so she said these words to William at once,   2295
"Ah, beloved lovely, listen now to me.
I am near maddened and mad by a dream this morning;
For I thought that there came to this cave right now

Wild bears and big apes, boars, bulls and badgers:
A host of brutish beasts all led by a lion,   2300
All encouraged to work by his keen command
To capture us two, together in this den.
Then there was a little lion, born of that leader,
That came with this company to see what now occurred:
For right as those brutish beasts should have snatched us both,   2305
Our worthy werewolf, who always helps us so well,
Comes with great courage up to all those keen beasts,
And laps up that young lion lightly in his mouth,
And went away with him wherever he liked;
And all those brutish beasts who were all about,   2310
Forsook us and followed him, for the sake of that lion cub.
And certainly, sire, that dream so woke me up,
And now I dread to death what destiny might bring us!"

"No, beloved lady," said William, "let go of such sorrow.
For surely it is a falsehood that you foretell;   2315
We may readily relax here securely at will."
But surely, just as she said, and in the same manner,
They heard a huge group of horses on the hill all about,
And heard them circling that quarry across the country all round.
At once, William wisely watched from out of a hole,   2320
And sees busy bold nobles all bearing bright arms,
Strutting with boastful bluster, speaking of those bears,
And in what way they would work with wit to catch them.
The provost of all those people pressed forth the foremost,
And many mighty men then made ready manfully.   2325
And, assuredly to say, God lent such grace
That the son of the provost, a seemly young boy,
Was brought forth with those nobles to behold the bears
And the splendid strange sight of seeing how they'd be caught.
When William was aware of how close they were,   2330
Then meekly, with mourning, he said to Melior,
"Alas, my beloved lovely, that ever I was alive,
To be in such bleakness and brought to such an end!
Alas, beloved, that our love should be broken so vilely,

That we must now die so dreadfully! So now, God, by Your grace, 2335
Let me have all the harm, I beseech You most highly,
Because I have wrought all this woe and deserve all of what comes.
For Melior, my dear heart, by Mary in heaven,
Wholly all of your hardship is through my heinous work!
Thus, if God were to will it, I would take the whole punishment, 2340
If you might escape quietly from this quarry in return.
And, dear heart, please directly do as I advise,
Briskly remove this bear skin and be still in your clothes;
And as soon as you are seen they shall soon know you;
Then your life will be lengthened by the love of your father. 2345
Thus you might surely be saved, if, in truth, nothing else;
And they will murder me then, for this matters not to me.
But if God, through His great grace, gave me to have here
A horse and fine harness as behoves to war;
I would rush out on them now, without stinting at all, 2350
And do what I might dare, until I suffered death;
Some of those braggarts now in arms should soon be bleeding or more!
Ah, but I am all beyond hope, yet God wills it to be!
So briskly be done of that bear skin I say,
And wander lightly hence and leave me to what comes; 2355
Save yourself swiftly, for this is for the best."
Weeping with wondrous sorrow, Melior then said to William,
"What? Leave you dear loved one? Why should I leave you
For any death or duress men might do unto me?
No, by Him who by His blood saved our lives through His, 2360
Be sure, never shall this bear skin be moved from my back!
Though I may win worldly life, I would rather be lifeless,
For sure, than to see you suffer through death.
With good will, we take such grace as God will send to us."

When what was said was spoken, surely to say, 2365
The provost bade bold men to go and take those bears;
And at his behest, hastily, they headed in to those rocks.
But with goodness, as God willed, such grace then occurred,
For the werewolf was aware and knew of their woes,
And bethought the best way of saving the bears; 2370

And at once, as a wild beast, he went against them,
With his mouth gaping grimly he goes straight away
To that provost's seemly son and swiftly caught him
By the middle in his mouth, that was of immense size;
And ran forth through that rabble, with such a raucous noise,   2375
As if he would briskly have devoured that boy.
When the provost perceived this, he cried to the people,
"Help us hastily, high men, on your lives, hurry, I command!
He will win his reward who now speeds at once
So to save my son, lest for sorrow I die!"   2380
Soon after he said that, we might now see his men
And many a bold noble spur after that beast,
And other fellows on foot, as fast as they might,
All wholly to that hunt, I have to say truly,
That neither body nor boy be left at that quarry,   2385
But went after the werewolf and away from the bears,
Hooting loudly their horns and hallooing huge cries,
And pursued him steadfastly with such a splendid noise,
That all the men upon earth might well be astonished.
Whenever that werewolf was a good way ahead,   2390
By some half a mile, or more if possible,
Lest those chasers cease in their pursuit of him,
He would wait with that boy to make them more blithe,
And raise their hopes of snatching that high knave from him.
But when they were all near him no, he would wait no longer,   2395
But drove directly away, as he did before;
And thus truly he led them, all the long day,
Such that no man on earth might ever capture them;
And they dare not shoot either, for dread of hurting the child,
So followed forth as they might, as fast as they could.   2400
Way back in that quarry, when those white bears were aware
That all the people had departed in pursuit of that beast,
That wisest of werewolves, so to win back that child,
And they saw how well for their sakes he suffered those pains,
To succour and save them both from a sorry death,   2405
They both began briskly to pray for that beast,
So that God in His greatness might spare him from grief,

And then wholly they knew that they would have been dead,
Had it not been for God's greatness and that good beast's help.
And when they had said their prayers, that pair then thought   2410
It would be best if they briskly bustled from that cave;
And William at once said these words to Melior,
"My sweetest one, sure to say, it seems to me best
That we disrobe from these bear skins, and not be so obvious;
For more folk will be watching for those two white bears   2415
Than they would after anyone who was walking in clothes.
Thus, I suggest that we wander now in our own garments."
Then Melior said meekly, "Sire, by Mary in heaven,
I hope it will be for the best to do wholly as you have said."
Thus they briskly hurled those bear skins from their bodies,   2420
And at once they were entwined, I will tell you truly.
And they were both blithe then to behold one another,
As, for a fortnight, in faith, they had not seen either's face.
Then they clasped and they kissed for all their cold cares;

And William at once peeped outside that cave,   2425
And busily observed, on all sides thereabouts,
To see if anyone was out walking, but no one he sees.
He latched on to lovely Melior and led her by her hand;
Clothed in normal clothes, they walked out of the cave,
Bearing now in their arms both of those bear skins,   2430
So loathe were they to lose them or leave them behind;
And then they wandered directly, over dales and hills,
Walking by ways which were furthest from folk.
In distress and in dread they dare see not a soul,
Lest they meet any man who might then betray them.   2435
And thus, as God willed, and with no one seeing them,
They walked in that way well over three miles,
And found then a fair forest, flourishing full thickly,
And at once they went there, without being noticed.
What with the their hardened haste, and all that hot weather,   2440
Melior was most weak; she might not walk any further.
Promptly, in the thickest place of that precious wood,
Well away from all ways and, all weary, they rested,
And greatly thanked God, who had gracefully saved them.
Lying softly together, they then slipped into sleep,   2445
As do those who are weary from being so long awake.
But we will leave them for the moment and now will speak of another,
For I will tell for a while of that wise werewolf.

 For hours, those frightening folk followed after him
To win that boy back from him whom he had taken
   that time;   2450
They hunted all the whole day both on horse and on foot,
   Until that seemly sun settled down to rest.
And when it was nigh on night-time, to tell you the truth,
The werewolf knew well that there was no more need
To bear that boy any further for the sake of those bears;   2455
They had followed him so far, he knew this for certain,
That surely none of his pursuers could return home swiftly,
No matter how hard he hurried all through the long night.
Now, briskly, that beast then put down that boy,

117

Who was made none the worse in woe nor by wound;   2460
For none might find on his body not one bruise on the boy
As made by that beast; he was still bold and fair.
And as soon as he had set that boy down,
He at once went away without further ado,
Directly, as if that day he had run just half a mile.   2465
When the provost and people perceived this was so,
That the beast had left the boy, they were all blissful then.
The provost sped to that place before all the people,
And hoisted that boy hastily high and nobly in his arms,
And clasped him and kissed him copious times often,   2470
And looked about his body for sign of any blemish;
When he saw he was all sound, he was then so glad,
That no grief under God would gainsay his joy.
Promptly, all those people who had run in pursuit,
Greatly thanked God for the grace which had befallen them.   2475
And, swiftly, all these here once so troubled were now all turned to joy.
So they all bustled homeward, briskly with bliss,
With all the mirth on this earth that men might devise.
So each man that night lodged in inns or elsewhere;
And when the day dawned, they turned directly for home.   2480
And at once, when they came home, I will tell you truly,
The provost then promptly warned all the people
To bustle briskly to that quarry to capture those bears.
They went with a good will, but when they came there,
They found they were all gone away who had been there before.   2485
None knew in this world where to seek them now
So they hastened now, homeward hurrying as they might,
And took their rest readily, at their own leisure.
Plainly the provost then proffered round about,
To any man upon earth who might capture those bears,   2490
A great gainful reward of gold for a lifetime.
Many men with their might made to busy themselves
Upon every such side so to seek those beasts;
But, by the grace of God, no man might grab them,
So happily were they hidden, through such fortune they had.   2495
And to tell what betided that opportune werewolf?

That night, when the provost had quickly departed,
He went away again to William and to his worthy maid,
Well charged with wine and with excellent food
Which he won by those ways which he had done before;   2500
And all these things he bore he briskly laid before William,
Then he went away from them, quickly at once.
William was amazed at this, and Melior also,
Why that beast would not stay who had helped them so well;
And each said to the other, "Now surely and certainly,   2505
This beast has man's nature, it may be none other.
See what sorrow he suffers to save us two;
And namely, he has never failed whenever we had need
To bring such as behoves to us, wherever we be.
May He who suffered five sore wounds for our sake,   2510
Please save our humble beast and protect him for us!"
"Amen, sire," said Melior, "by Mother Mary!
Were it not for his high help, we would long have been dead."
They then made themselves merry with the meat that they had,
And ate it at their ease, for they were long hungry;   2515
And they rested there readily all that long day
And all the next night after to tell you the truth;
For Melior was so weary that she might not walk.
Then early the next day before the sun came to shine,
Colliers carrying charcoal came to walk beside there,[20]   2520
And other ones that were wont so to fetch wood,
Close by to where William and his worthy maid were.
The colliers began to speak keenly together;
One of them said, swiftly, these self-same words:
"Would God those white bears were here right now!   2525
For all the men upon earth should not save their lives;
For at once would I wend, to warn the provost,
And they would be taken promptly and suffer much trouble;
For brutal bears they are not, though they seem to be;
It is the daughter of the emperor who wends so disguised   2530
With a knight who has captured her afflicted heart.
Therefore these cries have been so keenly called –
Whichever man alive might find them first,

He may get so much gold so never to go poor.
Wondrously, a werewolf saved them yesterday,   2535
That plainly bore away the boy of the provost;
While the host hunted them, the other two wholly escaped.
By He who absolved us, if they were both here
They should well practise witchcraft if they wished to escape,
Even if fourscore werewolves went with them also!"   2540
Then Melior was near mad, almost, with fear
Lest all these foul fellows should have found them there,
And dwelled still in her den, for dread, without noise.
At once, another workman, who was also nearby,
Began to fight with that fellow who had spoken before,   2545
And said, "Do your duty instead, there is work to be done!
How would it be better if those bears were here,
To do them any distress? They have done you no harm!
They have suffered much hardship since they have escaped;
I hope they shall still get away, despite your sorry will.   2550

May God, in His great might, save them from grief,
And bring them both bliss where so ever they be!
Let us do our paid deeds, as we are ordained,
And earn ourselves honest silver from our loads in the city."
They loaded their burdens briskly and began to wend;   2555
Neither William nor his sweet one see them anymore,
Though they had wholly heard all their huge speech.
Then William, at once, said these same words:
"Melior, my sweetheart, we must now no more
Walk round about here with these bold bear skins,   2560
If we want to make things work better for us."
"Certainly, sire, that is so," said Melior then,
"If we walk in these clothes, I truly would know,
That all of this country would come to know our condition;
We may be recognised swiftly by whoever might meet us.   2565
But I know not in what way to make this work for the best."
"Indeed, nor do I," said William, "but good will come to pass!"

 While those two sweethearts talked together,
The werewolf had hunted a huge hart right there,
And right before both of them he brought it to death;   2570
And hastily it hurried and brought also a hind,
And served it in the same way as the hart before,
Then he at once went away without further ado.
Then William knew very well what the beast willed:
He had slain and placed there both that hart and that hind   2575
So that he and his loved one might dress in their pelts
And leave behind those bear skins which were now busily sought.
And meekly to Melior he then mentioned his thoughts,
And said, "See what splendid marvels this seemly beast works!
Therefore, Christ, crowned King, pray keep him from sorrow,   2580
And might no man ever let him come to harm!"
"Pray, God grant that," said Melior, "for His sweet might!
For without the Heavenly King's help and that kind-hearted beast,
Our lives would have been lost many a long day since."
"Yes, indeed so," said William, "my worthy dear heart;   2585
Thus now we must work at what that beast wills;

We must skin the hides hastily of both this hart and hind
And grace ourselves in these garments if we are to go further."
William took the hart hastily and Melior the hind,
And they removed both the skins as craftily as they could.   2590
Each then gamely started to grace the other grandly therein,
Such that, sewn on them both, the skins fitted as tightly
As they had been to those beasts which they had once grown upon.
And, in sight, they seemed better dressed as seemly harts,
Than they seemed before, when they were bears,   2595
So closely to each of them were those skins now joined.[21]

 And when they were graced gaily in that garb,
They stayed there at their leisure until the sun set.
When it was nearly night-time and they could no longer
    remain,
    They went forth on their way, for it was as well they were
gone;   2600

And their seemly werewolf followed swiftly after,
Who had so wisely taught them the best ways to wend,[22]
To seek the path towards Sicily by the subtlest of ways.
The next day, most namely, many men sought them
In woodland and wilderness, far and wide about there;   2605
And as they walked in the woods with their loyal hounds,
They found both the bear skins and those flayed beasts.
They knew wholly forthwith they were a hart and hind,
And they knew those whom they sought were wrapped in these skins,
Who before would have been dressed like two white bears;   2610
And they knew then they had been working thus far in waste,
For all the hard hunting which they had been doing.
But they dare follow them no further because of a great war
That was wondrously violent, in the next land;
And so they ceased their pursuit of those sweet beasts.   2615
Thus I will mention no more of those chasing men;
So of the hart and the hind, pray harken now further.

 They went fast on their way; the werewolf led them
Over mountain and moorland and many fair plains;
But always, as they went, they found it all waste.   2620
For boroughs and bold towns had all been burned down,
Despite being well fortified with walls all around them.
And all this land was William's, I will tell you truly,
He who was now dressed as a hart. So here is the reason
Why that war and such woe was there in that land: 2625
You have heard here before, as I understand,*
Of Embrons, that acclaimed king, who ruled the kingdom throughout
Both Apulia and Sicily, Palermo and Calabria,
And was the father of William, who went there as a hart?
He was now long dead and duly buried, many a day before,   2630
Yet his comely queen, as God willed, was still quick and alive,
Who was William's mother, a lady of true renown.
She had since had a dear daughter, I tell you truly,

---

* The text suggests that the narrator himself – or possibly the author or scribe – may have changed during the telling of the story, although "as ich understonde" may well be formulaic.

Of the finest of face and the fairest of shape
That any man upon earth might ever imagine;   2635
She was younger than William by three full years.*
And the acclaimed king of Spain had a comely son,
Proclaimed as a skilled knight and a keen man of arms;
It was for his sake that the werewolf was so wickedly formed
Through the malice of his stepmother, as you may hear later,†   2640
And brothers were they both, sired by the same father.
That acclaimed king of Spain coveted for his son
That worthy maiden, who was William's sister,
But the queen would not grant that wedding, in any way.
Thus the king and his son had stirred up this war;   2645
For they had loathsomely burned and destroyed her land,
Burnt down bold boroughs and battered nobles to death;
And had besieged her so hard, to speak the truth surely,
That she fled with her people to Palermo most promptly;
And the king besieged that city savagely hard,   2650
And his son also made many a savage assault.
But doughty men defended it with diligence within;
Yet certainly, on both sides, many people were slain
And this lasted so long, believe me for sure,
That the citizens of that city soon became very weary,   2655
And came often to the queen, and counselled her earnestly
To accord with that king and grant what he craved,
For they might no longer maintain fighting, in any manner;
Because many of her folk were being felled by her foe,
And her men fast enfeebled for want of some food,   2660
That they might in no manner withstand more of that siege.

---

* The scribe here seems in error. The romance says elsewhere that William was abducted at the age of four (ll. A 35; 3498); at that time he was the only child of Embrons and Felice. Although it is possible that the lost leaves of the Middle English redaction may have said William was three when he was abducted, the subsequent reference to his age at l. 3498 points to an error.
† The MS reads, "as ʒe mow here after" (lit. "as you may hear later"). Although this is so (ll. 4096–4105), it seems unusual, given his normal behaviour, that the narrator doesn't refer to the story he has told earlier. The intention of the narrator here might instead be to say "of which more later". This general passage hints at some confusion with the narrator which may indicate a scribal change at this point.

Then that comely queen said, most courteously,
"Lords, you have been my liege men, both good and true,
Bold nobles in body, big to guide in battle;
I grant you, I know, that you are greatly aggrieved   2665
By these terrible troubles; but swiftly, I hope,
All will be well improved, for this you must know:
I have sent for support from my seemly father,
Whose grace is to guide Greece as sire and emperor,
And I know wholly and well that, without fail,   2670
He will send me assistance, or else come himself.
It is so far to that country, as you well comprehend,
That he might not sail forth as swiftly as he may.
Therefore, all my bold nobles, I beseech you and pray,
For the love which you owe to our life-giving Lord,   2675
Maintain all your manliness for a little time longer,
Until God in His grace might yet send us good tidings."
And thus she bade two bold barons to go briskly forth
To the king of Spain and say to him courteously,
That she prayed, politely through charity, to let her live in peace   2680
For a full fortnight, free from further grief,
From assaults to the city, or any other sorrows;
And unless her father comes by the end of a fortnight,
Or sends her some assistance by that said time,
She would with a good will, without any more let,   2685
Fall upon his manly mercy in the following manner:
To give him without grudging all of her goods,
So that safely she might, with her seemly daughter,
Journey elsewhere at once, to go where she liked.
Those manly messengers went as she had implored   2690
At speed to the Spanish king and told him of her speech.
But he swore on his oath that he would not assent,
Not for any man alive, for he must have her daughter;
So they promptly returned and told this to the queen.
And when she wholly knew the will of the king,   2695
She went to her chamber as a woman most woeful
And prayed fully and piteously to the Prince of Heaven,
For the love of Mother Mary, to maintain and help her,

So that her foes might not conquer her, in any fashion by force,
To win her most worthy daughter against her will.   2700
"Oh, madam," said her daughter. "Let Mary grant this,*
For the love of that blissful Babe who sucked at Her breast."
Thus they dwelled in distress, many days and nights,
Both that courteous queen and her comely daughter.
Had they known wholly the help which God had sent,   2705
All their grief should then gamely have turned into glee.
Now we cease speaking of those besieging that city
And of those serious assaults they launched on the same,
And of the doughty defence of those dwelling within;
And listen now for a little of those two beloved beasts,   2710
That as a hart and a hind happened on their way,
In whichever manner that wise werewolf would lead them.

Now listen, high ones, of this hart and this hind:
They carried on over countries, as Christ so willed,
Over dales and downs along discreet ways,   2715
Which the werewolf well knew, he who was their whole friend.
Then as one they sought out the rich city of Reggio,†
Which is most seemly situated upon the sea shores.
A grand number of ships belonged to that haven;
And there our humble beasts bided, waiting to cross.   2720
And so broad was that sea it behoved them to sail
All wholly by night; the whole way if possible.
All day the beasts dwelled, still, in their den,
Within some ragged rocks right by the harbour,
Until it was well into the night, when all were asleep.   2725
Then they hurried to that haven, with haste and quickly,
As the werewolf so willed them, he who was their guide;
And they stalked still and silent to where many ships stood.

---

* The MS reads, "No, mad(am)e," saide hire dauȝter, "Marie þat graunt . . . ", which appears to suggest a disagreement. Skeat in his glossary (p. 290) tells us " 'No' signifies assent to the previous speaker; 'nay' implies strong denial. Felice's daughter is therefore concurring with her mother's prayers."

† The MS reads "Rise". This is Reggio in Calabria (Reggio di Calabria), on the toe of Italy on the Straits of Messina opposite Sicily.

The werewolf, with wisdom, watched for which ship was ready
To fare forth on the waves, and he soon found one   2730
That was all gaily rigged and ready to go sailing,
And was faithfully filled, full of fine wines.
The werewolf went there to know who was around;
Every soul was asleep then, so it would seem,
All but the master mariners, to mention things truly,   2735
They had travelled into town, to be entertained,[23]
In mirth, till the moon rose; so they might not yet cross.
And when the werewolf knew that all there were fast asleep,
He returned once more to the hart and the hind,
And he soon showed his intent by using certain signs;   2740
And they followed him fairly, and willingly, on account of his kindness.
And he led them most lithely to that lovely ship,
And taught them to hide behind some tuns there.
When the moon rose, the masters came in most manly,
And when the full tide was fair they fared to sail,   2745
Having wind so to wend at will when they would.
The werewolf knew well when they were nearly over,
And bethought how best he might help the beasts,
So that they could escape, unscathed, from that ship.
When the sailors neared land, he leapt overboard   2750
At once in their sight, so that they would pursue him
And hunt him right down while the hart and hind fled.
As soon as the sailors see him leap down,
With haste, each man hoists a spar or an oar,
And loathsomely launched themselves at him, so to take his life.   2755
One hit him so harshly, as he leapt in the water,
That he dived to the ground from that dull dint,
And near nigh lost his life, but, as our Lord willed,
He quickly recovered, despite that stern stroke,
And swam swiftly away in the full sight of all,   2760
And alighted lightly on the land, a little distance away.
And because those folk were so eager to finish off that beast,
They sailed swift to the shore and sped after him.
But the werewolf was wily, and went with such skill,
That the sailors went wandering most wildly to take him,   2765

And everyone pursued him that belonged to that ship,
Except a barelegged boy, who was left on the barge.[24]
When those sailors and the wolf were long since gone,
The hart and the hind then hoped to escape,
And swiftly both of them bustled above all the hatches.   2770
But when the boy on that barge sees both the beasts,
He was near worried out of his wits, I will tell you, for fear,
And he bethought how best to quell those beasts.
As chance would so have it, he hits the hind first,
And set her such a stroke, so sorrowfully on her neck,   2775
That she went top over tail and tumbled over the decks.
But the hart full hastily hoisted her in his arms
And bore with her overboard on a broad plank,
And was not bold with that boy – he did not fight back –
But preferred to flee, for fear of more folk   2780
Far away on the shore, or else he would have stayed.
And when he knew that he was now well out of sight,
He examined that hind, seeking any heinous harm,
But found she was just affrighted, from fear of that blow.
Then the hart said to the hind, with high honour most fine,   2785
"Ah, worthiest one! How sorry is your fortune,
That all this hurt has harmed you that I should have deserved!
Oh, God through His grace, and all His great might,
That I had weapons right here which fall to warfare,
Then that boy in the barge should soon sorely be beaten;   2790
For the drubbing he dealt, he is marked to die!"
"No, my worthy man," said Melior then,
"For the love of God, who gave you life, pray, do not grieve!
We have escaped unscathed, so God may we thank,
And our worthy werewolf, may well he betide!   2795
Dear God, he has endured near death for us all,
Pray let no soul succeed in slaying our good beast!
Without his wit and his work, we would both be ruined."
"Yes, sweet one, this is certain," William said then;
"We must progress and go quickly, for the love of God,   2800
To reach now some refuge so that there we may rest."
Melior, full meekly, said without fear,

"Let us go now as God wills." Then they went with good speed,
Clasping each other closely, to speak but the truth.

 When the hart and the hind had escaped that hardship, 2805
The boy guarding the barge was astonished by those beasts;
How one had borne from that barge so boldly the other,
With so comely a bearing, clasped close in his arms,
And fared first on four feet and then upon two.
Meanwhile, the werewolf had escaped and was flown, 2810
From all those sorry seamen who sought to quell him by chase;
But, truly, none might take him, nor trouble him further,
And then he hurried fast, to the hart and the hind.
And when the hart and the hind had sight of their beast,
They were greatly glad and thanked God often 2815
That he was safe and sound, and had escaped those men.
Then they fared forth together, full of joy to be alive.
The shipmen who so swiftly had pursued that werewolf
Bustled back to their barge and the boy told them
How a hart and a hind had escaped from there, 2820
At once when they went to chase after that werewolf;
And he also told them how he had hit the hind,
And how the hart hoisted it and hastened overboard,
And how, with such careful bearing, he conducted her recovery
And then at once went away yet, to where, he knew not. 2825
They were astounded by this, but none knew what to do,
Or where for to fare so to find those beasts;
So they let things lie. Now learn some more about these beasts,
How they went through the wilderness and what happened next.

 Wherever they went, they found it all waste, 2830
Bold boroughs thereabouts were burned down on all sides;
And as ever, that wise werewolf would lead them onwards;
They followed him fairly as their faithful friend.
As he himself planned, who had led them so long,
He brought them to a borough that was bold and rich, 2835
And the fairest ever fashioned of any rich fortress
That any man upon earth might ever look on.

That palace was peerless and it was called Palermo.
The werewolf first took William away from that place,
When he was but in childhood, as I chanced to tell earlier.   2840
And truly, right at that time, to tell all the truth,
William's mother was imperilled there and all her many folk,
For the king of Spain besieged her severely,
In the manner and for the matter that was mentioned before.
Below that palace there was a prize place, a park as it were,   2845
That was once well stocked with many wild beasts;[25]
But those besieging soldiers had destroyed it all.
The hart and the hind then head there now, quickly –
As the werewolf so wanted, he who was their guide –
And to a well-crafted crag, below the rooms of the queen;   2850
And they dwelled in that den all the day and the night.
The werewolf went at once and won them meat and drink,
So that they made as merry as they might, at that time.
Now, of these humble beasts, we will be still a while,
And speak instead of that courteous queen, who lived in
    the castle.   2855

 She was besieged so hard, to speak the whole truth,
And so hard were the assaults given to that city,
That its comely crenellations were sent crumbling by engines,
And many of her mighty men were murdered to death.
Thus the queen was discouraged, and prayed often
    to Christ,   2860
To send her some assistance, so that she would be saved,
For the love of His mother Mary, who is most merciful.
She had lived such a life for a long time now,
And endured much distress for the sake of her daughter;
But on that self-same night, to speak the truth then,   2865
The hart and the hind and the third, their companion,
Caught their rest in that crag under the castle,
While the queen went to bed, all weary and weeping.
When asleep she soon dreamt a splendid sweet dream:
She dreamt she and her daughter, alone one day,   2870
Passed unattended from that palace by a postern gate,

To play privately in that park which belonged to the palace.
She dreamt one hundred thousand thronged about them -
Bold leopards and bears and beasts without number -
With mouths gaping grimly to grieve her and her daughter.   2875
And right as those brutal beasts should have snatched both of them,
She dreamt that a wise werewolf, and two white bears,
Hurried hard to them swiftly to help them in their need;
And when those two white bears both came near to them,
They seemed in her sight like two seemly harts;   2880
And both of them, on their foreheads, seemed to have a fair figure:
The bigger hart, on his head, had, it so seemed to her,
The fashion and form of a fair knight in the field,
And seemed like her own son, whom she had missed for so long;
That other hart, in her dream, had the shape of a maid,   2885
The fairest in her features than she had ever seen before;
And either hart on its head had, as so she thought,
A great crown of gold, full of good stones,
Most seemly to see, and which shone far and wide.
Then she dreamt that the werewolf and the maid stayed behind   2890
While the huge hart himself, hastily then,
Went alone briskly, against all those beasts,
And he bore down on both sides of them, always first at the boldest;
None was stout enough to withstand him, he fought so sternly.
He soon grabbed and caged the greatest of those grim beasts,   2895
A lion and a leopard, who were their leaders;
She dreamt that the huge hart had taken them quickly,
And put them in her prisons to punish at her will.
He soon stiffly defeated the stoutest and sternest;
The greatest he grabbed were all gaoled and caged;   2900
And, readily, all the rest of those rude beasts
Began to flee out of fear, as fast as they might,
Over dales and downs, for dread of that hart.
As soon as that high hart had given her deliverance,
And put her out of peril from those perilous beasts,   2905
She dreamt she went at once within the castle,
And climbed the tallest tower to behold all about;
And she dreamt that her right arm reached over Rome,

And truly her left arm lay all over Spain,
And both those comely kingdoms came under her will   2910
To harken at her behest and to work her wishes.
In wonder of all this, she wakened swiftly,
And, for dread of her dream, she quaked in distress
And wept sorrowfully in wonder, and at once dressed herself,
And then readily roamed to the chapel, right troubled,   2915
To seek out in God's goodness, what good things her dream predicted.

That comely queen had a priest, a clever man of learning,
Who knew much of many things, and was known as Moyses.
She called on him for his counsel and explained her case –
Truly all of her visions seen when sleeping that night –   2920
And as swiftly as she told it, the priest took his books,
And soon says of that dream how events should turn out.
He looked on that comely queen and courteously said,
"Madam, mourn you no more. You may well see
That the Prince of Heaven has you presently in mind,   2925
And soon will send you assistance, so this dream tells me.
The beasts which so beset you, and your seemly daughter,
And who would have done you to death, both of you direly,
They are surely those soldiers who besiege you so savagely
And, in doing so strenuously, seek here to destroy you.   2930
Now know of those white bears who then became harts,
And have on their heads the form of two handsome children,
And good crowns of gold, gracing their heads:
The hart who helped you, so hastily with his strength –
Who led that lion and leopard both into your prison,   2935
And brought under your will all those brutal beasts –
What that betokens I will tell you quickly.
It is a widely acclaimed knight who comes to your rescue,
And through his doughty deeds shall end this war,
And catch the king of Spain through his own clear strength –   2940
And then afterwards his son, the cause of all this sorrow –
And put them in your prison. The proudest of them all
Shall be humbled by your will, and bring these doings to an end,
And made meek at your mercy, those whose pride was misplaced.

And that ilk acclaimed knight who shall come to help you,   2945
I do not know whether he will take you as a wife,
But I know he will be the wise king of this realm.
And also that werewolf, who comes with the harts,
He is acclaimed also, a knight to be extolled,
And, for sure, I see through him that the king shall be delivered,   2950
Who you put in your prison, and that good peace will be made;
His son and all others shall be your whole friends
And restore all the wrongs, richly, which they have wrought.
Through that same werewolf, you shall know of your son,
Whom you have long lost, pray, believe me truly,   2955
And shall win him back once again within a short time.
And what of your right arm that reached over Rome?
I see well its significance; this shall befall:
Your son shall wed such a wife as to wield all of Rome,
Its lawful keeper and king, I can truly say.   2960
And, loyally, of your left arm which lay over Spain?
That betokens truthfully, as so my books tell me,
That your doughty son shall see your dear daughter given
To the Spanish king's son, when they make their accord;
Thus your left arm betokens her ladyship of that land.   2965
I have thus explained all your visions, and what surely will happen;
And, truly, all this shall befall, within a short time."

When that lovely lady had listened to these words,
And heard say that she would see her son once again,
She wept in wonderful joy, for all of those words,   2970
And sorrowfully she sighed lest anything should stop it,
And any false fortune fall on her son through sin.
Then, humbly, that bright lady bustled quickly to her chapel,
And prayed, for charity's sake, for her priest to sing a mass
To the all-enthroned Trinity, to turn her dream to bliss.   2975
He did this directly, devoutly and fairly,
And then that comely queen goes back to her chamber;
And she threw open a window which was toward that place
Where the hart and the hind had taken their rest.
There, that seemly lady sat so to look out,   2980

And, stuck in a stout study of her startling dream,
Watched out of her window while she was deep in thought.
And under a lovely laurel tree, in a green place,[26]
She saw the hart and the hind lying cuddled together,
Making the most joy that man might devise;   2985
With all the comely customs which they might contrive
They enjoyed all pleasures which paramours speak in private;
But surely nothing they said might the queen hear herself.
But, of their splendid pleasures which those sweethearts enjoyed,
The queen wielded great wonder of those worthy beasts,[27]   2990
And leaned there the long day to look out of the window
To see the strange gestures of those seemly beasts,
Until the day then withdrew, into the dark night,
And that lady, no longer, might look on those beasts.
Then she attired herself truly and returned to the hall,   2995
And made as merry as she could, among all her many folk.
When the same had all supped and washed themselves later,
Her acclaimed knights and councillors then came to speak,
Mentioning new misfortunes, how near they were to misery,
How their walls were all broken by the work of great engines, 3000
And their bastions about were all burned and destroyed,
And that they might not, anymore, maintain their defences.

 Then that comely queen full courteously said,
"Lords, you are my liegemen, all of you alike,
And each sworn on all sides to safeguard my rights,   3005
And any more such manly men may not live upon earth.
Therefore, my lords, for His love who let us be formed,
And for your own renown, work to keep me from harm
From these wicked men still who would spill my blood!
And if God, in His grace, will send us some good help,   3010
I will work to your will, without any fail,
Whether I beg for mercy or maintain this war.
Truly, if it betides me to escape this trouble,
I will reward you with riches to enrich you for ever,
So that truly, for your travails, you should not go without." 3015
And all her great men were glad of her good speech,

And said in assent that, what so would happen,
They would use all their manly might to maintain her will;
For as long as they lived, they would yield to no one.
Then that comely queen thanked them full courteously,   3020
And then afterwards, blithely, they bustled to bed,
And readily took their rest right to the next day.
Then that comely queen rises quickly,
And, so to say her prayers busily, bustles quickly to her chapel,
And made her priest, Moyses, swiftly sing a mass,   3025
Promptly, and in praise of the King of Heaven,
And to His mild Mother, who helps all men,
That They send her assistance, soon in good time.
When this mass was done, she went to her chamber
And waited at the window, where she sees the beasts,   3030
And she sees them in the same place as they were before;
Handsomely, both of them, embracing the other.
The hot sun had baked their hides so hard,
That their comely clothes, which their skins covered,
The queen saw as she sat, peeping from the seams,   3035
And was in wonder of them, I will tell you truly.
The queen called her priest to counsel her quickly,
And showed him the sight of those seemly beasts;
And as soon as he sees them, he said to the queen,
"For the love of Mary, madam, be dismayed no longer;   3040
For you might find right here the matter of your dreams,
As I described the other day, when you told me your dream.
And you have already heard how in Rome things have happened:*
How the emperor's daughter was given to the Greek heir in wedlock,
But that no man there might conduct that marriage,   3045
For she had first laid her love in a much better place,
On the most acclaimed knight known across the whole world,
The best in all body, bravest, boldest in arms?

* In ll. 3043–58 the scribe employs narrative transference in using the priest to fill us in on an
element of the story that has not occurred in the narrative as a whole. Although we the audi-
ence are aware of events, the queen's personal world knowledge of happenings in Rome has
not previously been revealed until now.

And how they both bustled from Rome in two bear skins;
And then hasped themselves in hart skins but how, I don't know?   3050
Well, I safely I say this, and will surely prove to you,
Those two yonder are himself, and his seemly maid.
He will, at once, bring this war to its end,
And bring you quick from all troubles to a brighter salvation,
And deliver all your lands back, in length and in breadth.   3055
Thus no more will I mention any more of this matter,
So bethink now how best to win those beasts to you,
That this knight and that comely maid might come quick to your
    chamber."

 Then that comely queen considered in her heart
That she would work in this way: to be well sewn   3060
In the hide of a huge hind, just like the others,
And then bustle out to those beasts, and lie under a bush,
Till she knew what they were, and if they would speak.
The priest then, promptly, purveyed such a hide,
And thus that day drove to night and all drew to rest.   3065
But the queen all that day had dressed well and proper,
Handsomely in that hind's skin, to appear as such a beast;
And she passed before daybreak through a private postern,
And waited under a bush near where those beasts lay,
Privately, where none but the priest might perceive her,   3070
And with but one of her chamber-maids, whom she loved the most,
Who stood still and waited within a postern gate;
And when the sun began to show, and to shine brightly,
The high hart and his hind began to awake,
And made together the most mirth that man might devise,   3075
With cuddling and kissing and numerous courtesies,
And between them they both talked many excellent words.[28]
Then William, without doubt, said the following words,
"Ah, my lovely beloved, I think it is a long time
Since I plainly saw your most seemly face;   3080
I long to see it intensely, if it should so occur."
"By Mary," said Melior, "I am too so longing
To behold your bright face, though we had better wait.

We will not creep from these skins unless we can escape,
Or until our humble beast says we can both do so.   3085
For he will signify when the time is right, and let us know swiftly
In what way that we might wear our own clothes."
"Truly, sweetheart, that is so," said William then;
"Though I think it will be a while before that time comes.
But if only God would let the queen know who we truly were,   3090
And would hastily help me with a horse and good arms,
I would soon bring her succour from all this sorry war,
And pull her out of this peril in a short time, most purely;
Although, as she knows not of us, woe is me therefore!
Were it not for your sake, sweetheart, I would not care for myself, 3095
For much mischief haunts you, and all due to me."
"Mischief, sire?" said Melior. "I will hear no more of this;
Truly, I would rather have this life, and live with you here,
Than to win all the world, yet want of your sight!"
Then they clasped and kissed, and stopped all that talk.   3100
And the queen, by a bush, lay alone by herself
And heard wholly all of the words which each of them said.
And Melior, in the meantime, said meekly to William,
"Sweet one, I was sore afraid, of a dream in my sleep;
I dreamt earlier of an eagle, which, before I was aware,   3105
Had taken us up and into that mighty high tower;
Whether great news or grim, I don't know how this gains us."
"No for certain," said William, "I well know for sure,
That it brings us good things, so God help us."
And as they lay in their leisure, they looked all about,   3110
And they both see at once, behind a bush,
How a huge hind lay here, at its rest.
"By Mary," said Melior, "I'm minded that this beast sleeps,
And seems unafraid of us, as I deem it, surely."
"Yes truly," said William, "I do not know why it should;   3115
It supposes that we are safe, we seem just like itself,
Because we are so suitably sewn in these hides.
For indeed, if it wisely knew what beasts we were,
It would flee from our fellowship for fear, very soon."
"No, by Christ," said the queen, "who shaped all mankind,   3120

137

I will not flee, fully nor far, for fear of you two!
I know well what you are, and from where you have come;
I know your case completely, what beckons you here."
William was most astounded when he heard these words,
And the meek Melior was made near mad by fear;   3125
But William, with haste, thus said to the hind,
"I compel you through Christ, who suffered on the cross,
That you promptly tell me, and tarry no longer,
Whether you are a good ghost who speaks in God's name,
Or instead some foul fiend, formed in this fashion,   3130
And if we should have from you some harm or some good?"

Then that comely queen full courteously said,
"I am a beast as you be, by Him who wrought us.
I hope you shall never have any harm from me;
For I speak as a good friendly ghost, in the name of God!   3135
We come from the same kind, as do you, by Christ;*
Except that other bold beasts, by their mastery and strength,
Have driven me with distress from my own dear pasture.
Therefore I sought you here, to seek your assistance;
And pray that through charity, and properly out of pity,   3140
You deliver me from distress and help restore my own pasture,
And truly, for all your life-time, you will be lord thereof;
And that eminent maiden who lies in there with you,
Shall be my elect lady to wield this lordship;
For the royal Emperor of Rome is really her father.   3145
I know well she is worthy to wield much more.
I know how by your cunning, you have crossed the country;
And I bid you be welcome here, by Christ that made me!
Of what sorrows I have suffered I will quickly now speak:
The proud king of Spain has besieged me with pride,   3150
And has wasted all my lands, loathsomely with his lords,
And all this distress he does to me on account of my daughter;

---

* The MS reads "Of swiche kinde ar we kome"; the queen appears to be using the "royal we".
The intention of the line may also be that the queen is suggesting all three of them are from
noble stock.

She would never assent to be wife to his son,
Thus he works me with woe, and wastes all my lands,
Save only for this city, where my stay is uncertain.   3155
But I hope, most hastily, to have your help alone;
I am meekly before you to amend my misfortune,
And I grant you plain power, promptly and swiftly,
To lead all my lordship however you like;
I make you master of all, with no rules or demands,   3160
With that you'll win back my realm, which I ruled before."
Then William was greatly glad, and thanked God often,
When he knew it was the queen, and at once he said,
"Madam, by that mighty Lord who made us all,
If I might at this time trust what you say truly,   3165
So you would loyally look after and save my beloved,
While I battle busily to beat off your sorrows,
Then you shall have, as you need, wholly all of my help.
In faith, without flinching, I shall never fail you,
For as long as any life is left surely in me!   3170
The queen was greatly gladdened, and thanked him gratefully,
And lovingly led him and his beloved by hand,
And they went forth on their feet, faithfully together,
Privately to the postern and passed through it quickly,
Where that maid was still stood, waiting for her queen;   3175
And, when she saw more thoroughly those three beasts coming near,
So hideous in their hides, as these harts were,
She went nearly out of her wits, I will tell you, for fear,
And began to run away rapidly, to recount matters truly!
But that comely queen called for her again;   3180
And she came back with care, when she heard her name called.
"Why carry on so?" said the queen. "Did you not recall,
That I was so attired when I departed from you?"
"Yes, madam," said the maid, "by Mary in heaven,
But I was nigh wracked out of my wits by those weirder beasts   3185
Who follow you in fellowship, and are so frightening."[29]
"They will do you no damage, by dear God of Heaven,
For it is they whom I went for to persuade to join me.
But look now, on your life, let no man know of this,

How these have come here, it is secret hereafter!" 3190
"No madam, by Mary," said that maid then,
"I will not divulge this deed, on pain of death."

 Then that comely queen takes Melior by the hand,
And before her went William. Then afterwards the queen
Brought them to a choice chamber beneath the
        chief tower, 3195
    And beds were brought there, fit for any rich noble;
And two baths were borne up by others, quite soon,
And were excellently attired for lords true and trustworthy.
The queen came quickly with a knife, and then both her comely self,
William and his worthy were all swiftly unlaced 3200
From those hideous hides, which were hurled in a corner.
And when they were seen in their own worthy clothes,[30]
No men upon earth might see any fairer couple
Than were this pair William and that worthy maid!
The queen clasped and kissed them, and made them comfortable, 3205
And they both bathed swiftly, those two, well and fair,
And graced themselves gaily in fine rich garments,
And they made manifest leisure, with the most noble meats,
And the most dainty dishes and drinks that there were;
To mention more is quite needless, for nothing they missed! 3210
When they had made themselves most merry with their meal,
That comely queen said, courteously to William,
"Sweet sire, might I ask, what sign would you like
To have shaped on your shield to show as your arms?"
"By Christ, madam," spoke the knight, "I covet nothing more 3215
But that I have a good shield graced most cleanly in gold,
With a werewolf depicted fairly within it,
That be hideous and huge, wholly in every way,
In the most striking colour to be clear in the field;*

---

* 3219: The MS reads "of þe covenablest colour to knowe in þe feld" (lit. "the most acceptable colour to be seen in the field"). Given the shield's background is said to be gold, we might interpret "acceptable" instead as a contrasting – or striking – colour so that William is more easily recognised on the battlefield.

All my life, I would aim to bear no other arms." 3220
The queen then commanded men with enough craft,
To draught the device he requested by the eve of that day,
To wend in war round the world wherever he liked,
In that peerless apparel, as proof of good things!

 Also that comely queen, as Christ willed, 3225
Had tied in her stable one of the sturdiest steeds
That any man upon earth might ever hear of,
And the doughtiest in all deeds that any horse might do.
King Embrons had owned it, who was her lord before;
And from the day that he died, no man dared go near it, 3230
Nor be so bold in his body as to climb on its back;
So it stood tied in the stable with stiff iron chains.
And a hole was cunningly crafted and cut in a fashion
So that men might leave him food, and much water at will.
The horse soon had a scent of our high noble knight, 3235
And knew, as God willed, it was his kind lord.
Thus, briskly he breaks all his bonds out of joy,
And began to flail with his feet, and frighteningly neighed,
So men thought he was mad, and so warned the queen
Of how sternly in the stable that steed now fared, 3240
And had broken his bonds, and that nobody dared near him.[31]
When William heard this he said these words to the queen,
"Madam, what steed is that, which is so stern to hold?
Can he do those doughty deeds that men do in arms?"
"Yes, certainly," said the queen, "the truth so to tell, 3245
I know of none in this world more worthy in that work,
If there were any man on earth who might handle him.
He belonged to my lord, whom I loved much when alive;
And out of love for him, certainly, I safeguard this steed."
"Madam," said William, "if it were to your will, 3250
I would pray through pure charity, and such profits that befall,
That I may have that horse, when I shall have its need.
I myself, on my own, will manfully go
And sit upon his saddle and most seemly harness him."
"Certainly," said the queen, "I say once and for all 3255

I make you wholly the master of all I hold here,
To do with, night and day, as you think for the good."
Thus William was glad, and thanks her at once.
Then they asked for wine and went to bed after,
For time had now stretched and fared far into the night.   3260

Directly in the morning, as the day began to dawn,
The steward of Spain, who was stern and bold,
Laid siege to that city with astonishing severity
With three thousand men, thoroughly fit for the fight.
Thus the soldiers of that city were soon prepared,   3265
As doughty men of deeds, to defend that place,
And shut all their great gates and guarded the walls,
Because none of those within would venture outside,
For their foe was so great, and so few were inside.
Cries now rudely arose, which were rueful to hear,   3270
For those within the town were in such distress,
That they wholly thought they would be seized that day.
Promptly, those tidings were told in the palace,
Of how fiercely their foe began to fight at the walls.
When William knew this, he started at once,   3275
As glad as any great man that God ever wrought,
Because he might fight his fill for that fine queen,
And so he was armed, in all manner of ways,
And went straight to that stable where that great steed stood;
And many folk followed him, to behold a fine marvel,   3280
Of how sternly he and that steed should contest together.
But no sooner had that kind knight come calmly to the stable,
Than the steed, upon seeing him, soon leapt up,
And knelt with his forefeet, fairly on the ground,
And made himself the most joyous that any might devise;   3285
And all the fellows who followed him were fully amazed.
The steed stood full still, despite all his sternness,
While the knight came to saddle him, and harness him cleanly,
And mounted that horse with ease, when he was ready,
And shoved a shield on his shoulder, a sharp spear in his hand,   3290
And girt himself with a good sword fit to grace the earth's finest.

The steed liked this load well, when he felt his lord;
He knew that just by his own skill, this one could ride well,
And brandished himself so boldly that everybody was in
    wonder,
Of the comely carriage of that knight he conveyed. 3295
He was so splendid to see, in his seemly arms,
That all nobles were blithe at once to behold him;
For so seemly a sire they had never seen before.
The queen and her daughter, and Melior the fair,
Watched out of a window, wilfully together, 3300
How that courteous knight carried himself on his steed.
The queen and her daughter admired him greatly,
And praised him the most peerless of any prince upon earth,
And said, "Happy indeed is the woman who would have him!
No knight under Christ could be described as so courtly!" 3305
When Melior heard all this matter, she thought what it meant,
And was frightened to death of how they might deceive her,
To win William from her, whom they so well praised,
And said softly to herself the same words as these:
"Dear Lord, if You had willed it, I would rather it be 3310
To have wandered the wilderness with my own loved one,
Than dwell here in the wealth of all this rich world,
Just to lose my beloved, who owns all my love."
Such mistrust had Melior, for those who praised him so much.

Now William, on his stern steed, rides stiffly forth 3315
On his own, and so stately, through all that city,
Such that everyone was in wonder who sees him with
    their eyes,
    So courageous was the countenance of that courtly
      knight.
William pressed promptly to where the people assembled,
And all the solemn souls who guarded that city; 3320
Bold barons and knights and other great nobles.
And when they were aware, all of them, of William,
Of the craft, the bold carriage, of this kingly knight,
They beheld him with heart, and were greatly happy,

That so manly a man would meet their foes with them.   3325
The noble horse which bore him they knew straightaway,
But wholly who he was, not one knew at all.
William went straight to them and said at once,
"Dear lords, listen to me, for the love of God!
It seems you are soldiers, both splendid and noble,   3330
And bold brave men to stand firm in the hardest of battles,
And you are also well armed, in many ways to perfection.
Why let your foe foully keep you fastened herein
And deal you all the distress which they might devise,
And you do nought to defy or avenge their derision   3335
But creep here so cowardly like curs in confinement?
Men, for your manhood, you will suffer no more,
But will head outwards at once and meet with your foe!
Right shall reward you, you shall speed readily;
For you know they do wrong so worse luck shall become
    them.   3340
If you meet with them manfully, we shall master them worthily,
Though they be five-fold the number that we few are.
And you who wish to win great worship in arms,
Follow me, for in faith, I shall be the first
That smartly shall smite the first with a blow!"   3345
And then he goes to the gates, and rides out at great speed.
When all those bold knights had heard the words of that noble,
And see him fiercely fare forth, before all of them,
They knew he was a warrior who would never fail,
And that he should help them, as they truly hoped.   3350
So four hundred fierce men followed after him,
All courageous skilled knights, and others so acclaimed,
Who were not worried whether they lived or died.
And when William was aware that this force now followed,
He was greatly glad that none gainsaid his words,   3355
And bided there till those nobles had come all about.
The Spaniards had spied them and, with speed, began riding
With great bravado and boast, blowing their trumpets;
For they saw that so few had come out of the city,
Against three thousand of them, that they took no heed   3360

To ride in ordered array. So, right out of sheer pride,*
Each noble before the other brashly spurred on his horse
To assail those soldiers who had come from the city.
William said to his own folk, at once, true to say,
"Lords and beloved friends, listen now to my words!   3365
Though you might fear your foe, never be first to flee!
We indeed should be bolder, they are not in battle order;
Let us stand our ground stoutly, all stiff as one force,
And we will not lose any land, my lords, God forbid!
Each lord, think of your beloved, and thus fight for her love,†   3370
To win lasting renown, for ever in this world,
And, in faith, though our foes might far outnumber us,
They shall die all the sooner, directly through your deeds!"
Those knights accompanying Sir William were greatly encouraged,
And were royally arrayed in a short while,   3375
Full stiffly, in strength, to stand and to fight.
Now came a cruel knight from the company of Spain,
A stiff man and stern, the steward of the king,
And the chieftain so chosen to lead that echelon;
And for his bold strength of body, he went before all   3380
Armed all completely, and on a noble steed.
William, at once, was aware of his arrival,
And gamely began to speak to his great men:
"By Christ, this cruel knight that comes here armed
Dreads little our deeds, whatever does he think?   3385
But by God, who gave me the Ghost and the soul,
I will be found on the field to meet with him first;

---

* Battle order was crucial to military success. At the battles of Crécy (1346) and Agincourt (1415), French lack of discipline in both cases played a major part in their ultimate defeat. The poet here illustrates how, instead of fighting in battle order, the Spanish appear to be racing pell-mell against William – each hoping from pride to be first into battle.

† Among the rules of chivalry was the notion of winning the renown of women. In the *Livre de Chevalerie*, Geffroi de Charny tells us ("The Lady who Sees her Knight Honoured") that ladies greatly favour knights who achieve great deeds over those who do not and that a lady who favours an unpromising knight will find herself "uneasy and disconsolate" ("A Knight's Own Book of Chivalry", p. 66). William's exhortation at this point is unique to the English text, possibly reflective of the renaissance of the chivalric ideal under Edward III whose Order of the Garter was founded in 1348.

But if I swiftly tumble never trust me again!"[32]
He then hoists his spear with speed after his speech,
And he ran with his steed, straight to that steward; 3390
And manfully, those mighty men met with each other,
And the spear of the other speedily split into splinters;
But William was so strong, I will tell you truly,
That he struck that steward, so sternly that time
Right through his bold body, that he bore him to the earth, 3395
As dead as a doornail, I would deem truly.
"Well certainly," said William, "I now surely well know,
You'll deal us no more distress by your deeds of arms!"
But, speedily, those Spaniards spied that he was slain;
They were out of their wits, I will tell you truly. 3400
They hastily heaved up his body and headed back to their tents,
To keep it safe from the fighting, and where horses trampled.
Now, briskly and boldly, the nobles of Spain
Thought to mete much revenge, to make their late lord happy,
For such a leader of lords, they said, had never lived, 3405
Nor was so doughty in deeds; his death must be avenged,
They thought at that time, and said that this is what must befall.

 A full brutal battle began now at that time,
When those stern soldiers on each side engaged.
Many spears then, with speed, were split into pieces, 3410
And many shining shields were shattered to shivers,
And many helmets were hewn, through strokes most huge.
And readily, to reckon what I think rightly true,
William and his warriors fought so wondrously
That they felled their foes, fast and quick to the ground. 3415
None might withstand their strokes more than a short stretch,
So well were they heartened by the works of William.
The Spanish steward had a nephew, and although of young age,
He was one of the most manful which men might ever know,
And the doughtiest in deeds which men should do in arms. 3420
As soon as he was aware that his uncle was slain,
He thought how deliberately he would avenge his death that day.
Armed all completely, he rode against them,

And pressed among the people where the fighting was thickest;
And soon he came to where those of the city were assembled,   3425
And fought then so fiercely for the sake of his uncle,
That he dealt out death to five good knights directly,
Who were bold in battle, standing by for their orders.
When William knew of this work, I will tell you truly,
There was no man on earth who might withstand him,   3430
As he pierced through that press, promptly that time,
Till he met with that man who was held as so mighty.
When the steward's nephew saw that William had come –
He knew him by the werewolf he wielded on his shield
And that this same sire had so slain his uncle -   3435
He at once, like a wild man, spurred himself towards William,
With his spear fixed in his fewter, so to kill his foe.
At the clash of those cruel knights, spears break on each other;
Then swiftly they swing their swords both together,
And dealt dreadful blows, deftly in that battle,   3440
But William was the more skilled and smote well sorely,
And set so hard a stroke, on that other soon after,
That it split his helm and head and hacked quick to the breast.
The sword then so swiftly swung right through the body,
That it tumbled dead to the ground, past the tail of his horse.*   3445
The steed of that stout man, and that other steward's too,
William swiftly sent to his seemly beloved,
Whereof she was gainly glad, and thanked God often
That he had worked so well, in warring that day.

William and his nobles, who were arrayed in that battle,   3450
All fought so fiercely with their foe at this time
That none was so strong in that struggle who might
    withstand them,
    And each was fain to flee, one before the other;
Happiest was he in the world who might run the fastest,
Whether on horse or on foot, for fear of his death!   3455
William and his warriors now went after them quickly,

* See Appendix 1 for a discussion on the moderation of violence in *William and the Werewolf*.

And made a manful chase for more than five miles,
And they gained, at that time, great prisoners and goods;
Those who failed to show meekness, they mainly slew without mercy.
And when the time was right, they turned for home again,   3460
Where they hailed God highly, that they had prospered so well.
But the whole of them knew it was the work of William:
Were it not for his doughty deeds, they would all be dead;
And they lauded him as their lord, the highest and the lowest,
And each man was greatly gladdened, who goes near where
    he rides.   3465
All that sorrow they had suffered for so long before,
They surely set at nought, so glad were they then
For the deeds of that doughty knight who had helped them that day.
With all earthly mirth, those mighty men together
Passed to the palace, proud of their deeds.   3470
The comely queen and her daughter came to him again,
With Melior the eminent, together with their maidens,
And welcomed William, as well they ought,
With clasping and kissing and every kind deed.
The queen led him lovingly along to her chamber,   3475
Where he was unarmed and then clothed afterwards
As cleanly as any who lived under Christ.
Then those three sat to please him at the window,
Right over that jolly place which belonged to that palace,
Where the queen first found William, and his fair maiden.   3480
And as they waited about, while they spoke there with mirth,
That werewolf of William was soon to be seen,
And looked up at the ladies and his lovely master,
And held up his forefeet in a merciful fashion,
And bent low to them lovingly and, truly thereafter,   3485
He went away at once, wherever he liked.
The queen was then in wonder and said to William,
"Sire, did you see this marvel of that seemly beast?
I wonder what he meant, what it might betoken?"
"Yes, certainly madam," said William then,   3490
"I saw those signs myself, and in truth I so hope
It betokens great good which shall, with grace, fall to us."

"Yes, if Christ wills," said the queen, "who died on the cross!
But sire, when I see that beast, who made those signs,
A sorrow sinks in my heart; I shall now tell you why.   3495
Some time ago, sire, I once had a seemly son
Who was called William, indeed, as you are.
In faith, when that child was just four years of age,
As my lord and I, and many other liegemen,
Pleased ourselves in that park, the place where I found you,   3500
For all the world, such a wolf as we have seen here -
It seems the same one, by its semblance and hue -
Came gaping at great pace and caught up my son
Right before his father and many other fellows,
And went away with him, so wondrously fast.   3505
My lord and many others manfully pursued him
Over mire and mountain and many wild ways;
At the last he lost them, for all of their might.
That sorry beast with my son leapt into the sea,
And since then I have heard not one more word of him.   3510

And certainly, sire, I had great sorrow for my son;
When I think on that sorrow it pierces my heart."

William was greatly troubled that this boy may be himself;
What the cowherd told the king now came to his mind,*
That he had found him in the forest in fine rich clothes; 3515
But she said that her son had been drowned in the sea,
And the wolf also, which bore him away.
But that whole thought vexed him so thoroughly at this time
That he soon dismissed it, and said to the queen,
That she should make herself merry to please all her company, 3520
And he would stand in, instead, for her son, when so needed.
She gave thanks to him graciously, and granted him all the power
To maintain all her possessions as master, in his own right.
They talked then of other tales, until it was time to eat,
And were served with ease, as was right for themselves, 3525
And so they drifted that day towards the dark night,
With all the merriment on earth that man might devise.
But we will hear less of them, and listen now of the others;
I will speak of the Spaniards, those who speedily fled,
And who went running for their lives away from that battle. 3530
At that time they sped speedily to the King of Spain,
And spoke to him and his son of the story as it happened;
How a knight came crashing, and conquered them and all others,
Who was so strong and stout, and delivered such strokes,
That no stiff nor steel armour might withstand his weapon; 3535
And how he, in that struggle, slew the stout steward,
And his noble nephew not long afterwards;
And they bid him at once to avenge this wicked wrong,
Lest every man upon earth might speak of them with shame;
So many of their friends had fallen in that field, 3540
That it was a sorrowful sight to see how they fared.

---

* There is a scribal error here; the scribe refers to the conversation between the cowherd and the
emperor, rather than the king. Similarly, the queen has made no mention of her son and the
wolf being drowned, although a reference to the King of Spain believing his own son drowned
at sea appears at ll. 4046 and 4111.

When the king and his council heard this case as related,
He was stunned by sorrow, and so was his son,
Who was a keen courteous knight, and a courageous man
    of arms.
He was worn out of his wits with wrath at this deed,   3545
And now promptly pressed this point to his father,
That he must, on the morrow, with a mighty host,
Ride out to wreak revenge for that wicked deed;
And if he met with that knight who was beheld so mighty,
He swore swiftly this oath, fast and quick to his father,   3550
That he would have his head soon from the body,
Or fast take him alive; and no flight would be allowed.
The king was so grandly gladdened, he granted this wish,
And urged him to work as he would, and go when he wanted.
Swiftly, the king's son assembled many people,   3555
And picked a well-tested host of the trustiest knights,
Which he might in the meantime gather by any manner.
Immediately, on the morrow, he prepared all his men,
As gaily in their good arms as great men might be;
Then, with these fair folk, he went to the field,   3560
Riding boldly before them, to array all his battles.
He briskly set all his nobles within ten battalions,
As readily arrayed as any warrior would think;
And there were some three thousand brave men in his own
    troop,
And more bold nobles, laid out in big strong battles.[33]   3565
And then the king's son said to his bold soldiers,
"Beloved lords, for my love, pray tell me loyally,
If I encounter this cruel knight who has worked this calamity,
How shall I recognise him, what is his coat of arms?"
"Certainly, sire," said a knight, "I know this so well,   3570
That cruel knight can be known by his keen deeds with ease,
And bears on his blouson of a bright hue,
A werewolf, well huge, and wondrously depicted;
That man drives to death all who he strikes down."
"Well, we shall soon see," said king's son then,   3575
"Which of us be more powerful, who will win or lose."

Now I will, for a while, tell here of William,
Of what manner on the morrow his men were arrayed.
Duly, at daybreak, they were all dressed
Truly in the attire which belonged to battle.   3580
And William at once, as he well knew best,
Set out all his soldiers as they should well be,
In six seemly battles in the best way;
And he was foremost at the front, before them all in the vanguard.
King Embrons' Saundbruel was thus his noble warhorse.   3585
And as soon as he saw him coming, the Spanish king's son
Fast asked of his folk who this fellow was;
And they said full swiftly, "For sure, it is that knight
Who has wrought all this woe; well ought we to hate him,
He drives to their deaths all he downs with his blows."   3590
The king's son, for certain, said no more words
But girds his steed and goes galloping straight to him,
With his spear firmly fastened to his fewter at that time.
When William was aware and knew of his coming,
His men soon swiftly said he was the Spanish king's son,   3595
And a doughty man, and deft in great deeds of arms.
"Leave this one to me," said William, "who I shall know soon.
In faith, even if he had the force of four of such men,
I will fight with him first, even if I fare worse."
He then started at good speed, on his sturdy steed,   3600
Towards that keen kingly son, acclaimed as knightly and noble.
So keenly they encountered when they crashed together
That the knight saw his spear shiver into splinters.
But William's spear stayed firm, you can be quite sure,
And met with that other man in the middle of his shield,   3605
Such that both he, and his horse, he hurls to the ground,
And he near broke his back, his horse buffeted him so.
William at once hoists him by the aventail*
To have, with his sword, to swipe off his head;
But the sure men of Spain sped to him quickly,   3610
Hurrying, with haste, that they might help their lord;

* Aventail: a skirt of chain mail attached to the helmet to protect the neck and upper shoulders.

And William's warriors, at once, now went against them.
So that battle began, brutally on both sides;
Never were fellows any fiercer, from Adam's day until now!
Soon, many bold nobles were brought to the ground,   3615
Many shields were shattered, and many helmets hewn,
And many a stiff steed strode around in their blood.
Bodies of those bold men lay around on both sides,
Who preferred to fight and hated to flee.
But William fought so well and wondrously that time,   3620
That no man that he hit might withstand him,
And he always kept the king's son away from his keen men,
That none might win him away, for better or for worse.
And whether they liked or loathed it, William at the last
Came with the king's son from out of that keen press,   3625
And brought him out on horseback from that great battle,
And assigned from his citizens such sufficient men
To keep guard of the king's son, until they came back to town;
And they were blithe at that bidding and busily fared
To ferry him forth fairly, as fast as they might.   3630
When the Spaniards spied that, they speedily followed him,
And delivered as much distress as they might so do.
A fierce host came there, with haste, to help them,
Hidden nearby, in a burnt grove, and ready for ambush.[34]
But when William was aware and knew of their coming,   3635
With manly demeanour, to make his men braver,
He bade them all be bold and fight the more busily,
For their foe had grown faint, and many had been felled.
That knight's typical actions, which encouraged his folk,
Made them as fresh for fighting as if it had been that morning.   3640
Yet William sees that the other side, was so fierce and so bold,
That all his men might not maintain their position
And withstand appropriately those pressing in pursuit.
So directly, he ordered his men to draw towards town,
And keep watch over that king's son, for what may yet occur.   3645
Despite all that their enemies might ever attempt,
They cut their way cleanly with him back to the town
And all of its citizens, except those who were slain.

And, with great haste, good yeomen shut the gates quickly,
And they went straight to the walls to defend them with haste, 3650
So, in faith, none of their foes might force their way in.

 William, with his warriors, within the noble city
Has conquered with clear strength the Spanish king's son,
Who passes with him and his people direct to the palace
With the most merriment on earth that man might devise. 3655
The queen met him meekly, along with those maidens,
Her dear daughter and Melior, to speak of matters most truly.
They welcomed William with a most wealthy worship,
And clasping and kissing, and all kinds of good deeds.
And William at once, without further delay, 3660
Yielded speedily to her the Spanish king's son,
To put into her prison and punish him as she wished.
And courteously she came to kneel before that knight
So to thank him thoroughly for that fine gift;
For he was the man she most hated of all men on earth, 3665
For the distress he had dealt on account of her daughter.
Then she hurried soon with them into the hall,
And she led William as lord of that lovely land;
And briskly, those bright ladies brought him to her chamber,
And then removed all his armour before afterwards clothing him 3670
As comely as any knight had been clad under Christ.
Then those same went to sit, to rest and play at leisure,
By a wide window which was in that chamber,
And made meekly to talk, with many good words.
And at the summit of their bliss, as they all sat there, 3675
The queen quickly beheld that keen young knight;
And her thoughts, at that time, were that never in this world
Did one living lord truly look like another,
As that comely keen knight so resembled King Embrons,
Who was lord here, when alive, and had wielded that lordship. 3680
And such a sorrow then soon sank in her heart
That at once she began to weep, wondrously sorely.
When William saw her weeping, he said with hard words,[35]
"For the love of Saint Mary, madam, why do you make such sorrow?

You should make yourself merry, so to gladden your company, 3685
Who are so faint from fighting or from wounds in the field;
To some you should give now gifts full good,
Or bestow on them promises, the more blithe to make them![36]
On this matter, you have much to make yourself most merry;
You have your foe in your hands, and through him you shall have, 3690
Once again, the renown which you wielded before."

 "Certainly, sire," said the queen, "you speak the whole
        truth,
     You make of this matter enough for me to be merry.
     I realise, from my weeping, that my conduct was poor,
        But I could not help myself, sire, certainly and truly, 3695
For a sorry thought, so thoroughly, has pierced through my heart!"
And she said to him the true reason for this,
How she thought that he looked like her lord the king then,
And how the sorrow for her son had made her weep so.
Then William at once said these words to her, 3700
"Madam, think of this matter, not one moment more.
How will you be made better by weeping so bitterly,
Since your sire and your son are both of them dead?
Though you endure such distress for all your life days,
You will not again get them back! Let God have their souls, 3705
And make yourself merry, to make your people glad."
Then the queen was most woeful, you will know truly,
That William had said that her son should be dead,
For her heart had convinced her that he should be her son,
On account of his countenance being so like that of her king. 3710
But they mentioned no more of this matter that time,
As they turned towards other tales, which touched upon mirth.
And watching outside the window, while they spoke their tales,
They then see the werewolf, who had come to them before,
Kneeling kindly with courtesy in his accustomed way, 3715
And he bowed low to the ladies, and to that lord also,
As humbly as any beast should, by any reason,
And then went on his way, to wherever he would.
The queen said these words, to William at once,

"Sire this seemly beast makes a miraculous sight! 3720
Behold now how lovingly he has bowed low to us twice;
It betokens something, truly; may God turn it to good!"
"Yes, in truth," said William, "have you no doubt,
For that blessed beast never bodes nought but good.
May He that harrowed hell save him from harm!"* 3725
"Amen," they all said, who sat with him there.
Thus they dallied through the day with many playful diversions,
And truly, when it was time, they turned to their meal,
And each was served of their sustenance, as they themselves liked.
But now we speak of the Spaniards, and what ensued for them. 3730

 As soon as the king's son was taken to the city,
And his own mighty men knew they might help him
no more,
There was an intense sorrow, amongst all of his soldiers,
And anxiously they carried themselves back to the king,
And told him wholly their troubles, how his son had been taken, 3735
And how their soldiers were slain in substantial numbers.
When the king knew of this, he was like a mad man,
And said with wrath to his warriors, those who were there,
"Why have you suffered my son to be taken so swiftly?
You should be hanged with haste and drawn by horses!" 3740
He raved, deranged at that deed, as if all should die.
But some knights of his counsel came to him quickly
And said to him seriously, so to cool his wrath,
That a knight cleanly conquered him by his own clear strength,
And had snatched him from them, despite all of their host. 3745
"One knight!" spoke the king. "What is he called,
Who so won my son? Is he really so doughty?"
"Yes, truly," said one. "Sire, with your leave,
I may say that no man on earth might stand against him.
He drives to their deaths who is so dealt of his blows. 3750

* In Christian theology, the harrowing of hell refers to the time after Christ was crucified when
he descended into hell for three days until his Resurrection; during which time he brought to
salvation all the righteous in the world who had died since its creation.

His doughty deeds do to us more damage than any other;
It is he who so wields the werewolf on his shield."
"I make this vow," spoke the king, "to Christ who wields all,
Before I eat any more meat, I will assay his might;
And, if any edged-blade at all might enter into his body,   3755
I will do him to death, and deal him more disgrace too;
He shall be hanged up aloft, high before their gates,
So that every soul in that city shall see him right there;
And then, next, I will set that whole city on fire,
And bludgeon dead every noble that be now therein;   3760
No man on God's ground shall grant it be otherwise!"
Then that king commanded a great cry be made quickly,
That all his warriors be ready, right early on the morrow,
Armed all completely so that none would perish;
And, with handsome haste, they held to his will.   3765

Immediately on the morrow his men were arrayed,
Bold companies of men, a most brave and fierce host.
A more grandly geared army, no man had seen gathered,
With all manner of armour which belonged to war.
Then all the Spaniards passed into a fair plain,   3770
Where that brutal battle was held the day before.
There they found felled a great many of their friends;
More than five hundred, all loyal noble fellows.
Because of this, the king was then afflicted at heart,
And soon felt much sorrow on account of that sight.   3775
But then the king briskly bade that the bodies be taken
Of those great and good men, and be borne with grace,
To their tents, till they might have time to bury them later;
And this deed was duly done, as he had ordered.
The king then, most truly, in three strong battles,   3780
Set his folk out all fine, as fast as he would,
In as royal an array as any warrior should work.
There were in each battle some two thousand nobles,
Armed all completely, and appropriately horsed,
Set stout in each squadron, stood as should be.   3785
Now, I will tell you next about William and his warriors.

William and his warriors were soon quickly armed,
As seemly to see as any soldiers might be,
And sortied silently from the city, when they see it is time.
William went before all, as a wise noble man,   3790
And ordered his host then in three great parties;
And set in each of those battles some seven hundred bold nobles -
All clean, capable knights and other acclaimed men –
And spoke these words speedily, on seeing the Spaniards:
"Behold, lords," said William, "what a lovely sight,   3795
Our foe here before us, all bold and fierce men!
There is wholly all their host! Now be of good heart,
And we shall truly this day bring this war to an end,
Through God's grace alone, and by your own good deeds.
Though they outnumber us by many, men, be not dismayed;   3800
God will preserve us, and stand with the right.
We go to them in God's name, and with a good will!
And might I come by that king, by Christ, as I hope,
He shall soon, thereafter, wend to his son,
To sojourn in that city he has besieged for so long!   3805
Therefore, friends and fellows, for He who died for you,
Do your deeds today as doughty men should,
And you shall win great renown while all this world lasts!"
William, in this way, so comforted his warriors
That they held such great heart, as hardy men should.   3810
Then, all at once, they clashed together,
And all manner of minstrelsy was quickly made,
Of tabors and trumpets – none might tell the number.[37]
And swiftly, either host both fast accosted the other,
And both hosts clashed together, attacking swiftly and sternly,   3815
Greeting each other grimly, with sharpened ground spears.
Many a bold noble was soon brought to an end,
And many a stiff steed was stabbed to death there.
No man upon earth might assess the number
Of warriors who, in a while, were slain on both sides.   3820
But William, like a wild man, was ever here and there,
And laid down such blows, please truly believe me,
That his days were soon done, who was dinted by them!

The King of Spain and his knights, carried themselves keenly,
And so fiercely they fought that, at their first assault,   3825
Many fellows of William began swiftly to flee.
When William knew of this, he at once cried to them,
And encouraged them so craftily with his knightly speech,
That they turned again swiftly, to tell you the truth,
And bore themselves much better than they had done before.   3830

 The King of Spain then cried, keenly and shrill,
"Watch for him that wields the wolf on his shield,
He has murdered my men, and wrought much harm!
If I might happen to have the good fortune to see him,
I would hunt him down as hard as any hound upon earth   3835
Ever hunted a werewolf! But he is so well aware
That I have so many hounds unleashed on him,
That, for all his doughty deeds, he dare not show his face!
But whichever man on earth might bring him to me,
I shall royally reward him to be rich for ever,   3840
And make him my chief steward, to manage all my estate."
Then a cultured knight appeared, son of the Spanish constable,
Who had come three days earlier to help the king;
He had brought a hundred keen knights in his close company
And himself, a bold noble, was the best of them all;   3845
And he was called Meliadus by all mighty men.
When he had heard clearly the cry of the king,
Then he bound into battle with his nobles briskly,
And conducted himself doughtily, with damaging blows.
He slew of those citizens, in just a short while,   3850
Some six great lords and nearly a seventh.
When William was aware of his doughty deeds,
Directly, as a doughty man, he drew straight towards him.
They greeted each other so grimly, when they clashed together,
That speedily their spears split into splinters;   3855
And then so swiftly they swung their swords at each other
That many men were amazed at their doughty deeds.
And in a while, in their mingling, this mighty Meliadus
Set a stern stroke on William, right on his steel helm,

Which wounded him wickedly, I would have you know truly.　　3860
But when this bold William saw his own brave blood,
Then, light as a lion, he laid on all round about,
And marked such a blow on Meliadus, with all his might,
That through the helm and the head, to the girdle with haste,
His blade cleaved through the body, despite all its bright armour;　3865
And he tumbled fast to the earth over his horse's tail.
At this, William's warriors were wonderfully glad,
And the soldiers of Spain were just as sorry on the other side;
For they had held out much hope in the might of Meliadus,
To have conquered William by clear strength of arms.　　3870
But when they see him dead, they soon began to turn,
And to flee as fast as they might fare.
But William and his warriors so wrought battle that time
That no riders they might reach would recover later,
And no man upon earth might estimate the number　　3875
Of all the fine folk that lay slain in the field.

When this tale was told to the King of Spain,
Of how that mighty Meliadus, of all men, was slain,
And he beheld how his nobles then began to flee,
And how William and his warriors followed them at once,　　3880
And direly drove down to their deaths all those that they reached,
He was fast swept with sorrow, and he swooned for fear.
And when he quickly came to, wildly he fared,
So that all torn was his attire of that he might tear at,
And he said afterwards, "Alas, what am I to do!　　3885
I see all my folk flee for the deeds of that fellow;
Never did no man on earth ever wield such might;
It is some devil in disguise which deals out all this harm!"
With that, he saw William win full near to him,
And slay down in his sight all his soldiers thereabouts,　　3890
And saw none gain any grace that might get anywhere near him;
So briskly, with his banner, he began to flee.*

* The "banner" here either refers to his royal flag or, more likely, the troop of knights associated with it.

When William was aware of how he went away,
He promptly left that press and spurred his horse in pursuit,
And swiftly overtook him, and stoutly shouted,   3895
And bade him yield quickly, or yet he would swiftly die.
When the king saw him come he called to his knights,
"Defend ourselves doughtily or we shall soon die;
He gives no quarter gladly; it gains us nothing to flee.
And it is more majestic for us to die manfully   3900
Than for to flee as cowards, despite what may fall."
"Certainly, Sire, that is true," said all of his men,
"Thus now, through our deeds, we must do what we might!"
Then promptly they turned again, and began to fight truly,
And fought more fiercely than they had done before.   3905
But William and his warriors were all so bold,
And stirred themselves in that struggle so strong and well,
That they had, in a while, slain one hundred,
And had taken more than ten score of their truest men.
The king saw that all his soldiers were slain before him,   3910
And that none might conquer this werewolf in any way,
And he was do doleful and a-dread lest he should die too,
That he began to flee from his host as hard as he might;
And those men that might do so began immediately to flee.
But William perceived which way the king went,   3915
And hurried after him with haste, and then overtook him,
And cried to him keenly, "Sire king, yield swiftly,
Or death I'll deliver, directly right here!
Make amends, meekly, for all your misdeeds
That you have raised in this realm and maintained for too long,   3920
And all of them wrongly wrought, as all this realm knows."

 Thus he sees nothing better than that he must yield,
Or else be slain swiftly. Then soon he alights
At once before William, to yield up his weapon;
To wield as he would, and begged wholly for mercy.   3925
    And William, as a true knight, as courtly manners required,
Granted this with good grace, and begrudged nothing more,
And said he must submit to all terms on meeting the queen,

And proffer himself for prison, promptly at her will;
And give himself to her grace, without saying a word. 3930
As fast as the king was taken, to tell you the truth,
Every soldier on his side soon began to withdraw,
And full glad was each fellow who might go fastest from there;
And thus was that fierce fight finished that time.
William went to the city with his bold warriors, 3935
And he led, in his company, the King of Spain,
With all the merriment on earth which men might hear of;
And all that same passed to the palace most promptly.
The queen came towards them with all her company,
And received them as royally as such rulers ought, 3940
And the king, not delaying, yielded himself as her captive
To work with him as she would as she herself willed;
And truly, soon after him, some two hundred and seven
Of the most royal ranks of his realm did likewise.
The queen went to kneel, at once, before William; 3945
She was blithe that this battle was brought to an end,
And thanked William therefore many thousands of times.
But William was humbled and upbraided her harshly,
And said, "Madam, you mock yourself, by Mary in heaven,
You, the heir of an emperor and a queen yourself, 3950
To kneel before such a soldier as simple as I;
You do the greatest dishonour to yourself by that."
"No Sire," said the queen, "so Christ help me,
I set you as no soldier, but as a sovereign lord -
To lead all this lordship however you like! 3955
And blessed be that lady who bore you in this earth!
But for God's grace, and for your good deeds,
I would be bare, at this time, of all bliss that I had.
From what I was so balefully crushed beneath before,
You have brought me from such blight, and beaten my foes; 3960
Therefore, in all ways, your worship is worth more."

Now to touch in this tale on what later betided.
All their lordly adversaries were quickly disarmed,
And with that worthy queen they went into the hall.
And the eminent Melior and the queen's daughter 3965

Led the King of Spain courteously right between them,
And their meek maidens, merrily at that time,
Led all the other lords most lovingly between them;
And all those seemly same, they sat in the hall.
The queen sat the king most courteously beside her,   3970
And William on her other side, and with him his sister[38]
And the eminent Melior, who was made much joyous
For the lovely lauding won by her beloved;
And all the lords of the land were in that hall,
And the best burgesses, and other nobles together,   3975
And the peers of Spain, who were taken prisoner.
The king besought the queen, if it were her will,
That he may see his son, to bring him some solace,
And she granted this gracefully and urged for him to be fetched.
And certainly, as soon as he came, the king said this to him,   3980
"Lo, son, what great sorrow we have wrought on ourselves;
Through our own haughty hearts we bring great harm on ourselves,
To want of such wishes that will not be granted.
It has brought hopeless heartbreak, by God that formed me,
To wish for such a wife that is ever self-willed!"   3985
Then his son said, "In truth, Sire, you know
That we have wrought wrong; now indeed it is obvious.
We must be held to what harms us; it will help us but little
Lest we readily give in to the grace of this good lady,
And let her work with us, as her goodness so wills."   3990
The king began to sicken sorely, for the sake of his son;
And to that comely queen he most courteously said,
"Madam, for the love of Mary, the mild Queen of Heaven,
Grant me of your grace, if you think this good:
If your skilful council accords well with this,   3995
Let me make amends for all my misdeeds,
By which I have wrongly warred and laid waste to your lands.
As much as any man may ordain by right,
I am ready to restore them; and readily, moreover,
All the worship that I wield, I will now hold of you -   4000
All the lands and lords which belong to my realm,
Which, till this day, I held of no one but God.

And, madam, if your council accords well to this,
Let me know your own will, how you will bind me,
And I will fulfil your command as loyally as you like;   4005
Beyond that, on any account, I have nothing more to offer."

 The queen and her council were contented with this,
That he had so proffered to perform as she chose,
And they go to mull on this matter, how it might best be
      resolved.
And as they were walking to treat in this way,   4010
There hailed into that hall, right to the high dais,
That wise werewolf again, who had helped William;
And boldly, as if unafraid of those many nobles,
He sped straight and with speed to the King of Spain
And fell down at his feet, and kissed them most fairly,   4015
And worshipped him in this way, and wholly most wondrously.
And he saluted the queen shortly soon after,
And William after her, and his worthy maid,
Then the queen's daughter afterwards, before then departing
Hastily out the hall door, as fast as he might,   4020
And went forward on his way to wherever he would go.
But soon, stalwart men who sat in that hall
Hoist hastily to hand whatever they might have,
Some axes, some swords, or some take long spears,
To wend after him, so to quell him at once.   4025
But when William knew this, he became almost wild,
And swore swiftly this oath, by all that God wrought,
That if anybody be so bold as to harm that beast,
Be he knight or clerk, knave or common soldier,
He would do him to death, directly himself,   4030
For no man upon earth might make amends for this.
And, immediately in that hall, there was then none so hardy,
That dared follow that beast on foot for sheer dread,
For they were so wondrously fearful of William.
But why did that werewolf behave so, they all wondered,   4035
And why more with the king than with any other?
And the king wondered this more than anyone else,

And thus he struck straight away into a deep study,
What it betokened that this beast had bowed lowest to him,
And wrought him more worship than to anyone else.   4040
Then it came to his mind, in the meanwhile,
That he thought of his seemly son he had once, long ago,
And how truly he had been told, a long time hitherto,
That his wife, through witchcraft, had shaped him into a wolf;
But she, of that slander, denied it unceasingly,   4045
And said that child had drowned, long since sunk in the sea.
That king was long distracted in anxious thought;
But William with haste, once that wolf had escaped,
Commanded all of his knights to let cry in the city
That nobody be so bold, lest they be straight hanged,   4050
As to watch for that werewolf and prevent his escape,
But let him wend where he would, whatever the time of day.
His behest was well held; none would hardly dare otherwise.

Let us speak now of the king, who was cast in great thought.
He was dazed and dismayed by the deeds of that beast,   4055
And was so steeped in study that none might distract him.
When William knew of this, he went to him quickly,
And said, "King, I conjure you, in the name of holy Christ,
And by all cultured customs which belong to good kingship,
That you tell me promptly and truly the truth,   4060
If you know of the cause, whatever its kind,
Why this humble beast bowed to you so much more
Than to anyone else who was here in the hall;
It may be that in some manner, I might imagine,
That you know in some way what all this may betoken?   4065
Therefore, tell me fast and true what your thoughts are,
Otherwise I make this stark vow to the mighty King of Heaven,
You will not pass from prison, but be punished the hardest!"
Then that king sickened sorely and said these words,
"Sire, no dread of such distress, nor of death on earth,   4070
Will make me wander at all from what is in my mind.
Sire, some time here before, in my younger years,
I wedded with all my wealth a worshipful lady.

My bride was in beauty the brightest on earth,
And greatest in all goodness than any man may tell of.   4075
That good beauty was the daughter of the king of Navarre.[39]
And in that same time we begat together
One of the fairest of fellows that folk ever looked upon.
But my wife, as God willed, and as shall come to us all,
Died at the delivery of my dear son.   4080
And I had that fair child fostered a full three winters
With all the cultured keeping as becomes such upbringing.
By that time the boy had grown big for his age,
And the seemliest to look upon that any man should see.
He was given the name Alphonse by his good godfathers;   4085
His name was confirmed at church, to confess the truth.
Then it betided at that time that I took another wife,
A full lovely lady, as learned as the best,
Courteous and accomplished, and extremely clever,
Who came from a great kin, and very capably skilled.   4090
With grace we begat, as almighty God willed,
A son, as you will now see before yourselves here,
Who you have put in prison, to be punished at your will.
That child was cleanly kept, as so becomes him,
And he grew fine of feature and was fully much loved.   4095
But then, wickedly, my wife dwelled upon this,
That my eldest son should become my heir,
To keep my kingdom after me, as justice commands;
And she stirred stiffly inside, as all stepmothers will,
To find some way that she might best kill my bold boy,   4100
So that her own son, soon after my death,
Might enjoy that rich realm, as its rightful heir.
And as I have been told, by true men of my realm,
She changed my son, through charms and enchantments,
Into a wild werewolf; and I well now believe,   4105
That this humble beast be that one himself.
But my wife, through her wiles, so led me to believe –
When I touched on such tales as were told to me –
That they were fantasy and falsehood, and spoken through malice;
And she swore great oaths grimly, by all that God wrought,   4110

That my own seemly son was drowned, sunk out at sea,
As he passed out to play once privately and alone.
I believed her then, loyally, and let it all pass;
But now, wholly, I know this werewolf is my son,
That seeks after succour, as would seem by his deeds.　　　4115
Sire, surely to say, these are my great thoughts
As to this werewolf's ways, may I have good fortune;[40]
And if what I say be wrong, I am worthless for ever!"

 William, with discretion, then said these words,
"Sire, it may well thus be right, by Mary in heaven,　　　4120
That this beast seeks our support, it seems best to me.
For I know well without doubt, and well often have found,
That he has a man's mind, more than we both.[41]
Many a day, I would have been dead and rotted to dust,
Had it not been for God's grace, and the help of that beast;　　　4125
He has succoured and served me, when I was in great need.
Therefore, in faith, for the world, I will not fail him,
But I shall love him loyally as my own liege brother.
And, sire, you ought to be blithe, by He who wrought us,
That he is thus happily here whom you have missed for so long.　　　4130
And if he might, in some manner, be made man again,
I would wish for nothing more, for all the wealth in the world.
And certainly, as it seems, to say the whole truth,
If your wife, as you tell me, is so wise to witchcraft
That she wrought him as a werewolf, then right well I hope　　　4135
She can, through her craft and her clever charms,
Make him man again; it may not be otherwise.
And therefore, sire, by Christ, who died for us on the cross,
You will never pass from our prison, nor any of your people,
Without the discharge of this dearly loved beast;　　　4140
For he must, and needs to be, made man once again.
Send for your wife wisely this way: tell her beforehand
That she must come fast to you, no matter what befalls,
Without let or hindrance of any living soul.
And if she knocks you with a nay, and says she will not come
　　　quickly,　　　4145

Say that I will, most swiftly, come soon with my host
And ride over her realm and readily destroy it,
And fetch her with fine forces, for all that might happen.
For until she through her craft has helped the werewolf,
Then all the men made on earth will never free you from here."   4150

"By Christ," said the king, "who suffered on the cross,
I vouchsafe to you that the queen be sent for!
If she might in any manner make my son again
Into a man, as he first was, then I will be most happy.
But certainly, I don't know whom I might send,   4155
To make as the messenger to speed on my errand,
Unless you would please suffer they be some of my lords,
Who are leaders in my land, and whom men hold as loyal.
If you will, grant them leave, and have them go there;
I think they shall speed sooner than should any other."   4160
"That I will," said William, "choose who you like,
And have them hasten quickly, as hard as they might,
And so bring the queen for what case shall befall."
So to speed up this matter, the Spanish king spares no time
And he swiftly chose fifty of his finest great lords,   4165
All talented and, as told, the truest men of his realm;
And they took those letters fast which told of their errand,
And he bade them tell more by mouth, which they much understood,[42]
Of the case which befalls when they come to the queen.
"And say thus to her swiftly, sires, I pray to you,   4170
The cause she must come for or, by Christ in heaven,
She'll not gain gladness again from me, nor my son.
And say surely to her that it is for this reason;
For my son is found here, of whom she said in the past
Was drowned sunk in the sea – as she led me to think -   4175
But who now walks about here as a wild werewolf;
And tell of his search for succour, as you all saw.
Therefore, tell her truly to the end, as all these things happened.
And bid her bring briskly what may be the remedy
To make him man again, as mighty as before,   4180
Lest all our lands be made worthless, and our lives also;

There is no alternative, you must tell her truly."
Those eminent messengers all then meekly said,
"We will work to your will, as well as we can."

Immediately on the morrow, the messengers were ready,   4185
Graced in all their gear, gaily at their best,
With their horses harnessed and all they had need of,
And they went on their way, at once and fast.
    Going always along ways which gained them truly the most,
They sped ever speedily, until they came to Spain,   4190
And they came to a city where the queen was sojourned.
She was promptly told that they had come with tidings,
And, gleeful and glad, she goes towards them,
With all the lovely ladies who belonged to her chamber,
And other eminent maidens – some fourscore and more.   4195
And they greeted the messengers meekly, when they met them,
With clasping and kissing, most kindly together.
But swiftly that comely queen asked them most courteously,
"How fares my lord king, for Christ's love in heaven,
And my seemly son, since they left here?   4200
Have they won, at their will, all that they went there for?
How fares my lord with that lady, and her lovely daughter?
Will she let my son wed her and take her as his wife?"
"Madam," said the messenger most worthy of all,
"It has worked otherwise than how you would think,   4205
It helps not to hold back; I have so much to say.
Ever since the King of Heaven died for us on the cross,
Worse never fell on anyone than it has for a while;
For all the royal warriors of this realm are all slain,
And are dug deep underground, many a day since: 4210
The stout steward of this land, and his strong nephew,
And the constable's son, a courteous knight proven,
And un-numbered noblemen, to mention the truth.
My lord the king was caught there in a keen struggle,
And your son also, and both are in prison,   4215
And we too also, madam, and many more others[43]
Of the lords of this land, who are left alive.

And never might any man see freedom once more,
Nor be plucked from his prison, lest helped purely by you,
Although we had that queen, through our craft and strength,   4220
Brought almost to breaking with such brutal assaults,
And wasted her lands and won many of her towns,
And promptly placed them at our will, all except for Palermo.
Certainly, they were so besieged until, at last,
She craved our mercy many times, in this manner: 4225
That she might wend away, with her daughter alone,
Without danger of distress or any wicked deed,
And let my lord have that land to his liking for ever.
But my lord in no way would grant this to her,
And this by chance hit us hard, for hastily thereafter   4230
A knight came to her call, the most courtly on earth,
And the most mighty in arms that men ever heard of.
He slew the best of our soldiers, surely in truth,
And captured with clean might the king and his son,
And truly many other lords who are still alive.   4235
And when they were captive, imprisoned at her will,
Then in wanders a werewolf, wonderfully huge;
With a comely comportment he went to the king,
And fell down at his feet, and kissed them most fairly,
And wrought him great worship; and everyone who saw it   4240
Said it seemed, to all appearances, as if it sought succour;
But then, just as briskly, that beast went on its way.
And then that cultured knight, who had conquered us cleanly,
Conjured my lord the king, by all that Christ wrought,
That he should, at once, tell him the whole certain truth,   4245
If he knew, in any way, what or who that beast was.
And with truth he said certainly, to cut this tale short,
That it was Alphonse his son, he knew sure enough,
Which you by your witchcraft had made into a werewolf.
About which, eminent madam, by Mary in heaven,   4250
We were made into messengers to make you aware
That neither your lord, nor your son, nor any of us,
Will ever be delivered from the danger which we now dwell in,
Till you come to that country and, with your crafty skills,

Have healed that werewolf well, in every way,   4255
And made him man once again, in the manner he should be.
And if you begrudge but one grain of this grace so to work,
Then all the men upon earth may never halt nor prevent
That same conquering knight, who keeps us all captive,
From coming to this country with all his clear strength,   4260
And brutally burning you in bitter fire[44]
And over-riding this realm and readily destroying it;
And, whether you will it or not, he shall win you through strength,
And then do us all dreadfully to death shortly after;
Thus, let us know at once what your thoughts are."   4265
Before long, when this bold queen, who was known as Braundine,
Had heard how now things fared, all wholly and entirely,
She swiftly fainted through sorrow and swooned right there,
And afterwards wept, it was no wonder;
And then she said, meekly, to those eminent messengers,   4270
"Now sires, since it so, whatsoever happens next,
I will wend with you all and see you well freed,
With the help of the heavenly King, hastily and soon."
Then she goes grandly to gather all the things
It behoved them to have as they hastened on their way,   4275
And a right royal company to ride by her side
Of lords and ladies, the best in all her land.
And surely to say, no soul under heaven
Ever saw such a royal group arrayed any better,
Nor one more gaily graced, in truth I grant,   4280
With its horses all harnessed and all its other gear.
The queen had with her all that behoved
To cure that werewolf well, and in the best way.

 When all were gathered gaily, geared in the best way,
She moved on her way with her majestic company,   4285
And they hastened on their journey as fast as they might,
Till they came to Palermo, to tell the pure truth.
William and his warriors were aware of their coming;
And he rode out to meet her, with his regal party,
And when he met her he welcomed her worthily,   4290

172

And her splendid company, eloquently and with courtesy;
And then he led that procession promptly to the palace.
The courteous queen of that land came towards them,
With the King of Spain and his son, and other courteous knights,
Who had been put into prison purely for their deeds.   4295
There was both mirth and mourning to be seen at that meeting;
When the Queen of Spain saw her lord being held,
And her seemly son, and all those sundry other
Great lords of her land; she did not like this at all.
The comely queen of that land, William's own mother,*   4300
Welcomed them all with wealth, and with great worship;
William kindly helped the queen to come down from her palfrey,
Then, most meekly, she kissed his eminent mother,
And her own lord and son, sweetly thereafter.
Her lord the king was much comforted that his wife had come,   4305
And her son also, and all those others as well -
The lords of that land who were held there locked up -
For they hoped to have help from her hastily thereafter.
William and his famed mother, most meekly and fair,
Led the Queen of Spain between them, most lovingly,   4310
And brought her into the hall, most handsomely then,
And then they all sat down dearly, at the high dais.
The King of Spain sat alongside his wife,
And their son beside them, to speak altogether,
To make them as merry as could be in the meanwhile.   4315
The Queen of Palermo and her daughter, that majestic damsel,
And the eminent Melior were matched together
To enjoy the same pleasure, and say what they liked.
Then all that huge hall was hastily filled
With barons and knights all about on each side: 4320
The royal ranks of that realm were on the right side,
And all those Spanish sires, certainly, were sat on the other;
So that peerless palace was filled with fine people.
Then spices were spread with speed all about

---

* As noted earlier, the narrator shares his knowledge only with the audience; William as yet is
unaware the queen is his mother.

Fulsomely to the fill of each fellow therein,   4325
And therewith also those wines, which they might like the best.

 And as they made themselves so merry, to mention it truly,
The werewolf you know of was in William's chamber,
And he had been in bliss there, both night and day,
From the moment those messengers had marched off to
    the queen,   4330
His own stern stepmother, until that instant then.
But the wolf knew full well when she had arrived,
And hurried with haste to the hall that time
To do her to death, directly, if he might;
He was so angry with her, and who could blame him?   4335
As briskly as that beast had broken into the hall,
He passed before all the people and proceeded straight on
And drew towards the dais. Then, in a dreadful manner,
He stared at his stepmother sternly for a while,
When he saw her with his father sitting in mirth.   4340
At first sight, the werewolf was full of great wrath,
And all of his bristles then began to rise terribly;
And gaping most grisly, with a grim noise,
He rushed briskly to the queen to kill her quickly.
And as soon as the queen saw him come towards her,   4345
She was nearly out of her wits, you will have no doubt,
And, much disquieted and crying, she said to the king,
"Ah! Beloved lord, I have not long to live!
Please save me now, or full soon I will die;
For this brutal beast will work blight on me,   4350
Though I know he's not wrong, as you must all know.
I have deserved death; but think dearly of me,*
And let me live longer, for the love of our heavenly King!
I am meek in your mercy, I may ask nothing more."
Swiftly, the King of Spain started up sternly,   4355
And his son also, to save the queen.

---

* The MS reads, "I have served þe deþ, ȝif ȝou dere þinkes", which might also be read as
"While I may deserve death, please forgive me".

William, at once, then went to the werewolf
And then wrapped his arms around his neck,
And said to him softly, "My dear, sweet beast,
Trust me most truly as you would trust a brother,   4360
Or as faithfully befits a father to his son;
And make less of your melancholy, so not to harm yourself.
I sent for her for your sake, I truly assure you,
To help heal you hastily, if she might do so.
And she has brought a remedy, by Christ, I hope,   4365
And if not, be right sure, by God who wrought us,
She shall be burned to cold coals, before evening comes;*
And the ashes of her body will weave with the wind,
And your sire, and his son, and all his stern noble lords,
Shall be put into prison and punished for ever,   4370
In distress all their days, until death shall take them.
Thus leave this all to me, my beloved sweet friend,
Be annoyed no more, for you shall have no need
To do her any distress, if you dearly love me."

 The werewolf was fully glad of William's words,   4375
Which promised to help him with haste thereafter,
And he fell down most fairly at his feet to kiss them,
And full kindly he granted, as much as he could convey,
To work in all the ways which William would say,
And made no more debate in any manner.   4380
As soon as the queen saw how matters fared,
That the werewolf would not work her any harm,
She was greatly glad, thanking God many times;
And passing straight to him promptly, before all the people,
She briskly fell down, on both knees, before that beast,   4385
And meekly, in this manner, craved his mercy.
"Sweet Alphonse," she said, "my seemly lord,
I have brought here a remedy to bring an end to your blight.
Soon all the people shall see your seemly face,

---

* The MS reads, "to cold coles sche schal be brent ȝit or come eve". The intention is that she will
be burned so completely that in the end the coals will have gone out and she will be just ash.

In manhood as in mind, as it ought to be.   4390
I have greatly grieved you, as I have confessed to God,
By readily robbing you of your right to inheritance,
So that this man, my own son, might have it instead,
Faithfully after your father's death. I transformed you then
In this way to a werewolf to roam and bring woe;   4395
But God would not let it be that you be so lost.
Therefore, I crave your mercy for all of my mischief;
Alphonse, I beg you, let me live, if you will,
And I will humbly be at your bidding for ever,
And I will serve you loyally, as my lord, all my life,   4400
And will never wrong you again, in game nor in earnest;
And I beseech you graciously, grant this now through your goodness,
For His love that made man; please forgive me this guilt."
And then, weeping, she said to William at once,
"Ah! Courteous kind knight, for Christ's love in heaven,   4405
Bid this humble beast to be merciful now;
For he will work to your will, I know well and true,
Far more than for any man that might live upon earth!
And all you, highest lords, help me in my plea
To this courteous kind knight to accede to this favour!   4410
I bow completely to the mercy of this beast,
To work his will with me, however he likes."

 The people felt great sorrow for the proffering queen,
For she fell before that beast, flat on the ground;
There was weeping and woe, most wondrously widespread. 4415
But the king and all that company of knights, most keenly,
Beseeched William so earnestly for the queen's sake,
That he gave up with good grace the last of his anger,
So that she might hurry hastily to help that beast;
And he swiftly granted this blithely, begrudging nothing.   4420
Then she waited no longer and went, without strife,
Into a choice chamber which was brightly painted[45]
And none went in there with her, except for the werewolf.
Then she brought forth a round ring, both rich and noble;
The stone stuck thereon was of such striking virtue   4425

That no man upon earth, who might wear it about him,
Should ever be bewitched by any witchcraft,
Nor perish by any poison nor be envenomed at all,
Nor wrong his wife while he should wear it.[46]
That rich ring, full readily, with a red silk thread,   4430
The queen now bore briskly about the neck of the wolf.
Then she fetched a fair book faithfully from a casket,
And read from it readily for a right long while,
So that then, in a moment, she made him a man,
As fair, as well featured, and as finely shaped,   4435
As any man upon earth might ever contrive;
There was none fairer in the world, but for William alone,
For he was, in his fairness, the flower of all fellows.
When the werewolf was aware that he was now a man,
Fair in all of his features as it so befell him,   4440
He was greatly glad, no man would blame him;
He liked that lesson full well, which the lady had read him!
Yet he was so surely naked that he was sorely ashamed.
When the queen saw that, she said to him swiftly,
"Ah, Alphonse, beloved lord, let be all your thoughts!   4445
I see well you are ashamed, but there is no need for this,
There is nobody in this bower, but for us two.
I see no blemish on you, sire, it is all as should be,
You fail not in one thing it falls on a man to have.[47]
Fare now forth to your bath, which has been finely prepared,   4450
For it is readied most grandly and graced in a good manner."
Then after her words, Alphonse afterwards
Blithely enters that bath, without further objection,
And found it truly attired and suitably warm.
The queen comforted him and served him with courtesy,   4455
As meekly as she might, in all manner of ways,
For nobody was nearby, but that pair themselves.

Then that courtly queen most courteously said,
"Sweet sire, please say now, so Christ may help you,
Which man would you designate to grant your arms and
    garments?[48]   4460

I suspect you have never taken the orders of knighthood;
Therefore tell me from whom you will accept them,
For you know well which man is the worthiest one here."
"Madam," Alphonse said, "by Mary in heaven,
I will take my attire and that true order   4465
From the worthiest one now wielding life."
"Who is that?" said the queen; "Is it your father?"
"No, by God," replied Alphonse, "who granted me birth,
It is that kind, courteous knight you have come all to know,
Who delivered you from death this day from myself.   4470
No one knows in this world anyone more worthy -
Of my kin, king nor knight - for his courteous deeds.
I will take my attire from him, and that true knightly order,
And love him as my liege lord for all of my life."
The queen then went to the hall, looking for William,   4475
And took him slightly by the sleeve and said in his ear,
"Sire, if it were your will, the werewolf beseeches
That you come to him promptly to clothe and attire him;
He will have none other to whom he will give worship."
"Is that truly so," said William, "my sweet high lady?   4480
That he asks after clothes, for Christ's love in heaven?
Do not deceive me through your deeds, but speak the absolute truth."
"Yes, by Christ," says the queen, "he asks for clothes;
He is as whole, hailed be God, as he ever was before,
And manly in every manner, as should fall to man.   4485
Hurry hastily to him, and help him to get ready,
For I know that these folk would be full pleased to see him.
But he wishes that no one comes with you to the chamber
But your eminent maid Melior and the queen's daughter,
Dame Florence the fair, for whom this war was fought;   4490
He bids that you bring them both, and nobody else."
Then William at once, as a man full of joy,
Clasped and kissed the queen, and gives thanks to Christ often
That this fellow was made whole who had helped him so often.
Thus, all was brought briskly which it so behoved   4495
Should cover a knight as his comely clothing;
No man upon earth might devise any richer.

Then William, at once, with Melior and his sister,
And the comely queen, went speedily forth
Into that choice chamber where that beast had changed   4500
From the way of a werewolf to a most worthy knight.
Then they beheld the bath and a bed beside,
And in that bed, immediately, they behold that noble,
They had never seen before such a one so seemly;
But, by Christ, none of that company recognised him!   4505
Nonetheless, William at once greeted him worthily,
And those eminent maidens did the same meekly.
And then Alphonse, after this, answered and said,
"May Christ, crowned King, kindly save you, sire knight
And your fair fellowship, who all follow you.   4510
Sire, I am in your country, and come into your court,
Yet you make for me now but this mean reception!
I have often near perished to put you out of peril,
And many a sharp shock have I suffered for your sake.
How little you can know me or the kindness I've shown!"   4515
"Certainly, sire, that is true," said William then;
"I know not in this world who it is that you are!
But I command you, by Christ, who was punished on the cross,
That you say to me swiftly who it is you so be!"*
"I am he, the werewolf," Alphonse said then,   4520
"Who has suffered many sorry pains, all for your sake,
And preserved you from perils from which you should have perished
Without great God's might, and my own good help."
"Certainly, sire, this is true," William said then,
And he leaps lightly to him, and clasps him in his arms.   4525
With clasping and kissing, they declared great joy;
All the men upon earth might not tell the half
Of the mirth that was made in that company then!
And if William was glad, I will tell you truly,
Melior was much more so, if that might be possible.   4530
And Florence was dumbfounded at what befell;

---

* Once more we see how the medieval narrator plays with the concept of disguise and revelation (see note to line 3971 above).

As soon as she saw him, she greeted him lovingly,
And he greeted that good maid gracefully in return.
And then his heart bright and fast, for the beauty she bore,
Turned to her truly, to love for evermore.   4535
When they had sat in that gladness for a great while,
Alphonse then asked to have some attire,
So to fare out swiftly, to speak with his father,
The lord of that land whom he had long missed.
And William at once, without further delay,   4540
Graced him as gaily as any grown man had been
With all the finest attire that belonged to a knight,
So that none might make it better, by one mite, I believe!
And when they were all ready, as would be their will,
Each held the other by the hand, handsomely and fair,   4545
And they hurried together to the high hall, with haste.
When those peerless people perceived they had come,
Many a full lovely lord leaps towards them,
As they were gamely glad to look on that good man.
Great mirth was made at that meeting, be assured!   4550
The King of Spain, for certain, recognised his son quickly,
And, as a glad man, greets him first, and thanks God often
That he so fairly had found his own firstborn son.
Then the lords of that lovely land greet him most lovingly,
And his bold brother, above all the others,   4555
Except the king himself, who greeted him the seemliest
And made the most joy at that meeting that time.
No tongue might tell truly all the whole truth
Of the joy that was wrought among all who were there!
The comely Queen of Palermo often thanked Christ,   4560
Who had sent her so much joy through His own dispensation
And settled her sorrow so swiftly, which had been so huge.
Soon those seemly sires were sat in the hall;
The royal ranks at the dais, as is rightly reasoned.
And all the others afterwards, along the side benches;   4565
And they sat in so much pleasure straight through the hall,
Each as their degree deigned, to tell you the truth.
When the noise of these seemly folk began soon to die down,

The King of Spain spoke to Alphonse, his son,
And said, "Seemly son, I have sorely longed   4570
To see your graceful face, which I felt I had lost;
Now this comely queen, through her knight's actions,
Has us all in her hold to harm us at her will,
Yet, sweet son, it has been so foretold[49]
That our deliverance would be down to you alone;   4575
Through you, help would come, and not from anyone else.
Thus we must praise highly He, our heavenly King,
Who has so lent your life to deliver us all."
"Sweet sire," said Alphonse, "may Christ help you,
Pray, how at first did it fall that these things so fared?"   4580
"By Christ, son," said the king, "to speak the truth,
All this war and this woe is down to our wrongdoing.
I desired this damsel, who is noble and dignified,
To have wed your brother, who is sitting by you;
But her mother, in no manner, would grant me my wish.   4585
Thus we at once went to war; I laid all her lands to waste,
And brought so much blight on her that she craved for mercy,
In such a manner that she, most meekly and fair,
Might go away with her daughter without further harm.
She desired nothing more, but I would not grant her this.   4590
But then this keen knight came and, through his clear strength,
He boldly bore down on us all, in battle,
And placed us in prison, to be punished at his grace.
Thus we aspired to win this, when we sped out Spain."

 Alphonse afterwards then answered and said,   4595
"Fair father, by my faith, foolishly you have worked
To implore someone to wed, who would not assent!
You should have known by your works how badly you
    would fare!
Your counsel was wicked, and your will after it;
You have now won much worse, you know it yourself.   4600
But I hope, by heaven's King, if you will hear my words,
That all this sad blight shall be brought to an end."
Alphonse then said, to the Queen of Palermo,

"Ah! Eminent madam, implore your people be silent
And spare no more time speaking, until I have spoken."   4605
Then all were made silent, I will say truly.
"Ladies and other lords, listen now to my words.
May you know this well, without any falsehood;
That this land would have been lost, at last in the end,
If these wars here had lasted any while longer.   4610
But God sent you through His grace and His great might
This courteous true knight who, through his clear strength,
Has banished all your troubles, and brought to your will
All your foes who have afflicted you with force for so long.
Yet you are unaware as to where he comes from,   4615
What or who he is; but you shall know this soon.
If that noble bears himself well, I can hardly blame him;
For each man has much good cause, to mention the truth,
So to champion his mother when she suffers mischief,
And of course he shall come to her, if he loves Christ."   4620
"What does this tale betoken? Tell us now, I beseech you;
Why do you speak you so?" said the queen then.
"Certainly, madam," said Alphonse, "believe me assuredly;
This comely knight is your son, by Christ who created me.
You bore him from your body, King Embrons was his father;   4625
All the lordship of this land is faithfully his own.
And I am that werewolf, I would have you know truly,
Who abducted him long ago, before you and his father,
And departed on my way with him, promptly from you all.
The king and his courtly knights with cries full huge,   4630
Pursued me right to the sea, to slay me if they might.
But, briskly and boat-less, I swam the broad water,
With neither hurt nor harm, let God's grace be hailed,[50]
Who sent me over the sea with your son safe and sound!
And good lady, please, do not love me the less   4635
That I bore your boy away; for I would otherwise be blamed,
As I knew full well what woe was planned for him;
For had I not done this, he would long since have been dead.
The brother of King Embrons thought about this often:
That if this same bold knight could be robbed of his life,   4640

His heir should take entire possession, and hold all his estates,
After the king's death, due to hereditary right.
And, as should such a rascal, he soon thought shameful things:
He acquainted himself craftily with the two ladies
That kept ward at that time over your son,   4645
And tempted them so much, with all manner of things,
And bribed them so well, more than I can tell you –
Great lordships of land according to their desire –
That they promised him, within a short time,
To poison, in private, the king and his son,   4650
So he would be crowned king and take the realm.
But when I knew of their cause, and their wicked intentions,
I could not suffer it, for sorrow nor woe,
That their wicked will would result in this.
And therefore I took him, I have now told the truth,   4655
And have helped him hitherto, whenever he had need,
As much as I might, in any manner of ways;
And so I brought him here, be you sure, to bring an end to your
     troubles.
Take him now in your hand; I yield him to you here."

 When the comely queen had heard all that speaking,   4660
And saw that this was her son, as so surely proven,
There was not one man upon earth who might tell of that joy
Which was, in the meantime, made amongst them,
Between the dame and the daughter and her dear son,
With clasping and kissing and other kindly deeds!   4665
And if any might be more so, Melior was the gladdest,
That her lovely beloved was lord of that realm -
By true kind, a king's son, and an excellent knight.
Now such mirth was made, at that meeting then,
By all of the people who were there in that palace,   4670
That not one tongue might tell any more than a tenth of it!
And then, afterwards, Alphonse told them
Of all that had happened to him, all wholly to the end,
From that time that he took the child from his friends:
How the father had followed him, fervent to kill him;   4675

And how he bore forth the boy over the broad waters;
And how since he had passed, along secluded ways,
Always bearing that boy, by night and by day,
Till he came to a forest, seven miles from Rome;
And how the cowherd came to him and kept the child after;   4680
And how since the emperor sought to go hunting,
And found him in the forest, and fared home with him,
And took him to be ward of his dear daughter;
And how he and the meek maiden talked much of love,
And had love to their liking, for a long time often;   4685
And how the son of the King of Greece came there to wed her,
And on the morning of the marriage, which she should have made,
How they went away from there in white bear skins.
"Thereafter, I truly saved you, sire, as you know surely,
When all of the people promptly pursued you,   4690
To have you done to death, and your dear maid.
And at Benevento I brought you from that bleak quarry,

When all the country was enclosed by cruel men of arms
All wanting to take you quickly and put you to death;
I seized their provost's son and so I saved you there." 4695
Then he told how he intended to change their hides,
And brought them harts' skins to have, so to hide them both.
"Then I won you both over that wide strait of water;
Further testament to that time? Let me tell of the maid –
A boy buffeted her, with a brutal oar, 4700
Such that, most truly, she nearly lost her life."
Alphonse tells all there all of what happened to them,
And of what he had suffered to save their lives.

When William had wholly heard all of these words,
He was greatly glad, and who could blame him, 4705
When all the people in that place openly knew
That he was the son of kindly King Embrons?
At once, he locked Alphonse in his lovely arms,
And clasped him and kissed him, and kindly said,
"Ah! fair friend Alphonse, may joy betide you, 4710
And may God yield you goodness, in all His great might,
For all those trying travails that you have suffered for me
And for my lovely beloved; may the Lord repay you!
For I know not in this world in what way that I might
Repay you a tenth of such debt in all my lifetime! 4715
There's no gold under God that I might ever gain
Which shall not readily be yours to have at your will,
Nor no deed I might do that shan't be done soon enough;
And I shall love all that you love, loyally all of my days,
And I shall hate with my heart all that which you think to hate, 4720
So that my heart shall, all wholly, hold himself to your will.
And thus I hold myself, wholeheartedly, for wholly I know
That you have spoken the truth in what you said previously;
You have suffered many grievous sorrows, and all for my sake."
"Certainly, sire, that is so," said Alphonse then, 4725
"I think you might be so held to recompense me;
And so I desire that you do, if you dearly think so!"
"Yes!" said William. "May God will it that I know

In what manner that I might most especially please you,
Or which of my worldly goods you would most desire."   4730
"Yes sire," said Alphonse, "so Christ help me,
There is nothing more under God that I desire more greatly
Than this one thing which I hope you would willingly grant me."[51]
"Yes, indeed," replied William, "wish what you will
Of that which you would have hastily, from the whole of
    my realm;   4735
I would withhold not one jot of my worth, except Melior alone."
At once, Alphonse answered and then he said,
"I crave nothing of your kingdom, by Christ who redeemed me,
Nor of your lovely beloved, truly in good faith.
I want for nought but your sister, and to be wedded to the same,   4740
To wield here as my wife for the whole of my life."
"Yes, by worthy God," said William, "I would be most happy
Just to know that you were to have her as your wife;
It would be a most wondrous deed, if it be that you would

Make yourself so meek as to marry so humbly." 4745
"By Peter, yes sire," said Alphonse, "I pray of you nothing more
For all the sorrow I have suffered, always for your sake;
Pray grant me, without begrudging, that graceful maid."
"By God, sire," said William, "who granted me life,
You shall have her at your behest, and with her, of my realm, 4750
Wholly one half, without any let."
"No, Christ forbid," said Alphonse, "for all His holy blood,
That I were ever so wicked to want any of your wealth!
I bid for nothing of worth but that beautiful maid."
Then William thanked him with grace, as a glad man, 4755
And said, "Now certainly we shall be such true friends together,
Loyally brethren in law, may Our Lord be thanked;
For now all the world's well-being falls on us as we please!"
Then all the people in that palace, openly for joy,
Made all the mirth that men might devise; 4760
And the comely queen thanked Christ, fully and often,
Who had comforted her so well, during all of her woes.
Those tidings were told, promptly, far and wide
Of that fabulous story which befell there; then swiftly thereafter
A great press of people, to tell you the truth, were drawn to
    Palermo 4765
To look on those lords, at their will, to their liking.

Now for to mention further as befalls in this matter:
When these tidings were told to all alike,
Of those two treacherous hags who would have betrayed
    William,[52]
Those ladies who, in his youth, taught and looked after
    the lad 4770
Then each wholly knew, and without any doubt,
That they should be done to death, cruelly and speedily,
And burned in bright fire, and then drawn or hanged,
In such a way most deserving for their wicked deeds.
Those two ladies who were called Gloriande and Acelone,* 4775

---

* It is notable that the narrator does not interject with "as you will remember" at this point.

Then they bethought briskly what might be their best remedy,
Since their treason was common knowledge, and known all about.
Hastily they hurried, in shirts of rough horsehair
Next to their bare bodies, and on barefoot they went,
And they both fell on their knees in front of William   4780
And submitted themselves to his grace, because of their great guilt,
And confessed the whole case of how they had contrived
To have slain most insidiously himself and his father,
By order of the king's brother, in bringing such blight.
"Let us keep our lives, sire, if Our Lord would will it.   4785
We make ourselves at your mercy, in every manner,
To slay or to save us, whatsoever your whim!
That we are worthy of our deaths, we know this well;
But would you grant us, in your grace, by God's love in heaven,
To put us in some place where we may serve our penance,   4790
And let us live, as long as Our Lord wills it,
So that we might make amends, at least, for some of our guilt,
And for us to pray faithfully for you and your father?
If you were to do so, you might gain more renown,
And, dear lord, while no good deed may come from our deaths   4795
A little wicked will would instead be assuaged."
Then briskly, all the barons bade their lord earnestly
That those women, in every manner, must make amends for their crime;
And William at once granted their will
So they would, in that way, work good deeds thereafter.   4800
Thus the ladies were brought to a hermitage soon,
And virtuously lived there, as Our Lord so willed,
In penance and in prayers, whether peacefully or aloud,
Till they went from this world when God would call them.
Now I will leave those ladies; listen now of another,   4805
Of what betides in this tale, as this story tells us.

 Without wasting more time, William at once
Summoned eminent messengers who, to tell matters truly,
Were the greatest lords of that land, known as the most loyal
And finely cultured in courtesy, and the most well-spoken.   4810
He sent them readily to the Emperor of Rome,

And loyally besought him, with loving letters,
That, if it were his will, and without any let,
To be there with his best men, by a certain time,
To come and honour the marriage of Melior his daughter.   4815
And if Alisaundrine were still alive,
He prayed courteously that she must come with him.
Then, in all manner of ways, those messengers were
So excellently equipped, to tell you the truth,
With horses, fine harnesses and whatever they needed,   4820
That no one in this world would want for better.
And they went on their way, fast and at once,
Till they had ridden readily, straight to great Rome.
When those bold barons came before the emperor,
They greeted him with grace, and gladly, as they ought,   4825
First on behalf of Alphonse, who was king of Spain,*
For the emperor and he had been fellows before,[53]
Then, on behalf of worthy William, who was king of Apulia
And sovereign of Sicily, which as king he should be,[54]
And then in the name of Melior, his esteemed cheerful
    daughter.   4830
So, on behalf of the King of Apulia, they prayed him most fair
To come presently to Palermo with his people, and soon,
By a certain day, which was set soon after,
To come and honour the marriage of Melior his daughter,
For he would take her as his wife, to wield that realm.   4835
When the messengers had mentioned Melior the fair,
He was greatly gladdened, and began to say thus,
"Lords, for your loyalty, truly tell me,
If you know, in any way, where that maid is."
"By Mary, Sire," said the messengers, "you must trust us well,   4840
The mild maid Melior dwells now in Palermo.
Look, here are her letters, to believe matters better."
The king commanded a clerk, both swiftly and keenly

---

* This is the first time the manuscript has mentioned Alphonse as King of Spain. It is assumed that the monarch carries the same name as his first-born son. *Guillaume* (l. 8426) also refers to King Alphonse of Spain.

To look on those letters, and loyally read them,
So that he might at once know all of their meaning.   4845
Directly, the clerk then undid those letters,
And found in them the matter those messengers mentioned;
How the King of Apulia had plainly arranged
To wed his seemly daughter, on a certain day.

 Then the emperor knew well that they spoke the truth,   4850
And made for those messengers all the merriment he knew;
Never were such royal ranks more well received in a place!
The emperor made his own messengers wend forth immediately
To summon, most loyally, all the lords of that land
To be readily arrayed in their richest manner,   4855
To wend with him, at once, to that noble wedding.
And when they heard his request, they all hastened fast.
Thus surely, on the same day which was assigned to them,
Such a royal troop in Rome was regally assembled,
That not one soul under the sun ever saw such another   4860
So excellently attired as all those from that land.
And they went their way at once, when they were all ready,
And Alisaundrine with them, who I mentioned already.
And as they were wending on their way that time,
The emperor then asked those eminent messengers   4865
By what way did his daughter come to fare to that land;
How it was so confirmed that a king would wed her?[55]
And then they promptly told him all the whole truth
Of the fortune which befell them, from beginning to end,
In all the manner I have mentioned of this matter before.   4870
And when the emperor had heard of how it all fared,
He was greatly gladdened, and often thanked Christ,
For the fortune which befell them, so fair and so noble,
And he soon informed his company of all of this matter,
As those eminent messengers had made it clear to him.   4875
No tongue might tell of such mirth as was made
As made so swiftly by them, when those tidings were told!
Thus they hurried hard on their way, both fast and with haste,
Until presently that procession came to Palermo's gates.

William at once then with his fairest people –   4880
Fine crowned kings and countless hundreds of knights –
Went towards the emperor with great gladness and cheer.
Great and glorious was the greeting when they met together.
William and the emperor went forward to each other first,
And Alphonse went next, and greeted him appropriately,   4885
With all the merriment on earth men might ever devise.
The King of Spain speedily hastened after him next,
For the emperor and he had been friends before,*
And they kissed each other kindly when they came together.
The mirth that was made at that meeting then,   4890
No tongue may tell of, it is truly so!
So these same folk next went, in a most seemly way together,
To the peerless palace, and, promptly at that moment,
The queen came towards them, with a courtly company -

* See note to l. 4827 above.

She the lady of that land – and led in her hands   4895
The eminent maid Melior, and her own daughter;
And next a group of seemly ladies followed them in splendour;
The Queen of Spain then, speedily, hastened swiftly after them.
That meeting was most merry when they all neared and met,
With clasping and kissing, and the most courtly manners.   4900
And, most surely, when the emperor sees his seemly daughter,
A gladder man under God none might glimpse upon earth!
No man might tell of all their manifest joy,
Nor were guests ever more gladly received, under God.
They willed nor wanted for nothing that they would wish for,   4905
They were so seemly served and supplied as their right.
But I will mention no more of their merry faring,
Because no one might think how to describe it any better.
As soon as Alisaundrine caught sight of her lady,
No tongue might tell of truly half of the joy   4910
That they made at their meeting when those two met!
And Melior, full meekly, brought her to her chamber,
And told her, when time let, wholly all of the truth
Of the sorrows she had suffered since she had last seen her.
Now of this matter too, I will mention no more.   4915
Thus every mirth was well made among all that company;
William and his worthy maid, when they find the right time,
Told the emperor truly of what had happened to them,
Of the mischief and mirth, and who had most helped them,
And how their troubles were abated when they were brought
     here.   4920
And all then had great joy in learning of their adventures,
And thanked God for His grace, who had spared them so greatly.

When it was time, they turned soon to their meal,
And all were served splendidly, as is rightly so,
With all the dearest delights in both meat and drink,   4925
And when those who sat at that meal were at their most
     festive,
Eminent messengers entered, most noble men,
From the Emperor of Greece, who greeted the queen well –

She the lady of that land, and he her dear father* –
With greetings too from Partenedon, her imperial brother.　　　4930
And when these messengers had made their greetings,
The most sovereign of those said to them all,
"Madam, make yourself merry, for Mary's love in heaven,
For your faithful father has not forgotten you:
For he has sent to assist you such a formidable host　　　4935
That there is not one man upon earth who might stand
　　　against you,
Lest they be quickly brought to ruin at your bidding.
They come sailing by sea, their sovereign is your brother;
Partenedon the peerless leads all of these people,
And you shall see him yourself soon, without fail　　　4940
Before a third day be done, have no doubt at all."†
And when that comely queen heard all of those tidings,
There was no gladder a woman alive in the world.
She made great joy by those eminent messengers,
And she welcomed them worthily, I will tell you truly.　　　4945
The comely queen and the king took counsel and concurred
That the bridal day be delayed until her brother came,
To make that marriage more honoured, if that might be so.
Then on the third day, her brother arrived there,
With an excellent company, to speak of the truth,　　　4950
Of the greatest lords of that land, who lived there at that time;
While his host, in the meantime, he left still on the sea.
When the queen knew of his coming, quickly and courteously
She gladly goes towards him with her own great lords,
The courtly Emperor of Rome, and the King of Spain,　　　4955
And his comely queen, and all their excellent knights.
William the worthy was the first to welcome him fairly,
And Alphonse after him, after those kings.⁵⁶
The Queen of Palermo then promptly pressed to her brother,
And received him as royally as any regal one might;　　　4960
The King and Queen of Spain then courteously greet him,

---

* The romance has already made clear Queen Felice's ancestry; see lines A 27–A 30 above.
† The MS reads "er þis þridde day be don" – i.e., the day after tomorrow.

And the Emperor of Rome, with right great joy.
There was a most ceremonial sight, when this same all met,
With clasping and kissing in mutual affection.
The lady, full lovingly, then led her brother forth,   4965
Promptly, to Palermo and that rich palace.
More merriment on earth might no man devise
Than was made by those men, to mention the truth.
None wanted for nothing that they would wish to have;
The people were served plenteously, at their own places.   4970
And as they sat in satisfaction, the queen swiftly told
Her brother, most humbly, of what there had betided,
How William was her son who, by his doughty deeds,
Had conquered the Spanish king, and ended that war;
And in what way the werewolf was brought to his state;   4975
And wholly all of the happenings, as you have heard before,
And how they both went away, in white bear skins.
Then she told of how Alphonse should wed his niece,
And, too, William worthy Melior, with wealth, the next day.
Then the Greek emperor's son was sorely aggrieved,   4980
When he knew on the morrow that this marriage should happen,
For he was meant to have wed her, when he went to Rome
    before.
And although he now knew that William was his noble nephew,
Had he had his host with him, he would have tried there
To have won her back stoutly, with audacious strength.   4985
But he surely sees that this might not be so,
And so he must suffer it, though he rued it sorely,
And he composed his appearance so as to seem pleased;
But I tell you, in his heart, he liked it but little.
Then William and his mother, and Melior also,   4990
And Alphonse afterwards, turned now to Alisaundrine,
And, who among those just then, she might marry with eminence.
And so they concurred between them, to tell you the truth,
That the brother of Alphonse, Braundinis, be her match,
The King of Spain's son, who had caused this war;   4995
And, at his father's behest, this was humbly granted,
And at the bidding of his brother and by William too.

Then they whiled away that day in diversions and mirth,
And they had all that they wished for, wholly at their will,
And then each bore themselves briskly to bed at that time.   5000
But immediately in the morning, to tell matters truly,
Men might be seen there arrayed, extremely graciously,
And in ways more worthy than were ever seen before,
Since He who absolved us was born in Bethlehem!
All the clerks under God could not describe,   5005
Rightly and properly, the royalty that day
Who were in that city for that sacred feast -
All the most seemly men who might ever be assembled
Among such glorious grandees all graced their midst.
It might also be difficult to mention the minstrelsy;   5010
For all manner of musician was there at that marriage,
And when they made their music, every man wondered
Whether heaven and earth should hurtle together;
That sound was so extraordinary that all the earth shook!
The streets were all strewn and stoutly bedecked   5015
With good cloth of gold, of many gay hues.
And burgesses with wives, in ways best becoming,
Waited at their windows each way thereabouts,
To peep at those people who paraded the streets,
And to look on their lord who loyally then should   5020
Be crowned king on that day, to keep all that realm.

 But, the truth for to tell, when the time came that day
For those blissful brides to bestir themselves to church,
My powers are too poor to tell of their attire,
For all the men upon earth might never describe it   5025
Readily and correctly, so richly dressed were they all!
Both those kings and queens, and those other courtly lords,
Were all expertly apparelled, and conformed perfectly
In both horse and their harness, and all that which they needed;
Truly none might amend not one whit of the dress   5030
Of each guest, by his degree, as befitting his graciousness.
Therefore, no more of that matter will I mention now,
But will touch on more of this tale, as the story tells.

When everybody was able to bustle to the church,
The Emperor of Rome led William's sister, 5035
The woman who Alphonse would take to his wife;
And the courtly King of Spain, most courteous and fair,
Led Melior, with eminence, among all the people;
Bold Partenedon, the brother of the Queen of Palermo,
Appropriately led Alisaundrine next. 5040
On horseback, and blissful, they bustled to the church,
With all the merriment on earth that any man might imagine.
The clergy came towards them, attired most gaily,
Expertly in procession, promptly as is right,
And came to their king, and bade him kiss the cross, 5045
Then, with worship and well-being, they went into the church.
The patriarchs and other prelates were promptly robed
To solemnise that marriage in the appropriate manner.
And by the law of that land, I tell you loyally,
They were thus wedded, finely and wondrously. 5050
And sincerely, though Alisaundrine's lord had no land of
    his own,
He was promptly given, truly, several towns,
Comely castles and more, and a number of counties,
For both to live well with renown all their worldly lives.
No cleric under Christ could ever describe 5055
The mirth at that marriage which was all made then,
Its regal splendour nor richness, to reckon the truth,
Nor the sumptuous service which was seen at that time.
But when that service was said as it should have been,
As befalls to a marriage so made in a church, 5060
Those people again promptly went to the palace
With all the mirth and minstrelsy which men might think of.
And truly, when it was time, they turned to their meal,
And were served as splendidly, and as each so wished,
With any delicacy or drink which they might desire. 5065
It is tortuous to tell of it all to be perfectly truthful,
And to recount the array of that rich feast correctly.
Thus I will leave this alone now, but believe this truly -
I believe that no man might amend one whit more of it!

When the boards were brought down, and those nobles had
    washed,   5070
Men might be seen giving many good gifts to the minstrels;
Stern and stiff steeds, and rich stout robes,
Great glories of gold, and good jewels given freely.[57]
The feast for that marriage lasted a full month,
And, on each day, great gold was given all about   5075
Amongst all of the multitude who were at that marriage.
Then those lords took their leave at the end of the month;
Partenedon parted first, the Queen of Palermo's brother;
For he had farthest to fare, so left there before the others.
And William, with his warriors, went with him some way,   5080
And splendidly, with much pleasure, brought him to the sea,
With Melior, and his sister, and his eminent mother.
The Queen of Palermo, promptly, prayed that her brother
Greet her faithful father full many times, and often,
"And thank him kindly for the help that he sent to me,   5085
And do tell him truly of all which betides here."
Then each took leave of the other, to tell of it loyally.
Partenedon passed on board ship, and his people after,
And went at once to sail – the wind was at its best –
And they sailed all gamely with glee until they came to Greece.   5090
Then he promptly told his father, truly and soundly,
Of the fortune that befell, from beginning to end;
How his seemly sister was helped through her son,
And how that maid Melior was wedded that time
To his own nephew, although he liked it not.   5095
And when the emperor had heard all of those words,
He was greatly in wonder, as well he might be;
But he was glad that his nephew turned out now to be noble,
And praised as the most peerless by all others that he passed
Of all the knights under Christ who were then known,   5100
And that his daughter was now delivered from her distress.
He greatly thanked God, for all His great might,
And lived then in bliss, for the rest of his life.
But now we go from those Greeks and begin talking of others;
We will tell of what passed with the people in Palermo.   5105

The royal Emperor of Rome then departed soon after,
Readily towards Rome with all his rich noble band.
William and his mother, Melior and his sister,
The King of Spain and his sons, and their seemly people,
Went with him on his way, for well over five miles,　　5110
To convey him with courtesy, as kindness demands,
With all the mirth in the world which men might imagine.
And as they went on their way, I will tell you truly,
The emperor, with full meekness, said to Melior,
"Now, my dear daughter, I pray do learn from my words.　　5115
Look that you bear yourself humbly, and be good and noble,
Be competent and courteous with commoner or lord.
Be meek and merciful to all men whom you serve,
And be loyal to your lord, and to this lady after,
Who is his eminent mother, and see that you much love her,　　5120
And after her, love as well all the lords of this land.
And daughter, look, on your life, as you love me dearly,
That the poor and impoverished are never plundered for you,
Nor taxed by unjust tolls; but attentively help
That all this land be so ruled in law as it ought.　　5125
Then will all the poor people yearn and pray for you
To live a long and good life, and your lord also.
Look that you strive stoutly, for the state of Holy Church,
To maintain it manfully in all manner of ways;
Give greatly of your goods, for the sake of God in heaven;　　5130
Be merciful to all men who are in much need;
Thus you shall you gain glorious renown, and be greatly honoured,
As have all of your ancestors, from whom you were begotten.
Do this, my dear daughter, and may you never dread
That you will not have heavenly bliss after life."　　5135
Melior said meekly, words mingling through tears,
"I hope, Sire, by our heavenly King, to work at your behest;
That nobody ever born shall blame me for my deeds."
At once, after talking, they then took their leave,
Courteously kissing and clasping each other.　　5140
But the mourning which Melior made at that time,
Because her father should fare far from her so soon,

Was truly troubling, to tell you the truth.
But the emperor most highly held her in his arms
And comforted her kindly, and prayed that the queen   5145
Be meek and merciful to Melior his daughter,
And cherish her – and chasten her, if ever it so chanced
That she would act wrongly or work any mistake.
"Yes, by Christ, sire," said the queen, "do not worry in this cause,
For I love her like myself, believe this truly.   5150
I know well that she will always work to the good;
Therefore her will shall be wrought, and of what she so desires,
She will not want for one thing of what pleases the heart."
The emperor thanked her thoroughly, many thousands of times,
And immediately, after that, he said to Alisaundrine,   5155
"God has not forgotten you, my good noble maid,
For you are most worshipfully wedded to rule with a king's son.[58]
I bid you, most soberly, always to honour that noble,
And work him all the worship in the world that you may;[59]
Then shall all loyal folk love you, and pray for your life."   5160
"I shall hold to your behest, sire," Alisaundrine said then,
"So that you shall hear of me nothing but good,
I hope, through God's grace, unless men tell gross lies."
The emperor then, promptly, took leave of them all
And wends forth on his way at once towards Rome,   5165
And lived there most likeably, for a long time after.
Now let those Romans rest, and we will instead recount more,
And speak of the Spaniards, while we have space,
And of how they sped, with speed, thereafter to Spain.

 When the King of Palermo and his peerless mother,   5170
And the meek Melior, his eminent queen,
Came once more to court, to speak of things truly,
They passed through Palermo into the royal palace
With all the merriment on earth that men might imagine.
But immediately on the morrow, to mention the truth,   5175
The King of Spain speedily spoke, and asked permission for leave,
Both for him and all his fellowship to fare forth at that time;
Both himself and Braundine, who was his bold queen,

And his seemly sons, both Alphonse and his brother,
And their worthy wives, simultaneously at once.   5180
The King of Spain now thanks King William
For all the fine, friendly deeds which he had wrought for them,
Through all the great grace which God had granted him;
For they would return to their country, and they commended him
      to Christ.
When the king was aware that they were ready to wend,   5185
His heart felt great sorrow for the sake of Alphonse,
Because he felt of the fellowship he must now forgo.
And when he felt the need most, he then took him by the hand,
And said, sorely sighing, "Now Alphonse, sweet brother,
Since you cross to your country to keep your own realm,   5190
I bid you as humbly, as one brother should to another,
If at any time it betides that you suffer trouble,
Through war, or other wrong, with anyone on earth,
Or should you suffer such from any sorry Saracens,[60]
Send your message to me, swiftly and fast,   5195
And I shall hastily hurry there, by Him who died for me,
To avenge you truly for anything which betides."
"I say the same to you, sire," said Alphonse then;
"And nothing shall stop me from coming swiftly to your
      summons."
Both then thanked the other many thousand times,   5200
And let each other take their leave, though they were loath to do so.

Then meekly, he kissed William's mother and Melior,
Commended them both to Christ, who was punished
      on cross;
And meekly, the queen then implored her daughter,
And asked her with courtesy to keep her honour well,   5205
She bade her be humble and love her noble lord,
And have pity on the poor, and be prompt to help them,
And give praise to God, and always do good deeds.
And she, sighing sorely, said that she would,
She hoped, through God's grace; and quickly thereafter,   5210
Clasping and kissing, they commended them to Christ.[61]

And the Spaniards, with speed, then hastened to their ship;
When they were arrayed, the crew as they would[62]
Swiftly set up their sails and then set on their way,
With all manner of mirth that man might think of,   5215
For they had, at their will, both the wind and good weather:
And they sped with great speed till they came to Spain.
Then all the lords of that land, and others of all degree,
Who were in any way worthy of that wide realm,
All hurried to the harbour, handsomely towards them,   5220
And welcomed them worthily, as well they ought;[63]
And of the coming of Alphonse, all there were glad.
And so all the people swiftly passed to the palace
With all manner of mirth that man can possibly make.
The King of Spain, speedily, to speak only the truth,   5225
Crowned Alphonse as king to keep all that realm,
For he had himself grown feeble and old,
So to live at Our Lord's will thereafter in bliss.[64]
Thus was Alphonse king there after that time,
And ruled rightly and properly, over both rich and poor,   5230
So that everybody blessed him, by night and by day.
Now I will stop talking of him, while I speak of William,
That courteous King of Apulia, whom I spoke of before.

 As speedily as the Spaniards had sped to sail,
William with his folk at once went again   5235
To the palace of Palermo; his people followed
With all the mirth of minstrelsy which men might think of.
        Then William at once, as a wise king should,
Put peace back in his realm among all his people,
And annulled all loathsome laws which had long been in use,   5240
And granted good ones to be made, and promulgated more
Which were upheld by his people and proved so profitable
That never did a Christian king capture more affection
Than did William in a short while, I will honestly tell you.
And if he gained much good, by all his great works,   5245
And was well beloved in his land by all, low and high,
So was Melior as much, his eminent queen,

Or more so, if she might be, in any such manner,
So promptly did she please both the poor and the rich.
Then it betided at that time, to tell you the truth,   5250
That the rich Roman emperor ended his days,
He died and was duly buried, as dear God willed;
And all the lords of that land, loyally in assent,
Sent word to William to say what had so befallen –
And to his queen Melior – by noble messenger,   5255
As to their liege lord, loyally as is appropriate,
By means of his marriage to Melior the fair.
Handsomely, and all in haste, they prayed him most highly
To take in rightful possession all of that fair realm,
And ever live in that empire, as emperor and master.   5260
Once that worthy William was aware of all this,
And had truly understood all these tidings to their end,
Then he was most hospitable to those eminent messengers
And welcomed them worthily, I will tell you truly.
Nonetheless, he and Melior both made much sorrow   5265
That the emperor was faring forth now fairly to Christ.
But they were quickly comforted, for this they both clearly knew –
That death comes to all whom Christ has formed,
To emperors and to earls, to everyone who has lived.*
Then they thanked God, with goodness and grace,   5270
And said they would suffer His summons and His will.
Then William, at once, and without further delay,
Swiftly sent for despatches to go surely to Spain
By his mild messengers, who were good loyal men,
And bid that Alphonse his brother should swiftly come,   5275
And bring his wife with him, his own worthy sister.
He bade Alphonse also that Alisaundrine and her lord
Might also, at all costs, come with him too,
And his faithful father, if he was still alive.
But he was dead and deep buried, as dear God had willed,   5280
And Alphonse now held that whole realm in his hands

* This reference is missing in *Guillaume*, instead Melior is happy that she and William will
become emperor and empress (ll. 9272–5)

As its kind king so crowned by a council of his peers.*
And when those eminent messengers fully understood their message,
And had letters from their lord to uphold what they said,
They went at once on their way, without further ado,   5285
And sped then towards Spain, with speed in a while,
And they conveyed their message to the courteous king Alphonse.

 When Alphonse was aware of the whole of their message,
That the royal Roman emperor was truly in God's hands,
And that his humble brother should be lord thereafter,   5290
He was greatly gladdened, and often thanked God,
        And Mary, His mother, who sent him such grace,
And swiftly he summoned all his noble men,
Then the lords of his land, the higher and the lower,
And other peerless people, to come promptly in attendance.   5295
When they were grandly gathered, as they thought good and proper,
They then passed to Palermo, as fast as they might:
Alphonse and his worthy wife, the sister of William,
And Braundinis his bold brother, and Alisaundrine his wife,
With hundreds of keen knights, I don't know their names.   5300
And when they came readily to where they should arrive,
William with his warriors went out towards them.
And no man upon earth might tell of the joy
That those bold brethren made between themselves,
William with Alphonse, when they mutually met,   5305
And then with his seemly sister, very soon after,
And with his other brother, Braundinis the bold,
And after that with Alisaundrine, and then all the others.
With that, all the people promptly went to Palermo,
And made themselves as merry as man might devise   5310
With all the dearest and daintiest of meat and of drink.
And thus those peerless people rested in Palermo,
For full seven nights, to ease themselves.

* This passage is unique to the English redaction; the description of Alphonse's coronation by
dint of the counsel of his peers reinforces the theme of legitimacy that runs through the romance
and the need for acceptance rather than autocracy in the delivery of good government.

And by that everybody, in the best way,
Was perfectly provisioned with all that they needed,   5315
And then William, that worthy king, was immediately ready
To depart for Rome with all his regal party.
Then he arranged for his mother to be mounted in eminence,
Between him and Queen Melior, to wend their way in mirth,
Along with his seemly sister, to please their hearts.   5320
Then, with his rich retinue, he rides on his way,
Readily towards Rome, by all the right roads,
With all manner of mirth that men might think of.
And as they carried on through that country, and came near
        to Rome,
Kings then came towards him, and other great kin,   5325
The fairest retinue of folk that was ever seen before;
Not one man upon earth might guess at their number.
And they welcomed William, as their lord, with worship,
And they greeted, most freely, all his fine noble fellowship,
And received them as royally as any retinue might;   5330
So they ride right into Rome, with richness and mirth.
But no tongue may tell how that city was attired,
So richly was Rome all arrayed for his coming.
The prelates emerge in a priestly procession,
And all the bells of the borough were busily rung   5335
For joy that their liege lord should take up his lordship.
Then all of those people passed straight to the palace,
And each man was made at ease, exactly as he pleased;
They wanted for nothing that they might wish for,
So plenteously the people were fully provided for.   5340
And at mass on the morrow, to mention the truth,
William was made emperor with worship and renown,
And his comely queen, Melior, was crowned empress.
There is no clerk under Christ who could half describe
The richness all arrayed for that feast in Rome,   5345
Nor a tenth of the attire, to tell of it rightly,
For all men upon earth might not improve on it,
What befell to such a feast, full sure, not a jot!
So I will leave off, for a while, you should know truly,

From recounting the adornments of that royal feast,   5350
To tell more of this tale, and what happened next.

For full fifteen days that feast was held,
With all the royalty of Rome that anyone might recall.
No tongue might tell of one twentieth the part
Of the rewards given many times to all of the minstrels,   5355
Whether robes with rich pelts or other great riches,
Stern and strong steeds or other stout gifts,
Such that each man amongst them might deem himself well paid.
And before that feast had fully fared right to the end,
William, who was crowned as the new emperor,   5360
As a courteous king, he thought of the cowherd,
Who had fostered him formerly for full seven years,
And so he soon sent for him and his seemly wife.
And when the cowherd came, the king said to him,
"Sire cowherd, Christ help you, do you recognise me?"   5365
The cowherd knelt quickly, and spoke these words,
"Yes Lord, by your leave, I knew you when you were little;[65]
I fostered you in my farmstead, and fully thought
And said that you were my son, for seven years or more.
The rich Emperor of Rome, who reigned here at that time,   5370
Won you away from me; woe was I then!
But hailed be the High King, who has since helped you thus,
And put you in this fine place, free from poverty for ever!"
William, the worthy emperor, said fully at once,
"By Christ, sire, you have said the truth, fully and straight; 5375
You fostered me most finely, as befalls your estate,
And by Our Lord, as I live, you shall not fail to be rewarded!"
And so he then, with haste, commanded come to him
His steward, without delay, who managed his lands and estates;
And, before courteous knights and other keen lords,   5380
He gave to that cowherd a full noble castle,
The finest on fair earth that any fellow might see;
The best place to be seen, to keep for himself,
And all that which touched upon it as a tidy earldom.
The king gave this to the cowherd, and his wife at this time, 5385

207

As freely as any fellow could devise, forever;
And with haste he assigned bailiffs to hold all their lands,
And that each be obedient by night and by day,
To the command of the cowherd, as much as to their kind lord,
If they valued their lives, and not to obstruct his will;   5390
And he sent his steward swiftly to settle him therein,
And his will was wrought quickly, I will tell you truly.
Thus was the cowherd kindly rescued from struggling,
As he and his gentle wife went to live well for ever.
Now I will speak of no more of that kind cowherd,   5395
But leave him to his bliss, and his wife besides;
And let us talk further, as this tale fares onwards.

 When this fair feast finished after fifteen days,
Each lord, most lovingly, began to take his leave
Of the emperor and empress and thanked them often   5400
For the worship and wealth which they had wrought
    upon them.
The emperor commended them, with grace, to great God above,
But first he took homage handsomely from them,
Meekly, in the right manner, as becoming such men,
So they would keenly come to his call, as to their kind lord;   5405
Then he thanked them with goodness and commended them to God,
And they went on their way, wherever they liked to go,
Each lord to his own land, where they lived in bliss.
And after they had all gone, so then King Alphonse
Came before William with his worshipful wife,   5410
And Braundinis, his brother, with Alisaundrine, his bride;
Then each one at once, of the emperor and empress,
Lovingly took their leave of them so to wend to their lands.
Soon great sorrow abounded, surely to say,
When William was aware that all would depart;   5415
Much mourning each made, and Melior also;
But since things might be no better, it behoved them so to suffer.
William led Alphonse, his brother, wholly by the hand,
And, near weeping with woe, at once said these words,
"Brother, if it be so, by God who wrought us,   5420

I wish it were your will to live with us here;
It grieves me with sorrow that we should part company,
But since there is no alternative, I will not fight it;
I commend you to Christ, who was punished on the cross.
And brother, I bid you, by all that you ever loved,   5425
If destiny befalls that some deed be done to you,
That anyone, by war, works against your peace,
Then swiftly send me a message and I will soon come to you,
For no lord alive shall ever hold me back,
Not for love nor for money, while all my life lasts;   5430
I will never hold back, till you be well avenged."
"Ah, blessed may you be, bold brother," said Alphonse,
"I say the same to you, if such fortune allows."
No fellow upon earth ever saw a more faithful friendship,
That was so perfectly proffered as to please each other,   5435
And help each other with haste, whosoever had the need.
Emperor William's mother, and Melior also,
Said to her daughter, that seemly Queen of Spain,
"Lovely daughter, beloved, always love your lord,
And be always busy about him to serve him obediently,   5440
And always, by your learning, advise him how to keep his land;
And you shall always be loved by all, low or high."
And, kneeling crouched on her knees, she replied courteously,
That she hoped, by heaven's King, while all her life lasted,
To work as they wished her, and without any let.   5445
And afterwards, they said to Alisaundrine,
That she should in the same way likewise love her lord,
And she, sighing sorrowfully, said that she would.
And when those same had said what so they should,
And the time came at last that they should part asunder,   5450
There was sighing and sorrow on both sides with sadness,
Hands wringing, and much weeping, for the woe in their hearts.
And with clasping and kissing, they comforted each other,
Commended each other to Christ, who was punished on the cross,
And then they themselves separated, though it sorely
    grieved them.   5455
The King of Spain, speedily, then sped to horse,

And went forth on his way, without further ado,
And all his fair fellowship followed after him,
And so they sped with speed, until they came to Spain.
They were royally received, as right and proper, on arrival,   5460
With all manner of mirth which men might think of;
And they lived there in bliss all their lives after,
And led all that land well, always with good laws,
So that everybody felt blessed that they were ever born.
I will cease my speech and speaking now of all those in Spain,   5465
And let them live in bliss at the will of Our Lord;
I return now to tell, readily, of that royal Roman emperor.

 When the King of Spain had fared speedily from there,
William took with him all his worthy company,
And his eminent mother, and all of her maidens,   5470
And rides through the Roman empire in fine regal state,
        To all its splendid cities and fortified strongholds,
So to know all of his country, as a skilful king should;
Taking homage from each lord who lived in the realm.
And when that deed was done, then duly and soon   5475
Good laws were set loyally throughout that land,
And were held so hard and fast, I have to say truly,
That neither robbers nor rascals might raid anyone,
Lest they be hanged with haste, or drawn with horses.
Flatterers and false men he soon chased from there;   5480
He held no love at all for neither liars nor sweet-talkers,
But he himself, always, took true and excellent counsel,
Such that all people prayed for him, the poor and the rich,
So wisely he worked to safeguard his realm.
And if he was meek in his manner, Melior, his queen,   5485
Was the same on her side, to tell the truth.
She was so generous to God's men and to all good works,
So compassionate to the poor, helping them promptly,
That each man had great joy to hear of her spoken,
And said prayers for her busily, both by night and by day.   5490
And also of William's mother, that most eminent queen;
She was so good and gracious to the great pleasure of all,

So wise and so willing to work good deeds always,
That all blessed her busily, everybody, for ever,
And prayed highly to heaven's King to protect all her livings.   5495
Then, once, in the meanwhile, it came into her mind
That her dream was so true which she had some time past,
That her right arm had readily stretched all over Rome,
And her left arm, whole-heartedly, lay all over Spain.
Then at once she knew what it all betokened: 5500
That her right arm reflected her son reigning in Rome;
And that her dearest daughter, who was drawn to Spain
To live her life as its lady, was shown by her left arm.
She thanked God, with much grace, for all of His might,
And His eminent Mother, the mild Queen of Heaven,   5505
Who had borne her from her troubles and brought her to such bliss.

Thus William and his worthy queen, through many winters,
Lived likeably in bliss, as Our Lord willed,
And they had two sons between them, most seemly children,
Who since then, through God's grace, were great lords
    thereafter.   5510
One reigned after his father as the Emperor of Rome,
The other was an acclaimed King of Apulia and Calabria;
And both were mighty and eminent men in their time,
And as faithful as their father to free man or serf.
Thus this worthy William rose to Emperor of Rome,   5515
Who had, here before, suffered much hardship,
And borne many troubles and burdens in his life.
But he was freed from those troubles, blessed be God's might;
And so shall every soul who seeks to be good,
And gives himself to God's grace, and always works to the good. 5520
In this way has this William ended his work too,*
As fully as the French book would fairly ask of him,
And as his wits would serve, although they were feeble.
So though this poem may not be to the pleasure of all men,

---

* For a discussion of the identity of William, the romance's narrator-scribe, see Historical
Introduction.

Do not blame he who wrought it; he would have done better 5525
If his wit, in any way, would have served him so.
But, fair friends, for God's love, and for your own renown,
You who like and love to hear such things,
Please praise that good lord who granted this to be made,
The high Earl of Hereford, Humphrey de Bohun; 5530
Good King Edward's daughter was his dear mother;
He caused this poem to be composed in this manner of speech
For those who know no French, nor ever understood it.
Bid that blissful Lord, who redeemed us on the cross,
And his mother Mary, that fountain of mercy, 5535
That this lord enjoys a good life, while he lives here on earth,
And, when he wends from this world, enjoys wealth without end,
To dwell in that pleasing joy which lasts for evermore.
And may God give such good grace, to all who gladly pray so,
And to have their own such place, plainly in Paradise. Amen. 5540

APPENDIX 1: The Character of the Narrator in *William and the Werewolf*

Anyone reading *The Romance of William and the Werewolf* for the first time will be struck immediately by the presence of the narrator; his voice is present in the first line of the romance and continues to be felt right until the last. His setting out of the story and of its importance to his audience – assuming of course that the missing passages of the Middle English redaction follow that of the Old French – seem critical to how he wants us to judge what follows. He reminds us frequently of his presence, albeit often formulaically (e.g. "I wittow forsoþ" – "I would tell you truly/I assure you") and his frequent references to the intervention of God or Christ also reveal that he is concerned throughout for his characters and the justice of their actions. Finally, of course, the narrator reminds us of his own patron – in this case, Humphrey de Bohun, one of the wealthiest and most influential earls in fourteenth-century England.* The narrator appears real, authoritative and relevant while also being compassionate, religious and didactic; but who is he really and what is he trying to achieve?

The role of the narrator in Middle English popular romance varies considerably. In some romances the narrative begins with what appears to be a performer in a public place, gathering his audience about him. In *King Horn*, the narrator's opening words announce, "Alle beon he blithe / That to my song lythe" ("May all be happy who listen to my song")

* See Historical Introduction.

while in *Havelok the Dane* he says "Herkneth to me, gode men ..."
("Listen to me, good men").[1] In these romances, we see him as a medi-
eval diseur, seemingly (at least in the case of *Horn*) about to sing the
romance. But if this is a conceit of certain romances, his role is not uni-
form; there is considerable debate about how romances were performed
and, indeed, if they were sung at all.[2] In the Anglo-Norman *Boeve de
Haumtone*, we encounter specifically a *reader* (l. 5) who collects money
for his performance at the end (ll. 3849–50).[3] But, by the fourteenth cen-
tury, we encounter someone who, in the later Middle English redactions
of *Boeve*, says either that he will "sing" what follows in a manner merrier
than the nightingale or, in one redaction, whose "song" in itself is mer-
rier than the nightingale.[4]

   Singing, it seems, may be real or metaphorical but it is also clear
that the presentation of romances could occur in a variety of ways. In
the memorable and somewhat waspish words of Robert Mannyng of
Brunne:*

> I mad noght for no disours,
> Ne for no seggers, no harpours,
> Bot for the luf of simple men
> That strange Inglis can not ken."
> (I didn't write this for any storyteller,
> Nor for any reciter or harper,
> But for the enjoyment of simple folk
> Who don't understand unfamiliar English)
> (Robert Mannyng, *Chronicle*, ll. 75–8)[5]

Mannyng's words, written possibly in the 1330s, reveal that romances
and other texts were delivered in a variety of ways, sometimes in ways
which, even if in English, could be difficult to comprehend by "simple
men" (seemingly, folk who understood English but not the sophistica-
tion of its flexibility and use). Indeed, romances and other texts did not
necessarily have to be read aloud; as Hollie Morgan has shown, private
chambers could be used for readings to small groups or, significantly,
were places where books could be read to assert a reader's individuality;

* Brunne is the medieval spelling of Bourne, in Lincolnshire.

contemporary illuminations often show readers alone with books.[6] As well as being read aloud, with the reader potentially taking the role of the narrator, books could also be read in silence, the narrator himself now becoming one of many imaginary characters to populate the reader's mind.

Irrespective of whether the narrator in *William* took the form of those in texts such as *Bevis* or *Horn*, whether he was a "disour", "segger" or "harper", the English romance's ancephalous form means that the only evidence we have for his character at the opening of the story is that given in its Old French source. *Guillaume*'s narrator does not position himself as a character; we are not told specifically that he is a reader, nor is he seen as a singer with an accompanying harpist. Instead, he is someone who intends to "tell" or "relate" the story to us (ll. A3, A7, A17, A20, A50) and to do so from memory (l. A19) in order to bring pleasure to himself and his audience (l. A18). Notwithstanding the missing lines, it is clear throughout the English redaction that the narrator is here to stay, resurfacing throughout as a character within it, whether helping us navigate from one strand of the story to another (ll. 78–9; 1923–5; 5104–5); recapping the story to remind us of events (ll. 1361–72); using idioms to bring the story to life ("dead as a doornail", ll. 628; 3396), or reminding us of his source to emphasise his credibility ("but then it happened one time, as this tale tells", l. 787). Often he appears weary of his tale ("therefore no more of this matter will I mention now", l. 5032), unwilling to describe events ("it is tortuous to tell of it all to be perfectly truthful", l. 5066),* or happy simply to revert to formulaic shorthand in order to capture a moment ("with all the mirth in the world which men might imagine", l. 5112).

In Mannyng's categorisation, the narrator in *William and the Werewolf* appears to be a "segger" – a reciter but nonetheless one whom, like Mannyng himself, appears to have an agenda beyond simply telling his story. Despite never introducing himself, nor showing any evidence of his physical manifestation, the narrator nevertheless has an opinion: he

---

* The unwillingness of narrators to describe events such as feasts and weddings is not unusual and, as in *William*, a formulaic approach to the narrative. Notwithstanding, anyone who has read the description of the feast (ll. 176–219) in the near-contemporary *Alliterative Morte Arthure* might understand the unwillingness of scribes to commit time to such writing.

believes that secrets are "better out than in" and that the wicked will suffer by the telling of things which bring only good (ll. A8–10). The narrator's subtle introduction of his opinions is not something that fades away either; his views predominate throughout, usually guided by religious morality or substantiated by references to his source, sometimes with quite revolutionary intent. Crucially, the positioning of his story in the past (ll. A21–22) enables him to distance himself from what he says; in the parlance of modern films, any resemblance to persons living or dead is entirely coincidental. This is an old story that must come out for the good of all; it is a story demanding to be told.

However, *Guillaume*'s portrayal and positioning of this unknown "segger" means that we now enter the territory of the "reliable narrator" – one who tells the tale in good faith – and the "unreliable narrator" – one who seems potentially compromised. So who is this man who tells us that nothing must be kept secret if, by its telling, it will bring good to others? Why should we believe this to be so; what information do we have to accept him as a credible deliverer of what is to follow? We know, of course, that the Middle English *William* is drawn from the French *Guillaume de Palerne*, which means straightaway that the "English" narrator is a fictional creation; he is mimicking the telling of his story as told by his French source. Yet we also know that the French narrator himself claims that even his work is drawn from that in an older tongue; as *Guillaume*'s scribe says of his patron, Countess Yolande:

> Cest livre fist diter et faire
> Et de latin en roumans traire.

> (She ordered this book to be written and made
> and translated from Latin into romance [French])
> *Guillaume de Palerne*, ll. 9658–9

Assuming the text is broadly similar in all its redactions, the real narrator of the tale – the one who is telling this from memory – lies somewhere in the depths of time, beyond the French scribe's twelfth-century original, in a text written in Latin that has now been lost. Our narrator is instead a conduit for the story, fundamental to its telling, but the story itself is not his and nor is it fully reliable.

While holding fundamentally to the characters and plots of its French source, the English narrator himself is not a perfect or reliable figure either, frequently transferring narrative responsibility to the dialogue of the characters and at one point even using a character to create a plot element that hadn't previously been explained.* Furthermore, the English narrative contains a number of subtle variations from its source, indicating that the narrator's "memory" may either be fallible, his translation and/or transcription skills are at fault, or that he is adapting the story for his English patron or his audience. Amongst these variations are the English redaction's negative view of stepmothers (ll. 130–32); the potential threat of Alisaundrine (l. 953) and the lovers' appeal to her (l. 1037); the Roman emperor's resource to the counsel of his peers (ll. 1456–60; 2105); the boy attacking Melior at the straits of Messina (ll. 2767–91); and the coronation of Alphonse by the agreement of his peers (l. 5282). However, as Renée Ward has discussed in some depth,[7] a significant variation between the two narratives appears to be how the English version has been "sanitized" of the gratuitous violence of its French source. We know from the graphic scenes of violence shown repeatedly in texts such as the *Alliterative Morte Arthure*, *Richard Coer de Lyon* and others that English audiences were not averse to the brutal representation of battle in texts, yet *William and the Werewolf* redacts practically all such violent depictions during the attack by the Duke of Saxony's armies and during the siege of Palermo itself. In *Guillaume*, we see a hero so enraged against the duke's forces that he is likened to a dragon (l. 2037), a lion (l. 2038), or a boar (l. 2213), as he goes about slaughtering and eviscerating his enemies, one of whom, Tosson du Pré, is relieved of his liver (*foie*) and lungs (*poumon*), which spill out onto his saddle bow or pommel (*l'arçon*) (ll. 2065–8). By contrast, the English redaction, while describing its hero as a lion once (l. 3862), prefers instead to tells us of many "stunning strokes" (l. 1158) and of forces being bludgeoned to death (l. 1163) or slain (l. 1165). The English text, significantly, reduces the gory personal details associated

---

* When the priest Moyses explains the meaning of the beasts in the palace garden, he is seen to remind Queen Felice of her apparent prior knowledge of the story of the lovers' elopement (ll. 3043–58). The narrator has not previously made the audience aware that the queen knows of the story.

with these acts,* seeming more content to portray William as a virtuous knight fighting a just war rather than being some bloodthirsty monster.

The English text also seems to redact some of the more intimate passages of its French source; while it retains the absorbing passages on the pains of love felt by William (ll. 656–85) and by Melior (ll. 433–537), it loses the French source's more eroticised delivery. In *William*, while we suffer the hero's anguish as he dreams of Melior, nowhere do we encounter the more overt physical passion so prevalent in the French:

> Puis li baisoit, ci li ert vis,
> Et bouche et nés et iex et vis;
> Et il li tot si faitement,
> Com sel tenist apertement
> Tot nu a nu entre sa brace,
> Li rebaisoit la soie face,
> Son col le blanc et sa poitrine.
> Sauve l'onor a la meschine,
> Souvent embrace l'orillier
> Quant Melior cuide baisier . . .

(Then it seemed to him that he was kissing her mouth, nose, eyes and face; and indeed did all of this as if he held her openly, both all naked, in his arms; again he kissed her face, her white neck and her breast. [But] he saves the honour of that noble maiden; often he embraces his pillow when he believes he is kissing Melior . . .)

Guillaume de Palerne, ll. 1145–54

The answer to these sensitivities appears to lie ultimately in the English and French narrators' fundamental links to their scribes, an identity that both texts confirm at the end of their narratives when each laud their patrons. If we did not know at the beginning that the English narrator is

---

* There are three significant references to William's personal acts of violence (ll. 3441–5; 3609; 3863–6), but, although we may see bodies cleaved, the text redacts the more brutal descriptions of bodily organs being severed or gored. This may also reflect the sensitivities of the scribe to the brutal death of his patron's father (see Historical Introduction).

in fact a poet-scribe who is placing the text before his audience, by the end we are conscious not only of this but that he is also following his patron's instructions by writing it down and then presenting it. As both English and French narrators make clear, they are also carrying out their duties with the express purpose of conveying a story to a broader audience by writing it in a tongue less difficult to access than that of their source. More, in the case of the English redaction, this process also involves not only writing the story in English but in delivering it in a completely different way; if *Guillaume* was written in tail-rhyming French couplets, *William* is written in a distinctive English style: non-rhyming alliterative long line.

In editing the text, transcribing it in a different poetic style and then presenting the text to a non-French speaking audience, we can begin to understand this narrator-scribe in a different way, attaching to him a character unknown at the beginning of the romance. Despite what he says, we learn that the English narrator, a certain "William" (l. 5521), is not in fact relating his story truly from memory but instead is telling it with a distinct agenda – one based on the express instructions of a patron and one which, as we have seen, varies in delivery according to a variety of sensitivities. By mentioning Humphrey de Bohun twice in his narrative (ll. 161–9; 5527–40), he is also telling us that his message is one not just passed on by a patron alone but by a lord who is none other than the Hereditary Constable of England; he has the medieval equivalent of "state approval".

While we cannot be certain how the English narrator originally opened his poem, what is clear throughout the narrative is that he continually attests that he speaks the truth or truthfully relates what he knows. We also witness frequent praise to God, Christ and Mary, irrespective of whether these words are uttered by the characters themselves or by himself on their behalf. Even if such interjections have been interpreted by some as "pious formulae" used by the scribe to fill metrical gaps, it also seems likely, as Roger Dalrymple has argued, that they are nonetheless used with deliberate skill to suit and engender the narrative themes.[8] Throughout, phrases such as "for Crist þat þe made" (by Christ who made you) (l. 987), "bi grete God þat gart me be fourmed" (by great God that granted me to be born/created) (l. 2082), and "bi God, þat me gaf þe gost and þe soule" (by God who gave me the Holy Spirit and my soul) (l. 3386), enforce a profound and benign religious force in control of the characters and their world which is much more prevalent than in the French source.[9] Similarly, God's providence is evident in the characters' own dialogue when in their darkest moments, such as when William wonders where he and Melior will find food (ll. 1801–5), or when considering the motivations of the Werewolf (ll. 1869–75).

But these references are more than formulaic; instead they offer a supportive context to the more substantial broader message of the romance as seemingly intended by the narrator's patron. We know that Humphrey de Bohun was not only deeply religious but also an Augustinian; St Augustine's view was that God could not be loved unless he loves us already[10] – we must strive to be perfect. Augustine accepted that man, as a finite being, has profound limitations in himself[11] and that Original Sin made it impossible for peace to be sustained by an inherent goodliness of spirit in man; with their place on this earth a gift of divine judgement, rulers had a duty to safeguard the property of all and to prevent war. Being a ruler, in fact, was a potential remedy for man's sin[12] and, in order to achieve this aim, kingship must be conducted justly and in a way that brings pleasure to God. It is in this light that *William and the Werewolf* becomes more manifest in its intention and meaning. Not only are we asked to contemplate the human condition through the impact of animal disguise, the otherness of exile and the distancing from God, we are also asked specifically to reflect upon government and society and what makes a good king in God's name.

In this context, the advice given by the Cowherd to William (ll. 328–44), and the guidance on lordship to Melior (ll. 5115–35), Florence (ll. 5205–8) and Alisaundrine (ll. 5156–60), all highlight the need for God to be able to see leadership being conducted well and to the benefit of the poor. Similarly, in their forgiveness of Braundine (ll. 4416–20), Gloriande and Acelone (ll. 4797–4804), both William and Alphonse reveal by their actions – and by taking advice from their counsellors – that they are seeking to please God rather than mete out revenge. War too must be just; in his redaction of the graphic horrors of war so beloved of the *Guillaume* narrator, the English narrator highlights that a much broader picture – that of righteous cause – is what matters;[13] we are frequently reminded of the "wrongness" of the wars fought against Rome (ll. 1070; 1108; 1128; 1172–8) and Palermo (ll. 3340; 3921; 3995–7). And when

William dreams of Melior, his dreams reflect a purity of love rather than the more lustful eroticisation of the French source; too close for comfort, perhaps, for Augustinian taste. Even Melior's agency can be seen as part of this message; in eloping and then marrying through the purity of love rather than the forced arrangement of a dynastic marriage, she succumbs to the will of God rather than the coercion of two emperors.* Even her elopement itself takes on a new, broader meaning in the English telling; travelling in their own clothes yet sewn within bear skins, any suggestion of carnal activity is denied, irrespective of whether in contemporary society they are deemed to be married.† Love is pure not forced; as Alphonse says to his father (ll. 4596–7), "foolishly you have worked to implore someone to wed who would not assent" ("folili ȝe wrouȝten to wilne after wedlok þat wold nouȝt asente"). While the sentiment is expressed in both the French and English redactions, it is in the broader message of the English text that the dynastic obsession of kings seems depicted as aggressively coercive rather than something that should be facilitated by the free will of both marital parties.

Whether directly (through the text's own modifications) or indirectly (by moulding the source to an Augustinian message), the English narrator-scribe seems to prefer us to dwell on higher matters than pure earthly existence; his characters' actions do their best to atone for Original Sin and reveal a strong desire for God to love us. In such a way, the text's constant references to "truth" and veracity in the telling also come to morph into the higher message: the narrator is telling us "the truth" because he wants us to be sure of his "truth". Nor is the story's seemingly endless tying up of narrative loose ends entirely trivial; in showing how each and every king is there by right, shaped by the advice of their wives and ultimately approved by William, the narrator is rebuilding the world in the eyes of God under the good overlordship of William himself. It is in this light that we must reflect on what is perhaps the English redaction's most haunting and potentially revolutionary lines, delivered in a

---

* In both the French (ll. 3592–3610) and English (ll. 2006–17) redactions, Alisaundrine asserts that Melior elopes because she has heard that Greek emperors lock up their wives in a tower, living lives of misery, a fact that Sconduto (p. 104) suggests also alludes to Chrétien der Troyes' *Cliges*.

† See Historical Introduction for perceptions of marriage in medieval society.

manner completely different to those of its source. When William and Melior learn of the death of the emperor, the narrator tells us:

> Naþeles Meliors and he made moche sorwe
> For þemperour was forþ fare faire to Crist.
> Sone þei cauȝt cumfort, for þis þei knewe boþe,
> Þat deþ wold come to alle þat Crist hade fourmed,
> To emperours and erles, to eche þat lif hadde

> (Nonetheless, he and Melior both made much sorrow
> That the emperor was faring forth now fairly to Christ.
> But they were quickly comforted for this they both clearly knew –
> That death comes to all whom Christ has formed,
> To emperors and to earls, to everyone who has lived.)

(ll. 5265–9)

Death, says the narrator in dramatic fashion, is the great leveller and no recogniser of status or wealth. In saying as much, he reminds his audience that the pursuit of truth and of beauty, in order to please God, is the true way to redemption; in the end we all return to earth and dust.

Just as Humphrey de Bohun asked in his own will, so the narrator repeats also, that we pray for his soul so he can rest in eternal peace; even Humphrey, despite his power on earth, was afraid of God's judgement. Good lordship and justice are the essential messages of the narrator to his audience of English folk; if indeed the narrator tells us at the beginning that this story needs to be told for the good of all so that the wicked will not thrive, he goes on to reveal how good government is fundamental to legitimate and effective statehood. In his telling, God is not pleased by oppression, by wickedness, lies and deceit; kings and emperors must always act to please Him so that all humanity can live in harmony. But in telling this story anew, in a different age with different moral codes, does our narrator still exist in our own mind, in a world so many centuries from Humphrey de Bohun and his Augustinian poet-scribe William? Like William, your translator – your redactor – has drawn from all his knowledge to bring this ancient story once more to life to the best of his abilities; he himself would have done better if his wit had served him so. While the world has moved on since the turbulent days of the fourteenth century, some things remain the same. Pandemics and pathogens, if not plagues, still abound; wars still ravage this world and debase mankind; leaders still grasp at power and cling to it by lies and duplicity and the promotion of bad laws, bigotry and prejudice. If we cannot quite envisage the scribe or his patron in our minds, we can still hear their words and understand their relevance. *William and the Werewolf*, Humphrey de Bohun and his narrator-scribe William still call out to us from those far-off days, holding up a mirror to the vanity, greed and degeneracy of those today who really should know better.

APPENDIX 2: The Old French text of *Guillaume de Palerne*

The text below shows the Old French text of *Guillaume de Palerne* that scholars accept reflects the missing content of the Middle English romance, albeit written in tail-rhyme form rather than the alliterative long line of *William and the Werewolf*. The text is transcribed from Henri Michelant's 1876 redaction from the manuscript in the Bibliothèque de l'Arsenal in Paris, alongside which I offer my (unrhymed) parallel translation. This translation thus forms the basis of my creative work for the missing sections of the Middle English romance. All mistakes in the translation are my own; as Scribe William might have said, I had not the wit to make it better.

The two passages of Old French, which I have named A and B, are denoted by lines A 1–186 and B 690–834 in the body of my main text. Their line references correspond with those in Michelant's text.

Passage A: Lines A1–186

Guillaume de Palerne	*William of Palerne*
Nus ne se doit celer ne taire,	No one must keep secret nor be silent
S'il set chose qui doie plaire,	If he knows of something which is able to please
K'il ne le desponde en apert;	But which he does not recount publicly;
Car bien repont son sens et pert	For truly, to his loss, he hides his knowledge

Qui nel despont apertement	When he does not reveal it openly A5
En la presence de la gent.	In the presence of all.
Por ce ne voel mon sens repondre	Hence, I will not keep secret what I know
Que tot li mauvais puissent fondre,	So that all the wicked may founder
Et cil qui me vaurront entendre	And those who may wish to hear me
I puissent sens et bien aprendre;	Might themselves learn well its sense; A10
Car sens celés qui n'est ois	For such unheard wisdom
Est autresi, ce m'est avis,	Is similar, it seems to me,
Com maint tresor enfermé sont,	To much treasure locked away
Qui nului bien ne preu ne font,	Which brings neither profit nor good to anyone
Tant comme il soient si enclos.	As long as it is locked up. A15
Autresi est de sens repos:	Likewise is hidden knowledge:
Por ce ne voel le mien celer,	Therefore I will not conceal mine,
Ançois me plaist a raconter,	And so it pleases me to recount,
Selonc mon sens et mon memoire,	Subject to my knowledge and memory,
Le fait d'une anciene estoire	The details of an ancient story A20
Qui en Puille jadis avint	Which occurred once in Apulia
A un roi qui la terre tint.	To a king who held that land.
Li rois Embrons fu apelés;	The king was called Embrons;
Mult par fu grans sa poestés.	His power was considerable.
Bien tint cm pais sa region	He kept the peace of his lands well A25
Et mult par fu de grant renon.	And was held in great renown.
Moillier avoit gente roine,	His wife, the queen, was gracious,
Gentil dame de franche orine	A high-born woman of noble birth
Et fille au riche empereor	And the daughter of a powerful emperor
Qui de Gresse tenoit l'ounor.	Who held dominion over all of Greece. A30
Felise avoit a non la dame;	The name of this queen was Felise;
Mult fu amée en son roiame.	She was well-loved throughout her realm.

N'avoient c'un tot seul enfent,	Between them they had but one child,
Petit tousel ne gaires grant.	A small lad, not yet full grown.
De quatre ans ert li damoisiax	This young gentleman, just four years old, A35
Qui a merveilles estoit biax.	Was exceedingly handsome.
Guillaumes ot l'enfes a non;	The name of this child was William;
Mais la roine tout par non	But the queen above all
L'ot a deus dames commandé	Had commended him to the care of two women
Qu'ele amena de son regné.	Whom she had brought from her land. A40
Gloriande est l'une noumee,	One was called Gloriande,
Acelone est l'autre apelee.	The other, Acelone.
Celes le commande a garder	She ordered them to watch over,
A enseignier et doctriner,	Instruct and educate him,
Moustre et enseignier la loi,	And to explain and teach him the law, A45
Comme on doit faire fil a roi.	As is befitting for the son of a king.
En eles s'est asseuree,	She trusted these women intently
Mais traie est et euganee	But she was tricked and betrayed
Et deceue laidement:	And ignominiously deceived:
Mult porrés bien oir comment.	Very soon indeed, you will hear how. A50
Li rois Embrons un frere avoit	King Embrons had a brother
A cui li regnes escaoit,	To whom the kingdom would fall;
Et cil douna tant et promist	This brother greatly courted, promised,
Et tant porchaça et tant fist	Bribed and did so much
As gardes qui l'enfant gardoient,	For those women who guarded the child A55
Qui dit li ont qu'il l'ocirroient	That they said that they would kill him
Et le roi meisme ensement.	And the aforesaid king also.
Ja ont porquis l'enherbement	Truly, they purchased a poison
Don't il andoi mort recevront,	From which both would die
Se Diex nel fait, li rois del mont.	If God, the king of the world, did not intervene. A60

En Palerne orent sejorné	They had been living in Palermo
Un mois entier, en la cité,	An entire month in that city,
Entre le roi et la roine.	In the king and the queen's company.
Desous le maistre tor marbrine	Under its marble keep
Ot un vergier merveilles gent,	Was a most beautiful orchard, A65
Tot clos de mur et de cyment;	Enclosed all round with a mortared wall;
S'i ot mainte sauvage beste.	Within this were many wild animals.*
Un jor par une haute feste	One day, during a high festival,
I vint esbanoier li rois.	The king came there to enjoy himself.
Si chevalier et si borjois	His knights, his chief householders A70
Et maint baron i sont venu;	And many noblemen had come;
La roine meisme i fu.	The queen herself was there.
Celes qui l'enfant ont en garde,	Those who are in charge of the child –
Cui male flambe et maus fus arde,	Whom evil inflames and the wicked fire burns
Mais por ce ne le font noient,	But who have yet to harm him – A75
L'ont mené avoec l'autre gent;	Have brought him along with others;
Que s'el seussent la dolour	If only they had known the suffering
Qui de l'enfant avint le jour . . .	Which that day would befall on account of that child . . . †
[LACUNA]	[LACUNA]
Parl le vergier li rois ombroie	In the orchard, the king seeks the shade
Et la roine a mult grant joie;	And the queen is extremely happy; A80
Mais ne sevent com lor grans dex	But they are ignorant of the great sorrow
Lor est presens devant lor ex.	Which will unfold before their eyes.
L'enfes florretes va cuellant:	The child goes picking flowers,
De l'une a l'autre va jouant.	Playfully going from one to another.
A tant esgardent la ramee:	At that moment, they look at the bushes: A85

* The suggestion is that this was a walled garden in the manner of a private park where the animals were free to roam but were not fundamentally dangerous to humans.
† A brief lacuna occurs in the French text at this point (Sconduto, *Guillaume*, p. 13). Skeat makes no reference to this while also transposing lines 75–6.

Saut uns grans leus, goule baee.	A great wolf springs out, mouth wide open.
Afondant vient comme tempeste;	He comes rushing forth like a tempest;
Tuit se destornent por la beste:	Everyone turns away because of that beast.
Devant le roi demainement	Right in front of the king himself
Son fil travers sa goule prent.	The wolf takes his son crosswise in his mouth. A90
A tant s'en va, mais la criee	Immediately, he goes off, but the cry
Fu après lui mult tost levee.	Was raised very soon after him.
Lieve li dels, lieve li cris	So rises the grief, so rise the cries
Del fil le roi qui est trais.	For the son of the king who is taken away.
La roine souvent s'escrie:	The queen cries out repeatedly: A95
"Aidiés, aidiés, Saint Marie!	"Help, help, Holy Mary!
Maisnle au roi, que faites vous?	My lord's retinue, what are you doing?
Je me morrai, s'il nest rescous."	I will kill myself if he is not rescued!"
Li rois demande ses chevax	The king calls for his horse
Et fait monter tous ses vassax:	And orders all his vassals mount: A100
Toute la ville s'i esmuet;	All the city is in uproar;
Cascuns I keurt plus tost qu'il puet.	Each of them rushes there as fast as they could.
Li rois le siut a esperon.	The king pursues the wolf at the spur.
Le gart açaignent environ;	The orchard is enclosed all round
Mais li leus en est fors saillis;	But the wolf has leapt well away; A105
A la campaigne s'estoit mis.	He has escaped to the countryside.
L'enfes sovent s'escrie et brait:	The child often cries out and shrieks:
Li rois l'entent qui après vait,	The king, following him, hears him,
Garde, sel voit monter un mont;	He watches and sees them ascend a mountain;
De tost aler sa gent semont:	He summons his men to go faster: A110
Donques se paresforcent tuit.	At which all gain strength.
Li leus a tout l'enfant s'enfuit.	But the wolf flees with the boy.
Fuit s'en li leus et cil après	The wolf flees and the others follow after
Qui de l'ataindre sont engrès;	Who are eager to catch it;
De si au Far le vont chaçant:	They chase it to the Straits of Messina: A115

Il saut en l'eve a tout l'enfant.	It leaps into the water with the child.
Le Far trespasse, perdu l'ont	It crosses the Straits and they are lost
Li rois et cil qui o lui sont.	To the king and those who are with him.
Ensi s'en va en tel maniere	And so in this way it flees,
A tout l'enfant la beste fiere.	That fierce beast with the child. A120
Li rois arriere s'en retorne.	The king halts and turns back,
Mult a la cuer et triste et morne	Greatly sad and mournful at heart
De son enfant qu'a si perdu;	For his son who has been lost;
A la cité sont revenu.	They returned to the city.
La roine maine tel duel,	The queen is so mournful, A125
Morte voudroit estre son vuel;	Her wish would be to be dead;
Pleure sovent et crie et brait,	Often she laments, cries and wails,
A la beste son fil retrait:	And recounts of her son taken by that beast:
"Fix, dous amis," fait la roine,	"Son, sweet love," says the queen,
"Tendre bouche, coulor rosine,	"You of tender rose-coloured mouth, A130
Chose devine, espiritex,	Divine, heavenly thing,
Qui cuidast que beste ne leus	Who would believe that a beast or wolf
Vos devorast? Dix, quel eur!	Would devour you? Lord God, what fortune!
Lasse, por coi vif tant ne dur?	Alas! Why do I live or endure so much?
Fix, ou sont ore ti bel oiel,	Son, where now are your beautiful eyes, A135
Li bel, li simple, sans orğuel,	So beautiful, so innocent, without arrogance;
Tes frons li gens, et ti bel crin	Your handsome forehead, and your fair hair
Qui tuit sembloient fait d'or fin,	Which all seemed made of fine gold;
Ta tandre face et tes clers vis?	Your tender expression and your shining face?
Ha! cuers, por coi ne me partis?	Oh my heart! Why do you not leave me? – A140
Qu'est devenue ta biautés	What will become of your beauty?
Et tes gens cors et ta clartés;	Your gracious body and your brightness;

Tes nés, ta bouche et tes mentons	Your nose, your mouth and your chin
Et ta figure et ta façons,	And your form and your appearance,
Et li bel brac et les mains blanches	Your lovely arms and white hands A145
Et tes rains beles et tes hanches,	And your pleasing waist[1] and your hips,
Tes beles jambes et ti pié?	Your beautiful legs and your feet?
Lasse, quel duel et quel pechié!	Alas, what sorrow, what misery!
Ja devoies tu estre fais	Surely you were intended to be made
Por devises et por souhais;	For sharing and for pleasure;[2] A150
Or es a leu garoul peuture,	Now you are nourishment for a werewolf,*
Li miens enfes; quele aventure!	My dear child; what [mis]fortune![†]
Mais je ne cuit, por nule chose	But I do not believe for any reason
Beste sauvage soit si ose	That a savage beast would be so rash
Que ton gent cors ost adamer,	As to dare to harm your gentle body, A155
Plaier, sanc fair ne navrer;	To injure, draw its blood, nor wound it;
Ne cuit que ja Dame Dieu place	I do not believe it would please Lord God
Ne que tel cruauté en face."	Nor that He would enable such cruelty to happen."
Ensi la dame se demente	Thus the lady is so tormented
Ensi por son fil se gaimente	And in this way she laments for her son, A160
Ensi le ploure, ensi le plaint.	Weeps for him and bewails his fate.
Mais tant la castoie et constraint	But she is so greatly reproved and restrained
Li rois, que tout laissier li fait	By the king such that the great sadness
La dolor qu'ele maine et fait.	She is feeling soon recedes.
Ensi la dame se rapaie;	In this way the lady is placated; A165

---

* Until this point, the werewolf has been described either as a beast or a wolf; now seen as an outcast, he is a werewolf or "garoul".

† The text does not preface "aventure" with "male", to give "what misfortune", but the context is clear.

Mais or est drois que vos retraie
Del leu qui o l'enfant s'enfuit.

But now it is right that I tell you
About the wolf which had fled with the child.

Tant l'a porté et jor et nuit
Et tante terre trespassee
Que près de Roume, en la contree,
En une grant forest s'arreste
Ou ot mainte sauvage beste.
La se repose huit jors entiers.
L'enfant de quanques fu mestiers
Li a porquis la beste franche:

He carried him far, day and night,
And crossed much land
Until, in the countryside
near to Rome   A170
He stops in a great forest
In which are many savage beasts.
He rests here for eight whole days.
Whatsoever the child required
The beast provided for him
freely: A175

Onques de rien n'ot mesestance.
En terre a une fosse faite
Et dedans herbe mise et traite
Et la feuchiere et la lihue
Que par dedans a espandeu.
La nuit le couche joste soi
Li leus garous le fil le roi,
L'acole de ses. iiii. piés;
Si est de lui aprivoisiés
Li fix le roi que tost li plaist

The child wanted for nothing.
It dug a den in the earth
And in it placed grass,
Bracken and rushes
Which it spread about inside.   A180
At night, it lies just by him;
The werewolf embraces the king's son
With his four paws;
In this way, the king's son
Comes to trust him and is pleased
by everything   A185

Ce que la beste de lui fait.

Which the beast does for him.

Passage B: Lines B690–837

"Fille, Guillaumes a a non

"My daughter, William is the
name   B690

Li damoisiax," fait l'emperere.
"Je cuit par le baron saint Pere
Qu'il est de mult tres hautes gens,

Of the young man," says the emperor.
"I believe by the most Holy Father
That he is of very noble birth,

Car mult par est et biax et gens,	For he is extremely fair and handsome,
De cors, de vis et de faiture;	In body, in face and in features; B695
Encor orrons par aventure	We may yet hear, perhaps,
De quex gens est estrais et nés.	Who bore him and from whom he is descended.
Ma douce fille, or retenés	My sweet daughter, now look after
L'enfant que je vos amain ci".	This child whom I bring to you here."
"Ce soit la vostre grant merci,"	"Great thanks belong to you for this," B700
Dist Meliors, "biau sire chiers;	Said Melior, "my own dear father;
Je le retieng mult volentiers".	I will nurture him most gladly."
Puis prent l'enfant et si l'enmaine	Then she takes the child and leads him
En la soie chambre demaine;	Into her private chamber;
Uns dras li a fait aporter,	She has robes brought for him, B705
Sel fait vestir et conreer.	And has him clothed and provided for.
Quant des dras fu apareilliés	When he was dressed in the clothes
Et a sa guise fu chauciés,	And provided with shoes to his liking,
Or fu si gens et si trés biax	Now so noble, so handsome
Et si apers li damoisiax	And so fine was the boy B710
C'on ne recovrast son pareil	That one could not find his equal
Desos la clarté du soleil	Anywhere under the bright sun
De sa biauté, de sa semblance.	To match his beauty and appearance.
Et Meliors qui tant ert france	And Meliors, who is so noble,
Li a fait par un sien sergant	Caused one of her servants B715
Aporter le mangier devant;	To bring food before him;
Et cil manga qui fain avoit.	And this he ate because he was hungry.
Or, revient auques a son droit:	Now, to return for a while to his duty;
Por çou se il est fix de roi,	Because, if he is the son of a king,
N'est desonors, si com je croi,	It is no dishonour, I believe, B720
S'il sert a cort d'empereor,	If he serves at the emperor's court,
Et pucele de tel valor	And a maiden of such merit
Com Meliors estoit la bele.	As the beautiful Meliors.
Ensi remest o la pucele	Thus William remained with the maiden,

Guillaumes, com poés oir.	As you can hear. B725
Mult se paine de li servir	He makes every effort to serve her
Et des autres tous ensement;	And everyone else in a similar way;
Mult s'i acointe belement,	He learns to do this most fittingly,
Si com li hom qui n'estoit mie	Just like a man who has never been
Norris en cort n'entre maisnie;	Raised at court nor amongst the household, B730
Mais auques se prueve nature,	But Nature reveals him somewhat.
Et il sor tote creature	And he, above every creature,
S'entente et tot son cuer velt metre	Pays close attention and wants to put his whole heart
A quanque se doit entremetre	Into whatever must be undertaken
Nus damoisiax de nul service	As any young man in any service B735
A cort si haute ne si rice.	At so noble nor so rich a court.
Tant i a l'enfes son cuer mis	The child put his heart into so much there
Et tant entendu et apris	And was so attentive and cultured
Qu'ançois que fust passés li ans	That before the year was out
Fu il si prex et si sachans	He was so expert and so skilled B740
Qu'il n'est hon qui le puist reprendre,	That not one man could fault him,
Tant i sache garder n'entendre,	No matter how closely he might watch or pay attention
De riens nule que veoir sace,	To anything he might see,
Que riens mesprenge ne mesface.	Because William neither behaved badly nor made a mistake.
Oi avés pieça retraire	You have heard told long ago B745
Que li oisiax de gentil aire	That the bird of noble breed
S'afaite meisme a par lui	Educates even himself
Tot sans chastiement d'autrui.	Completely without rebuke from another.
Comme vos ci oir poés,	Thus, as you too may hear,
S'est si Guillaumes doctrinés.	William indeed so taught himself. B750
Ensi Guillaumes est a cort;	Thus, William is at court;
A tos desert que on l'ounort,	By everything meritorious in which people honour him,

Ne fait riens qui doie desplaire;

Nothing he does is able to displease;

Mult par est frans et
debounaire,

He is most gracious and full of
noble sentiment,

Scrviçables, cortois et prous,

Willing, courteous and wise, B755

Et mult se fait amer a tous,

And makes himself much loved by
everyone,

Et larges de quanqu'avoir puet;

And is generous as much as he is able;

Et sachiés bien, pas ne l'estuet

And, know this well, it was not necessary

A chastoier de ses paroles

To chastise him for his words

Qu'eles soient laides ne foles,

Which were neither rude nor
foolish, B760

Mais asises et delitables.

But charming and delightful.

Si set plus d'eschès et de tables,

Indeed, he knew more about chess
and draughts,

D'oisiax, de bois, de chacerie

Of falconry, woodland and the hunt

Que nus qui soit en Lombardie;

Than anyone in Lombardy;

N'en toute la terre de Rome

Nor is there anyone in all
Rome's land, B765

N'i a vallet, fil a haut home

Whether servant, the son of a rich man

N'a riche prince natural,

Or wealthy prince by birth who,

Quant Guillaumes siet a cheval,

When William sits on horseback,

L'escu au col, el poing la lance,

His shield at his shoulder, his lance
in his hand,

Tant par soit de fiere semblance,

Seems of such fierce resemblance, B770

Si gens ne si amanevis.

So noble nor so prepared for battle.

Ne sai que plus vos un devis,

I know not of more I can mention to you;

Que tuit semblent a lui vilain

Except that all seemed base, compared
to him,

Et li Lombart et li Romain;

Whether Lombard or Roman;

Bien samble a tos estre lor sire.

He seemed so well to be the
lord of them all. B775

En tot la regne n'en l'empire

In neither the whole kingdom nor
the empire

N'i a un seul, ne bas ne haut . . .

There was no one, whether base or
noble . . .

[LACUNA]

A cui il soit, du ce me vant,

Des biens de lui que le gens
   conte;

Chascuns en fabloie et raconte

Tous li pueples communement;

Et l'empereres ensement

Li porte honor, aime et tient chier,

Comme le fil de sa moillier.

Et quant il va en esbanoi,

Toudis maine Guillaume o soi,

En grant afaire ou en besoing

Tos jors i va, soit près ou loing;

Et cil del regne d'environ,

Li grant signor et li baron,

Por l'amor a l'empereor

L'aiment et portent grant honor,

Et plus encor por sa franchise

Dont chascuns tant le loe et
   prise.

Et ke diroie des puchieles,

Des dames et des damoisieles?

Certes, et se Diex me doinst joie,

Ne cuit que nule qui le voie

Ne qui son los oie retraire,

Tant par i soit de haut afaire,

Bele, cortoise, ne prisie,

N'estraite de haute lignie,

Ne sage, orgeilleuse, ne cointe

Qui ne vausist estre s'acointe.

[LACUNA]

Who has – I boast of this –

Such virtues of which other people speak;

Everyone speaks and tells
   stories of them,   B780

All the people of the community.

And the emperor, similarly,

Honours, loves and holds him dearly,

As if he were the son of his own wife.

And when he goes off to amuse
   himself   B785

Always he takes William with him,

On great business or more functional
   errands;

Whether near or far, he always goes along.

And those of the kingdom round about,

Its great lords and barons,   B790

For their love of the emperor,

Love and honour him

And even more so for his magnanimity

For which everyone lauds and esteems
   him.

And what can I say of
   the maidens,   B795

The noblewomen and young ladies?

Certainly, and may God grant me joy,

I do not believe that any who see him,

Nor who hear related any praise of him,

No matter her status,   B800

However beautiful, refined, or esteemed,

However noble by birth,

However wise, proud or knowledgeable,

Did not want to be his love!

Mult a boin los par la contree;	He receives much praise
	throughout the country; B805
Par tot en va sa renoumee.	His renown spreads everywhere.
Si fu a cort trois ans tos plains	So William was at court three whole years
Guillaumes entre les Romains,	Amongst the Romans,
Com vos dire m'avés oi.	As you have heard me say.
Forment crut et bien embarni	He grew exceedingly noble B810
Et devint gens li damoisiax,	And the young man became gracious,
Et fors et aformés et biax.	Strong, well-formed and handsome.
De la chambre est merveilles bien;	He is wonderful in the chamber;
Les puceles sor tote rien,	Above everything, the maidens –
Por sa franchise et sa valor	For his generosity and virtue – B815
Li portent mult trés grant honor.	Accord him much great honour.
Quant Mellors la debonaire	When the gentle Meliors
Ot del vallet le los retraire	Hears praise told of the squire
Et les grans biens qui en lui sont,	And the great qualities he possesses,
Et voit qu'il n'a si bel el mont	And she sees that there is none so fair in the world, B820
Ne damoisel de sa valor,	No youth of such virtue,
Fil de roi ne d'empereor,	Whether king's son or emperor's,
Ne de si boine renoumee,	Nor any of such fine repute,
Trestot son cuer et sa pensee	Soon her heart and her thoughts
Tot maintenant vers lui atorne.	All immediately turn towards him. B825
Or est si trés pensive et morne	Now she becomes very pensive and sorrowful
Qu'ele n'entent a autre chose.	Such that she cannot think of anything else.
Son cuer reprent et blasme et chose	She berates, blames and scolds her heart
Et dist souvent: "Cuers, que es tu?	And frequently says, "My heart, what has become of you?
Qu'as tu esgardé ne veu?	What have you witnessed or seen? B830

Que t'ont mi oel monstré ne fait,   What have my eyes done or shown
           to you,

Qui m'as embatue en cest   That have placed me so on trial,
  plait,

Que je ne sai que puisse   Such that I do not know what ails me
  avoir

Ne quel error me fait doloir   Nor what uncertainties make me
           grieve

Ne plaindre plus que je   And lament more than I am
  ne suel?   prone to do?   B835

Diex! quex maus est dont   Lord God! What malady gives
  tant me duel,   me so much grief,

Qui si me fait estendillier   That makes me writhe about so
  [. . .]?"   much [. . .]?"

NOTES

Historical Introduction

1 The incomplete poem *Wynnere and Wastoure* is seen as the earliest Revival poem due to its references to the Statute of Treasons of 1352 (Turville-Petre: *The Alliterative Revival*, p. 1), although *William and the Werewolf,* with its references to its patron Humphrey de Bohun, 6th Earl of Hereford (earl from 1336 to 1361), indicates a similar time frame. The notion of an alliterative "revival" has been contested by others such as Erik Weiskott, who have argued for a continuous development of the alliterative technique from the earliest times to an eventual demise in the sixteenth century.

2 Madden tells us in his introduction, reprinted in Skeat, *William of Palerne* (pp. vii–ix), that the "first notice of the poem in its English dress" was as part of the "Rowleian controversy", a debate concerning works by Thomas Chatterton that were attributed by some to his medieval fictional creation, Thomas Rowley.

3 To fill the gaps in the Middle English text, Skeat's EETS edition of *William of Palerne,* published in 1867, drew originally from the Old French prose edition of *Guillaume de Palerne* printed by N. Bonfons (Skeat, EETS, p. 219), a work itself derived from versions of the poem produced subsequent to the poetic original. An edition of the only extant example of the poetic original was finally prepared by Henri Michelant on behalf of La Société des Anciens Textes Français

in 1876; scholars were then able to see more clearly the original text for the first time. Michelant's work was subsequently incorporated into later editions of Skeat's EETS volume.

4 In Marie's twelfth-century story of *Bisclavret* – The Werewolf – a treacherous wife discovers her husband is a werewolf by night and, on finding out his secret, steals his clothes from the place where he hides them when he transitions, compelling him to roam the world forever as a wolf. The husband is eventually returned to his human status when – as in *William and the Werewolf* – he is recognised by his noble behaviour as being human and, with his clothes returned, becomes a man once more.

5 For a discussion of werewolves in social history, see Nicole Jacques-Lefevre's chapter in Edwards (ed.), *Werewolves, Witches and Wandering Spirits*, pp. 181–97. A general history of werewolves and their appearance in mythology and literature can be found in Adam Douglas's work, *The Beast Within: A History of the Werewolf*; while *On Werewolves*, an introductory section to Madden's own text, also incorporates a contribution to the history.

6 Holmes, *The Estates of the Higher Nobility in Fourteenth-Century England*, p. 20. The reader is referred in particular to Chapter 1 in Holmes, where the complexity of estate management and growth through inheritance is discussed in detail.

7 The death of Humphrey's father was particularly gruesome, having been stabbed from below by a spear thrust into his bowels (R. Ward, "Sanitizing Violence in 'William of Palerne'", p. 488).

8 The need for kings to elect earls in their own mould to ensure loyalty and exert power was fundamental to governance in medieval England. The circumstances surrounding the death of Edward II, the power of Roger Mortimer, and the vulnerability and brutal response of a young Edward III to his influence, are discussed in detail in Given-Wilson: *The English Nobility in the Late Middle Ages*, Chapter 1, and Underhill: *For Her Good Estate, The Life of Elizabeth de Burgh, Lady of Clare*, Chapter 1.

9 Davies, *Conquest, Co-Existence and Change: Wales, 1063–1515*, p. 397. In his description of Humphrey, Davies may be drawing on his 1978 text, *Lordship and Society in the March of Wales: 1282–1400*.

10 For a summary of these codices and their production together, see Sandler, *Illuminators and Patrons in Fourteenth-Century England*, pp. 1–20.

11 The reader is referred to Melville M. Bigelow, "The Bohun Wills" *The American Historical Review*, Vol. 1, No. 3, April 1896, pp. 414–435 and in particular p. 425.

12 William was ultimately also to predecease Humphrey, although he did father the 7th Earl of Hereford, also called Humphrey, who died in 1373 (Holmes, *The Estates of the Higher Nobility in Fourteenth-Century England*, p. 21). See also Madden, *The Ancient English Romance of William and the Werewolf*, p. v.

13 See R. Ward, "Sanitizing Violence in 'William of Palerne' ".

14 Turville-Petre, *The Alliterative Revival*, p. 41.

15 Salter, *Fourteenth-Century English Poetry*, p. 44.

16 Bunt, *William of Palerne*, p. 19.

17 Bunt, *William of Palerne*, p. 75

18 Bunt, *Localizing William of Palerne*, p. 84.

19 Oakden (*Alliterative Poetry in Middle English – A Survey of the Traditions*, pp. 38-9) dates the original composition to around 1350; the extant redaction has been dated to either 1350–75 or 1360–75 (see Bunt, p. 3), suggesting the extant MS is either contemporary with the original redaction or was produced very shortly afterwards.

20 Pascual, *The Bohun Dynasty*, p. 210.

21 Dillon and St John-Hope, "Inventory of the Goods and Chattels belonging to Thomas, Duke of Gloucester", pp. 280–81.

22 Nichols, *A Collection of all the Wills Known to be Extant, of the Kings and Queens of England*, pp. 44–56.

23 Dennison, *The Stylistic Sources*, pp. 271–2.

24 Sandler, "A Note on the Illuminators of the de Bohun Manuscripts", pp. 366–7.

25 Sandler, *Illuminators and Patrons in Fourteenth-Century England*, p. 18.

26 Holder, *The Friaries of Medieval London*, p. 119.

27 Sandler, "A Note on the Illuminators of the de Bohun Manuscripts", p. 364.

28 Pascual, *The Bohun Dynasty*, p. 212. Humphrey died on 15 October 1361.

29 Sandler, *Illuminators and Patrons in Fourteenth-Century England*, p. 9.

30 Pascual, "The Heraldry of the de Bohun Earls", pp. 156–7.

31 Pascual, *The Bohun Dynasty*, p. 150.

32 Pascual, *The Bohun Dynasty*, p. 215.

33 Warner, "Langland and the Problem of 'William of Palerne'", p. 399.

34 Turville-Petre, "Humphrey de Bohun and 'William of Palerne'", p. 252.

35 Oakden, *Alliterative Poetry in Middle English – A Survey of the Traditions*, pp. 39–40.

36 Turville-Petre, *The Alliterative Revival*, p. 41.

37 Barron, *English Medieval Romance*, p. 197.

38 Warner, *The Myth of Piers Plowman*, p. 22.

39 Warner, *The Myth of Piers Plowman*, pp. 26–7.

40 For a discussion of the appeal of the romance in Europe, and also in subsequent editions in English, see Bunt, *William of Palerne*, pp. 20–29.

41 Diamond, "Loving Beasts", p. 142.

42 McDonald, *A Polemical Introduction*, p. 1.

43 Neal, *The Masculine Self in Late Medieval England*, pp. 192-3.

44 Dickson, *Verbal and Visual Disguise*, p. 41.

45 Diamond, "Loving Beasts", p. 150.

46 Diamond, "Loving Beasts", p. 151.

47 Dalrymple, *Language and Piety*, p. 64. See also Appendix 1.

48 Fernyhough (ed.), *Others*, p. ix.

49 See Neal, *The Masculine Self in Late Medieval England*, p. 13.

The Romance of William and the Werewolf

1 Lines 1–2 of the Middle English text are similar to lines 185–6 of the French introduction. I have followed Skeat in allowing both couplets to stand, although the reader might wish to see this as a point of elision between the two texts.

2 The MS reads, "For spakly speke it couþe þo and spedeliche towawe", which reads as "for it quickly learned to speak and move around speedily"; I have changed the beginning of the line to give it a more meaningful reading in its context.

3 The text states that the boy rushed out of the bushes ("and buskede him out of þe buschys þat were blowed grene"), although l. 25 later says he leaves the cave/barrow; I have therefore altered the

meaning of l. 21 to suggest the attractiveness of the bushes is what lures him from the cave.

4 The MS reads "nigramauncy"; Skeat glosses this as necromancy, although Bunt's gloss of black magic seems more appropriate in this context.

5 Both Skeat and Bunt suggest that the original manuscript is corrupted at this point since the princess's wickedness seems overplayed. *Guillaume* (l. 290) also describes her as "well praised" here, which paints a slightly more balanced picture and enables her redemption, to some degree, at the end of the poem. Bunt (p. 285) concurs with Skeat that the English text omits some key lines here that fundamentally introduce Braundine's son as Braundinis (see note 6, below).

6 In *Guillaume*, ll. 290-4, the French text makes clear that Braundine has a son, Brandin, by the Spanish king. The Middle English text, or at least the extant manuscript, misses these key lines although we later learn her son is called Braundinis (l. 5299).

7 The MS describes a variety of William's friends who live in the forest with him; the lines appear corrupt. In *Guillaume*, Akarin and Christian are two distinctive friends whereas in the English poem, the manuscript is specific in describing "þe Cristen Akarin". In *Guillaume*, a further friend Thomassin the son of Paien (l. 598) is described, which in the English is redacted as "and þe trewe kinnesman, þe payenes sone", which appears to translate clumsily, given the previous line, as "and his true kinsman, the pagan's son". An alternative translation might be "and that true kinsman, Payen's son."

8 ll. 433-442 represent a considerable challenge in translation. As Bunt notes, the English text "emphasises the emotional aspects of [Melior's] love-sickness, whereas in the French its outward symptoms are stressed" (Bunt: *William of Palerne*, p. 288). The requirement for a relatively seamless transition between the French and English texts means that ll 435, 439 and 442 have been subtly adjusted in translation to maintain the narrative flow.

9 The inclusion of a sycamore tree is intriguing. The Woodland Trust (a UK charity dedicated to the preservation of ancient woodlands and a greater understanding of woodland in general) states that

the sycamore may have been introduced by the Romans or appeared in Britain around 1500. The use of the sycamore by the poet (*sikamour*, from *sicamour* in Old French) is unambiguous, which would favour the earlier date. *Guillaume* does not mention the species of tree, suggesting that for the *William*-poet to refer to it means it already existed in England at that time or the French name was known by the poet and anglicised for alliterative purposes. Its use here may also be intended as a pun on sick-amour, a tree to hide the lovesick.

10 Knighthood was a fluid status in the Middle Ages and the term was used to describe men of many different ranks. A bachelor is a knight who served under a banneret, a more senior knight commander with sufficient status to command his own troops with his own banner. In being described as a knight or a bachelor, William is therefore being described more as a novice, or young knight; possibly a squire. This fits with his youthfulness at this stage of the poem.

11 In *Guillaume*, Alisaundrine is not spoken of as a potential threat; Bunt (p. 296) says this line is unique to the English edition. The French poem unravels William's thoughts by means of the hero describing himself by means of a metaphor of a ship lost on the waves. Alisaundrine understands William's predicament, is shown as his potential saviour, and listens to him favourably (*Guillaume*, ll. 1527–1664).

12 A medieval army was typically comprised of three main "battles": the vanguard, middle ward and rear guard; in battle the middle ward would form the central battle, usually to the rear of the army. At Crécy, in 1346, the vanguard, under the Black Prince and the Earl of Warwick, was positioned to the right, the rear guard, under the Earls of Northampton and Suffolk, to the left. Edward III commanded the middle ward to the rear, able to intervene if necessary as the battle progressed.

13 The Greek emperor, as upholder of Christianity in the eastern Mediterranean, is seen as an equal to the Roman emperor himself and his visit of huge significance. Nameless in the Middle English redaction, he is known as Patrichidus in *Guillaume*, possibly in reflection of the religious and political supremacy of his position in Constantinople.

14 In his note to this line, Gerrit Bunt references K. W. Tibbals who, in 1904, argued that in an earlier (lost) version of the story, it may have been the case William and Melior, rather than donning animal skins as described by Alisaundrine, were in fact transformed into wild beasts in the manner of Alphonse's transformation into a werewolf (Bunt, *William of Palerne*, pp. 106 and 302).

15 In *Guillaume*, Alisaundrine also takes the skin of a serpent (l. 3063) from the kitchen; almost certainly this was used to create the robust thongs the poet describes. The serpent skin is missing in the Middle English edition.

16 In *Guillaume* (ll. 3465–3502), the Roman emperor, whom it names as Nathaniax (Nathaniel), is described as being more than eighty years old yet wearing clothes which seem ageless. By comparison, the Middle English text leaves the age and appearance of the emperor to the imagination of the audience; in showing the great age of the emperor, the French text may be emphasising the fragility of his position without a (male) heir.

17 The MS reads *timbired*, or built. The suggestion is that the tower would be like some mighty keep; she would be locked behind stout doors, with hefty timber draw bars to keep out others. Leslie Sconduto, in his note to *Guillaume*, line 3597, cites the end of the poem *Cligès* by Chrétien de Troyes, which "states that royal wives were locked up and guarded because Fenice had deceived her husband Alis".

18 Bunt, in his critical edition (p. 305), points out the emperor's summoning and listening to his counsel is not a feature of the French source, citing also lines 1457–60 above. This may be a particular feature of the English telling, emphasising the importance of advice and good lordship that we see elsewhere in the romance. Counsel is not unique to *William and the Werewolf*, however, and features in numerous romances including the Old French *Chanson de Roland*. For detailed coverage of the topic, see Geraldine Barnes, *Counsel and Strategy in Middle English Romance*.

19 *Guillaume* (ll. 3888–91) explains that Benevento was held by the Pope but that the Emperor of Rome was responsible for justice. It is possible a medieval audience would have been aware of this and would consequently understand William's fear of the city.

20 Licences to produce charcoal were granted by local lords; the process itself not being the peasant's primary occupation. Jean Birrell, "Peasant Craftsmen in the Medieval Forest", tells us of a John Cokeson who, in 1326–7, paid 2s for a licence to burn charcoal in the forest of Inglewood in Cumberland. Birrell has shown that some were also involved in the illegal assart of land (conversion of forest land to arable) in the 1270s and 1280s; their status on the edges of society may have been included by the poet to engender a sense of lawlessness and danger.

21 As with the *Guillaume* poet, the English poet ignores how the two might have sewn the skins together. In *Guillaume*, a soliloquy by William during this passage also gives a greater depth to his understanding of the werewolf's sorry condition when he exclaims: "Je ne sai que ce est de vous / que an nule riens ne fus lous" ("I do not know what you are / But you are in no way a wolf") (*Guillaume*, ll. 4379–80).

22 The MS reads, "þat wittily tauȝt hem þe weis whider þei wende scholde". The intention seems to be that the Werewolf has by his own cunning ("wit") taught the pair to find the routes to Sicily; he is deliberately bringing them to Palermo, where they will be outside the jurisdiction of the Roman emperor (see in particular l. 2834). At the time of *Guillaume* (ca. 1200), Sicily was the centre of the Kingdom of Sicily; by the time of *William* (ca. 1350) the island and much of southern Italy notionally fell under the kingdom, known also as the Kingdom of Naples. Contemporary audiences would not have seen Italy as a unified country but as a peninsula home to various kingdoms and states, as touched upon in ll. 2613–25.

23 The Middle English translator describes the master mariner – the "mest maister" – as a single individual, although in *Guillaume* (ll. 4577–9) there are several. In l. 2736, however, the English translator renders the master mariners plural ("þei" – "they"), which suggests a scribal error in the previous line, which I have, too, rendered plural.

24 The introduction of the boy is unique to the Middle English telling. Descriptions of vessels in English poems of the period often use common names without necessarily meaning the vessel they are describing. For a descriptions of different vessel types in this period

(including cogs, crayers, and dromons) and descriptions of certain nautical shipbuilding terms, see the glossary to Smith, MTA: *King Arthur's Death* pp. 192–201.

25 The poet has returned us to the very garden William was stolen from at the beginning of the romance. A menagerie was kept at Palermo by the Holy Roman Emperor Frederick II (1194–1250), who became King of Sicily in 1198. It is possible that the original poet of *Guillaume* was aware of this (*Guillaume*, ll. 4671–7).

26 Although an alliterative insertion, the laurel tree may have been included here by the author as a metaphor for victory. In *Guillaume* (l. 4899), the pair sleep beside a hazel bush ("Dalés un bus de coudre estoient").

27 The MS reads "So gret wonder walt þe quen of þe worþ bestes". Skeat (p. 316) glosses "walt" as suggesting the enjoyment of a possession wrongfully. The text may therefore be implying that the queen's watching is almost voyeuristic, which may suggest why on l. 2988 the text makes it clear she cannot hear the words spoken by the lovers.

28 In its abbreviation of its source, the English text excludes considerable portions of the original. In this section, for example, a key passage is redacted showing William and Melior discussing how they might meet the queen and how the queen talks with her warriors about the siege (*Guillaume*, ll. 4909–5168). As a consequence, some of the subtlety behind the decisions of individual characters is lost.

29 Bunt tells us (his note to ll. 3129–30, p. 311) that in this period ghosts assumed a visible shape in order to deceive their intended human victims. This may explain William's reaction to the queen appearing as a huge hind and the terror of the queen's maid when she sees her mistress returning accompanied by similar "ghosts".

30 The manuscript is confusing here ("and whan þei were cloþed worþli in here wedes"), which suggests they put on their own clothes; however, we know already (l. 3034) that they are wearing their own clothes under the skins (including the queen's previous observations of the clothes being visible beneath the skins (l. 3035), and also mirrors the more comprehensive description of the disrobing in *Guillaume* (ll. 5344–9).

31 In the various redactions of the Anglo-Norman and Middle English romance, *Sir Bevis of Hampton*, we read of a similar horse, Arundel, which cannot be mastered except by its lord and which, when stolen by the Saracen king, is also retained by iron chains and frees himself only when he recognises his true master. Arundel is emblematic of Bevis's power as a knight, essential to the vanquishing of his enemies; at the climax of the romance, with the near simultaneous natural deaths of Bevis, his wife Josian and Arundel, the narrator asks the audience to pray for the souls of all three – knight, wife and horse. In *Guillaume*, King Embrons' former horse is called Brunsaudebruel (l. 5407); in the English redaction, the horse is called Saundbruel, although we learn this at a later point in the narrative (l. 3585).

32 The MS reads "but our on titly tumbel, trowe me never after". Bunt (p. 313) suggests "our on" translates as "one of us". While this is true to *Guillaume*, in which William makes it clear that one or other of them will win (ll. 5653–6), in this telling it might be more compelling to read "our on" as "our own", as in the royal "we" or "I". This makes the second part of the sentence, "never trust me again", a more effective irony on behalf of William and a more encouraging battle cry.

33 The MS reads "and þre þousand þro men in his eschel were, and all bold burnes in batailes strong and bigge". The description is confusing as to whether the 3,000 men represent the whole army or merely the number in the battle of the king's son. It is suggested, therefore, that the prince's own battle numbers 3,000; the other men (previously described as forming ten battalions) are laid out around the main battle of the prince to create a larger army. In *Guillaume*, the Spanish army is cited as 22,000 men (l. 6050); the English scribe may therefore have redacted core elements but retained the sense of the Spanish army's size.

34 This is one of many elements in the English telling that abridges significant details in the French source. In Michelant's redaction of *Guillaume* (ll. 6101–9) we are told that the Spaniards "mis quatre mil de lor gent" ("put four thousand men of their men") in reserve ready to ambush William's armies if events turn against them. However, as Sconduto (p. 168) reminds us, Michelant's note to this line reveals the

original manuscript reads that the Spaniards "Mis .IIII et .IIII. de lor gent" ("put eight of their men") in the ambush group. We might expect a small force of picked men ready for such a purpose rather than a huge number hiding almost impossibly in a valley although even the Middle English redaction refers to a "fierce host".

35 The MS reads "wroþli he seide" (lit. "angrily he said"). Anger seems indelicate here; the scribe may have intended "worþli" ("worthily") although neither Bunt nor Skeat suggest a scribal error and the queen's subsequent words suggest she responds well to being admonished. *Guillaume* (l. 6312) does not describe anger but reads, "Guillaumes dist: 'trop faites mal, Dame . . . ' " ("William said, 'Madam, you're behaving badly' ").

36 In a feudal society, and one that rested on the generosity of its rulers to ensure mutual management of the kingdom, monarchs rewarded knights and others with a wide range of gifts or honours, sometimes for the most trivial of actions. In the *Alliterative Morte Arthure* (l. 3031), King Arthur rewards a herald with a "hundred pound holding" in reward for bringing good news of Sir Gawain.

37 During medieval battles, communication between different groups of men was conducted by the use of musical instruments as well as by banners and flags. The oldest surviving complete medieval war trumpet, dating from the late fourteenth century, is held at the Museum of London (see Curry and Mercer, *The Battle of Agincourt*, p. 93).

38 Although we have already been told of William's sister (l. 2643), William himself at this stage is unaware of the fact; the gradual revelation forms part of the theme of "disguise" in the romance whereby secrets known to the audience are gradually revealed to the characters. For further reading on the use and importance of disguise in medieval romance, see Dickson, *Verbal and Visual Disguise*.

39 In *Guillaume*, we read King of Gascony, which in English alliterates the *c* in Gascony on the *k* of king. The English version chooses Navarre; Bunt (p. 319) suggests that the scribe made the change because Gascony was not a kingdom, although this results in the manuscript lacking strong alliteration in the resultant line: "þe kinges douȝter of Naverne was þat god burde".

40 The MS reads, "so me wel time" in the b-verse, which might translate to an idiom such as "so help me God", "in all sincerity" or "as luck would have it" .

41 The MS reads, "þat he as mannes munde more þan we both". The text may suggest the werewolf has a greater intellectual capacity than William and the king combined or it may instead be suggesting that "on more than one occasion both Melior and I thought the werewolf had the mind of a man".

42 The MS reads "and het hem munge bi mouþe more, and þei couþe" ("and told them to do it by word of mouth, which they were able to"). The intent appears to be that, once they have presented the queen with the king's written instructions, they are to explain the full details from what the king has told them.

43 The conduct of a chivalrous knight was to know his obligations as a prisoner. Although the messengers are technically free, they know they are actually William's prisoners and must return to him. In such a way, after the treaty of Brétigny in 1360, King Jean II of France, who was freed from prison to raise his ransom, returned to captivity when his son, left as surety in his stead, escaped.

44 There is a suggestion here that William will burn the queen as a witch or a heretic on account of her craft. The manuscript is clear that the subject of this is the queen rather than the kingdom: "and balfulli do þe brenne in bitter fire". This appears to be unique to the English version; *Guillaume* (l. 7518) merely suggests she will be done to as she deserves.

45 Wealthier medieval homes incorporated painted chambers; in England, the best preserved can be seen at Longthorpe Tower near Peterborough. The Middle English romance *Sir Degrevant* (ll. 1441–96) contains a rich description of one such chamber; Longthorpe reveals that the scribe's words are far from an exaggeration.

46 The MS reads "ne wrongli schuld he wive þat it in wold hadde" ("nor wrongly take a wife while in his possession"). The English redaction appears singular unless the scribe is ironically referencing Alphonse's stepmother. An alternative reading may interpret "wive" as "to take a woman" rather than a wife; in *Guillaume* (l. 7740) the text reads "ne fortraire de sa moiller" ("nor avoid/betray

his wife"), which may hint at the intent of the line and which ties in with the central themes of love and loyalty in the romance.

47 The intimacy of this passage and the fact that the queen has no blood relationship with Alphonse highlights the sexual tension in the room as the "male gaze" is clearly transferred here to the woman. One possibility is that the poet, in converting Alphonse to a man is also converting Braundine to his dutiful mother, whereby the sexual context is lessened and she admires him as her own son; metaphorically, he has been born anew and naked in this world while she also undergoes metamorphosis as a caring woman. For an insight into the medieval theory of looking, see Spearing, *The Medieval Poet as Voyeur*, Chapter 1.

48 The MS reads "what gom wol ȝe þat ȝou give ȝour garnemens nouþe?" ("from which man do you wish to receive your equipment now?"). The context of the line in relation to the subsequent text suggests that the queen is asking Alphonse from whom he would prefer to receive his knighthood; the meaning of "garnemens" now becomes "arms".

49 The MS reads, "But, swete sone, saide it haþ ben oft" ("But, sweet son, it has been often said"). *Guillaume* (ll. 8003–4) reveals the likely intent of this line when it reads, "mais si comme est dit et parlé, par toi seromes delivré" ("but as it is said and spoken that we will be delivered by you").

50 The MS reads "boute hurt oþer harm; heriȝed be Goddes grace". The text may also be read as "without harm or hurt to the other, let God's grace be praised". Bunt notes (pp. 321–2) that the werewolf's choice not to swim the crossing on the return journey may have been due to difficulties he may have experienced in the initial crossing. However, the return journey would also have meant swimming the crossing with two adults; the boat journey is therefore more logical.

51 The MS (ll. 4732–3) reads, "þer nis god under God þat I gretli willne / as o þing þat þou woldest wilfulli me graunt" ("There is not one good under God which I desire greatly as one thing that you would grant me willingly"). I concur with Bunt (p. 323) that the sense is that Alphonse desires nothing more than one thing from William; this is substantiated by what follows.

52 The MS reads "trattes". Bunt glosses the word as meaning "old hags"; Skeat as "old women, spoken contemptuously" whilst also alluding to the Teutonic "trot", meaning "a woman, an old woman, a witch".

53 The reference to the friendship between the King of Spain and the emperor is not supported by any of the earlier text. *Guillaume* (l. 8427) contains a similar reference at this point; the scribe has clearly lifted the reference from here.

54 *Guillaume* (l. 8429) is more explicit in linking Sicily and Apulia as one kingdom under William, reading "Te puis de par le fil Embron / Cui est Puille et toute Sezille" ("and then on behalf of Embron's son who is [king] of Apulia and all Sicily"). At the time of *Guillaume*, Sicily and much of southern Italy was referred to as the Kingdom of Sicily until the Angevins were removed from Sicily in 1282. The line "as schold a king bene" (which as king he should be) may be a scribal reference to the way southern Italy and Sicily had become separate.

55 The MS reads, "and how kendeli sche was knowe" ("how she was correctly known"). The emperor, aware that his daughter had run away and therefore unproven as a princess, appears also to want to know himself how she was recognised as royal. Once more, the theme of disguise and recognition comes to the fore in the romance.

56 The MS is confusing on this point, reading "and Alphouns after him, and after þe kinges". Bunt suggests the word "sone" is missing, suggesting the line to mean "and Alphonse, the king's son, after him". However, the line might also be read (as here) as Alphonse following after those more senior than him (William, the emperor, and his own father).

57 For an assessment of how medieval minstrels and poets lived at court and were rewarded, see Green, *Poets and Princepleasers*.

58 The MS reads, "For worchipfulli artou wedded to welde a kinges sone." "Welde" carries numerous meanings in Middle English, although here it implies that Alisaundrine's marriage is one where she will wield power with her husband.

59 The MS reads, "to wirche him al þe worchip" which, literally translated, means "to bring him honour".

60 The romance refers here to the Reconquista, the centuries' long conflict between the Moors and various Christian kings on the Iberian Peninsula. For a detailed examination of the military organisation of the Hispanic Christian kingdoms at the time when *Guillaume* was first transcribed into French, see Powers, *A Society Organized for War*.

61 The MS reads, "to Crist þei hem bitauȝt". The subject and object of the line is unclear; the intention may be that they commended each other to Christ.

62 The MS reads "whan þei were arayde, eche ring as þei wold"; "eche ring" could be read either as each of the nobles on board or each crew member.

63 Bunt (p. 325) suggests the subject of this line ("him") is the Spanish king rather than the complete royal party. However, "hem" (them) is assumed here for contextual sense; *Guillaume* also suggests the latter (ll. 9211–14).

64 The reference to the Spanish king's age and the reason for Alphonse becoming king at this point is unique to the English telling. For line 5228, the subject is unclear with the MS reading "to live þerafter in lisse wil our Lord wold". In the context of the preceding line, it most likely refers to the old king rather than Alphonse.

65 This reads, "ful littel I ȝe knewe", which appears to suggest English self-deprecation on behalf of the cowherd. *Guillaume* (l. 9395) is more forthright, having the cowherd recognise William more fulsomely. Bunt suggests additionally, "I knew you as a little boy" or "little did I know who you really were", preferring the first option.

Appendix 1: The Character of the Narrator in *William and the Werewolf*

1 Both texts cited from Herzman et al., *Four Romances of England*.

2 For an insight into the musical performance of medieval romance, see Zaerr, *Performance and the Middle English Romance*. A recent overview can also be found in Putter, *The Singing of Medieval Romance*.

3 In the narrator's words, "Jeo le vus ay lui e vus l'avez oye / Rendez m'un servise si freyez curteysei" ("I have read it to you and you have heard it / in return it would be courteous to reward me").

4 The reader is invited to compare two redactions of this romance laid out in Jennifer Fellows' 2017 edition of the poem for the Early English Text Society.

5 *Chronicle* of Robert Mannyng of Brunne, cited in *Putter: The Singing of Middle English romance*, p. 73.

6 Morgan, *Beds and Chambers in Medieval England*, pp. 123–5.

7 See Ward, *Sanitizing Violence in William of Palerne*.

8 Dalrymple, *Language and Piety*, pp. 65–6.

9 Dalrymple, *Language and Piety*, p. 67.

10 Leff, *Medieval Thought*, p. 37.

11 Leff, *Medieval Thought*, p. 38.

12 Leff, *Medieval Thought*, p. 46.

13 For a discussion of Just War theory and its understanding, up to and including the fourteenth century, see Cox, *John Wyclif on War and Peace*; in particular, Chapter 1.

Appendix 2: The Old French text of *Guillaume de Palerne*

1 Hindley et al., *Old French-English Dictionary* (p. 522), gloss "rain/rein" as having various meanings including: "small of back, waist, hips, loins, sexual parts". The waist is referred to as a figure of admiration in the (much later) *Sir Gawain and the Green Knight* ("both his womb and his waist were worthily small", l. 144).

2 Both Skeat (p. 5) and Sconduto (p. 15) have this line as "for pleasure and for desires". Hindley et al. gloss "por sohaidier" as "for all one's wishes" (p. 558) while "devise" is more complex, largely suggestive of allocation and sharing out, although "faire devise" is glossed as "to wish" in terms of a legal will; "a droite devise" is glossed as "to tell the truth, wish, will desire" (p. 231). I have translated the line, therefore, to suggest that William's mother sees her son as intended for elegance and princely activities, who pleases the rooms he chooses to enter. Both "devises" and "souhais" used together may be intended as a literary pun by the original poet, to fulfil wishes and to be wished for.

BIBLIOGRAPHY

Editions of *William of Palerne*

Bunt, Gerrit H. V. *William of Palerne, an Alliterative Romance.* Bouma's Bookhuis, bv, 1985

Madden, Sir Frederic. *The Ancient English Romance of William and the Werwolf; Edited from a Unique Copy in King's College Library, Cambridge.* William Nicol, Shakspeare-Press, 1832

Michelant, Henri. *Guillaume de Palerne: Publié d'après le Manuscrit de la Bibliothèque de l'Arsenal à Paris.* Société des Anciens Textes Français, Librairie Firmin-Didot, Paris, 1876

Sconduto, Leslie A. *Guillaume de Palerne: An English Translation of the 12th Century French Verse Romance.* McFarland & Company Inc, 2004

Skeat, Walter W. *William of Palerne (Otherwise Known as the Romance of "William and the Werwolf"); Translated from the French at the Command of Sir Humphrey de Bohun, About A.D. 1350, now first edited from the unique MS in the Library of King's College, Cambridge.* Early English Text Society, 1898

Secondary Sources

Allen, Patrick. "Rethinking Pleshey Castle: New Discoveries from Old Records". *Current Archaeology*, November 2018: pp. 40–44

Barnes, Geraldine. *Counsel and Strategy in Middle English Romance.* D. S. Brewer, 1993

Barron, W. R. J. *English Medieval Romance.* Longman, 1987

Benson, Larry D. "The Beginnings of Chaucer's English Style". *Contradictions – from Beowulf to Chaucer: Selected Studies of Larry D. Benson*, edited by Theodore M. Andersson and Stephen A. Barney, Scolar Press, 1995

Bigelow, Melville M. "The Bohun Wills". *The American Historical Review*, Vol. 1, No. 3, April 1896, pp. 414–435

Birrell, Jean. "Peasant Craftsmen in the Medieval Forest". *The Agricultural History Review* Vol. 17, No. 2 (1969), pp. 91–107

Bradbury, Nancy M. *Reading Aloud: Storytelling in Late Medieval England*. University of Illinois Press, 1998

Bunt, Gerrit H. V. "Localizing William of Palerne". *Historical Linguistics and Philology -Trends in Linguistics, Studies and Monographs 46*, edited by Jacek Fisiak. Mouton de Gruyter, 1990.

Cable, Thomas. *The English Alliterative Tradition*. University of Pennsylvania Press, 1991

Casson, L. F. *The Romance of Sir Degrevant, a Parallel-Text Edition from MSS. Lincoln Cathedral A.5.2 and Cambridge University Ff.1.6*. Early English Text Society, 1949

Christianson, C. Paul. "Evidence for the Study of London's Late Medieval Manuscript-Book Trade". *Book Production and Publishing in Britain, 1375–1475*, edited by Jeremy Griffiths and Derek Pearsall, Cambridge University Press, 1989

Coleman, Joyce. *Public Reading and the Reading Public in Late Medieval England and France*. Cambridge University Press, 1996

Cox, Rory. *John Wyclif on War and Peace*. Boydell & Brewer, 2014

Creighton, Oliver H. *Castles and Landscapes*. Continuum, 2002

Curry, Anne and Mercer, Malcolm. *The Battle of Agincourt*. Yale University Press, 2015

Dalrymple, Roger. *Language and Piety in Middle English Romance*. D. S. Brewer, 2000

Davies, R. R. *Conquest, Co-existence and Change: Wales, 1063–1515*. Oxford University Press, 1987

Davies, R. R. *Lordship and Society in the March of Wales: 1282–1400*. Clarendon Press, 1978

De Hamel, Christopher and Lovett, Patricia: *The Macclesfield Alphabet Book, BL Additional MS 88887 – a Facsimile*. British Library Publishing, 2010

Dennison, Lynda E. "*The Stylistic Sources, Dating and Development of the*

De Bohun Workshop ca 1340–1400", 1988. Westfield College, University of London. PhD dissertation. Queen Mary College, University of London open access

Diamond, Arlyn. "Loving Beasts – the Romance of William of Palerne". *The Spirit of Medieval English Popular Romance*, edited by Ad Putter and Jane Gilbert, Longman, 2000.

Dickson, Morgan. "Verbal and Visual Disguise: Society and Identity in Some Twelfth-Century Texts". *Medieval Insular Romance – Translation and Innovation*, edited by Judith Weiss, Jennifer Fellows and Morgan Dickson. D. S. Brewer, 1997

Dillon, Viscount and St John-Hope, W. H. "Inventory of the Goods and Chattels belonging to Thomas, Duke of Gloucester, and Seized in his Castle at Pleshy, Co. Essex, 21 Richard II. (1397); with their Values, as shown in the Escheator's Accounts". *Archaeological Journal*, Vol. 54, No. 1, 1897, pp. 275–308

Douglas, Adam. *The Beast Within: A History of the Werewolf.* Chapmans, 1992

Edwards, Kathryn A. (ed.). *Werewolves, Witches and Wandering Spirits: Traditional Beliefs and Folklore in Early Modern Europe.* Truman State University Press, 2002

Einhorn, E. *Old French: A Concise Handbook.* Cambridge University Press, 1974

Fellows, Jennifer. *Sir Bevis of Hampton Edited from Naples, Biblioteca Nazionale, MS XIII.B.29 and Cambridge, University Library, MS Ff.2.38.* Early English Text Society, 2017

Fernyhough, C. (ed.). *Others: Writers on the Power of Words to Help us See Beyond Ourselves.* Unbound, 2019

Given-Wilson, Christopher. *The English Nobility in the Late Middle Ages.* Routledge & Kegan Paul, 1987

Green, Richard F. *Poets and Princepleasers, Literature and the English Court in the Late Middle Ages.* University of Toronto Press, 1980

Helmholz, Richard H., *Marriage Litigation in Medieval England.* Cambridge University Press, 1975

Herzman, Ronald; Drake, Graham; and Salisbury, Eve. *Four Romances of England: King Horn, Havelok the Dane, Bevis of Hampton, Athelston.* Medieval Institute Publications, 1999

Hindley, A., Langley, F. W., and Levy, B. J. *Old French-English Dictionary,* Cambridge University Press, 2000

Holder, Nick. *The Friaries of Medieval London: From Foundation to Dissolution*. Boydell & Brewer: Boydell Press, 2017

Holmes, George A. *The Estates of the Higher Nobility in Fourteenth-Century England*. Cambridge University Press, 1957

Johnston, Michael. *Romance and the Gentry in Late Medieval England*. Oxford University Press, 2014

Kaeuper, R. W. (intro.) and Kennedy, E. (trans.). *A Knight's Own Book of Chivalry by Geoffroi de Charny*. University of Philadelphia Press, 2005

Kölbing, Eugen. *Sir Beves of Hamtoun Edited from Six Manuscripts and the Old Printed Copy*. Early English Text Society, 1885–6

Leff, Gordon A. *Medieval Thought – St Augustine to Ockham*. Merlin Press, 1980

McDonald, Nicola. "A Polemical Introduction", *Pulp Fictions of Medieval England: Essays in Popular Romance*, edited by Nicola McDonald, Manchester University Press, 2004

McFarlane, Kenneth B. *The Nobility of Later Medieval England: The Ford Lectures for 1953 and Related Studies*. Oxford University Press, 1973

Morgan, Hollie L. S. *Beds and Chambers in Late Medieval England, Readings, Representations and Realities*. York Medieval Press, 2017

Neal, Derek G. *The Masculine Self in Late Medieval England*. Chicago University Press, 2008

Nichols, John. *A Collection of all the Wills Known to be Extant, of the Kings and Queens of England, Princes and Princesses of Wales, and Every Branch of the Blood Royal*. London, Printed by J. Nichols, printer to the Society of Antiquities, 1780, pp. 44–186

Oakden, J. P. *Alliterative Poetry in Middle English: A Survey of the Traditions*. Manchester University Press, 1935

Oakden, J. P. *Alliterative Poetry in Middle English: The Dialectical and Metrical Survey*. Manchester University Press, 1930

Pascual, Lucia D. "The Heraldry of the de Bohun Earls". *The Antiquaries Journal*, Vol. 100, 2020, pp. 141–64

Pascual, Lucia D. *The Bohun Dynasty: Power, Identity and Piety 1066–1399*. Royal Holloway, University of London. PhD dissertation 2017. Royal Holloway open access.

Pounds, Norman J. G. *The Medieval Castle in England and Wales: A Social and Political History*. Cambridge University Press, 1994.

Powers, James F. *A Society Organized for War – The Iberian Municipal Militias in the Central Middle Ages, 1000–1284*. University of California Press, 1988.

Putter, Ad. "The Singing of Middle English Romance – Stanza Forms and *Contrafacta*". *The Transmission of Medieval Romance: Metres, Manuscripts and Early Prints*, edited by Ad Putter and Judith A. Jefferson, D. S. Brewer, 2018

Putter, Ad, Jefferson, Judith, and Stokes, Myra. *Studies in the Metre of Alliterative Verse*. The Society for the Study of Medieval Languages and Literature, Oxford, 2007

Salter, Elizabeth. *Fourteenth-Century English Poetry: Contexts and Readings*. Oxford University Press, 1983

Sandler, Lucy F. "A Note on the Illuminators of the Bohun Manuscripts". *Speculum*, Vol. 60, No. 2, April,1985, pp. 364–72

Sandler, Lucy F. *Illuminators and Patrons in Fourteenth-Century England: The Psalters and Hours of Humphrey de Bohun and the Manuscripts of the Bohun Family*. University of Toronto Press, 2014

Smith, Michael T. A. *King Arthur's Death – the Alliterative Morte Arthure*. Unbound, 2021

Spearing, Anthony C. *Textual Subjectivity: The Encoding of Subjectivity in Medieval Narrative and Lyrics*. Oxford University Press, 2005

Spearing, Anthony C. *The Medieval Poet as Voyeur: Looking and Listening in Medieval Love-Narratives*. Cambridge University Press, 1993

Stimming, Albert, ed. *Der anglonormannische Boeve de Haumtone*. Bibliotecha Normannica VII. Max Niemeyer, 1899.

Stratmann, Francis Henry. *A Middle-English Dictionary, Containing Words Used by English Writers from the Twelfth to the Fifteenth Century – A New Edition, Re-arranged, Revised and Enlarged by Henry Bradley*. Oxford University Press, 1940.

Trigg, Stephanie. *Wynnere and Wastoure*. Early English Text Society, Oxford, 1990

Turner, T. H. "The Will of Humphrey de Bohun, Earl of Hereford and Essex, with Extracts of his Inventory and Effects. 1319–1322". *Archaeological Journal*, Vol. 2, No.1, 1845, pp. 339–49.

Turville-Petre, Thorlac. *Alliterative Poetry of the Later Middle Ages, an Anthology*. Routledge, 1989

Turville-Petre, Thorlac. "Humphrey de Bohun and 'William of Palerne' ". *Neuphilologische Mitteilungen*, Vol. 75, No.2, 1974, pp. 250–252

Turville-Petre, Thorlac. *The Alliterative Revival*. D. S. Brewer, 1977.

Underhill, Frances A. *For Her Good Estate, The Life of Elizabeth de Burgh, Lady of Clare*. Moonwort Press, 2020.

Ward, Jennifer. "Appendix 3: Bibliophile cousins: the Bohun Family". *For Her Good Estate, The Life of Elizabeth de Burgh*, by Frances A. Underhill (Moonwort Press, 2020), pp. 190–196

Ward, Renée. "Sanitizing Violence in 'William of Palerne'". *Studies in Philology*, Vol. 112, No. 3, Summer 2015, pp. 469–89

Warner, Lawrence. "Langland and the Problem of 'William of Palerne'". *Viator*, Vol. 37, 2006, pp. 397–415

Warner, Lawrence. *The Myth of Piers Plowman: Constructing a Medieval Library Archive*. Cambridge University Press, 2014

Weiskott, Eric: *English Alliterative Verse: Poetic Tradition and Literary History*, Cambridge University Press, 2016

Yakovlev, Nikolay: *The Development of Alliterative Metre from Old to Middle English*. 2008. Wolfson College, Oxford University. PhD dissertation, University of Oxford open access.

Zaerr, Linda M. *Performance and the Middle English Romance*. D. S. Brewer, 2012

Ziegler, Philip. *The Black Death*. Penguin Books, 1982

ACKNOWLEDGEMENTS

I am indebted once more to my wife, Nicky, and the rest of my family for tolerating me being locked away on this translation for so long. In particular, I wish to thank Gerrit Bunt, whose 1985 critical edition of the Middle English *William of Palerne* has formed the base text for my translation and who has graciously given permission for me to quote extracts from his work in this translation as appropriate. Huge thanks also go to Nick Wray, for his continued support of my work and direction, and to Sue Jones of Stoneman Press, whose encouragement, advice and guidance on the illustrations have been invaluable. I am also indebted – tangentially – to the teachers and staff at the University of York; in particular, Dr Nicola McDonald but also Dr Holly James-Maddocks, and Dr Shelagh Sneddon. Although they were not involved directly in this work, their influence on its outcome in terms of how I have thought about this translation has been profound, not forgetting two fellow students Madeline Fox and Katherine Willett, who supported me so generously on my particularly arduous journey with Old French. To Rob Jeffs and Sam Hellmuth I would like to extend a special thank you for supporting me in so many different ways over the last few years as all this work came to a head. At Unbound, I am grateful to Mathew Clayton, Anna Simpson, Richard Mason, Mark Ecob and the rest of the team for helping see this book over the line and turning it into the magnificent item it is. And finally, my heartfelt thanks go to each and every supporter of this book who invested in a dream and helped make it happen. Middle English romance is hardly the stuff of commercial dreams for many publishers; without every supporter's pledge and Unbound's unique platform, *The Romance of William and the Werewolf* would never have existed. Now it lives again to tell its story and message to an audience it could hardly have imagined six centuries ago.

Unbound is the world's first crowdfunding publisher, established in 2011.

We believe that wonderful things can happen when you clear a path for people who share a passion. That's why we've built a platform that brings together readers and authors to crowdfund books they believe in – and give fresh ideas that don't fit the traditional mould the chance they deserve.

This book is in your hands because readers made it possible. Everyone who pledged their support is listed below. Join them by visiting unbound.com and supporting a book today.

Mark Bowsher
Fiona Boyd
Orla Breslin
Christopher Brett
Arlene Brown
Rachael Buckland-Spector
Peter John Paul Buckley
Emma Bull
Erica Bullivant
Steve Bulman
Claire Burton
Sarah EC Byrne
Tom Callaghan
Dan Callahan
Rosalie Callway
Rodman Campbell
Debbie Cannon
David Carney-Haworth OBE
Morwenna Carr
David Lars Chamberlain
Thalia Charles
Theo Clarke
Matthew Cleaver
GMark Cole
Ady Coles
Adrian Congdon
Charlotte Coombs
Julie Cooper
Mark E Cooper
Jo Cosgriff
Geoff Cox
Sarah Crabtree
Greg Crawford
Peter da Silva
Maarten Daalder
Kev Daniels
Elizabeth Darracott

Julia Davies
Katrina and John Davies
Andrew Davison
Eleanor de Bohun
Humphrey de Bohun, 7th Earl
    of Hereford, Essex and
    Northampton
Humphrey de Bohun, 4th Earl of
    Hereford and Essex
Humphrey de Bohun, 6th Earl of
    Hereford and Essex
Alex de Campi
Elizabeth de Clare
William de Monklane
John de Teye
Fiona de Wolfe
deadmanjones
Shaun Dean
Bobby Derie
Yova Djiganska
Richard Dobell
Ben Doran
Cressida Downing
Jen Drake
Adam Drew
Stephen Drury
Melanie J Duck
Sheila Dunn
Paul Dunthorne
Lynden Easton
Sarah Elkins
Dror Elkvity
Debbie Elliott
Susanne Emde
Michael Evans
Jane Everard
Neil Fallon

Matthew Farenden

Peter Faulkner

Simon Filbrun

Ellen Finch

Jean Forbes

Brian Foster

Nicky Foy

Frankie & Alexander

Lisa Fryer

Richard Furniss

Mark Gamble

Tiffany Garbiso

Graham Garner

Alex Georgalla & Ashlea Woods

Victoria Gerrard

Barbara Gittes

Dave Goddard

Jon Goerner

Terence Gould

Keith Gregory

Tony Grice

Eamonn Griffin

Richard Griffiths

Jen Grosz

Abel Guerrero

Anthony Christopher Hackett

Christopher Hadley

Simon Hagberg

Daniel Hahn

Monica & William Haig

Stephen Hampshire

Jeanne Hand-Boniakowski

Russell Handelman

Jeremy Hanks

Mathias Hansson

CY Harkin

William Hart

James Harvey

Tim Harwood

Andrew Hearse

Emma Heasman-Hunt

Sam Hellmuth

Alex Hewins

Jan Hilborn

Andrew Hingston

F & C Hobbin

Lisa Hobbs

Emily Hodder

Wayne Hollis

Johnny Horth

Sara Howers

John Huddlestone

Matt Huggins

Jessica Hurtgen

Damian Hutt

GP Hyde

Damien Hyland

In Honor of Avi ASner

Not Interested

Brent M. Isaacs

Nika Jablonski

Paul Jabore

Daniel Jackson

Jesse James

Mike James

Braden Jeffs

Dan Jenkins

Rob Jenkins

Gregory Jennings

David Jesson

Tristan John

Brian B Jones

Michael Jones

Mary Jordan-Smith

Paul Joyce
Roderick Joyce
Louis and Tilly K
Daniel Kaseforth
David Kellett
Maura Keniston
Lyn Kenny
Gregory Kindall
Jason Kingsley
Allan Kirton
Daniel Kleinman
Burkhard Kloss
Michael Knight
Knight of Words
Patricia Knott
Koen Koggel
Helene Kreysa
Gus Kuffel-Bronson
Sumitra Lahiri
Mr Peter Lake
Luke Lambert
Pete Lambert
Douglas Lanier
Nick Lansbury
Richard Lansdall-Welfare
Suzanne LaPrade
Alison Layland
Caroline Lee
Lesley Lee
Jeff Leven
Jenny Linford
Kim Locke
Kari Long
Adam Lowe
Iain Lowson
Jacquelyn Loyd
Brigitte Colleen Luckett

Anthony Lynch
Diana Lynn & Jared Emry
Jonathan Macartney
Iain B MacDonald
Josh MacLeod
Philippa Manasseh
Ava Mandeville
Greg Manizza
Phil Manning
Keith Mantell
Juliet Marillier
Andrew Marriott
Nico Marrone
Emma Marsden
Bill Marshall
David Matkins
Susan Mattheus
Ralph Mazza
Charleen McCready
John A C McGowan
Tommy McGuire
Sarah McKinlay
Patrick Mark Meredith
Roger Miles
Katrin Miller
Ed Millie
Luciana Bulhões Miranda
James Moakes
Fran Moldaschl
Alan Montgomery
Cameron Moore
Kirsty Morgan
Rosemary Morgan
Ed Morland
Bernard Moxham
Carlton Mullis
Lauren Mulville

Debbie Nairn
Georgia Nakos
Carlo Navato
Jack Nicholas
Ian Nichols
Sally Norris
Conrad Nowikow
Beth Nuyens
Kevin O'Connor
Jonathan O'Donnell
Brian O'Neill
Douglas Oberg
Heather Oldfield
Valentine Page
Nicoletta Pagliai
Michael Paley
Richard Palmer
Adam Parmenter
Lisa Pearce Collins
Bianca Pellet and Steve Uomini
Hugo Perks
Jonathan Perks
Elizabeth Perry
Shelley W. Peterson
Neil Philip
Mark Phillips
Robert Phillips
Dani Pines
Mark Pinto
Steve Porter
Christopher Potash
Dion Potter
Nick Powell
Baker Pratt
Ian Preece
Susanne Press
Janet Pretty

Michael Pretty
Nikita Ptashnik
Caroline Pulver
Ben Quant
Nicky Quint
Andrew Radford
Rebecca Rajendra
Chad Randall
Andy Randle
Leeds Reader
Helen Reid
James Reid
Joel Rein
William McFarlane Rennie and
    Nicola Joy Rennie
Andy Rixon
Victoria Roberts
Anthea Robertson
Simon Robertson
Mark Robinson
Nick Robles
Max Rohleder
Kalina Rose
Elizabeth Rowlands
Rui & Tita
Melissa Rung-Blue
Eoin Ryan
Sara Sahlin
Mira T. Sandaaker
Nicola Sard
Anne Sauntson
Keith Savage
Nick Scarr
Arthur Schiller
Eric Schneider
Janette Schubert
Jenny Schwarz

Tony Sears
Katharine Secretan
Dick Selwood
Kal-El Sengnouanchanh
Eric Shaffstall
Christopher Sharp
Fiona Shaw
Kevin Shrapnell
David Shriver
Alan Sims
Fran Sluman
Alan C Smith
Kirsty Smith
Margaret and Stuart Smith
Michael Smith
Nigel Smith
Simon Smith
Laurence Smither
Jeremy Sowden
Rob Spence
Ann Speyer
Andrew Staff
Louise Starkowsky Dancause
Mary Steele
Gabriela Steinke
Diana Stevens
Ruth Stevens
Sharon Steward
Catherine Stewart
Matthew Stillman
Andrew D N Stocker
Tyson Stolte
Corinne Stone
Brice Stratford
Rae Streets
Brendan Strong
Nina Stutler

Martha and Bill Sullivan
Dan Sumption
Tim Suter
Penelope Swan
Audry Taylor
Bridget & Paul Taylor
Jane Teather
The Development Team
    Unbound
Emma Thimbleby
Claire Thomas
Gareth Thomas
Holly Thomas
Thomas, Duke of Gloucester
Brewer Thompson
Marian Thorpe
Christopher Trapp
Lindsay Trevarthen
Christopher Turner
Karen Turner
Mike Turner
Zoë Twelvetrees
Lewis Tyrrell
Lindy Usher
van Beijnum Hilje
Vera van Dalen
Mark Vent
Gregor Venters
Stephanie Volk
Sir Harold Walker
Philip Walter
Carole-Ann Warburton
Olivia Watchman
Andrew Wawn
Jessica Webb
Stephen Webb
Jack Weeland

Liz Weldrake

Alexandra Welsby

James Whinfrey

Kerrie White

Laura White

Russell Whitehead

Steven Whitehead

Daniel Wickstrom

Thomas Wigley

Rachael Wildman

James Wilkinson

Shen William

William, Earl of Northampton

Arnold Williams

Mike Williams

Thom Willis

Joanna Willmott

Juliet Wilson

Peter Wilson

Peter Wood

William Wootten

Wendalynn Wordsmith

Andrew Wright

Rachel Wright

Sarah and David Wyatt

Kate Yates

Siu Ying Wat

Andrew Zeiner

A NOTE ON THE AUTHOR

Michael Smith is a British translator and linocut illustrator of Middle English alliterative romances. Born in Warrington, Cheshire, he holds an honours degree in History and an MA in Medieval Literature and Languages from the University of York. He has now returned to the city to study for his PhD, where he is conducting research into the translation, performance and effective modern representation of late medieval Middle English stanzaic poetry. A former student of the Curwen Print Study Centre near Cambridge, Michael is also an active printmaker whose work graces many private collections around the world. *The Romance of William and the Werewolf* is the third in his series of illustrated translations for Unbound. He lives in Ware, Hertfordshire.

www.mythicalbritain.co.uk

NOTE ON THE TYPE

The text of this book is set in Palatino. Designed by Hermann Zapf, the typeface is an old-style serif font. It was first released in 1949 by the Stempel foundry and later by Linotype.

Zapf named his typeface after the 16th-century Italian master of calligraphy Giambattista Palatino. Palatino is based on the humanist types of the Italian Renaissance, created during the time of Leonardo da Vinci. Zapf optimised the design for legibility with larger proportions and a sold, wide structure. These adjustments meant it could be read clearly on the poor-quality papers of the post World War II period, as well as at a distance in display printing or when printed at smaller sizes in advertisements.